22 STORIES

Also by Penelope Gilliatt

22
STORIES

Penelope Gilliatt

�֍

DODD, MEAD & COMPANY
New York

Most of these stories appeared originally in *The New Yorker*. "The Redhead" and "Phone-In" appeared originally in *Transatlantic Review*. "Autumn of a Dormouse" appeared originally in *Atlantic Monthly*. "When Are You Going Back?" appeared originally in *Encounter*.

No part of this book may be reproduced in any form
without permission in writing from the publisher.
Published by Dodd, Mead & Company, Inc.
79 Madison Avenue, New York, N.Y. 10016
Distributed in Canada by
McClelland and Stewart Limited, Toronto
Manufactured in the United States of America

Designed by Claire B. Counihan

First Edition

Library of Congress Cataloging-in-Publication Data

Gilliatt, Penelope.
22 stories.

I. Title. II. Title: Twenty-two stories.
PR6057.I58A6 1986   823'.914   86-6307
ISBN 0-396-08491-5

1 2 3 4 5 6 7 8 9 10

FOR
Vincent Canby

Contents

22 STORIES

Fred and Arthur

" *'Friends, Romans, countrymen,'* " shouted Fred Stokes at the top of the Forum steps, carrying Arthur Moe in his arms center stage. They wore togas, sandals, and short white socks. Fred was thin, Arthur very fat, and Fred's head made a pecking movement over the bulk of his friend with the effort of bearing the load.

Arthur felt anxiety in the grip and spoke into the pullet neck on the upstage side. "You've got your weight wrong."

" *'Lend me your ears,'* " Fred orated, altering his hold and guttering at the knees.

"It's your right foot."

" *'I come to bury Caesar, not to praise him.'* " Fred was still concentrated on his clasp instead of his balance, and getting sworn at for it. Their manager, standing in the wings, wondered what Arthur was yakking about, and at the same time had a moment of seeing them as Gandhi carrying a buffalo.

"I'll have to do a fall," Arthur muttered. He gathered his great weight neatly to a point against Fred's sickly-looking chest, said "Serve you right" in a cheery tone under the roar of the music-hall audience and shoved away, grounding delicately at the foot of the Forum steps and watching his partner with one eye. Fred was thundering on with the speech as though the corpse hadn't fled, and at the same time bobbing up onto the balls of his feet with relief from the lost burden. Arthur scrutinized the business and thought it makeshift but not bad. He started taking apart the engineering of the scene, keeping count of the timing in his head.

They went back to their dressing room in a hurry as soon as the act was over, and Arthur started a metronome. Fred tucked his toga between his legs like a baby's nappy and picked his friend up.

"I don't see what I did different," he said, facing front to inspect the two of them in the mirror and then turning round to have a look from the side.

"I told you. Your weight was on the wrong foot. It still is. You can't hardly maneuver."

"It wasn't bad, what we did."

"Best get it straight the old way first. Seventeen, eighteen, *'Lend me your ears,'* then my sneeze on nineteen, and your slap on twenty."

"I liked the fall better myself," Fred said. "Let's keep it. Long time since we did a fall."

"Bit old-fashioned, isn't it?" said Arthur.

"What are you talking about? Falls don't date."

"Take it from fourteen," said Arthur.

" *'Friends, Romans.'* My shoulders is busting."

"Fifteen, sixteen. Carry on, I'm counting. You've got to *'come to.'* Nineteen, twenty."

" *'Bury Caesar, not to.'* Now I'm on my left foot. Suppose I stay on it. *'Praise him.'* "

"Twenty-four, twenty-five."

"Are you going or not? I said *'praise him.'* That's where you did it before." Fred watched carefully in the mirror for some muscular indication of what his friend had in mind.

The bulk lay poleaxed. "Twenty-five," it said again.

" *'The evil that men do.'* You've gone and left it far too late. *'Lives after them, the good is oft interred with their bones.'* You'll have to go, I've run out of words." But by now Arthur had quit, flying smoothly through the air like a zeppelin and saying "Thirty-one, thirty-two" as he went. "All right," he said, rolling lightly onto the floor. "Again."

Their manager came into the room. "If you don't keep in that fall, I'm stopping your sweets," he said, and then looked down at the mass of Arthur on the ground. "I haven't seen you do one like that since your old dad was alive."

"It's all in the position of the head," said Fred, sitting down and having a beer. "I can't do it. Not like he can. You use the head as the rudder." He stopped the metronome and put his hands on his bony kneecaps, looking into the mirror at his gloomy Indian-brave's face.

Arthur watched him, pulled in his stomach, listened to the loudspeaker to hear how the performing dog was doing, and thought seriously enough that he hadn't seen Fred so exhilarated since last August at Blackpool. "Good date, this. I've always liked Huddersfield," he said.

"You're putting on weight," said the manager, picking up Arthur's belt and looking at the notches.

"No, he's not," Fred said loyally. "That's muscle."

After the second house the two of them went out to supper. It was their ninth year together, and they had been top of the bill at the Palladium in the West End six years running. It was a buoyant evening. They had four pints of beer each and a slap-up dinner in one of Huddersfield's new swinging joints.

"Changed a bit," said Arthur, looking at a girl dancing in a miniskirt not much deeper than a belt.

"My old dad used to sing Handel here in the workingmen's choir," Fred said. "Came up from London by coach. They like Handel here. Here and Newcastle."

"Newcastle's a good date, too."

Arthur and Fred had been to school together. Their partnership seemed freakishly fortunate. When they went out on their own with girls, they tended to fix things for the same evening so as not to spend two nights separated where one would do. Fred's father had owned a pub near a music hall where Arthur's father had often played, and before their sons were even born the men had sometimes had Saturday-night booze-ups together. Arthur's father had been a famous comic called Willie Moe, and his mother, Queenie, was the butt in Willie's routine. When he married her, she was a reserved, very plain girl who played the harp in a provincial symphony orchestra. She had learned the harp because she had once been told that she had beautiful elbows, and harp playing seemed to make better use than most careers of the Lord's stingy gift. Her husband admired her serious-mindedness, and at the same time saw that her absence of humor held comic promise for his act. He would plant her downstage and get her to start playing "I dreamt that I dwelt in marble halls," and then sabotage her work from the back wall.

As soon as the infant Arthur was old enough to be propped

against the proscenium arch, he was included in the turn. There was nothing else to do with him; theatrical landladies didn't offer babysitting with the rent. When he strayed, his mother would shove him back into position with her foot as she harped. Then one night the child fell onto the bass drum, plummeting ten feet into the orchestra pit without seeming to harbor a grudge, and it occurred to his father to try bouncing him. Arthur commanded fame and respect in the profession for several years as "The Living Football," followed by "The Living Boomerang" and "The Living Dart." The characterizations consisted of being rolled up into a sphere by Willie, or swung by one arm, or aimed at a dartboard while wearing a trick suction device on his head. The cap fixed him securely to the board, with his airborne body trembling behind him like the handle of a plunged dagger. Later on, when he was five and too heavy to play a dart satisfactorily, he became "The Living Gladstone Bag." He wore a handle on the back of his costume, stitched there by his hard-driven mother herself because she wasn't going to have some theatrical costumier treating her son as if he were a sequin. His onstage father would unsnap the child's clothes, which were held together at the back by a clasp, pack them with toothbrush, pajamas, and reading matter, and throw the patient luggage at an assistant stage manager dressed as a railway porter. The boy went without a name until he was six. His father dismissed the notion that it was any necessity and called for his son by clearing his throat, like Henry Irving demanding a prompt. His mother felt wretched about the matter and often suggested Roland. She liked this name because it was romantic and well-bred, which were precisely Willie Moe's objections to it. Her alternative was Percy; Willie said it was wet, and she said it was *Henry IV*. When she moaned and said, well, what did he suggest instead, Willie would affably juggle the child and two oranges, and reply with the obvious oath. And his wife would flinch at the coarse life that harp playing had brought her to, and go off her kipper, and mash up the remains with some potatoes for the boy's breakfast next morning. If her son hadn't got a name, at least she was going to see that he had a proper lining to his stomach. He went to bed on porridge, got up on potatoes, and did his twice-nightly work on scones, baps, cottage loaves, crumpets, and Yorkshire parkin. The boy adored his father exclusively; his mother's recourse was starch, and his bulk therefore waxed and waxed. The process didn't perturb him for the simple reason that it didn't repel Willie. The jibes of the kids at his scattered schools, which he attended sometimes for a token day or two to throw a sop to the government, struck him as neither here nor there. What he watched for anxiously was any sign that his father found fatness unprofessional. But on the contrary Willie made it seem a prop of the work, like ripe thighs in a chorus girl or the swivel eye of Ben Turpin. Nor was it a disadvantage technically. The child was agile enough to seem filled with helium, as if he had mass without weight.

He was named on his seventh birthday. His mother had hopelessly suggested Cyril. Willie Moe snorted and picked up the boy by the leg and started to whirl him as if winding him up, which was part of a new routine called "The Living Propeller." Then he dropped the weight with a glow on his face and said, "I've got it."

"What?" his wife asked.

"Arthur," he said, pronouncing it "Arfer" because he was a Cockney of the old generation. "Arfer Moe. 'Alf a mo. We can work it into the act."

His wife felt unspeakably lowered and lit the gas for the baked beans. Everything was grist.

The child's own feelings were split between mortification at a christening that doomed him to live out for good a pun that he could already see to be gruesome and pride that his father had cared for him enough to embed him into his act by the very roots of his name. The ambiguity lasted long after Willie died. So did Arthur's torn attitude to his weight. He could never entirely regret it, because it reminded him of working with Willie, and the passing resolves he made as a grownup to lose some of it always contained a tang of unease about betraying his professional qualifications in the eyes of a man who would have belted him for such a thing.

After Willie's death Queenie packed in the theatre. She gave harp lessons and sent her son firmly to school. It was wartime and the boys called him Barrage Balloon. The normal childhood that other people wished on him struck him as mostly

plaguing and tawdry; his own lost norm, a life spent in the
company of ribald sopranos and tap dancers and hard-pressed
comedians in fear of the sack, seemed to have more decency
and purpose. When Fred Stokes arrived at the school, Arthur
had spent a year in hell. But as soon as their friendship was
struck the memory faded and the bad time seemed no worse
than some null interlude between two boon companions. To
be with Fred was as naturally convivial as to be with Willie. At
the age of nine Fred was already very much like the man he
was going to be at thirty-five or forty. He was tacit, bold, and
weedy, with a miraculous sense of humor at work behind the
face of a tomahawk. He could make his friend laugh convul-
sively enough to fall off schoolroom chairs, and once even out
of a hammock. Arthur would lie on the floor heaving, dead
silent apart from a rusty creak at the moments when he managed to catch a breath. Within himself he would have a sensation of liquefying with giggles and of becoming extremely
thin, like a puddle.

The two fitted together even in the way the day took them.
Fred woke up lugubriously, and the spectacle of Arthur's ca-
pacious morning optimism lifted his spirits. After the last show,
or earlier if they weren't working, Arthur would often fall prey
to the bite of melancholy, with such sharp dread of all endings
that he would greatly fear going to sleep, as if nothing would
be left to him unless he kept watch on it. He hated other people's leaving him for bed, and when he saw a hard mood ahead
he often took a sleeping pill at supper to stop himself from
being clamorous, though at the same time he found his terror
about the end of a day daft in a creature who was surely in-
tended by build to signify immortal fun.

While they were walking back from the Huddersfield dis-
cothèque, it suddenly dawned on Fred and Arthur that they
had eaten three main meals that day instead of two. The usual
sausages and spuds had been brought to them between the
shows.

"We had lunch. That's what put us out," Arthur said. A
producer had fed them silly in an effort to woo them to do a
film. Arthur had eaten large helpings of *scampi* and steak-and-
kidney pudding, refrained from the damson pie as a gesture,
and taken his mind off the others' plates by saying that they

would do the film if he and Fred were allowed to write it, direct it, find the props, and put together the sound track. He also said that he would want to do his own stunt work in an escape sequence. The appalled producer took refuge in the unions and his insurance company, and Fred and Arthur composed their faces into the necessary combination of artistic bloody-mindedness and guestly sympathy to scotch the project without actually seeming to throw their good lunch back into the producer's face. Neither of them had liked him at all.

"I've never had a good experience of a boss with a short upper lip," said Fred.

"The *scampi* was O.K.," Arthur said, bumping a penny along the railings in groups of four and muttering "Breakfast, lunch, dinner, supper. Breakfast, lunch, dinner, supper. No more than the Tudors had, I bet."

"You should have had the damson pie," Fred said.

"No, I shouldn't. I'm blowing up again."

Nearer to their hotel, Fred did an improvisation about the homelife of an air hostess who was taken over in bed by her working phrases and asked her husband if he would care to recline and have a beverage. Arthur leaned against a lamppost and felt thinned.

The mirror in their tatty hotel suite exposed that delusion. "My face looks as if it's going to drop off a fruit tree," he said at himself. "It's like a medlar. *Purple.* It seems to be *running.*"

"It's the light," Fred said.

The telephone rang. Arthur left Fred to it and lay on his back in his own bedroom, reading a book about ballistics. He felt himself to be so uneducated that it seemed hopeless even to try to catch up with the ordinary things that people knew.

"Daisy said to give you her love," Fred said, coming into the room half an hour later. Daisy was Fred's bird, a freckled teen-ager with red tabby hair whom Arthur had entrusted with a slice of his savings so that she could open a boutique. He often caught himself liking her better than his own girlfriend. Per-haps this was because she belonged to Fred, which meant that there was no call to—Oh, all that, he thought, shutting up in his own head. He had a striking decorum even in his thoughts. Fred sat on the end of the bed with his elbows on his knees and his hands hanging down with their knuckles back to back, like a tired football-player in a dressing room. He was looking at a beautiful textbook about race horses that Arthur had laid out on the floor.

"She says the shop's raking it in," he said. "She's going to pay you back the loan at the end of the week."

"No hurry."

"You like making people's fortunes for them, don't you?" Fred said.

Arthur immediately started to tell a story about a time in music hall when he had set out to behave less admirably and had cost a theatre manager a packet. After a couple of sentences he went into the present tense, which was a habit he had in speaking of the past, as if it were the plot of some play he was about to do. "So even the performing seals are disgusted with his cheeseparing by now, and that night the lyric soprano breaks one of the hoops of her crinoline in the middle of her best love song because he wouldn't run to proper whalebone, and I take myself aside and say to myself . . ." This was another characteristic that he had: he often talked about himself as if he had custody of someone who needed a lot of upbringing.

"Tell that story to Daisy sometime," Fred said at the end of it.

"You two should get married," said Arthur, scaring himself. His thoughts teetered nastily, and he wondered if he had uttered the possibility in order to ward it off.

"Why don't you marry Peg?" Fred rinsed the old tea out of a cup and poured some Scotch and tap water into it.

"It mightn't suit the work."

"What?"

"We'd be three, and all that." But the same thing was true of Fred's marrying Daisy. "It would be different if it was you and Daisy. I mean, I like her."

"I like Peg."

"Anyway, I'm too fat to get married."

"Don't be so sorry for yourself."

"I'm not sorry. I'm just fat."

"What about King Farouk? He never stopped getting married."

They hadn't spoken like this before. Arthur tightened. Constraint stung his skin like a wave of hornets. The conversation was alien and impossible. At the same time he had the clearest image in his mind of the three of them: Fred, Daisy, and himself, and it was a spectacle of nothing but pleasure. He was hanging his head over the edge of the bed and wondering what to do next when a spring burst in the mattress.

"I still think you should try marrying Peg," Fred said, starting for the door and giving Arthur as sharp a seizure as he had ever had of longing and hatred for an ally who was deserting him to go to sleep. "You could always split up," said his friend. Another ending. A second swarm of enemies attacked Arthur's skin and he swore at them blue murder.

"I've got a new idea for the fall," he said. "I keep the arms still and move off from your downstage shoulder. Your weight's on your back foot, same as before, but now you can brace it better against the step." Peg was all right, but to marry her seemed a deal of foreign new trouble to face for the sake of off-loading the known old pain of loneliness before sleep. He remembered some story about a primitive farmer who discovered roast pork when his house and his pig barn burned down and then imagined that he had to set fire to the place again every time he fancied a bit of crackling. "Hang on to the house," said Arthur, taking himself aside. "Hang on to the house." He lay on his elbow and hip along the top of a bureau, looking more like a Turkish sultan in a harem than he felt. Then he flung himself neatly across to the bed, thinking agreeably of life with Fred and Daisy as he went, and another spring broke. Mankind (me), he thought, mashing up the rest of the mattress because he wasn't going to spend the night braced for a lot of bedsprings to bust in their own time, is idyllic in his intentions, tragic in his fate, and farcical in his functions.

No: *ludicrous,* he thought next morning, when the first thing in his waking head was the image of his sea-lion self with a wife.

Fred and Daisy got married later that year. Arthur was their best man and there were jolly pictures of the wedding in the papers. He took them out on a spree the night before, just the three of them.

"It's a stag night, only with a girl," he said. "You don't want a lot of people, do you?"

Daisy asked Fred privately whether they shouldn't get him

to invite Peg. Fred had already thought of it and shook his head.

At the Savoy Grill, Arthur told Daisy that they were going to drink Dom Pérignon. "We've gone off beer since you decided to get spliced," he said, looking at Fred.

"*Fred* hasn't. *We* always drink beer," said Daisy, collaring the "we." Then she regretted it, and touched Arthur's arm and laughed. "I don't know anything about wine. Is Dom Pérignon good?"

"Also very pricey," said Fred.

"That's what money's for," Arthur said.

Fred said, "The only other time he ever ordered it was the night you rang us up in Leeds to say you'd got the house and we could move in by the week we were spliced."

Then Arthur took them to a night club called The Scotch, and made them dance, and thought they looked good together. "Half the room is wearing clothes they've bought from your posh shop," he said to Daisy. "Best investment I ever made was in that place. In fact, the *only* one I ever made."

"Haven't you got any stocks and shares, then?"

"He hardly even trusts the bank," Fred said. "I know what he means. He'd much sooner keep it in an old pair of tights."

"What you put into the business," Daisy said, "you should have treated it as a loan and let me pay you back the capital. I always thought of it as a loan. Two thousand quid is a lot of loot. You might need it. Or I might go bankrupt."

"I like getting dividends," said Arthur. "The other day I got twenty-two pounds five and six from your accountants. It seems like real money, your dividends. Like getting a wage packet again, instead of voting myself a salary as my own director or whatever it is they make me do."

He saw them off on honeymoon and didn't know what to do with the weeks they were going to be away, until he thought of taking a total-immersion course in Italian. Daisy had once said that the three of them might spend a holiday together next year in San Gimignano. He worked at the course twelve hours a day and found it exhausting but staggeringly easy. Once he was over the edge of extreme fatigue his brain drank up the language by the pint. He thought of startling Fred and Daisy with a flood of Italian when he met them off the boat train at Victoria Station, but at the sight of them his plans fled for excitement. Intruding on a newly married couple sounded a textbook mistake when he surveyed it, but plainly both of them were glad he was there; he could see it in their faces and ran up the platform with joy, not shy at all about the reflection of his hurtling bulk in the glass of a news-agent's stall.

It was a couple of months before he felt in Daisy's way. He tried to find himself a girl to take his mind off it: some new girl, because Peg had gone wrong. He invented engagements when he had nothing to do, and ordered *La Stampa* to keep up his Italian as a surprise for Fred when the present stage was over. Surely it was too predictable that Daisy was going to want to elbow him out; the feelings that existed between the three of them were substantial enough to forbid anything so trite. He started keeping Fred and himself to timetables, so that she knew where she was, and cut out eating with Fred after the show or seeing him in the daytime at weekends. Working together was more enviable than ever, and professionally they seemed infallible. By good luck, they were in the middle of a long stint in London. The next provincial tour was months ahead, and by then Fred would have seen Daisy through whatever was bothering her. Arthur liked her very much, and when he heard from Fred that she was going into hospital overnight to have a minor operation he packed her room with flowers and clownish notes. Fred was jumpy while they were working together the next morning, so Arthur opened a bottle of Bollinger in their businesslike new office and then took him out to lunch.

"What's she in there for?" he said.

"Children," said Fred.

Arthur changed the champagne to Dom Pérignon. They had two bottles. He looked at his watch. "Is it over yet?"

"I don't know."

"When were they doing it, then?"

"I don't know."

"You don't *know?*"

"She didn't want me to think about it too much. She just went in last night and said she'd be back today as soon as she could. She wouldn't let me take her."

"I understand that," Arthur said. "She knew you'd hate the

lousy place. Couldn't she have had it done at home?"

"She doesn't mind hospitals like you do."

They had a brandy, and then another. Arthur saw Fred looking at his watch. "Do you want to go?" he said.

"I don't much want to be at home on my own. She won't be back for ages."

"Let's have a Calvados."

They forgot the hospital and invented a new sketch. The restaurant closed in the end, so Arthur took Fred to Fortnum's and they floated through the food department arm in arm. They ordered chicken breasts in jelly and invalid grapes for Daisy, and grouse in aspic to be sent when she was better. Then they went down the stairs to the wine counter and Arthur bought Fred some port—a lot of port, what the noble-nosed assistant called a *pipe* of port. Arthur told the lordly one that it was to be sent to Mr. and Mrs. Stokes, but Fred knew whom it was tacitly meant for, because he had read in newspaper gossip columns about dukes laying down pipes of port when heirs were born.

"Why do you hate hospitals so much?" Fred said when they had dropped into Jacksons of Piccadilly to buy Daisy some out-of-season strawberries that they hadn't thought of in Fortnum's.

"Dunno," Arthur said.

Fred waited and looked at him, knowing that only forbearance might call it out.

"Heart," Arthur said loudly. The morning-coated manager had recognized them and was being proprietary with them in front of a dowager customer. Taking the word—"heart" or "art"?—for a signal of entertainment, he brought his dowager nearer.

Fred, drunk though he was, saw what was happening and pushed Arthur toward the Stiltons. "The old bag's got her ear trumpet out," he said too clearly. "What do you mean, heart? All right, aren't you?"

"You know how it is," Arthur said.

Fred stumbled and steadied himself by putting his hand on a York ham. "Yes," he said. The dowager looked on and smiled and thought courteously about the people. Fred was suddenly felled with booze. "You're all right, though?" he said at last, holding on to a Gorgonzola.

"I always think the old thing's conking out, you see. They keep telling me it isn't, but it's all bluff, isn't it? Doctors. Look at the common cold. They don't even know about that. I mean, obviously I've got it coming. A man of my weight." He focussed on a birthday cake that interested him. "I once saw a film about a girl in love with a man who had a dickey heart," he said. "I think he was a composer. Thin, of course."

"Anton Walbrook."

"Can't remember who the girl was. I wish it had been Carole Lombard. I'd like to have married Carole Lombard. Do you remember what you and me were doing when she was killed?"

"Bleeding French dictation."

"No we wasn't, it was bleeding basketwork. They was making us make *baskets*, for the *war effort*. Carole Lombard was a nice girl. She had the nicest forehead I ever saw." Arthur thought of her dead, and reacted to a reflection of his own mortal hulk with more sympathy toward it than usual. "Poor child."

"What do you mean, child? She wasn't any younger when she died than we are now."

"But she feels younger, because we've gone on living longer," said Arthur. He glimpsed a fallacy, said "Longer to *us*, I mean" with a vague interest in nailing it, and then thought the hell with it and bought some very expensive soap. So after that they staggered happily to Hamley's in search of mechanical toys for themselves, and passed a record shop on the way that reminded Arthur of something. "Daft of me not to be able to remember who the girl was," he said, "but I tell you what I do remember. They played the Grieg Concerto every time the composer was going to have an attack."

He hummed and sounded quite at ease, so Fred asked if he would like the record.

"Thanks very much," Arthur said furiously. "I can never hear the damned thing without wanting a cardiogram."

When they got back to Fred's house, it was eight o'clock. They had had tea at the Ritz and drinks at the Café Royal, and then more drinks at Lyons' Corner House in Coventry Street because they were fed up with swish places and Lyons' seemed like home. They were more than fairly high, merry as grigs, and prepared to go on all night.

Daisy had been back for a long time; she looked white and pinched. "Where have you been?" she said, crying. "I rang everyone. I was out of my mind with worry."

"Shopping," said Fred.

"He didn't think you'd be back for ages," Arthur said protectively.

"You're drunk," she said to Fred, and turned on Arthur. "You've made Fred drunk. How *could* you? When I was in *hospital*." She cried some more. "I came out faster than anyone's ever left before. As soon as I could walk straight, I got out. They said I had to lie down for two hours because I was going to be groggy, but I thought Fred would be worried. I had to get back."

"You shouldn't have done that," Fred said.

"He's only drunk because he *was* worried," Arthur said.

"People should do what doctors say." Fred's voice was acid. "After operations."

"It wasn't an operation. How can you call it an *operation?* It was for a *baby.*"

"You're being a soppy date," Arthur said. "Funny, you're not usually."

"Perhaps it's the anesthetic," Fred said.

"Anesthetics can upset people for hours," Arthur said.

Daisy screamed at them. "Stop ganging up. Even when I've been in *hospital,* for *this,* the two of you gang up."

The humiliation and jealousy that had surfaced in her didn't abate in the weeks ahead, and the prospect of the friends' provincial tour together made her behave like a vixen. She broke up the partnership with exhaustive cunning, prizing Arthur away with weapons of sexual mortification that she knew he would never describe to a living soul, least of all to Fred, because she was Fred's loved wife. She made Fred see himself here only as she described him—as a man who was deliberately making his now pregnant wife unhappy. All the same, he insisted on doing a final tour. He did it because he wanted to, because he wasn't going to be her victim, and because he cared very much for Arthur. The time together wasn't at all the funeral wake it might have been. On the contrary, it was brilliant and buoyant: two months of boon nights. They had actors' temperaments, and they forgot London because it wasn't there. Future separation didn't exist, except when the long arm of the telephone reached into the room.

"It's only for a time," Fred said on the last night of the tour. "We'll give it till the baby's a year old, say. Or six months. Probably she'll be so wrapped up in it she'll feel differently."

Daisy had one baby and then another, and Fred and Arthur did a television series together directly after the first child was born, but a reserve had come between them and their companionship wasn't quite the same. Arthur went back to life alone in his rooms in South Kensington and wondered how to proceed. He dipped into books, but couldn't get his brain to bite. He went to Italy on his own and eventually made himself pick up a girl in Rome, mostly for the sake of having someone to speak his new Italian to, but she thought his intense shyness some sort of perversion and kicked him out. Arthur wandered the streets and ate pasta on his own and learned the intricate history of Christian heresy in an Italian-language library. It was plainly not a useful thing for a comedian to do. But then being a comedian was plainly not a useful thing to do either. He came back to England and went on drinking champagne alone, and nerved himself to do a TV series without Fred. The endeavor was professionally abysmal as well as painful, and his money started to run out. Life seemed more exacting than God himself.

Then the Aldwych Theatre suddenly asked him to play Bottom in *A Midsummer Night's Dream* for the Royal Shakespeare Company. He waited until it was nearly too late, and then set his alarm for the old confident time of the morning and rang up his agent to tell him to say yes. As soon as the offer was accepted, it seemed the clearest piece of luck. Arthur remade his day, for he had let it disintegrate stupidly. His new habit of sleeping on and on to rid himself of as much time as possible and then of staying up drinking alone until very late only left him with none of his natural good time and hour upon hour of his bad. So he started getting up early again, at five or even four, and going into heavy sleep with the waning light. The work ahead began to make him feel over-rested and dangerous, like a fat lion. Every now and then he would walk through Covent Garden fruit market toward the Aldwych to make sure that the theatre was still there. He refrained from ringing Fred up and stored Daisy's dividend checks in a drawer without cashing them, although he could have done with the money.

The rehearsals were as pleasurable as they generally are. The director was a small, pink-cheeked man with bottle-shaped shoulders and an expression of misleading blankness. He took rehearsals in an ancient overcoat that might have come from Gogol's dustbin. It hung to his mid-calves and he was devoted to it. Instead of talking from the stalls to actors in front of one another, he would always shamble up onto the stage with his peculiar hedgehog gait and take them aside separately. He spoke very shrewdly and at alarming speed, in a low voice that seemed to come from elsewhere; though his lips might be moving in front of Arthur, the shafts of help would sound as if they came from the wings or the orchestra pit. The director had a knack of giving elegant voice to exactly the thought that was currently in poorish shape at the back of Arthur's head, and this was infuriating, though to feel resentment at having your skull so stylishly looted seemed small-minded and a blunder of taste. Halfway through the rehearsals Arthur started to feel anxious, and after nights of floundering he concluded that he should stop trying to put aside what he knew from music hall. Next day, of course, the director shuffled up onto the stage, stopped the rehearsal, took Arthur on one side, and lifted the ass's mask to murmur, fluttering the hairs on the bearded jawbone, "You're cutting yourself off from your technique."

"I know," Arthur said impatiently. "I thought that Shakespeare . . . I mean, I thought . . ."

"Bottom is a music-hall character," said the director over him. "People always make him too pathetic. Try playing him as George Robey."

"Blast," Arthur said to himself. "There goes what I was thinking again."

After a traditionally disastrous dress rehearsal the director came into Arthur's dressing room, which he shared with Flute the Bellows Mender, and said cheerily, "I tell you what, why don't you go back to the awful way you used to do it? Then the production will be integrated because it will be *all* bad."

"I think it's disgusting, him talking like that," Flute said afterward in a thin voice. "As if the conception hadn't got anything to do with him." He slammed down a tin of cleansing cream. Flute was a mirthless man who often used words like "conception," "subtext," and "seminal," and also "Jarry-esque," which appeared to have something to do with a play called *Ubu Roi*. Four weeks of being cooped up with Flute had taught Arthur that *Ubu Roi* was somewhere held to be the most seminal possible thing about funniness, and if it was a book he was prepared to try getting it out of the public library one day.

Arthur looked at Flute's cross face and thought longingly of Fred's horse sense at dress rehearsals. With as much robustness as he could spare, he said that he didn't think the director had meant to be flippant. This added fuel to Flute's chilly little fire, and Arthur's shoulder was given a painful thwack with a rolled-up copy of the *Tulane Drama Review*.

"Comedy should be taken seriously," Flute said.

Arthur grunted a serviceable yes or no, perfected in combat with supercilious wine waiters who had tried to test his strength, or his French, or both.

Cheek, he thought later, with his usual time lag, pouring himself a glass of champagne from the half bottles that he kept in the fridge. He nearly rang Fred up, but he would be seeing him tomorrow at the first night. Then the telephone rang, and the director said he had been very good, and did he like pâté? Because his wife had made dishes of it as first-night presents for the cast, apart from Titania, who was on a diet and would have to be dealt with in some other way. At the idea of pâté in the offing, Arthur's voice leaped like a salmon. "Oh, blow Titania," he said, putting four fingers into his waistband, which was on the loose side at the moment. "Give her the pâté anyway and let her get on with it. She can always hand it on to Peaseblossom or Mustardseed. They both look starving."

"That's their ballet background," said the director.

"You could give yourself a nasty cut on those shoulder blades," Arthur said, suddenly remembering the whole girl subject after his respite from it and feeling unusually breezy. The sight of Fred and Daisy after the first night added to his nerve, and he scooped the skeletal Peaseblossom out of a dressing room full of tulle to take her out to dinner with them. She stayed mute through two rounds of drinks and potted shrimps.

"You *did* have a crush of fans in your dressing room," said Daisy, doing her best.

"Mashed up Mustardseed's wings," Peaseblossom said.

"What?" Daisy asked.

Arthur inquired further and relayed his findings. Her colleague's fairy costume had been badly injured by an admirer who had sat on it.

"What rotten luck," Daisy said, putting on the upper-class voice that she used only when she was feeling guarded. But what about? Not about the sight of me *acting*, thought Arthur; surely not. He asked after Fred's new play and she ran on with unconvincing enthusiasm about a young actress who was going to be in it.

"She's a dish," said Fred. "Only sixteen. We'll all be up for child rape. I don't know whether she can act, but she looks a treat."

"She's the bird with the two Afghans," said Arthur, who had seen pictures of the dogs in the papers.

"She's a fearfully nice girl. Have you met her?" Daisy said graciously to Peaseblossom, who was in contemplation with spaghetti.

"You sound like a royal going round a factory," Fred said. He ladled some of his stew onto Daisy's plate. "Go on, shut your cake hole with that." They laughed together with such intimacy that Arthur had to look away. Then Fred took Peaseblossom off to dance and Arthur gave Daisy an envelope of the uncashed dividend checks, saying that he wanted her to plow them back into the business. She missed the quality of his action altogether, or chose to pretend to, and said crisply, "Oh, you can tear them up, love. I had them stopped ages ago."

When Fred came back to the table, the two old friends suddenly fused and started to laugh, while Daisy had to wait upon them as their natural audience. "This is the way things really are, isn't it?" Arthur cried in his head. "It can't have been lost. Dear God, they'll pick their things up in a minute and leave me on my tod with that Peaseblossom. I'm tired, it's not fair.

What shall I do with her when she'd had enough to eat?" He took her back to her flat in Putney, which was a long way, and she turned out to be keen on cocoa. Arthur left her to a mug of it and a Beatles record.

He began to be asked to act in play after play. There was something awry with directors' reasons for casting him and something unnourishing in the West End audiences' response, but he smothered the knowledge of it. Intellectual reviewers took him up in left-wing papers because of his music-hall background and appreciated him in a way that made him wretched. They wrote as though finding him funny were something radical and upright, of a kind with rallying good will toward colored immigrants. One director used him in *Waiting for Godot,* and he felt at home in a straight play at last, but unfortunately a critic wrote four hundred words about the Christly nature of the moment when he took his hat off. After Arthur read that, the piece of business became impossible and it was only after Fred rang him up and ribbed him about it that he could manage to get the thing off his head again.

It was summer, though, and life was working in its careless way. Arthur went to the Kings Road one hot afternoon to buy some sausages at Sainsbury's.

"That's Arthur Moe," said a young man on the street outside. He looked like a male model.

"So it is," said his girlfriend.

"Ask him for his autograph, then."

Arthur was used to people talking about him in his presence as if he couldn't hear. It made him feel as if he were a television set. The man long-sufferingly tore apart a paper bag for him to autograph, shoved it into his hand, and said furiously, "Haven't you even got anything to write with?" Arthur's affability began to be tinctured with a faint new sarcasm. He asked them into Sainsbury's, borrowed a pencil from the sausage assistant, and wrote his name on the paper bag.

"Phony writing," the man said severely.

"What?" said his girl, leaning over his shoulder to look.

"I said phony, not funny. I haven't laughed at him for years."

Arthur bought two pints of Devonshire cream as an act of aggression. Life being what it is, he thought, one dreams of revenge. He came out into the sun and wondered what next. Defend myself! I'm fed up with my place. I'd like a cat. A man must have somewhere to go.

Then he saw a wonderfully pretty girl who had obviously been watching him for a long time. It was Sukie, Sukie something, the nymphet Fred was working with; he knew her by the Afghans.

"You were even cooler than Fred," she said, laughing at him admiringly and leaning her two dogs against her as if they were supporting a fine book. He was glad she thought he had been cool. He decided not to wipe his face, which had started to run in its usual sleepy-fruit way, because to do so might have destroyed the impression.

"Come home and have a drink," she said. "You're not playing tonight, are you?" She imparted her knowledge of him so agreeably, and her kneecaps looked so trustworthy, that the glancingly unkind afternoon improved out of all recognition. He had an obscure faith that he was in the presence of some tributary of Fred's staunch temperament. They walked to her car: two lean and amazing dogs, one lean and amazing girl, and the old bladdery wineskin. Oh, well. Oh, hell. She bought a choc-bar ice cream on the way, and this immediately gave him the illusion of proxy license that he always felt upon seeing the thin and flawless elude the rules. Indeed, he even had a buccaneering moment when it seemed to him that to have a choc-bar himself would do the trick of making him exactly like her. So he bought one. Her car was a red M.G. with the hood down, parked closely; there was room for her to get in, but not for him. She realized this openly and laughed at him in the sun, saying that the Afghans couldn't manage it either, and her blatant flirtatiousness fuelled him to perform one of his music-hall leaps over the back of the car into the bucket seat.

"Fred never told me you did that sort of thing."

"I don't usually. Not in private life."

"He said you were shy. Do it again." She really was a child. O.K.: one more when we get home and that's all before bedtime, he thought, facing the fact that bedtime was probably all too literally what she had in mind. Well, in that case, he told himself, there are ways of quieting kids down. Meaning no when you say it, for instance, and hot-milk drinks.

"Not here," he said maturely. "I'll do you one more when we get to your place." Her chin was shaped like a baby's heel.

She gave him a Coke out of a fridge that held caviar, half-empty tins of sardines and water chestnuts, and medicine bottles for the dogs. There was also a cold-cream jar containing marijuana jam. The drawing room was full of rugs that looked upsettingly as if they had been made from earlier Afghans. She sat on one of the longest-haired mats, draped the dogs around her, and catechized him about Fred with an insistence that he took for childishness. He tried asking her about herself, but she had a knack of averting his questions with an apparently bashful stammer, looking at him with kohl-lined eyes that rolled around like the globules in a bricklayer's balance. Her beauty was so startling it mysteriously approached the comic. Arthur found the reasons for this unfathomable, but took it that they had to do with a comparison to his own looks. The sight of her bare toes made him feel slightly religious. When she wanted not to reply to something, she would lift her ravishing upper lip over her opened teeth in a way that put him alarmingly in mind of a horse wanting to be bridled. He grew very hot and thought that he was probably looking runnier than ever, but felt it would be courting horse-trouble to take off his jacket. She was wearing schoolboy shorts herself, and what seemed to be an eleven-year-old's prep-school cricket blazer. Her hair was in a single pigtail tied with a black bow, like one of Nelson's sailors. Merely to connect her with the Battle of Trafalgar liquefied him a little further because it moved him. He assumed the pigtail to be her own, but it wasn't. When she came back from changing, her haircut was a boy's, except that it had newborn-looking curls at the nape of her neck, which knocked him out for a bit. He went into her giant bathroom to take his mind off things and stood there awhile between her mirrors, thinking not particularly of how he looked himself but mostly of the inflections that she had caught from Fred, and also of how it must feel to be this negligently perfect child, who had obviously never in her life spent herself combating a flaw.

"You shouldn't wear a switch, you know," he said when he came back. "Your own hair's nicer."

"It's fun, that's all. It's boring to be the same all the time."

"When you're as pretty as you are, you should leave yourself alone."

She wavered her eyes at him, but he wasn't going to hand her anything more, for she knew perfectly well she was pretty. Not that her vanity took away from her; in some eerie way that he didn't relish, her self-absorption even made her harder to withstand. He found himself thinking solemnly about her bone structure, going on and on about it in his head, but put a stop to that because his thoughts sounded like the conversation of fashion photographers.

"Promise me not to wear a switch again," he said, after a fool's pause.

"Why? That's the whole *point* of living now. We can change ourselves. We can be anyone we want." She read too much newsprint, perhaps. "I've got dozens of wigs. I suppose you think that's frivolous of me. But I get so bored with myself. Don't you? What I mean is, you can choose now in the mornings whether you're going to be Marie Antoinette or a plumber's mate. As far as your hair's concerned, I mean. Or you can learn something. Like, er, Spanish. Anything. Shorthand. You can decide to have kids or not. You can be fat or thin. You just have to know what you want. Of course, it doesn't matter for a man about being fat. Women don't mind that sort of thing in men. I'd kill myself if I was fat." She poured a glass of Perrier water for herself and asked if he would like to smoke some pot. "If I was fat I simply couldn't stand it."

He watched her as she moved around the room. She was smoking her joint with quick snatches of breath, like a swimmer doing the crawl. He forgot for a moment that it was pot and thought of nicotine, and then of cancer, cells in delirium, the inroads that living would make one day even on this varnished little icon of the exempt: the flab of tiredness, children, overwork, sitting up too late at night listening to people, indulging buoyant childish appetites as a device to sustain good nature against foreshadows of the senile self.

"I hate Daisy, don't you?" said the little beauty, sitting cataclysmically on his knee, with a baby sparkle hard to tell from old-age mischief.

He put his huge right hand on her polished gold kneecaps,

because it suddenly looked ridiculous lying around on the arm of a chair, and said, "No."

"Tell me about Fred. No. Tell me later, when we're in bed. I'll cook us some shepherd's pie. I'm a super cook. Did you know that? Fred told me you used to have shepherd's pie three or four times a week when you were in music hall. He said you liked it best the way they did it in Derby. Fred's a smashing man, isn't he? He's taught me everything. I even feel I know all about you. I mean, I know about your mother the harpist, and your father, and why you're called Arthur, and about the way you can fall. I wasn't really surprised when you jumped into the car like that, you know. I wanted you to." She was a witch, then, because he had never before in his life done such a thing with a girl in the street. She must have put the idea into his head herself: pinned it onto the back of his mind, like one of her flaming hairpieces.

The room was full of photographs of her. He looked at them. There was one of her dandling a baby, and he took it into the kitchen to her.

"It's my godchild," she said. "I adore babies. I'm going to have eight."

He looked at the back of her knees, nearly fainted with the beauty of them and went into the drawing room again to convalesce, holding the photograph on his big lap. What was she doing? He couldn't see his way. He seemed to have become her creature, though she was the one on a drug supposed to make her passive. The cadences of Fred in her speech were cruelly deluding. She struck him now as perilous and avid, and he had the sensation of going into a skid. He looked again at the photograph, and recognized at last that the baby who looked familiar was Fred's. No, Daisy's, with the child in the kitchen as her surrogate mother.

"How on earth did you get this?" he said. "It's Daisy's kid."

"I want Fred to see it." She smiled gaily, and a freezing wind howled in his guts.

"You need locking up."

"We'd better get on with it if you're going to be nasty, hadn't we? What a waste of my beautiful cooking. Still, I'm not really hungry. Are you?" She came and kissed him like an anteater, and he went out of the door. "You're frightened of me, aren't you?" she shrieked at him. "Come on, we could have fun. I think you're nice. I think you're attractive." He went down the stairs, and she stood at the top of them screaming. "I admire your work. Help, I'm falling."

"Hang on to the doorpost, then." He hesitated. She had certainly gone ashen, but it was probably pique. "Go to sleep," he said. "Have something to eat and go to sleep. It was a bad idea, that's all. And leave Fred and Daisy alone."

"I'll kill myself."

As soon as he got home, the telephone was ringing and she told him the same thing many times. "I'll kill myself."

"Where did you get my number?"

"From Fred."

"What've you done to him?"

"I'll kill myself if you don't come back."

"Eat your nice shepherd's pie and lay off. I've got to work tomorrow."

"So I'll never see you again."

"All right, I'll take you out to lunch one day."

"You don't love me. Mine's Flaxman 9424. You grab what you can get and then you desert me."

"Don't talk such bollocks. We've only just met."

"I can't bear being deserted. I won't have it. You're just like Fred. If you don't come back I'll take the whole bottle."

"You mean you did this to *Fred.*"

"I can't stand it—I'm taking them—I'm giving them to the dogs . . ."

She made her voice fade and left the receiver knocking against a table leg. Arthur listened carefully and heard her tiptoeing away. An hour later he dialled the number, but it was still engaged. The night seemed the longest he had endured. He sat for many hours in front of a mirror, moving his joints, detecting stiffness in a knee, juggling with cakes of soap to see if he could still do it. He was rehearsing Sir Toby Belch in *Twelfth Night* and the lines had fled; what he hung on to was the physical business, and when he did some of it to the mirror it seemed poor stuff for the old Living Boomerang. "I am not doing what I ought to do," he kept saying to himself. Was Fred free of that girl? He tried to reach her again, and told the operator to put the howler on the line because the phone was off the hook, but the girl said reprovingly that it couldn't be done in the middle of the night in case it woke people up. "It might be an emergency," Arthur said, though he didn't believe it. Then he got out his old square-toed athlete's shoes and practiced falls onto the bed. His heart seemed to be beating too hard, and he started to test his twenty-twenty eyesight by leaping with alternate eyes closed. He thought the right one seemed weak. Perhaps it was tiredness. *I am not doing what I ought to do.*

The next day the press was onto him. Sukie had been rushed to hospital after taking an overdose of sleeping tablets, and she had left an incriminating love letter to him. It was printed next Sunday in one of the gutter tabloids. There were also photographs of himself, and of her bedroom as the police and reporters had found it, with the two Afghans poisoned on the floor.

Sukie recovered, and there were no charges to be brought, but she was a favored public child as well as a minor and something stuck. After he opened in *Twelfth Night,* Arthur was hissed by a crowd of women waiting for him outside the stage door. It happened again, out of the blue, a few days later in Oxford Street. He thought of something he had read once about Fielding, who had heard the watermen at Rotherhithe mocking his body when it had grown ugly with the dropsy.

Fred understood Sukie's vengeful ruse, and most people could have guessed it if they had cared to, which they didn't. Often it isn't the truth that punishes but what's believed. After a fortnight, Fred saw what was likely to happen and went to a lawyer whom he trusted. "The girl's practically a nut. Can't he make a statement?"

"It'd do more harm than good."

"You think it'll die down?"

The lawyer looked out of the window. "You know what I really think? His weight will damn him. He'll become a monster."

Arthur survived. Defeat was too great a compliment to pay to society. He merely changed. He started to smoke incessantly, carrying around a cigarette box as big as a biscuit tin.

He lost so much weight that he wore two suits, one on top of the other, because he despised the sign of toll.

> *I'm the kind you can trample for a time,*
> *But then I quit.*
> *God hear,*
> *That's it.*

He woke up in the middle of some night with this composed in his head. He had practically no money left in the world, but he went on drinking champagne on credit. After he had been out of work for months his telephone rang and a manager asked to see him. In his office the manager said that he thought he might have a part going, and then looked at Arthur for a long time. Arthur looked back grimly. "No," the manager said. "It isn't for you. But keep in touch." Arthur left without a word. What had he been expected to do? Go down on his knees?

Fred was killed in a car crash at the end of the year. By that time Arthur had started again as near as possible to the place where he had begun. He played in workingmen's clubs in the North of England. They didn't pay much, but they were more like the old music halls than anything left in the South. With an enjoyment that came back as soon as he started to work, he invented a solo routine that was deliberately and taxingly physical. The audiences at the first show of the evening were sparse but hair-raisingly alert. The second houses were packed, but the people were generally too drunk to pay much attention. The roaring, boozing Saturday nights were always great.

Daisy found him by telephone in Harrogate with the news of Fred's death and asked him to identify the body for her. She seemed to be asking not so much to save herself as because of some instinct for the men's friendship. Arthur flew to London and stayed in the police morgue a long time with the body that he knew as closely as his own, thinking of Fred's splendid good nature, his tough-mindedness, and his humor about the absurd and even the terrible. Daisy let Arthur pay for the funeral, although she knew he had no money. His choices were old-fashioned and lavish, with a full choir and more flowers than he could possibly afford. The bills came on the morning of the burial, and he suddenly drew them from his pocket during the service, opening them without knowing what he was doing. He crushed them in his hand as he passed the coffin and shouted at the lid, weeping. "Even when you're dead you cost me too much."

Come Back If It
Doesn't Get Better

My mother is such a terrible doctor that she has left a stamp
on the district. The villages around are full of faith healers
and health-food shops, and there is a prodigious local resistance to infection because she has never in her life sterilized a
hypodermic needle properly. Though the average life expec-
tancy of the population is low, the children are as tough as
Neanderthal kids must have been, and no one could say that
people aren't happy. Most of the women have developed the
strength of oxen, and when they do fall ill they dislike admitting it. The men, who suffer more, especially from hypochon-
dria, buy gypsy remedies and herb teas. For a dormitory town
in Sussex in the nineteen-sixties, the number of jolly babies is
amazing—more like a South Sea island before monogamy.

To imagine my mother, you have to think of a mixture of
a missionary and a duchess, though Left Wing. My mother has
always been entirely Left. I think the reason why my father
went away, apart from their unhappiness, which seems to be
worse on her side now than it was before, is that he had Tory
doubts. He grew up in a grand house and Mamma's convictions upset Papa's father, a nice old barnacle with a gale of a
voice who unfairly blames her for the state of the economy.
He also goes on at her about the Americanization of England,
especially for the tendency to put brand names on things such
as the emblem on his 1926 Rolls-Royce, which is pretty silly of

him and obviously no more the fault of America than it is of my mother, who is English through to her bootheels.

In any case, I don't know why a grown woman should be penalized for riding a bicycle into somebody's stable yard. My grandfather, who said that she should be capable of getting about on a horse like anyone else, yelled at her that there had never been anything but horses in that yard since Henry VIII. (This was actually a lie, because there has always been a lawn-mower in one of the loose boxes.) My mother said back that she found horses phenomenally alarming to sit on, and that she needed a bicycle for her work just as much when she was spending Saturday to Monday with people who hunted foxes for a career as when she was pigging it in a semi, which is the way she tends to talk when she is protecting herself.

We live in a semidetached house with a vengeance, she and I, and pig it is hardly the phrase. Mother practically exists on debris and rubble, like a sheepdog I know that hates meat and only seems to eat rock. When I finally took a room in London in the week, it was mostly because I'd been pushed out by the lava of Mother's sardine tins and medical journals and inventions and bicycle pumps and mounds of freakish makeup, which she buys in bulk from a mail-order firm, though it doesn't usually work for her any better than her medicines.

It came out later that what my grandfather really objected to was not so much the bicycle as the basket on the front of it. I think he was braced to the idea of a period that included bicycles, because the gardeners' boys had been using them on the estate since the beginning of the First World War. What he detested was a female relation pedalling about in front of people he knew with a bicycle basket full of books. My grandfather is against the further education of women. For me this has had the nice effect of his not minding about my being dim and illiterate. He has an enormous medieval library himself, but he doesn't use it because the books are all in Latin and he says that reading Latin again would make him forget Greek, which he uses to make up crossword puzzles. His reading consists mostly of *Horse and Hound, Country Life,* and *Field.* In the evenings he also has an hour with a detective thriller or a sci-fi before bed, standing up at a lectern in the library and reading the book as if it were chained up like the Caxton Psalter.

My grandmother, who died a year ago, leaving him lonely, never used to be allowed into the library at all. After her death my grandfather seemed to think of his connection with the sex as severed, he having five sons and not being a man to count the cook. So my mother had to pay for belonging to a gender that didn't quite exist in his head any longer, and there were many rows about more than bicycles, and my father got more and more Right Wing and miserable, though he never failed to back up my mother against opposition.

As to me, she has always wanted me to be an intellectual, and the disappointment to her must be constant. I wish she had never begot me. Nor that my father had either, for that matter, though I assume that the mother must be held mostly responsible. I also wish that I were bright, and that she wouldn't go out of the room so conspicuously when my brain stalls, which she does so as not to be squashing, of course, but it has the same effect.

It strikes me often that Oedipus must have been the only child in history who ever really loved his mother. I don't, I'm afraid. Not if I am honest. A lot of other feelings pass for love between us a good deal of the time—compunction, for one. She provokes more of that in me than I like to admit. It seems a puny response to a temperament that I know I would admire and like a lot if I weren't related to it. Other people can see that she is remarkable in spite of the rubble tendencies, and that she deserves the license of her originality, not to mention her guts. I do try to extend this license to her, but it is easier when I am away from her, which is the old story about mothers and children, I suppose. Back at home for weekends, I feel inept and dream of revenge—revenge on life, if possible, without involving her. She is a startling woman, and I would dearly like to startle her back by being brainy and intellectually dashing. But what I mostly haven't is brilliance. That and concentration. The combination of the two lacks is bad. My school reports were always making it clear and so does my mother, however hard she tries not to.

I daresay I arouse as much compunction in her as she does in me. I can see that my rotten jokes hammer her into the ground, for instance, but even so she generally makes an effort to laugh, snorting through her nose and looking handsome, as she sometimes can, and I feel worse than ever. When I was seventeen, last Christmas, after four years at a viciously expensive English public school paid for by my father, where she justly said that I did nothing but fiddle and moon, she sent me for a college term to America. How she did it out of her doctor's income I daren't think, because she never sends in a bill if her patients don't get better and this means a good deal of work for nothing. Anyway, the Americans were encouraging, and I felt more capable and thought I might even be some good at acting. I don't know if it could ever have led anywhere. I did comedy at college and it went down quite well and my nose was an adjunct. My mother regrets my nose, but in America I think they thought the abnormal size of it was just something to do with being European, like not liking bacon frizzled into a crisp, or not getting upset about homosexuals. I am also peculiar physically because of being nearly six foot. My mother's pie-eyed theory of medicine holds this responsible for my dimness. She says the strain on the vertebrae drains something essential out of the cerebral cortex. This sounds absurd even to me, but it makes a kindly excuse, and one that I am not above grabbing when life gets me down.

If only being an intellectual were more physical. When I sit and read, a good seven-eighths of me simply isn't being used. I keep thinking about my feet and my legs and my spine all doing nothing, and the result is very destructive to the feeble work going on in my brain—as bad as thinking about the pedalling when you are playing the piano, which is a sure way of wrecking what your fingers are supposed to be doing.

I also keep getting tripped up by thoughts of food. Being so tall, and non-cerebral, which is what they told me I was in America in vocational guidance, I seem to need a lot to eat. As soon as I have a decent thought—I mean a genuine intellectual idea, a sentence that doesn't have the name of anyone you know in it—as soon as I do happen to have such a thing, I immediately seem to think of food. It must be a lot easier for people to be intellectuals when they are shorter and need less nourishment, like my mother. Alexander Pope was a midget. I was out in the garden the other day in the middle of a not bad thought about the Common Market, peacefully watching a lark overhead that was going off like an alarm clock, and I suddenly thought, I'd love a bar of chocolate. Obviously, many people must be better than I am at getting their minds to stay where they put them. When I look at something like the leader page on the front of the *New Statesman*, two columns of intellectual sentences all following on properly from each other, I keep looking for the gaps where the man who was writing it must have got up for a cup of coffee and a biscuit. But there never seem to be any. In Mamma's house I catch myself having morbid thoughts of snacks all the time, what with the efforts about being an intellectual and also the lack of meals.

A family like mine is as departmental as a government ministry, and it has never been easy to communicate about basic rules like who does the cooking. Before Father left, my mother did it, I think, though meals didn't loom. Father was fond of boiled sweets and throat pastilles, and Mamma brought him back supplies of anything reasonably edible in the way of pastilles from her dispensary. I lived on doughnuts and Bovril, mostly. On the Sundays when my mother wasn't out on a case, we had stew. She used to cook it rather fast for stew, with a stethoscope round her neck and her bicycle propping the back door open because she always got too hot. Sunday tea was another huge binge: two blowouts in a row, with scones and slab cake and crumpets and Oxford marmalade and a new loaf. But when Father had gone the cooking stopped, and after a few months I realized there was probably a new set of rules in my mother's mind and it wouldn't hurt if I took over. She's much too thin now, especially by Fridays. She must have lost a good ten pounds since Father left. She spends hours going to sleep at night and then stays under for a long time in the mornings, which is what women seem to do when they're unhappy, and the opposite way round to the insomnia of unhappy men. This means there is never time now for her to have breakfast, which was the one meal she used to tuck into in the old days, being upper-class. For her birthday I bought her a Norwegian steel pan with a petroleum jelly flare under it, and I left it in her room at night with some bacon and eggs ready, in the hope that she'd cook herself something when she couldn't sleep, but a couple of months ago it disappeared, and then I saw it in her surgery being used for one of her experiments. If only my mother would read the medical journals that pile up in the house, instead of trying to find things out from scratch herself. I'm sure other people must have discovered a lot of the answers already. I hate the worry the experiments give her and the spectacle of more and more patients joining the ranks of faith healers.

"I've had a letter from your father," she said when I came down one weekend. In the week, I live in a Maida Vale basement with a sculptor I might marry, and my father sometimes comes for food. She doesn't know that I'm living with anyone. Even Father has only just been able to nerve himself to say that he has a mistress. He was never married to Mamma, because of her Socialism, but this didn't make the news any less hard for her to bear. Father and I both seem to find it impossibly difficult to tell her things.

"What did the letter say?" I asked Mamma, buttering both of us a muffin. Her fingers were yellow from some experiment or other and the house reeked of sulphur; I think she had been pursuing a theory in the bathroom. She had her cardigan sleeve rolled up and her right arm was peppered with needle jabs.

"Myra's taking him into hospital," she said. Myra is the mistress.

"Why?"

"He doesn't say."

"He must say *something*."

"She's putting him into the private wing. Not on the Health Service. The nurses are terrible in the private wing. He won't get looked after properly. Responsible people shouldn't give their support to the old system, anyway. If there weren't the ambiguity of private practice still going on, the National Health Service would be better. It must be something worrying or he'd never have agreed to go in. His heart."

"What's the matter with your arm?"

"What?"

"You look like a junkie."

"My electromyogram experiments."

"What are they?"

"You've forgotten. I told you."

I suppose she did. I seem to retain nothing. Her arm looked so poorly.

"Have you seen him lately?" she said as I was going to bed. She was walking away from me toward the back of the ugly little hall, with a load of books under her chin.

"Yes. This week. For dinner." She didn't reply and I felt I'd better go on because silence seemed deceptive, even though there was nothing much more to tell. "Minestrone and pasta and chocolate steamed pudding," I said.

"How was Myra?"

"All right. Quite chatty."

There was more silence.

"Do you hate her?" I asked, pretty stupidly, but I wanted to be sure.

Mamma spilled the books into a log basket in a cupboard and looked inside a gum boot for something. "I like the first twenty years of her life," she said.

Mother often speaks about people as if they weren't quite human beings—more like works of art that get slammed in the Sunday papers, books that pall, or plays that go off after the first act because of something to do with the author's intentions. People's middle age and retirement never seem to please her. But who *does* like the last chapter of a life? No one enjoys the sight of someone waning. Anyway, I don't want to be judged as if I were a novel that had to stand up in the sight of future generations. I hope to lie down, in fact. I hope to lie down and just *die* when I'm dead. I've had enough of justifying myself already with my mother. "Father looked fine," I said, because her silence might have meant she was worried, though maybe it was just because she was immersed in the gum boot. I never seem to be able to tell about this sort of thing, especially with Mamma. You allow for pain and then it isn't there, and then you don't and it is.

"I'm sure they're botching up his shots," she said.

"What?"

"He'll never go on with them on his own. He hates admitting he has rheumatism, to begin with."

"He's not on his own. There's Myra."

She ignored this. Or maybe couldn't cope with hearing the name. How can you tell?

"I don't suppose Myra would stop the shots just because you

started him on them," I said. "Surely no one could be jealous of cortisone, or whatever it is. It wouldn't be human."

"Did he move his arm like this?" She was inside the cupboard and invisible, and did a mime with only her arm showing round the edge of the door. The movement looked slow and difficult, like the arm of a man in privation signalling for help. The imitation was so graphic that it was hard to remember the pain wasn't my mother's.

"Easier than that. More like this." I demonstrated, but she didn't look. It must be because of this habit of not always looking that she's such a wretched doctor. "Are you worried?" I said.

She went into a golf-club cupboard at the very back of the house and roared, "Do I sound worried?"

A week later we heard that Father had had a stroke. It was late on a Saturday night and I had just got some baked beans into her. We drove up to London in fifty-three minutes. Usually it takes an hour and a half. We kept going past telephone boxes where we could have found out how he was now, but it was frightening to spend the time on it.

We found him alive and able to speak a little, but his left side was paralyzed. Myra was leaning over his bed, with her long black hair swinging near his face. His eyes were wild and staring and they looked like the openings of potholes. He seemed to want Myra to hold the hand that was paralyzed. The nurses had moved his watch onto his right wrist so that he might look at it, and though he was far too desperate to think of time passing, it seemed an affectionate thing to have done. In the middle of everything, the composure of Myra's head and voice had the power of art. She has a devotion about whatever she happens to be doing that you can't help being struck by. My mother is probably just as serious, but it is hard to see it. Mostly she seems cranky and somehow not to the point. For instance, she kept fussing about Papa's hair, his beautiful white hair, which she said they hadn't washed, though he had been in hospital not severely ill for a week. It had gone a little yellow. Yet she didn't show a trace of response to his illness, or even to what the nursing sister had said when we arrived.

"Mrs. Ponsonby is with him," the woman had said. "You

won't be too long." Ponsonby is our name, Papa's and mine, so my mother was suddenly the only person there with another surname. Had Papa married Myra without telling either of us? Or was she just adopting his name for the sake of the conventionalism of hospitals? Sometime in the interminable night I found out that she really was his wife; the name was on a check she had written out.

So Mamma had no rights. While Father was on the danger list, the Sister would hardly let her into his room, because she didn't fit into any official category of relation. She stayed in a waiting room for most of the next day. But that night Myra was to sleep in the hospital on a camp bed and there was nowhere for Mamma to go. She took a room at the Hyde Park Hotel. It was close to the hospital and offensively luxurious. It seemed the last place to be at the time, but somehow we failed to think of anywhere else. The management's cellophane-covered basket of flowers looked obscene, and we couldn't turn off the central heating. Mamma sat up all night in a mock Louis Quinze armchair and I slept for hours on the brocade bedspread without meaning to.

When I woke up at nine in the morning she had disappeared. I went to the hospital, where Father was a little better, and they said that she had come and gone. Walking back to the hotel, I suddenly looked into the park and saw her. There was no reason to have looked in her direction at all except perhaps that she was willing me to psychically, in spite of her dislike of me and her envy of the entrance I had to Father's room. She was sitting on a chair far away in the cold, staring up Rotten Row, where a few riders and policemen were exercising horses at a trot on the frozen turf.

She abused private patients and Father and Myra for a long time. It was a scabrous outburst and I hated her for it. But I scarcely had a moment to enjoy an interlude of indignation and contempt before my heart started banging away again and the old process of terror and attrition in her presence began. She was crying—something I had never seen—and I had no idea what to do with her. She looked ugly. Not like Myra, who cries beautifully. And her diatribes were vulgar and embarrassing, however much I said to myself that she was in extremity and meant something else by them. Then she said, "He gave Myra's name as next of kin."

"What else could he do?"

"He could have said you."

"I expect it was nothing more than the hospital keeping the letter of the rules."

"It should have been me."

"Mamma, she's his wife."

"How *could* he."

"It's only the hospital being bureaucratic. I don't understand you. You could have been married to him a hundred times over. That's all it's about. It doesn't mean anything."

"Belinda, you don't understand. You're far too young for your age."

"You don't know anything about me. I've been living with someone for a year." She didn't notice what I was saying, of course. It was a stupid time to have told her, anyway.

"By every right it should have been me. Twenty-two years." She wept furiously.

"I don't see why you're so upset. You never wanted those rights."

"I'm going to talk to Matron. He's going to fall out of bed and be hurt. They won't put sides on his bed. It's dangerous. I told them to last night, and they still haven't done it. I know he's terrified of falling."

A woman on a horse in the Row had ridden up to a nanny and a pram, and a baby was being lifted out of the pram onto the saddle.

"That horse is going to bolt," Mamma said. "Look at it. Women are so silly." She really meant Myra, I suppose.

The hard thing to respect about Mamma's instinct is that when it does putter into life at all it is so infallibly wrong. The woman rode very slowly down the track, with the child on the saddle in front of her, and the horse went perfectly.

When Papa started recovering and Mamma was still being pushed out by the nurses, I went to Matron in my turn. What I had to say seemed instantly frivolous. I felt a boor to be explaining about Mamma's position and saying I was illegitimate and all the rest of it, when people nearby were suffering and when the woman behind the desk obviously had reasons you couldn't dismiss for having decided to be conventional in her own life. I expected her to be a battle axe, but there was something attentive and benign about her. She listened to me for a time with her head hanging like a big dog's, as if something were awry and tiring and she wished to start afresh. "I'll tell the nursing staff in the wing," she said.

"Mother's a doctor, you know. She's worried about his not having sides on his bed in case he falls out."

"The Sister is one of the best we've had. She'd have put sides on the bed if they were necessary."

A week later Father was talking more easily. He asked me not to let Mamma see him without me or Myra there, because she fussed him. A nurse who was in the room when he said it must have told the Sister, because Sister herself then asked Mamma not to go in again for the moment: I daresay with a little triumph. Mamma simply nodded and said she anyway preferred not to, because she wasn't happy about the way the case was being nursed. The atmosphere was immediately impossible. Mamma didn't go to the hospital again, but made reasons for herself to stay in London all the same, and she behaved to me with a grim undertone of jealousy. She was far too stern with herself to pester me for news, yet at the same time I found it hard to grub up voluntarily the crumbs she depended on. Bearing tales of Father and Myra together in the awful, expensive hospital room stuck in my throat. I felt perfidious to everyone.

"Have they got the sides on the bed?" Mama asked me suddenly one day. And God help me, I lied and said yes. I can't think why. It made me an ally of Myra, of hospital politicking; no friend to Papa, or sense, or anything crucial, let alone to my plaguing mother and her perfectly decent anxiety. The sides *hadn't* been put on the bed, and I knew quite well that the Sister's reason was obstinacy, the old professional's obstinacy about knowing best. She was taking the sort of risks that hospitals get away with all the time: the ones that people never suspect of being as random as most other impulses, because we so badly want to believe that everything in medicine happens for less passing reasons than that. When someone is very ill, it's not pleasant to start thinking that medicine is obviously as open to silliness as, say, soldiering, and that lives can be altered because a doctor has pranged his new car, or a Sister thinks someone is trampling on her rights.

Not long afterward, Papa did fall out of bed. He would have

been in terror, lying there half paralyzed on the brown lino-
leum and not able to make himself heard. He had dreaded all
his life being a cripple, as some people dread lunacy. The first
time he fell, he was all right and only chipped a bone. Things
went on. Mother didn't know about it, and I couldn't tell her.
The doctors ordered sides to be put on the bed and Papa felt
safer.

The next thing that happened was that Mamma sent him a
parcel of the throat pastilles he liked from a chemist they had
both used once, and Myra cracked up about it.

"She didn't send a note," she said, weeping desperately in
the little anteroom. "It was so furtive of her. I don't know
what she's playing at. I don't understand anything." She
sounded just like Mamma about the next-of-kin form.

"Mamma never writes notes," I said. "Nobody can read her
writing except chemists. She's not playing at anything."

"*Chemists.* Even the chemist says that he's going back to her."

"What are you talking about?"

Everything seemed fabricated. Mamma couldn't have told a
chemist such a thing. And Myra surely couldn't have catechized a man in a dispensary? I asked again what she meant,
but she shook her head. And then when I asked her directly
if she had really gone all the way down to the chemist to talk
to him, she nodded, and cried more, and said, "Everything's
been shabby ever since he was ill. It's out of control. He was
so happy. I don't know what to do."

A little while later, Papa fell out of bed for the second time.
Again the sides weren't on the bed, perhaps because the nurses
were still cussed on principle, or perhaps just because they
were negligent. The fall concussed Papa and he died in a few
hours.

I took my mother down to stay with Grandfather, who was
unexpectedly imaginative enough to ask her to come, and she
behaved monstrously, though God knows she had the unwit-
ting right to, considering that her halting instinct had for once
gone so horribly home. Marriage licenses and throat pastilles
and chemist's gossip and Sister's little victories—they were all
smoke screens, I suppose, but they added up to a very powerful fog of fictitiousness, shifting the outlines of a calamity,

and while we were in it none of us had the nerve to tell Mamma the fact that was owing to her. I suppose a lot of people in a crisis will invent decoy reasons for feeling mortally threatened, but I don't really understand why no one but Mamma seemed to have been any good at seeing that the real threat was the possibility of Papa's death. Not who had said what to a chemist, or who had first thought of putting sides on a hospital bed. Yet then I remembered the jealousy she had been cast into herself about the next-of-kin form, and that seemed as disguised a response as anyone's—to fall prey to the pinch of that particular anguish when Papa was fatally ill, and when she had spent a good part of her life delivering small wounds to him by refusing to get married for the sake of her principles.

The next weekend, Grandfather said that Myra was coming down. Mamma seemed panicky and said something brutal and nerveless. Almost as soon as she got there, Myra told me I looked gaunt, which Mamma naturally interpreted as an insult to her, and I said I was fine, and went and had some Bovril with the cook. Then Mamma surprisingly suggested that Myra and I should go riding. When we came back into the stable yard, Mamma was waiting for us in the rain. Heaven knows how long she had been there. She was standing in the middle of the yard on the cobbles. Her arms looked long, like a monkey's, and they hung a little in front of her. Myra got off her horse at the mounting block, because her back was hurting— from the effort of lifting Papa, I suppose. Mamma made a drama about getting out of the horse's way, and I laughed. There hadn't been any humor anywhere for a long time, not from anyone, but it wasn't a particularly funny thing to have chosen as a start and I saw Myra looking at me sharply. She was practically on Mother's side, it seemed. Side, ally. You take my side. Side of the bed.

We had sherry indoors quickly, and Mother's face looked crusty with the alcohol after the cold. Grandfather was in his usual goldfish state, moving round people without speaking and avoiding bumping into them in instinctive ways of his own while he read a bound volume of *Punch,* and then standing still for twenty minutes in front of the bay window, with the draft waving fishy gills of white hair.

After he had been there for a time, Myra told Mamma qui-

etly that Father had died for exactly the reason she had fore-
seen. I thought it generous of her. Mother looked neither
triumphant nor grieved, only old. I started to cry, and Myra
got up and put her arm round me. And then Mamma suddenly swooped and hit Myra in the face, and folded me up as
if she were collapsing a camp bed and put me on her lap,
grabbing my head and shoving it into her chest. She stroked
my neck and it wasn't comforting at all. I felt as if I was suf-
focating. It was as bad as being inside her guts again, and I
suddenly remembered all too accurately what the first impris-
onment had been like. I tried laughing, and it helped a certain
amount. At least I can do that this time, though the prospect
of a second escape seems poorer.

Known For Her Frankness

"What *are* dialectics?" said Anthony, looking for his agent's kit bag and makeup case on the baggage trolley at Frankfurt Airport and speaking with as much truculence as he could ever muster.

Maud tapped her cigar and said, "You mean what *is* dialectics. I predict that the car will crash. Then I drive it at a brick wall. The car crashes. I am right."

"Ah."

"Though properly understood, dialectics is the muscle of the drama."

Anthony still wondered if it shouldn't be "are the muscle." No: "The wages of sin *is* death." But no one would actually ever say such a thing. Though that wasn't entirely true, for Maud would, and she would probably even bring it off. To have the character to give sanction to grammar—phew! Maud talked with a mixture of pedantry and horse sense that impressed him as singular and forcible. Sometimes he tried to catch her style in scraps of speech that he wrote down in a notebook, because she had often told him to listen to the way strangers talked and to keep a record of conversations overheard in the underground. But for reasons that he took to be his own error in transcription anything that he pilfered straight from life never sounded convincing. She could make him doubt most things about himself, but not the accuracy of his ear. He might put down until kingdom come the dully literal truth of the way she talked, but when it was written out it was clearly not credible, except maybe as the English of Nkrumah, or of an Eskimo who had studied the language by Gramophone record.

Her style on paper, in her manuals about how to write, was rather different. It was terse and practical, a little like a dog trainer's. In the quiet of his own skull he called it manly, but he would never have used such a word to her, not only because she was privately decorous but also because the way she talked about her children made him sense that she dreaded being thought Lesbian. The blight she cast on his work was something he didn't care to inspect, for she certainly wished him well. Before she had taken him over, he must have written too easily. Then he had read a textbook of hers about the craft of the dramatist and it had stopped him from showing her anything for a year. There was a chapter in it titled "So You Think You're Chekhov." The very thought had crossed his mind only the day before, when he had contemplated giving up doctoring, as she kept telling him to. He felt appalled at her insight, and at his own cheek. There was another chapter called "Study Your Market, Not Your Navel."

"I'd like something to drink," she said while he was putting the luggage together.

He spoke to the porters in English, because he was trying to forget that he had spent the first ten years of his life in Berlin.

"Practice your German," she said.

In the airport restaurant, he asked her what she would like.

"A plain soda water. With ice."

"It seems to be all beer," he said, after reading the menu for a long time. "They don't give you any alternatives. How German."

"*An* alternative. They don't seem to give you *an* alternative. There can never be more than one alternative. *Alter, alter—* one of two."

"Aren't you feeling well? No, I didn't mean—I meant about wanting soda water?"

"Aeroplane food is inspissating. My tongue feels like a rug. We ate better in Hall at Oxford." The days of reading philosophy, politics, and economics, called P.P.E., came up a good deal. "I've just sold a comedy of Philip's about air travel," she said. "It's ill-executed, I'm afraid. My fault. It was my topic. I gave it away to the wrong person. No, I correct myself: for the wrong reason. I'd hoped to get the poor man writing again. But he's sold out. My God, he's sold out. Still, I suppose the play's commercially viable. Everyone abominates air travel, though they all do it. What a travesty of Mary Wortley Montagu." She ran a comb through her cropped hair.

"It's awfully good of you to have come with me," he said, feeling he should apologize for something, and kicking as powerfully as possible against the fancy that he was Philip.

"It's a poor play. I hate it, frankly."

He remembered a girl he had known once who used to say *"franchement"* whenever she meant "frankly"—rather a soupy girl, and far from frank, but consoling all the same on despairing Sundays, and she had made beautiful casseroles.

"Philip hasn't written a real play for four years," Maud said, looking around for the waiter. "I've told him so perfectly frankly. He's funking it."

"I must get you your soda water."

"It looks to me as if there's some system of getting service that you don't grasp."

"No, I don't think so. Really? Oh." He floundered, and then clicked his fingers, doing it hesitantly, because it seemed like the worst of the British Raj in India. But no one can click his fingers hesitantly.

"Why don't you shout something to him?"

"I hadn't realized how much I was going to hate speaking German again."

She snorted. "You mustn't funk it. Once you get over it, there's your play."

"Two soda waters with ice, please," he said eventually to a waiter who looked like Himmler.

"It is absolutely forbidden to have soda except with whiskey," Himmler said.

"Two coffees, then," Anthony said in German, trying a grin to rinse out the sounds in his mouth.

"What's happening?" Maud asked. "Why are you laughing?"

"He says it is absolutely forbidden to have soda except with whiskey. It's so German, that's all. It's exactly what I remember." Kindergarten in Berlin in 1936. Special Jewish Kindergarten. His Jewish mother pretending there was nothing special about it at all, and pouring chicken soup with barley down his throat.

Maud made a swatting gesture against his amusement.

"Why didn't you ask for Perrier water, then?" she said. "They must surely possess Perrier water."

"I wonder if you have Perrier water," Anthony said. "Or Pellegrino?"

"Mineral water," said the waiter. "You have to have."

"Is the mineral water still or sparkling?" Anthony asked, trying to foresee snags. In his consulting room he was good at it.

"Yes," the waiter said.

"What?" Maud said.

"He says mineral water we have to have," Anthony said. "I mean, we have to have mineral water." He laughed again, without looking forward to a thing.

"I hope it's sparkling," Maud said. "Surely mineral water's *bound* to be still. They must have *something* sparkling. *Something* like soda."

"Soda is absolutely forbidden except with whiskey," the waiter said. "Because it is permitted only to charge a profit of sixty pfennigs if soda is served with whiskey."

Anthony started to translate this, out of an inability to do anything else with it, and when he turned round again the waiter had disappeared. There was a silence of a sort that he knew very well. It seemed especially designed to give weight to his ineptitudes, lending a ridiculous dignity in space to what he had screwed up, like making a free-hanging sculpture of a broken egg whisk.

Maud salvaged him as usual by noticing nothing, and he mistakenly respected her instinct for dealing with his doldrums. She went on talking strongly, attacking Philip's decline as a playwright, the way he had compromised and run dry by doing translations and hack comedies. And once he had been at *Oxford,* she said. He had got a *Double First.* In *P.P.E.*

Then the waiter came back, with two glasses of soda. "I have brought you what you absolutely insisted upon having," he said.

"What's he saying now? He's brought the soda perfectly agreeably. You must have misunderstood him. Your German can't be as fluent as you think."

"He did say one couldn't . . ." Anthony said. But the next

thing to be said was "Thank you very much" in German, as quickly as possible. No point in behaving like some second German. But he *was* German, of course. Ex-German, rather. Jewish. A Londoner. A doctor. A future playwright. No, a playwright already, by gum. ("So You Think You're Che-khov.") He thought with envy of the young *locum* doctor standing in for him at home, seeing his patients at this very moment, and then he thought of his ex-wife, and his ex-cat, which used to sleep on their bed, and then with interest and longing of flukes, the flukes of absorption that can at least put the unforgettable at some merciful remove.

The waiter set down the glasses, saying, "It should be entirely forbidden."

Maud smiled at the man, which struck Anthony as expedient of her, and said to Anthony, "How do I say thank you?"

"I've said it already," Anthony said.

She ignored it. "He's been charming," she said. "I'm afraid you've been churlish. It's understandable, of course, with your history."

They went out through a door that was marked "Hours of opening: 08.00 to 23.59." Anthony laughed again, at which Maud felt curious while her face stone-walled, a habit of disguise that she recognized as costly but could not be rid of. The waiter bawled at them triumphantly and kicked the door with his shoe to point out another notice, which said in English "No passing."

"No passing," Maud said. "Even I can read that."

"No *passing!*" Anthony laughed again in some torment. "*Everything* brings—brings things back." When words ran as thin on him as this, he sometimes managed to suppose that it meant he was unconsciously saving them to write with. But generally it was plain to him that the cause was his familiar and wringing insufficiency.

"You mustn't get subjective," Maud said. "Don't investigate *your* troubles. People don't want to hear about that. See it *their* way."

He was starting to feel like a bundle of notes about himself in a case-history folder in hospital, one of the folders labelled "NOT TO BE HANDLED BY PATIENT."

*   *   *

In Berlin his past rose to his teeth. Maud had put him into a small hotel near the street where he was born, telling him to absorb the atmosphere. He was supposed to be germinating a television program for her, on her own topic, about the conscience of an escaped East Berliner. She had told him she was fed up with plays about love—which she spelled out "L.U.V.," as if she were saying "B.E.D." to another grownup in front of a child who might be going to throw a tantrum—and that she wanted to hear about some public issues for a change. Sick with longing for his wife, Diana, and worn out with the public issues of doctoring that had apparently lost her to him, he had agreed.

He tried to think about the Wall. He could see the passion of the theme, but its substance eluded him. He was in the grip of more personal and random emotions. After a few days in his efficient hotel bedroom, the rage and shame of having any connection with West Berlin passed into glassy remorse. He felt more like a hole in the air than ever, and also frighteningly stupid. He could have stuck pins into himself and it would have taken ten seconds for his body to complain. He slept ten or twelve hours a day and didn't answer Maud when she telephoned. This was the furtiveness that could become fear: not owning up to a language he spoke, smuggling sausages into his bedroom, pretending he was out, plaguing the porters for a letter from his wife when he knew she didn't know where he was. He began to have the spy's terror, the terror caused by one's own silence. Once he saw Maud in the Kurfürstendamm, eating alone in a café and looking a little desolate, with a stack of coins already piled beside her plate although her meal had only just come. Instead of keeping her company he dodged into a doorway to watch her. She had ordered no wine. Perhaps her money was running out. In the middle of eating she got up to telephone. He thought her not easily distinguishable from the Berlin women, with their detestable white felt bowler hats, who still looked much as George Grosz had drawn them thirty-five years ago; but there was also something isolated about her, and the battered mannish briefcase against the leg of her chair was touching. She came back from the telephone booth quickly, looking distracted. When he got to the hotel, she had left another message. "Please telephone back urgently any time until 4 A.M."

He felt like a pursued husband, though not like any husband that he had ever been himself. In his own life it had always been he who was the supplicant, telephoning Diana from call boxes on his rounds in the hope of closing some nagging gap of intimacy left at breakfast, and always having to hide the agony of dread that her casualness could cause him, for fear of the danger of irritating her. She was never in now when he tried to make contact with her. Nor had she answered messages through friends, and she had written to him only twice: once to say she hoped he was well, and once about some dry cleaning. He couldn't even put together a picture of her day any longer, because she hadn't allowed him to see the Bloomsbury rooms where she lived, though he had mooned by them in his car often enough, at the starts of many nights doomed to reveries of longing and revenge. He spent the black hours best in the writing of hopelessly happy propositions to her that he kept for comfort in a drawer, as if they were love letters received from her instead of dead ones from himself that he saw no good in posting. His memory of her became dulled and blocked, a stalemate of the imagination that began to have the taste of sloth and suicide, like the evil torpor that can ensue from spending night after night without a dream. When he finally had a nightmare about the loss of her, at least it supplied him with a landscape to imagine her in again; there was some spasm of life in that, he supposed.

Maud caught him in the doorway of his hotel one evening. "You never ring me back," she said.

"I have tried. You've been out."

"There were never any messages."

"You know what hotels are like."

"I was concerned about you."

"I'm all right."

"I don't like not knowing what you're doing. Are you working?"

The muscles under her eyelids clenched, and the skin on the bone of her forehead moved back like the hood of a snake. Was she angry? Something else.

"I must talk to you," she said. "Otherwise there's no point in my being in Berlin at all."

"I thought you were here for lots of other reasons as well. You said you had to come anyway."

"Are you getting somewhere with the script?"

"I'm doing my puny best."

"Is it coming along?"

He felt precisely as if he were hiding something from her.

"Am I going to be pleased with it?" She pursued him to the porter's desk.

"There's nothing." What was he saying? Denying an affair, it seemed. He was in the middle of more grief than he could deal with, yet he was piling onto it the commonplace misery of subterfuge, as if he had to protect some clandestine happiness that didn't even exist.

To shake off the mood of secrecy, he took her out. The balance of power must have shifted between them, because he had a few glittering moments of objectivity about her as well as the old nuzzling gratitude of some broken-kneed dray horse. For once, too, she seemed to want him to order, and to pay the bill.

"Here's to your play," she said, when they had decided to have another brandy. "The play of public conscience."

"I don't know about that."

"A reprieve from the telly of L.U.V."

"I feel in more of a muddle about politics every moment."

"Not muddle. At least dignify it as ambiguity."

She was quite handsome in her own brazen key. He had had too much brandy, and he suddenly thought that her face looked like a Buick. To make up for the unkindness, he made a bad and nervous joke. She responded, not laughing but sucking in her cheeks like a man blowing onto his hands in cold weather. He saw himself as a buffoon with nasty reserves of observation, a man with goonish spectacles clamped round his ears and perfidy in his guts, and he felt so appalled by his mistrust of an old friend who must surely be taken for an ally that he tried as fast as possible to invent some headway on the project about Berlin.

"You're lying to me," she said.

"I don't know what you mean." It was like a B-feature about a married row.

"You haven't written a line." All he had written, she knew,

were letters to his ex-wife in his head; she could smell it. "You're unhappy. You're obsessed with Diana, aren't you?"

"No. Yes. I can't help it, anyway. Why should I?"

"You do extend a prodigious welcome to ghosts."

"Anyway, I have written quite a lot."

"Really."

"Quite a bit. I think it's going to be a comedy."

"You've never written a comedy. It's not a very promising subject for humor." She checked herself. "Well, it's a daring idea. I believe in you, you know." Because she had been aggressive again, she pulled out her wallet and showed him photographs of the children.

He had invented the idea of the comedy at that moment, and to prove it he had to offer her a joke in evidence. "I'm going to put in a few of those brutal German proverbs that don't mean anything. Like 'A hungry belly has no ears.' "

She started to say that to her this sounded more like Khrushchev, and then stopped herself again; the line was so clearly a proffering of comfort. He was surely telling her the truth. Not really intending to write about his wife. "You mustn't be unhappy," she said with an edge.

"I do try not to be."

She put on an adopted cozy accent to make him laugh, but she was no mimic and the effort was arthritic. "It's all in the mind."

"I know, but that's where I have to live." He smoked a cigarette and looked at her stubbly hair and bought her another brandy. "I can't think of a toast," he said. "Never mind the blessed television. Here's to—oh, all the other writers you look after. Here's to Philip."

"Have you ever heard of the Slavonic banquet?" she said. "It's a Polish image for the Russian method of killing off the inconvenient. The Russians invite any dangerous questioners to a sumptuous feast, and during the embraces and the toasts the guests are quietly poisoned."

"What do you mean by that? You don't mean that *you're* the guest?"

She made no answer.

"What do I do?" he said later, very drunk.

"There's nothing to do."

Next day, she sent him a huge parcel of books about Germany. She also enclosed a little leather-bound copy of Heine's love poetry, with a jocular luggage label on it that read "This is *not* what you are writing about! ! !" There was a plain white card inside as well, saying, "Only the artist realizes that some of us exert a Homeric effort simply to behave ordinarily," but she had translated her declaration to him into Latin in a self-defeating impulse to disown it, and he never troubled to puzzle it out.

He read some of the German books, soothed by her solicitude and fancying for a time that he really was being impregnated with ideas about the Wall. He felt like a potato in the soil dreaming of the vodka that was to be made of it. Then the endless writing of love-letters in his head crashed through the barrier into fiction, and he put his fierce lament onto paper.

Maud waited patiently for him to finish, with only a sliver of dread, and they came back together to London. They did the second half of the journey by train. The compartment was full of two middle-aged German couples with a sticky and unhappy child. Both couples mysteriously spoke in English, with heavy accents. The mood of the return was the opposite of the journey out. This time Maud was buoyant with collusion, and Anthony robust because he was free of his script.

"Would you like a cup of coffee?" he said to her at a station, and she grinned at him over the cardboard beaker, holding it with both hands.

One of the Germans, wearing a surprising black-and-white checked cloth cap, made an operation out of buying coffee through the window and held up the train while he got a missing straw. "I took up the cups of coffee, *five* cups, and they give me only *four* straws, not five," he explained carefully. He drew in his breath sharply and gave the change to his wife, who put it into a double-clasped purse, which was then hidden in the inner pocket of a locked handbag. He watched the method anxiously.

"Now we got to wash up our fingers and later we eat," said the second man, when he had collected the paper cups and straws.

"We might go and have lunch," Anthony said to Maud, looking at the preparations for eating in the compartment— napkins tucked into shirt collars, laps spread with paper bags. The code of agreement he assumed gave Maud pleasure.

When they came back an hour and a quarter later, the meal seemed scarcely begun.

"I got here tongue as well," the man in the checked cap was saying. "Tongue. I have various packets. These our sister-in-law put in. And the tin of milk. And a plum. And a peach."

"A straw for the tea," said the second man, pouring from a thermos.

"No."

"No?"

"No."

"Sugar?"

"No sugar."

"I take sugar never either."

"I without milk take it also."

"Have a cigarette," Anthony said to Maud.

"Thank you," Maud said.

"I haven't got anything to read."

"I'm not sure that I could concentrate," she said, as near to humor as he had ever seen her.

He wondered whether to give her his script to read. Perhaps she really wouldn't be able to concentrate. Yet he badly wanted a response to it. He thought it might be good.

"We will real Americans be and with our hands chicken eat," the second man said. He had kept on his hat. It was a brown derby, worn straight on the head without an air. "One half of a gherkin," he said, unwrapping a small thin package in disgust. "What can you do with one half of a gherkin?" He flapped it like a galosh.

"Would you like to read the blessed script?" Anthony asked.

"Are you sure?"

"I'd like you to."

He found it an impossible spectacle to watch, and walked up and down the corridor for nearly two hours. He thought it unlikely she would be influenced by the disappointment he had dealt to her plan for a play about the Wall. She was too generous an agent for that.

"Sorry about no Berlin," he said when he finally returned to the compartment.

"You can't be held responsible for your distaste for politics, I suppose." She had her fingers awkwardly in five or six places in the script.

"Are those parts that worry you?"

She pulled her fingers out quickly. "Things that struck me."

"Struck you how?"

One of the German men undid yet another thermos and offered Maud some chocolate in a cup, with a straw. She shook her head. The smell in the compartment was nauseating.

"How is the *strudel* consisted?" one of the women asked.

"Come into the corridor," Maud said. Her dislike and fear of the script burned in her head. This couldn't be jealousy, she told herself. No. More like ordinary disappointment, multiplied to a point that was nearly unbearable. "The blow fell with the merciless swiftness of all misfortune"; it was someone else's line, a client's presumably. "My dear boy," she said, lighting a cigar. "I'm probably not fitted to speak about this."

"Why?"

"Knowing your circumstances."

"What?"

"Your Diana."

"It's not autobiographical."

"No. The power of feeling is."

"That makes it sound good."

"Do you want me to speak frankly?"

"Of course."

"I think you shouldn't give up doctoring. I think there's less disappointment in it for you than in writing."

"What are you trying to say? That you think it's awful?"

She was silent.

"You're just peeved that it's not about your subject, that's all. All agents are eunuch writers. I wish you'd just take your ten percent and leave us alone." He looked round at her, standing beside him in the corridor bar staring out at the stupid countryside. She was crying, for heaven's sake.

"Do you know what it's like?" she said. "You use us as conveniences. We're not just secretaries to fix the Belgian rights."

"That's exactly what you are. You sound like all those parents who complain that their children use the house like a ho-tel. Of *course* they do. All children do. And so will *their* children. Writers have agents simply to do maths and whoring for them. And to get loot. And perfectly handsomely you do out of it. I don't begrudge your cut. But it doesn't mean I owe you anything, either."

"Except possibly friendship."

"Fine kind of friendship to kick a new script in the teeth."

"We were happy just now. And in Berlin."

"Happy? I'm very fond of you. You've been very good to me. But you're not being honest, not for a moment. We were both miserable in Berlin. I've never felt so lonely in my life. And you were just inventing errands to stay around."

"Because I wanted to."

"Out of benevolence. I missed Diana every moment. I was down a hole. I kept falling asleep at the wrong time like an old tramp. This play got me through, not you. It was a way of wangling with my own cowardice, that's all. You can get an edge on yourself by writing. I'm not saying it's great, but it's not bad."

"I think it may well be very good. I said I wasn't equipped."

"First you say you're not equipped, then you say go back to doctoring, then you say it may be good. You take a position and then you say things on either side of it. What *is* this frankness of yours?"

"*Each* side. You mean that I say things *each* side of it. Not 'either' side. 'Either' side isn't what you mean."

He looked explosive, and then laughed and gave her a kiss on her flushed and papery cheek and bought them both a bottle of wine in the wagon-restaurant for tea. He took his script with him from the compartment for fear of its vanish-ing. She told him she didn't want to be his agent any longer if he didn't need her advice, though it would be pleasant if he ever wanted her friendship. She behaved with dignity, in a pain that he perceived without comprehension of it.

In the taxi, while he was dropping her at her small house in Fulham, she made an effort to regain some inch of the in-dispensable contact she had squandered, but there seemed no way of doing it. The pint of milk and newspapers that she had ordered for her arrival were correctly outside the front door.

"Coming home is as difficult as going away," Anthony said, aware of having behaved wickedly. "Fear of the next step, I suppose."

"Cowardice isn't the worst vice."

"What a curious thing for you to say. When you can't ever have been guilty of it."

She shook her head vehemently, with tears flying out of her eyes each side, like water flying off a spaniel's ears.

He speculated about what she was coming back to. Empty house, chagrin perhaps about his script, loss of face with the TV company, negligent children? An old affair with some woman who had hurt her? The thought did come to his mind a week or so later that she might have been in love with him, but it seemed a ludicrous idea as well as self-congratulatory, and he put it by.

The Redhead

When the skulls in the crypt of St. Bride's Church were dis-interred, the wisps of hair remaining on them were found to have turned bright orange. The earth lying under the paving stones of Fleet Street had apparently had some extravagant chemical effect. This was what Harriet's hair looked like. When she was born she had two sprouts of what seemed to be orange hay on her head. It was shocking in its coarseness and to her gentle Victorian mother alarmingly primitive, nearly pre-moral. It gave the infant's presence the power of some furious Ancient Briton lying in the crib.

Neither the color nor the texture ever changed. The hair stayed orange, and to the end of her life it was as tough as a rocking horse's. When she was a child it was left uncut and grew down well below her waist. The tangles were tugged out three times a day by a Norland nurse who attacked the mane in a moral spirit as though it were some disagreeable piece of showing-off. By the time she was thirteen, the routine of agony and rebellion on one side and vengeful discipline on the other had worn everyone out and she was taken to a barber. The barber took a knife to the thicket, weighed it when it was off, and gave her two and a half pounds of hair wrapped up in tissue paper, which the nurse briskly took from her as soon as they were outside because she didn't believe in being morbid.

The operation had several effects. One of them was that the nurse, robbed of her pleasure in subduing the hair, turned her savagery more directly on to Harriet, and once in a temper broke both of her charge's thumbs when she was forcing her into a new pair of white kid gloves for Sunday School. Another was that the child, who had always been sickly and scared, as though all her fortitude were going into the stiff orange fence hanging down her back, seemed to begin another kind of life as soon as it was cut off. She grew four inches in a year. Her father, a dark, sarcastic, pharisaically proud man whom she worshipped, started to introduce her to people as "My fat daughter."

She wasn't really fat at all. With her hair cut off she didn't even look like any normal Victorian parent's idea of a daughter. She looked more like Swinburne streaming up Putney Hill. Her lavender-scented mother began to watch her distastefully, as though she were a cigar being smoked in the presence of a lady without permission. Mrs. Buckingham's dislike gave Harriet a sort of bristling resilience. She had from the beginning an immunity to other people's opinion of her, which isn't a characteristic that is much liked in women. Later in her life it made her impossible. Her critics found it crude of her not to care what they thought of her. It meant that she started off at an advantage, for as soon as they imagined they had caused her misery they found that they were only confirming her grim and ribald idea of the way things would always be. She lay in wait for pain, expecting no rewards from people, and this made her a hopelessly disconcerting friend. Her peculiar mixture of vehemence and quietism caused people discomfort. If she had had any talent, if she had been born in another period and perhaps if her spirit had been lodged in the body of a man, she might just have been heroic. As it was, her flamboyance struck people as unbecoming and her apparent phlegm as not very lovable. The only person who might have respected her independence was her father, and he was the one being in whose presence she lost it. His mockery, which he meant as love, frightened and cut her to the bone. At thirteen she felt trapped by the system of growing into a woman, which seemed to be separating them, and longed more than ever to be his son.

A year later her back began to hurt. At the girls' establishment where she had been sent at huge expense to learn music and French and to carry out the ornate disciplines conceived by the headmistress—including communal teethwashing in the gardens, winter and summer, and then communal gargling into the rosebeds, which the headmistress regarded as a form of manure-spreading—the pain was put down to growing too fast. It was only after she fainted at tennis that her father took her to a specialist, who found that she had an extra vertebra. For the next two years she was supposed to spend five hours a day lying flat on her back on an old Flemish seat in the hall of her parents' London house. Formal education was shelved, which was a relief, because the unctuous kind of diligence expected of her at school had convinced her that she was both stupid and sinful. The physical privation of lying for hours on cold wood suited her mood. She began to feel that she would like to become a Roman Catholic, partly to frighten her mother, who was one of the pioneer Christian Scientists in England, and partly because the rigorousness of the experience attracted her. Her father was a Presbyterian, and when she confronted him with her decision, doing it as pugnaciously as usual in spite of her nerves, they had a furious and ridiculous quarrel; a man of fifty for some reason threatened by the vast religious longings of a fifteen-year-old. She found herself capable of a courage that startled her. Maybe it was temper. She went upstairs, emptied her jewelbox into her pockets, and left the house.

In 1912 this was an extraordinary thing to do. For two nights she slept on the Thames Embankment. It was really the misleading start to her whole punishingly misled life, because it gave her an idea of herself that she was absolutely unequipped to realize. She started to think that she had a vocation for taking heroic decisions, but it was really nothing more sustaining than a rabid kind of recklessness that erupted suddenly and then left her feeling bleak and inept. As a small child, sick with temper when she was forced to do something against her will or even when she was strapped too tightly into a bed, she had risen to heights of defiance that genuinely alarmed her family. She had a ferocious and alienating attachment to independence, but very little idea of what to do with it. The row about Catholicism got her out of the house and carried her through two euphoric days, during which she thought about

the Trinity, existed on lollipops and stared at the Celebration
of the Mass from the back of Westminster Cathedral. After
that, the fuel was spent.

The priest whom she eventually accosted took one look at
her, an ill-proportioned, arrogant child with cheap clips in her
gaudy hair, and started grilling her for an address. She was
furious that he refused to talk about religion except in terms
of duty to her parents; what she wanted was a discussion of
Peter Abelard and an immediate place in a convent. She had
an exhaustive knowledge of Sunday Schools and it was depressing to find him full of the same bogus affability that she
detected on every Sabbath of the year. She wanted harshness,
remote ritual, a difficult kind of virtue; what she got was an
upholstered smile and an approach like a cozy London policeman's to a well-bred drunk on Boat Race night.

Declining to lie, she let the priest take her home, planning
to swear the maid to secrecy and slip out of the back door
again as soon as he had gone. When she got there she found
that her father was dying. The truancy was forgotten. Her
mother, supported by two Christian Science practitioners, was
in another room "knowing the truth" and trying to reconcile
her hysteria with Mary Baker Eddy's teaching that passing on
is a belief of mortal mind. The child was allowed into the bedroom and for two hours she watched her father die. He was
in coma, and as he breathed he made a terrible bubbling sound.
The nurse and the doctor left the room together for a moment and she grabbed him by the shoulders and shook him
desperately, with an air-lock in her throat as though she were
in a temper. When his bubbling stopped and he was dead, it
seemed to her that he suddenly grew much larger. He looked
enormous, like a shark on the sand.

After that no one in the family really bothered about her.
Though it was Edwardian England and though Harriet was
the sort of upper-class child who would normally have been
corseted with convention, Mrs. Buckingham's resolve collapsed after her husband's death. Her natural passivity, encouraged by her religion and perhaps by the fact that she was
pregnant, committed her to a mood of acceptance that was
sweetly and hermetically selfish. The nurse was sacked to keep
down the bills and the incoming maternity nurse was not in-

terested in an unattractive fifteen-year-old. It was agreed by Mrs. Buckingham, who had always resisted the false belief about the pain in her daughter's back, that Harriet should stop lying around on the hall seat and go to a school founded in the 1840s for the further education of gentlewomen. Having lost some of the true Christian Scientist's sanguinity about money and the faith that good Scientists should be able to demonstrate prosperity, she suggested faintly that Harriet had better take a secretarial course and equip herself to earn what she called a hat allowance, by which she meant a living.

The classes that Harriet in fact chose to go to were logic, history, English literature, and Greek. Logic, when she came to it, seemed to her as near to hell as she had ever been. She felt as though her brain were clambering around her skull like a wasp trying to get out of a jam jar. History was taught by a whiskery professor who thundered about the Origin and Destiny of Imperial Britain. His ferocious idealism made her think over and over again in terror of what her father would have said to her, and what she would have replied, if he had woken up when she shook him.

The English master baffled her. She hated Lamb, who was his favorite writer, and once terrified the class by saying so by mistake. Her own tastes were all wrong for the times; she liked the flaying moral tracts of the Christian Socialists and a kind of violent wit that had hardly existed since Pope. She felt a thousand miles away from the gentle professor, who used to cross out the expletives in Sheridan and even bowdlerized *Macbeth*. "Ladies," he said sweetly to the class one day, "before proceeding further we will turn to the next page. We will count one, two, three lines from the top. We will erase or cross out the second word and substitute the word 'thou.' The line will then read: 'Out, out thou spot. Out I say!' "

To begin with, she made friends. There was one girl called Clara whom she used to meet in the lower corridor an hour before classes began: they had long discussions about Tolstoy, Maeterlinck and Ibsen, and were suspected of immorality. But soon she began to detach herself from the girls sitting hand in hand in the Bun Shop and from their faintly rebuking way of going at their books. Life, she felt vaguely but powerfully, was more than fervent chats about great literature. Life as she wanted it to be was momentarily embodied by the don who taught her Greek, a brave and learned man who had fought the Turks in Modern Greece. As usual, her excitement burned out fast, like her courage. She had no gift for academic work; she simply longed to be able to dedicate her life to it.

Six months later she went to prison as a suffragette, having lied about her age and enrolled as a militant. It was the only time in her life when she was free of Doubts. She had found a cause, and the cause wasn't yet debased by her own incapacity to believe. She was thrilled with the suffragettes' tenacity and the expression it gave to her feelings about being in some kind of sexual trap.

But feminism, far from letting her out of the trap, turned out to be a hoax. She suddenly saw herself and her comrades not as prophets but as a howling and marauding mob. She prayed for faith, addressing a God whom she had never altogether managed to believe in, but clinging to the structure of the Roman Catholic Church as though it might do instead. During a hunger strike she asked to go to Confession. The prison doctor refused unless she agreed to drink a cup of tea and eat a piece of bread and butter. Confused, she agreed, and wrote a letter confessing the weakness to a friend outside, asking her not to tell the stonyhearts at Suffragette Headquarters. When she came back from Confession, uncomforted, she found her cellmate kicking the doctor who was trying to feed her, and at the same time yelling that he should take his hat off in the presence of a lady.

For Harriet this was the end of Votes for Women. She had no idea what she wanted, but it wasn't a license to have it both ways. She left, feeling cold and fraudulent. After making several trips to Headquarters in Lincoln's Inn and each time letting the bus take her on to Aldgate East, she managed to resign from the movement. Characteristically, she did it in the most abrasive and insulting way possible. Everyone was disagreeable.

Six months later the Great War had broken out and she had found a new cause. She became a ward maid in a hospital. For a girl brought up in a Christian Science home there was a certain frightening kind of excitement about medicine, like

drink for a teetotaler; but otherwise she found the work har-
rowing and repellent. Everyone else seemed to be roused by
the war, but she saw it as a giant emotional hoax. The roman-
ticism of the period upset her more than the blood. All the
house surgeons started to avoid her, preferring the pretty
V.A.D.'s. Her unnecessary decision to do the dirtiest work in
the place struck them as alarming. By now she was six foot
tall, and to the patients she looked like Boadicea with a bed-
pan; none of them found her calming, and the sisters regarded her hair with secret fear. The people she liked best
were the consultants. Longing as usual with her spirit to enact
the role that her flesh shrank from, she pined to be a doctor.
She knew that the one thing her mother would never provide
money for was a training in medicine, so she wrote eventually
to the *Boys' Own Paper* to ask them how to go about it, inventing a letter that was supposed to come from a badly-off boy
whom she thought would enlist their sympathy. The bullying
answer appeared in the correspondence columns:

> *Medical training is long and arduous. It is unsuitable for the*
> *working boy. Our advice is that you learn a trade.*

So the huge, blundering, privileged girl, now seventeen, went
back to her mother's comfortable house. She prayed, and she
took up vegetarianism, more as an extra religion than as part
of the war effort; after a while she made herself go back to
the hospital, and eventually she found higher mathematics. She
bought textbooks, studied in bed at dawn, and went every night
to evening classes given by a frock-coated seer who spoke about
calculus as though it were a way of life. "The language of
Newton!" he cried, scribbling figures on the blackboard and
immediately wiping them off with a damp rag as though he
were doing vanishing tricks. "O Newton!" He was the only living person whom she had ever heard using the vocative case.
He talked as though he had learned Latin construction before
English. "To read the language by which Galileo explored the
harmony of the celestial system! To look backward to the time
when first the morning stars sang together!" He treated the
mad redhead as though she were a fellow spirit, and she responded, until the moment when she finally admitted she was

incapable of understanding a word he was saying. After two months she loosened her grasp on the subject like a drowning man giving himself up to the sea.

Slogging away at the military hospital, sickened by the pain she saw and more muddled than ever, she decided that when the war was over she would become a tramp. She thought of it first when she spent her two nights on the Embankment, which was littered as soon as dark fell with sad, wild men and women stuffing bread into their mouths out of brown paper bags or staring at the barges on the river. She was attracted by the privation of the life, which she always linked with virtue, and she liked its sexual freedom. One woman derelict told her that after living with three husbands for twenty-five years she had decided to give them up and devote herself to the task of surveying the cathedrals and abbeys of the British Isles. This woman also had a passion to visit Russia, and she seemed to look on herself as a sort of tramp reformer. Besides being keen on Bolshevism she was deeply religious, and a great admirer of the Court of St. James. She told Harriet that she often met King Edward VII in her dreams and looked on him as a sort of uncle.

At the end of the war the Buckinghams decided that something had to be done; not Mrs. Buckingham, who was still repining, but Harriet's vast web of paternal relations. At Christmas her Uncle Bertie assembled the clan at his manor house in Wiltshire and announced that as a start she had better be presented at Court.

"But I don't want to be," she said.

Girls didn't speak like that then.

"Nonsense," he said breezily. "Fun for you. Get you out of yourself for a bit. Put some roses in your cheeks." And he bore down on her and pinched them, smelling of horse sweat and sherry. "Agnes will see to it, won't you?"

His wife stopped eating marrons glacés and nodded grimly.

"It's a waste of money," said Harriet, looking out of the window at the parkland, which seemed lush enough to feed the whole of the East End of London until the next war. She remembered going to harangue working women in the East End when she was in the suffragettes: their pale, pinched, dulled faces, dulled with years of lost endeavor. She had told them that once women got the vote everything would be all right: "Poverty will be swept away! Washing will be done by municipal machinery!" Not that she knew anything about washing. At home she had never been aware of it. But it seemed to her that the women in the East End never got away from it: everlasting wet linen in the kitchen, smells of flatirons and scorching, burns on their knuckles, and puffy skin up to their elbows.

Bertie was furious. His performance of the lecherous uncle collapsed. His glass eye—he had lost the original when he was cleaning a gun—seemed to swivel further out of true than usual and stared pleasantly at the fire; the real one looked like a razor.

"Waste of money! Questions of yield, my girl. A thousand pounds for a season and we might get you married off. No thousand pounds and your mother might find herself supporting you all her life. How much do you think you cost in a year? Eh? Add it up. Add it up."

The married women in the room looked righteous, as though they had made the unselfish decision. Harriet's Aunt Gertrude, a nervy spinster who lived with Uncle Bertie's household, sat as still as possible.

When they got back to London, Harriet packed and left forever. The fact that she had no money of her own didn't strike her as an obstacle; the suffragettes had reinforced her natural contempt for people who worried about money. One of her few friends in the movement, whom she used to meet at Lockharts in the Strand for a poached egg once a week, had come down from a mill town in Lancashire in 1916 with nothing but two brown paper parcels. (The smaller was her private luggage; the larger, which she called her public luggage, was full of pamphlets.) Harriet got a job as a dentist's receptionist and lived on lentils and sausages in a hostel until the dentist asked her to marry him. To her surprise, she said yes.

She was surprised because she had thought that she had a vocation not to marry. Her heroines were Queen Elizabeth and Mary Wollstonecraft and Edith Cavell and, when she was miserable, Mary and Martha, the maiden ladies of Bethany. Queen Victoria, whom she made perpetual coarse jokes about in a way that struck people as uncalled for, had put her off marriage in the same way that she had put her off Scotland. But the dentist supplied her with a religion for a while: the religion of giving up everything for someone else. As she saw it, this meant becoming as drab and acquiescent as possible, and until her temper and gaiety erupted again, it worked.

They lived in a depressing house in Finchley. She cooked abominably: boiled meat and blancmanges. After the birth of her second child, during the Depression, she began to dream violently of hell and her father and the Book of Revelation. The Queen Victoria jokes got more ferocious and they upset the dentist a good deal. There was one terrible day when she came into his surgery and found him sitting beside the gramophone playing "Soldiers of the Queen" with tears pouring down his face. She launched into a long mocking invention about patriotism and monarchists and the army, inspiring herself with hatred and feeling pleasurably like a pianist going into a cadenza. Afterward she repented it bitterly, but she was hopeless at apologizing: instead of retracting her feelings, what she always did was to say that she was sorry for expressing them, a kind of amends that costs nothing and carries the built-in rebuke that the other person is unable to bear the truth.

The fanatic voice of Revelation built up in her head like the air in a pressure chamber. "Nevertheless I have somewhat against thee, *because thou hast left thy first love*." She went over the final quarrel with her father again and again, and left her present loves to fend for themselves. She brought up her children in her sleep; her husband, who was a silent, kindly man, did a lot of the work. In the front room she started to hold prayer meetings that were almost like séances. Presently she found that she had the gift of tongues: notions of sacrifice and immolation and of a saviour with hair of sackcloth poured out of her mouth like a river of lava.

When the war began her husband was too old to be called up. He became an air raid warden and they kept allotments. She made touching things for the children called mock devil's-food cakes, concocted out of cocoa, golden syrup, carrots, and soya flour. Her back by now was giving her constant pain. She looked more odd than ever and her movements were beginning to stiffen. She smoked cheap cigars, and the ash lay on her cardigans like catkins. On her fortieth birthday, in 1943, she was taken to a hospital for a cancer operation and no one expected her to live. When she found she had survived she felt like Lazarus. She noticed that everyone was slightly embarrassed by her; she reminded them too much of the death around them, and they put on brutish cheerful voices with her. She felt, as so often, fraudulent, a corpse stuck together with glue.

In 1944, when she was out shopping, a flying bomb killed her elder child. It fell on a crowded school, and when she ran to the site from the High Street she could see some bodies still moving. The youngest children had been out in the playground; some of them survived. She found one little girl of about four under a pile of masonry. The child was on her back, unconscious. Just before she died she began to bicycle furiously with her legs, like a bee not quite crushed under a knife. Harriet carried the memory around with her as an image of horror, like the sickness in her own body.

After the war it became clear to her that the one heroic thing she was even faintly equipped to do with her life was to teach herself to die honorably, by which she meant without fear. This meant grappling with a panic that was like asphyxiation. Her wisps of belief in an afterlife had deserted her irrevocably with the flying bomb. "It is not death that is frightening, but the knowledge of death": she started from this. After cooking her watery stew one night and seeing her younger daughter into bed, she went to the public library and looked up "Death" in a concordance. She brought home piles of books every week: Seneca and the Stoics and *Measure for Measure* and the Jacobeans. Her husband watched her reading and finally lost touch with her. The daughter fidgeted through her long wild monologues and wished she wore prettier clothes. People said that she had become nicer, quieter, but harder to get at than ever, if you knew what they meant.

"I really must go up to Harriet's tonight."

"Oh God, she's so unrewarding."

"You feel you have to. She might be gone next week."

"I thought they got it out when they operated."

"You never know, do you?"

"But she's as tough as old boots."

"I can't bear her really, but I feel sorry for her husband."

"How can people make such a *mess* of themselves?"

*　　*　　*

She is still alive. When she dies I think she is going to be more frightened than she expects. It is an absurd ideal, really: a huge carcass inhabited by a blundering speck of dust and hoping to die as well as Nelson.

I put this down only because I have heard her daughter's friends call her "mannish," and her own generation "monstrous." This is true, perhaps, but not quite the point.

The Tactics of Hunger

"Algy is a she!" Lady Grubb shouted into the telephone to the young man from Fleet Street. "The he is called Guy. It's quite clear which is which in *Burke's Peerage*. Surely you have *Burke's Peerage?*"

The gossip reporter said that he had, but she overrode him. "If your newspaper can't afford it, then go to the public reference library. There is one beside a cinematographic house in Leicester Square. But surely you should possess a copy. Tell your proprietor I said so."

Her twin children, bitterly cold, fiddled with their sherry, which had been mixed with whiskey in the decanter by mistake, and took the reporter's side. "He's *got* a copy of it, Ma. He keeps telling you," said Algy, who was the girl, as her mother had bellowed.

Lady Grubb made a whirring noise like a pheasant going up. "Why didn't he say so?" She glared at the telephone dial as if it were the young man's face and held the receiver away from her ear. "What did you telephone for, then?" she said into the mouthpiece. "No, of course she's not engaged. She hasn't come *out* yet."

The fact was that Algy had been living for the last year with a working-class architect called Len in a basement flat in Maida Vale. But her mother, who was hostile to facts, had gone on entertaining for her as if she were a chaste child just emerging from school. The young men she rustled up as marriage candidates seemed to Algy to be all one person with different haircuts, well-born dullards on their way into industry who exclaimed "I say, how jolly enterprising!" when they heard that Algy was a scene painter, and who surprised her by still dancing fox trots and rumbas that she thought extinct. This weekend she had finally braced herself to the course of obtruding the existence of Len into the house. She had thought for months of trying to blow the gaffe on the fact that she was past marrying off, but it seemed a lot to put Len through, and her mother was anyway exceptionally good at not acknowledging that a gaffe had been blown.

At sixteen, three years ago, she and her brother had erupted together from home practically unnoticed. Their parents were elderly, though not as elderly as they seemed. Lady Grubb had fallen easily into the habit of behaving to her children as if she were some doggedly snobbish godmother, inviting them home every few months to look into their marriage prospects and treating the occasion as if it were a country weekend that put her to a lot of trouble, though her house was actually in the middle of London and fully staffed with unhappy *au pair* girls. Reality got through to her intermittently; her apprehension of it was uncommonly tuned, for though she was generally oblivious to the most apparent, she was often startled by things to which others were deaf. When Guy brought his girlfriend home for the weekend, for instance, the air was thick with sex, but Lady Grubb noticed nothing. On the other hand, when she had taken up the carpets for a dance for Algy and filled the house with sixteen-year-old boys from Harrow School and Marlborough, she twitched to the thin soprano signals of public-school lust like a dog hearing the squeak of a rat in its sleep. She was cruelly obsessed with class, and if her children had not come from a background that she knew to be reliable she would certainly have ignored them as she ignored the *au pair* girls.

"I wish she'd get her hair done," Algy said when Lady Grubb was out of the room.

"She looks all right," said her brother.

"No she doesn't. She used to be pretty."

"You're kidding yourself. When's Len coming?"

"Late as possible."

Lady Grubb's invitations to them were always by letter, and

led to a file of correspondence because she enjoyed making microscopic changes of plan. The first summons habitually began with a long and belligerent explanation of why some other weekend was not possible. As it had never been proposed in the first place, her children could read this only as a piece of unadmitted defensiveness about having ignored them in the past. They dreaded the prospect of accepting, but they were fond of their father, so they generally packed warm clothes and went.

Lady Grubb kept the house miserably cold. Occasionally she recited, as though it were a rule of life, a testy saw of her own invention maintaining that fifty-five degrees Fahrenheit was the correct temperature for a drawing room and fifty degrees for corridors and bedrooms. Bathrooms she regarded as outhouses. She was a clever woman with obscure sources of energy who would suddenly start to garden by torchlight late at night, or walk willfully all the way to Soho to buy vegetables at the times when the pin in her hipbone was especially painful. In other moods she would go to bed for days, and have trays sent up to her room that were laden with stingy nursery snacks of mashed fish and junket. Her interests, when they were detectable, were urgent and surprising. Sometimes she startled her mild husband by knowing all about African politics. Lord Grubb was an ancient hereditary peer who kept up eagerly with the times and was trying at the moment to unlock his capital to set up a chain of waffle shops. His wife, more canny than she seemed, had already witnessed huge losses over a scheme to promote detachable shirt cuffs, and so far she had managed to sit on the remaining money. Lately he had been troubled by rheumatism brought on by the damp in the house, and his doctor had set him up in sleeping quarters on the ground floor with independent heating arrangements. But his bathroom was in the conservatory, which had two doors onto the garden where his wife grew plants, and as she left these doors open all morning his part of the house was apt to be colder than anywhere.

The house was decorated almost entirely in weedy shades of green and looked to the children like a fish tank that needed cleaning out. Lady Grubb knew a great deal about antiques and owned some beautiful pieces, but she topped up the genuine furnishings with reproduction Jacobean coffee tables and plastic cruets. The cruets were said to have been bought in the cause of saving the work of cleaning silver ones, but she still made the *au pair* girls polish a hoard of Georgian silverware in the cellar every week. One of her hobbies was anesthetics, and she subscribed to an anesthetists' journal in which she had seen an advertisement for a chemist who outfitted doctors' waiting rooms and surgeries. This had appealed to her, and recently she had replaced a broken standard lamp in the drawing room with a hospital operating arc light. It had been refitted with a low-watt bulb practically too dim to see by, in order to save electricity.

Algy particularly was made miserable by the change in the house. Her only pleasure in it now was the notes left all over the place by her father: cheery instructions in a classical scholar's hand, written on the gummed labels used by the more pious English governments to get a second use out of old envelopes. "If this drawer sticks, don't despair," said a label on a Queen Anne chest in the spare room. "It will open if tugged sharply to the right." And on the bedside table, facing the sleeper: "Don't be alarmed by any irregular thudding noise in the night. It is probably the water tank. If in doubt, call for help." Lord Grubb knew well enough that Algy dreaded her visits, and to let her off the trial of breakfasting with her mother he had installed a complicated route of strings and pulleys that led from her second-story bedroom to the basement. This made a placard spring out in the kitchen. It said, "I'm ready for breakfast. Thank you." The idea of a bell didn't occur to him.

"Ma must have taken to cooking up bits of food in her bedroom," Algy said when Lady Grubb was doing something to the plants and she and Guy were alone with their father in his study.

"What do you mean?"

"She's got a Primus in there."

"I haven't been up for a while," her father said, implying total absence of mind, and some of body, too.

"She seems extra loopy today."

"Eh?"

"I wish she wouldn't wear those cardigans," Guy said. "She looks like a Scripture mistress out to grass."

"When does she expect us to leave?" Algy said. "Lord, it's only Friday."

"I don't know, my darling," Lord Grubb said. "Whenever you like. Sunday evening?"

"Last time she couldn't wait to be rid of us. She didn't say a word all Sunday."

"I think she was frightened to ask how long you were staying in case you left," said Lord Grubb, with a lunge of shrewdness.

When Len arrived, they seemed for some reason to talk about nothing but health. He was a tall, shy, bony man with a stoop, who cracked his fingers when he was worried. He expected to be patronized by Lady Grubb because he came from a lower class, about which he didn't generally care tuppence, but when he saw her effect on Algy he found it more difficult than usual to be ribald about it.

"You've got a cold," Lady Grubb said accusingly to her son.

"No I haven't. I don't *think* I have, at least. Have I?"

"I can *always* tell when you have a cold," she said, brooking no argument. "The whites of your eyes go pink." Then she said to Len, but without turning to him, "Do you get ill much, Mr. Warren?"

"Hardly ever."

"We've all had colds here. Cecil had a snorter. I could hear him honking all the way from my bedroom. He lives on the garden level because he suffers from gout."

"Rheumatism," Lord Grubb said softly.

"Did you know that tortoises get gout? If they're brought to a cold climate too young, that is. I persuaded our Member of Parliament to introduce a bill about it. About the importation of small tortoises. One can judge the age by the length."

"Daddy wouldn't have rheumatism if the house wasn't so damp," Guy said.

"The place isn't damp at all," said Lord Grubb. "You can always tell a damp house by the state of the cigars."

"It must be very different where you come from," Lady Grubb said enigmatically to Len, who came from Putney. Putney was two miles away at the most, but she implied that it was two thousand.

"I'm afraid this is what you'll have had every day of your life," she said to him as the *au pair* girl put a plate of mutton in front of him. Algy suddenly realized that her mother was engaged in an elaborate pretense that he was a New Zealander.

"Not a bit. Algy and I live off baked beans," Len said.

"Ma," Algy said, "Len was born in *Putney*."

Lady Grubb graciously ignored the rebuttals. "Would you like some ice in your drinking water?"

"Aren't you having wine?" Algy said to him.

"Don't press it on him," said Lady Grubb. "He's not accustomed to it. We had an American to dine the other day who wanted coffee with the sirloin."

"Len and I have wine all the time," Algy said, but facts led nowhere; they never had.

"Have you found somewhere pleasant to live in London?" Lady Grubb said.

"He lives with *me*, Ma. He's *always* lived in London."

"I expect you'd like to meet a few people. Algy must remember to ask you to come next time I give a little party for her. There are always plenty of spare girls."

The *au pair* maid went down to the basement and again started plotting with her friend how soon they would have enough money for the fare home to Zurich. When she came in with the junket, the row had obviously developed. There was a V-shaped vein sticking out in Algy's forehead. Lady Grubb looked triumphant. Lord Grubb was trying to concentrate on taking the band off a cigar. Guy had left his mutton, and Len was watching Algy.

"Where on earth did that trolley come from, Ma?" she said.

"The chemist."

"You're furnishing the whole place from a medical outfitter. It's starting to look like an obstetrician's lumber room."

"It's not your house."

"It's certainly never felt like it. You're dead right."

"*Too* right, as your friend would say," Lady Grubb replied, imitating a New Zealand accent. "Will you have some junket? Louise makes it very nicely."

"You must have rennet spilling out of your ears," Algy said to Louise, who by now was beyond taking pleasure in such moves of friendliness and simply handed round the dish with her left hand behind her back as she had been taught, feeling mutinous and thinking proudly of a homeland where not junket but fondue was the commonplace. "*Why* do you shop at the chemist's?" Algy said to her mother, stupidly pursuing the question of the trolley.

"I had to go there anyway and I saw it. I needed some things as presents." Her children knew at once the sort of things that these would be. Last year for Christmas she had given Louise a red rubber medical bathmat for the aged.

There was a silence, and then Lady Grubb said, "It was quite a pleasant walk."

"But why couldn't you telephone? They deliver."

"The delivery is very unreliable."

"Oh, Ma. The one thing that chemists are is reliable. That's what their profession is. Like those men in long white overalls who see schoolchildren across the road."

"Last week they made a mistake on a prescription label."

"Well," Algy said lightly, "don't be a nit—complain to the *Lancet*. Or go to another chemist."

" 'Nit' must be a local word that you taught her?" Lady Grubb said to Len.

Dislike ran round the table like electricity, and the lightning generated and struck. "Come off it, you old bag," Len said. "I'm not that outlandish. I was born two miles away. My mum probably did your scrubbing."

Then it was as if trees started crashing down and roots tearing out of the ground. Algy began abusing her mother. Lord Grubb, in terror and fragmentation, waved his hand at Algy with a patting motion of great violence and scattered cigar ash on his beautiful old green smoking jacket. "Don't rise to it, sweetheart!" he shouted. "Don't you see your mother's only trying to convince herself your friend doesn't belong here?"

"Don't you think it's time she realized he did?" Algy said coldly.

"Probably," said her father. "But she's old. We're both old. I hate her. She's going to die first and she won't notice it, and then I'll be on my own. It's not dying I'm afraid of; it's being dead."

Lady Grubb picked up her plate of junket and went to eat

it in the drawing room, shaking with a passion she didn't care to scrutinize because it contained not only fury but also amazement and fear.

"She's killing herself with what she eats," said Lord Grubb to the three left at the table, who felt they should be listening to nothing. "It's not fair. It's not fair to me. I don't want to be on my own. One more fall and she'll break her hip again and then she'll die. What she puts into her system isn't fit for a woman of her age. It's pap. It's food for premature lambs. But she won't do anything I say. I might as well not exist. I write her notes every day. Notes all over the house, in her potting shed, and on her food lift. I try to warn her and she pays no attention. She never replies. Sometimes I think she can't read any longer. For all she advises me of her condition she might be *blind* and I wouldn't know it. I hate her. I've written her notes and notes and notes and she's never answered one of them. Surely she could send me a message of some sort? She's only to give an envelope to Louise. I haven't seen her handwriting for so long that I can hardly remember what it's like. Perhaps she can't even hold a pen any longer. Perhaps she can't do *anything* any longer. Poor soul. Poor old cocky. She used to call me 'my old mate' when she was a girl, you know. It was a joke from a music-hall song. I hate the sight of her now. She's nearly dead. I know it."

"Father," Guy said. Then he could find nothing more to say at all. It was impossible to find any landmarks for the moment. The balance of power had moved like the contours of a desert after a night wind. What was happening? Before this, the twins' visits had always seemed extorted. Now it seemed neither here nor there that the two of them even happened to be present. They had always written off their mother's maneuvers as tribal tactics devised to keep the two of them for her kind, with their father as some sort of lower ally in the endeavor, more deeply absorbed by his autonomy and his cigars than by the dynamics of living with his wife. But now his needs seemed more urgent and primal than hers.

"You mean she won't admit she's ill?" Algy said.

"That's what he's been saying all the time," said Len. "Haven't you been listening? Lord Grubb says she won't admit anything. Blimey, she wouldn't even admit I'm English."

"Oh, shut up. Of *course* I've been listening," Algy said to Len. "I can't get . . ." She waited and tried again, to her father. "You mean she's frightened of the doctor and she thinks you're going to send for him behind her back?"

"You can't possibly be suggesting Father *intimidates* her," Guy said. "Not Mamma."

"She won't confess it," Lord Grubb said, hectoring the table but still powerfully giving the impression of talking sotto voce to himself. "She's blind, for all I know, and half starved. Probably even all those long walks she says she takes are a pretense to put me off. It's quite likely she calls a taxicab every time and has it waiting round the corner out of sight. It's perfectly probable she can't even get *about* now. I write to her about it again and again."

"You keep talking as if you live in different houses," Algy said.

"She's going to die, and she's keeping it from me. She was always secretive. I won't stand for it. She's got to put it in writing."

"Do you want me to talk to her?" Guy said. "If you're as worried as this . . . But she doesn't seem ill. That's what I don't understand. Does she, Algy? And if she is, surely she's perfectly capable of calling a doctor herself. Isn't she?"

"She does it to spite me," his father said. "Don't you see what I'm saying? She refuses to answer. I never hear from her."

"Daddy, you *live together*," Algy said.

"Talk to her when we've gone and tell her that *we're* going to get a doctor to come. Would that make it easier?" Guy said.

Lord Grubb snorted and looked sulky. The room was full of ire.

Len said carefully, "When my dad died, he and my mum hadn't spoken for three years. They'd had a fight." He watched, on an instinct. The block of paranoia sitting at the other end of the table minutely shifted shape.

"I certainly shan't speak to her until she starts replying to my letters," said Lord Grubb, cued in so that it was possible to say it at last.

Algy got up from the table and went into the drawing room. After a moment Len followed her.

"Ma," Algy said, as normally as possible. "Is it true that you and Daddy don't talk to each other?"

Lady Grubb suddenly wept over the magazine on her lap and the finished plate of junket. It was a spasm, over at once, like a sneeze. "My hip hurts," she said.

"You can't go on like this," Algy said.

"My mum and dad managed not to open their traps to each other for fourteen years," Len said. "Mum used to play the wireless and turn on all the bath taps as soon as he came in. Even in front of me they did it. At least you two don't do that." He tried a cliché, to seem breezy. "There's always somebody worse off than yourself."

"It's the only time I hear his voice, when you two come," Lady Grubb said. "He even leaves notes for the maids."

"Do *you* speak to *him?*" Algy said.

"I won't be bullied. Why should one? Getting nagging letters in one's own house. During the Labour landslide they used to be *love* letters. He hasn't even changed his handwriting. It's perfidy. Even the same black ink. Reminding and reminding me. He's trying to break into me."

"Which Labour landslide?" Len said softly.

"Ramsay MacDonald's."

"Why won't you speak to him?" Algy said, sitting on a low tapestry footstool by her mother's chair and putting her forefinger on Lady Grubb's big garnet ring as if she were pressing a doorbell, staring up at the implacable old head and thinking of nothing but of how to get her to look at one of the two people in the room.

"He's going to die," said Lady Grubb, eyes fixed on the carpet. "He'll die first and he knows it. Then I'll be on my own. I have to practice being on my own."

"Is that why he moved downstairs? To make you learn? I thought it was because of his gout."

"You silly goose. The young guess nothing."

"If you mean about being lonely," Len said. "If you mean we don't know much about being alone because we don't find it difficult, that's true."

"No one understands loneliness if they haven't been married," Lady Grubb said. "For forty years. You two! Fly-by-night affairs. You risk nothing."

Algy turned on Len. "It's not true at all. Do you really think

I don't know what isolation's like? What do you imagine goes on in my head all night when you've been talking about splitting up? You hope it takes the pain out of it to talk about it, but it doesn't. You said when we bought those bloody birds last Christmas, 'I wonder how long it'll be before we're yanking all this apart again and halving the furniture and carving up the doves.' I've never forgotten it. It's unbearable."

"Oh, come on," Len said. "Not unbearable. Inevitable. When it happens it'll just happen naturally, and that's all there'll be to it. It would be silly for us to say *if* it happens, because it's bound to. The things you can't avoid are the easy part."

"I see," Algy said angrily. "Like dying."

As We Have Learnt from Freud, There Are No Jokes

I married my Manhattan landlord. If I were a local, I suppose I would put that more delicately. But I come from Tobermory, a Scottish island village where it would not be such a craven blunder.

The beginnings with him were not auspicious, though.

I waited for him for an hour, outside his half-built apartment building. You could see him coming a block away. He wore a bright mustard suit. One of the Mafia? An evil-looking briefcase contributed. On the other hand, and leaving the suit aside, there was something pleasant about his stoop.

"Are you married?" he said at once, head turned toward the din from his workmen as he stepped past me over the rubble and put a key into the lock of the, I should have thought, not yet apt to be plundered building.

"I've been waiting an hour," I said. "The foreman promised you'd be here. I've got to find somewhere to live."

He scraped his shoes free of the mess outside, an act which interested, considering the dirt he was to step into. A piece of grit flew backward from his heel onto my eyeball. I had an impulse to say "Sorry," owing to my nationality, but managed to quench it.

"I'd like one of these apartments," I said.

He went in. "Married?" he said.

"No," I said, holding my eye. I suppose a New Yorker would

have said "Yes," for prudence, but there wasn't much lust in the air.

"I can't have unmarried women," he said. "They're always getting raped on the way to the laundry."

As I left, with all speed, I noticed a sign outside the apartment building that said "Beware of the Dog." Rage weakened here, and I thought quite fondly of the workman within who must be in the habit of bringing some overloyal pet to the site.

The next day, after the thirty-third night spent on the exitless side of a bed that was shoved up against a wall and that also housed a physiotherapist called Daphne, an air hostess called Olga, and Olga's dopey Teddy bear, I got out of the bottom of the bed unheard and thought, *No*.

I rang the building site. The foreman said the owner was there.

"Can I speak to him?"

"He don't speak on the telephone."

So.

Do something else. Buy a birthday present for my grandmother on the way to work.

"I want a nightdress to send airmail," I said to a saleswoman in a fair-to-lousy cut-price shop. "For an old lady."

"This."

"No, something to the floor, I think."

"This."

"Haven't you got anything that goes to the floor?"

"This is waltz-length."

"She's eighty-one. I think she'd rather have something full-length."

"Everything is waltz-length or bikini. You want she should trip over and break her neck?"

So.

Push on to work. My employer, Simpson Aird, a friendly capitalist who calls me Miss Nib when he feels rumbustious, dictated letters in bed. His wife, Tessa, ate fried bread and tomatoes. Their six-month-old son was kicking on the bottom of the eiderdown. I picked him up while Mr. Aird thought.

The baby treated me hospitably, being the age he is and there-fore still inclined to interpret the rest of the world as an annex of himself. To be organic to somebody else's idea is an expe-rience not to be sneezed at, in these divided times or any other. The Aird baby has a strong cast of thought and he imposes himself, philosophically speaking; as he stared at me, lying on my lap, he seemed like a hand of mine. Self and others. The usual tautology.

"How's the apartment hunt?" Mr. Aird said.

"Plugging on," I said.

"No luck?"

"Not yet."

Tessa said, "You'll suddenly find one."

"Or gradually," I said.

"You don't *gradually* find an apartment. You *suddenly* find an apartment," said Tessa.

"I might be inching up on it, mightn't I?"

"No," said Tessa, who sees things her own way as resolutely as any baby. "One day you'll simply have it, and then you won't remember what it was like to be without it."

"No?"

"You need some new clothes," said Tessa.

"Shall I get on with the letters?" I said.

Simpson peered at our two faces, scenting a row. Or a wound. "My dear Miss Nib," he said, hurling himself out of bed and into the bathroom, "take a letter. I think you look first-rate." He imitated my Scots accent. "Furst-rate. Scrumptious." He sang "D' ye ken John Peel?" into the bathroom mirror.

So.

Revived, go back in the lunch hour to the apartment build-ing, even if the landlord has twice more refused to come to the telephone. Swine.

He was standing in the foreman's office, looking troubled. Mustard jacket off; black pullover underneath. That stoop. A brooding and somewhat majestic effect. If swine, then big wild boar, hunting quietly in the woods for something, mooching about and turning things up.

The foreman was putting down the telephone. "They won't pay," he said to the landlord. "I told you."

"I've come about an apartment," I said. "I don't see why I have to be married. If it comes to getting raped on the way to the laundry, married women with a lot of washing must get raped more."

"Get them back on the phone," the landlord said to the foreman.

"You'll have to talk to them yourself," the foreman told him. "They're your insurers."

"No."

"You know what you've got, not talking on the telephone?" the foreman said. "You've got a hangup."

The landlord went on standing there, turned away from me.

"I want one of these apartments," I said to the foreman, who was drinking a Coke.

"Can't you see I'm busy?" he said.

"I've something on my mind," the landlord said softly to a concrete wall.

"What's happened?" I said.

"A *dog's* been stolen," the foreman said impatiently.

"Oh dear," I said. "Was it his?" looking at the large black back.

"It was to guard the plumbing," said the foreman, crushing the Coke tin with his hand and throwing it into a corner.

"What?" I said.

The landlord said, fast, "It was supposed to be guarding the plumbing, and if you think that's crazy then ask him about it. He told me to."

"It's you that's crazy," said the foreman. "What sort of a boss are you, doing what *I* say?"

"Trained to look after *plumbing*?" I said.

"These dogs are highly skilled," said the foreman.

"This one wasn't," the landlord said.

"Well," the foreman said, "what do you expect for eighty bucks a week? You got it cheap,"

"It seems a heavy thing to steal, a bath," I said. "Let alone baths."

"I know it was only eighty bucks a week," the landlord said over me. "But eight *hundred* for the loss of the dog."

"You should've taken out insurance. You should've thought of that," said the foreman.

"Also, it was a nice dog," the landlord said, now sorrowing and private.

The foreman yelled something to the ceiling in another language and stomped toward the door saying, "The whole world is crazy, I tell you. Make your own telephone calls. What kind of a landlord are you, not speaking on the telephone?"

"You should've got the four-inch ducts finished on schedule," the landlord said. He took a couple of steps toward the man. "Then the plumbing would have been connected and we'd never have had to *have* your guard dog."

"Listen," said the foreman, swinging the door handle to and fro. The landlord had come to a halt. "I'm going to take time out to tell you something."

"Well, I pay for the time," the landlord defended himself, though not as intimidatingly as I could have hoped.

"One: Plumbing has to be bought in *ahead of schedule*, in case you lose a month's rent, O.K.? Two: The four-inch ducts were finished *last month*. It's the Mayor's *inspector* we're waiting on now. And why? Because you were too goddam mean to drop the five-hundred-buck payment to City Hall for *special services*."

"Five-hundred-buck *bribe*."

"*Payment*. For *special services*, for getting it *done*. See what happens when you waste your time in line?"

The foreman left. The landlord stood there. Now, to contradict myself, he didn't look like one of the Mafia at all. On the contrary.

"Shall we have some lunch?" he said.

"Yes, please. Could I have an apartment as well?"

He laughed. His eyebrows looked permanently as if they had just shot up. They had big half circles of pure white skin below. His hair was dark brown, and his face so asymmetrical that a reflection of it in a piece of broken mirror on the wall was unrecognizable. An exuberant man, nervous, poetic, with a way of pulling his long fingers one by one when something was making him laugh to himself. He was fun. I have never had such fun with anybody.

At our first lunch I asked for canneloni to fill myself up.

"Good. Girls are always thinning themselves," he said.

"What's your name, by the way?" I said.

"Murray Lancaster," he said. Pause. "Huh?" he said. "What are you looking like that for?"

"Well," I said, "I thought you were in the Mafia, but it's not much of a Mafia name."

"Why do you think I was in the Mafia?"

"Because you're a landlord, I suppose," I said, holding back the next thing I had been going to say and then deciding he might not mind. "Perhaps also because of your mustard suit."

He looked angry. It took me some time—weeks—to discover that he was poor and wore clothes handed on by a negligently competent brother-in-law in the soft-drinks business.

He asked my name.

"Emm," I said. "Emm McKechnie. My parents christened me Empyrean, but there had to be a way out."

"Do you believe that, in general?" he said.

"Yes, with luck," I said. He looked up fast, extremely pleased in a philanthropic way but still hanging back for himself. One could tell. Something more needed to be said, obviously. Wondering whether this was it, I told him I had a mustard suit, too. Ah, no. He concentrated on the menu. Hell, I thought. Patronage. The British abroad at their old work. But when I bent down on some pretext and could see into his face it seemed possible that he was laughing at himself as well as flustered.

Still with his head down, he ordered his lunch. "A very rare steak," he said. And then, to me, "Vegetable?"

"Could I have a green salad?"

"And a very green salad," he said to the waiter before he could stop himself.

The foreman victimized him. Waiters made him feel a fool, this clever man. Spectres of poverty beset him, and he hankered after anything that would last. Perhaps that was why he had embarked, without capital, on trying to put up a building, though god knows this would have no long life in Manhattan. The little money he had saved was kept in seven different banks and also in his apartment, in the freezer locker of the fridge, inside a string beans packet. He made piles of quarters in his sock drawer when he emptied his pockets at night. After a few months, despite our best efforts, he went bankrupt and his knavish contractors were awarded all he had. We kept the loot that was in the freezer. We got married in a while. By then we were living in a dirt-cheap place on the Bowery. He hung on to his car. No bailiff would have touched it. He was deeply fond of it. It was a very old dark-green Hispano-Suiza, held together with beautiful leather straps like the ones my grand-parents had on their steamer trunks.

He was a moving man, bashful but debonair. He was the only man I have ever known who once actually fell out of a hammock with laughing.

He slept on his back, at the edge of the bed by the tele-phone, near the door. I think he was frightened something would happen to us.

The following year he turned over in his sleep and crashed his leg onto my hipbone. It was like a piece of falling timber. Next morning I limped.

"What's happened?" he said from bed.

"You hit me with five ton of leg in your sleep. I didn't know a leg could be so heavy. It was like being socked with a Wel-lington boot full of mud."

"Should you go to a doctor?"

"Oh, no."

"What's a Wellington boot?"

"Gumboot. Rubber boot."

"I'm so sorry."

"I was rather pleased. It's the first time you've ever slept anywhere near the middle of the bed."

He groaned and looked away. "And the first time I do it I hurt you. I do things wrong too often. One of me is too many."

He thought of himself as a bungler. He thought he was in-finitely dispensable and replaceable. From things he said in his sleep, I know he thought I was going to fall in love with some-body else. But we were allies. We were some sort of kin.

My husband died, my love, died in his car, on the night we put the clocks back, on the night of the extra hour that every-one else was glad of, though for my part I found no use to put it to. It was a Saturday night and I had a fortnight of holiday ahead of me while the Airds were unexpectedly away, not to speak of the obligatory Sunday to get through, the one that would have fallen to me in any case. I did what one does, moving myself about, reading the news, maintaining the circulation of the blood, for the accepted reasons. The heart and lungs carried on willy-nilly, keeping me going, keeping me awake. The need for sleep wasn't as merciful as it might have been. I would have to get my clothes cleaned, if I was to go on. I would have to telephone the grocer, if I was to go on. A pound of tea, I said; no, half a pound, thank you, and any bread that's got a European type of crust, and have you some Dundee marmalade? I don't like it here very much, not at the moment, I said, no doubt sounding like a dangerous recluse and a chauvinist to boot. Which would have been doubly misleading, for I had never felt more in search of company, nor indeed more indebted to Manhattan, the city without him being a great deal more like the city we had lived in together than anywhere else without him would have been. After a few days, nine or ten, I wondered if it would aid things to pay a visit to Scotland, but I hadn't the purpose for it, let alone the money. So I went and lived in public libraries and all-night cafés for a time. Someone moved me out, sooner or later, and it was probably just as well, for my attempts to find anyone to talk to had not prospered. "Do you think I could have a cup of tea, please?" I had said to a promising-looking man behind a counter, but it seems I should have said "Cup of tea" and left it at that, for he put his hands on his hips and shouted, "What's stopping you?"

When my holiday had the goodness to be over, I stood on the usual rush-hour bus and read a schoolboy's comic strips over his shoulder. There was sun outside. Life had several appearances of being on the mend. Halfway uptown, after a setback caused by a reminiscent cheekbone at the other end of the bus, I got a seat between a Chinaman and a Puerto Rican woman. I seemed to be taking up more than my share of the space, and the grief was bad again. I tried thinking of others, more as a device than a good, and clenched my thigh muscles for a start, to give half an inch more room to the neighbors.

"Excuse me," I said to the Chinaman. "My husband is dead."

The Chinaman grunted and dug his heel-shaped chin into his collar. It started to rain.

"Every morning this time the bus is full of nuts," the driver said with violence, not even visibly addressing me, though his right eye was glaring at me in his driving mirror. I spread my muscles again and took all the room I wanted. I should get my hair done, I thought. Widows slip if they let their hair go. Queen Victoria went downhill. It's a mistake to be wearing his watch.

"Hello," I said to the Puerto Rican child who was sitting on the lap of the woman beside me.

"Doan speak English," the mother said in the voice of a record, turning the child on her lap so that its back now faced me.

"Hi," said the Ukrainian doorman at the Airds' building, using the sum of the English that I had ever heard him speak, apart from "God bless," "Cab, sir?" and "You bet your ass." This morning he followed "Hi" with "How's life treats you?" so I thought he must have learned English while I was away.

I said, "My husband's dead."

He laughed and said, "You bet your ass."

In the Airds' duplex apartment I hung my raincoat over Tessa's second mink with a malign hope that it would drip, which involved me in turning in my tracks after a minute or two to take the gesture back. The Chinese manservant caught me at it. I'm afraid nothing of the sort is hidden from him. There is no meanness he does not recognize. He winked in the direction of the Airds' bedroom and said, "Having late breakfast."

"Yes," I said coldly.

He winked again and said, "Nice holiday? Nice time with hubby?"

"My husband isn't well," I said, having no mind to hand him the truth at that moment.

The Airds were good to me. Cheerful. They made me move in to live with them as something they called their *au pair* girl, mostly to exercise two new Great Dane puppies. The manservant, Wu, took me in hand in his own way and gave me makeup lessons. He sold cosmetics on commission. He had a fine and steady hand with an eyeline brush, like a miniaturist.

"You should go take Spanish at night school," he said one evening in the Airds' downstairs lavatory when we were clearing up after they had gone out to dine. He put one of their cocktail nuts into my mouth off a silver tray that he had balanced for the moment on the washbasin, and set himself to work on my mascara. "Meet Mr. Right," he said, twirling one of his makeup brushes in a half-empty glass of Simpson's after-office bourbon. Then the Airds came back for something they had forgotten. Wu panicked and locked the door.

One of the Airds tried to come in.

"Who's there?" said Simpson's voice.

Wu clapped his hand over my mouth and daftly said nothing himself.

"Who is it?" Simpson said again, firmly.

"It's only us," I said like a fool, through Wu's palm. Inapt. Wu and I were not us, not in any way.

The Great Danes slept in my room, unfortunately. I walked them for three or four hours a day, but nothing tired them or won their love. They seemed quite undevoted, except to each other. From an air hostess with a Teddy bear to two Great Dane pups. I lived in a room off the kitchen, so thin-walled that it was impossible not to hear what was happening in the dining room unless Wu had a gadget going. The garbage disposal, say, would drown things, but then it would stop and there I was, a living wiretap.

"We could send you our *au pair*," Tessa was saying one night. "She has a genius for sorting things out. You could pay her whatever you wanted."

"Can she really do filing?" said a woman's voice.

"She's Simpson's secretary," Tessa said. "She's got high speeds. She can even cope with the baby. She looks after the dogs at the moment to keep herself busy. She can do anything."

"It doesn't sound as if she's got much spare time."

"She doesn't know what to do with it. Her husband . . ."

Wu ran a beater for a short while. I had thoughts about the awesome hearings of eavesdroppers, of spies, of babies before memory. Then the beater was turned off, unmercifully.

"To tell you the truth, it'd be a relief to me if she did something adult. The dogs are too much of her life," Tessa said.

"She's a handsome girl," Simpson said. "She'll marry again. She's funny."

Tessa laughed gently. "Simpson worries about her. I think

he's a bit in love with her." There was the sound of a kiss. Merriment.

"—two defunct types of people now," the woman was saying. "Have you ever thought of that? It struck me the other day. The man of letters and the maiden aunt. Your *au pair* may be a born maiden aunt. From the sound of it, she's more like a relative to you than a servant."

"I don't think she wants to be a maiden aunt," Simpson said. "I don't get that feeling."

No, I thought. Though one can pretend, if required.

Some other day, Tessa came gaily into my room and pulled the dogs off the bed. "And what are you doing here, pray?" she said to them. "Emm doesn't want to see you today. It's Emm's day off." She kissed them.

"How can they tell it's my day off?" I said. "I'm here and they're here."

Tessa looked at me as if I had said something odd. "You should go out more," she said. "Take my charge plate and go shopping. How would you like to buy me a black cashmere sweater? No, that wouldn't be much of a holiday. Why don't you go and buy yourself a sweater, on me?"

"Or not?"

"That's something you say, isn't it? O.K., not, but for Christ's sake go out and enjoy yourself, my dear. You're sitting there like death warmed over."

It might be preferable, I thought, not to shop?

"She should get married again," I heard Tessa say to her mother-in-law on the telephone. "I'm going to send her to my doctor. She's got this thing about saying 'not' all the time."

So.

I went to her doctor. Tired to death, for some reason, and answering his questions in a doze.

"Perhaps you should get married again," he said.

"Why?"

"Sleeping all right?" he said, head down, plowing on.

"Who with?" I said, without thinking. Poor man.

"I meant, would you like some sleeping pills?"

"I'm fine. I don't need putting out. Do you think I should go and live in a commune in San Francisco? Somebody once asked me to. I wouldn't mind that."

"If you like the idea. Though people can get over-individuated in communes."

"Does that mean lonely?" I started to laugh.

He leaned forward. "Aha. Interesting. Now we have to ask ourselves why you're laughing, don't we? What you're avoiding." He shook his kindly head. "As we have learnt from Freud, there are no jokes."

So.

I coped with the amazingly uninteresting savories for one of the Airds' cocktail parties. I met a Bulgarian as I was handing round the cheese dip. He made some measure of pass at me. Given the circumstances of a cheese dip, it was cheering. However off the point.

Much later, I came back in to help Wu clear up the debris and to take the puppies out for a walk. Simpson looked at me. At this tall, broad-shouldered girl. I tried to shrink. One of the puppies suddenly flung itself through the air and banged its wet nose against my right eye in its flight to a tray of vol-au-vent. Wu looked at me and gestured to his own right eye and giggled. He meant that my mascara had been licked off. "Brrr," I said, shaking my head and pretending to myself that I had dog's jowls. Any disguise to slink into, any animal mask.

"Perhaps you should go to an analyst," Tessa said. She put her arm around me. I laughed, and she said, "Laughing is a way of protecting yourself from the truth."

What? I thought, a laugh being pretty well the only dealing with the truth that offered itself at the moment, and so nothing to run down.

The Bulgarian took me out. I think he thought I was younger than I am. I think he thought I didn't recall anything about the war.

"I have to leave Bulgaria," he said. "You know where Bulgaria is?"

"Yes."

"You English girls are so educated."

"Scottish. But thank you."

"I have to leave," he said heavily, "because my conscience dictated that I inform on the Nazis."

"So you came here what year?"

"You have heard of the Nazis?"

"Yes."

"They were brutes. My conscience shouted that I had to inform. Bulgaria is a proud country."

"Bulgaria wasn't so proud in the war," I said. I thought about this, and then said, "I'm sorry," for he was a good-natured man. "I'm sorry, I've never even been there."

But he took no notice of either thing I had said, anyway, and laughed heartily at nothing evident about Sixth Avenue, and grabbed at my knee. "I do what I have to do, as they say in Western films," he declaimed, ogling my ear. "Bulgarians are masterly. In Bulgaria the woman is the man's slave."

"Are you hungry?" I said.

"Where shall we eat?"

"Where would you like?"

"When I take you out, you have to be my slave. You have to decide," he said, looking waggish, and also beginning to whine.

"What do you mean, your slave?"

"The man is superior."

"Oh," I said, glad of surrealism, though wondering who was to cope.

Silence unseated him. "What is it you do for the Airds, our friends?" he said desperately. "Apart from making succulent eats such as sardines?"

"I'm their nanny," I said. "To their Great Danes. Also their secretary, sometimes."

"So the Airds are Danish," he said. "Danish in ancestry. A proud race." He beat his chest and sang a song that turned out to be the old monarchist Bulgarian anthem.

"Slave," he said when it was over, "where shall we eat?"

"I like being mastered," I said, not sure how much money he had.

He looked suddenly suspicious that I was making fun of him, which I wasn't, and grabbed me to look down the front of my dress. "Aha. I spy a bra," he said. "I was thinking you were a member of Women's Liberation."

"I told you, I'm a sort of nanny."

"Women are inferior."

"Yes," I said. But now he looked inescapably furious, and also seemed stalemated about what to say to the cabdriver. So I tried for a calming course, feeling thankful to this man for his dogged clasp on difficulties that wouldn't cause me any recall of my dead love in a million years, and I pursued the wisp of a path suggested by the word "nanny." "Women have babies," I said firmly to my redeeming friend, "so it's men who have to decide about spending money, such as money on restaurant bills."

"Bulgarian women have babies in hedges," he said, looking vaguely about him at the north end of Sixth Avenue.

I got him out at an ice-cream parlor after a while. I paid for the taxi because he had no change. We ate waffles. Perhaps he had no money whatever.

"You see," he said, maple syrup on his chin, "we are celebrating."

Celebrating, my fellow in farce, although neither of us belongs, to waffles or to one another. Of course, belonging may be gone by the board, historically speaking, she advises herself, wiping her face with this American paper dinner napkin and not wishing to be personal, to use a bygone phrase.

"What shall we celebrate?" I said.

"I give you a toast," he said, waving a doubled-over piece of waffle on his fork in salute. "To your beauty," he said, though my looks at the time were nothing to write home about, "coupled with the birthday of the king of Bulgaria."

"The ex-King?" I said, which was hurtful, so I toasted the man in coffee. "His Majesty," I said. "Will he be having a party?"

"We have sent him a loyal birthday telegram in exile," he said. "My name is at the head of the list. Boris Blagov, chairman."

"Chairman?" Now I knew his name.

The heartening nature of repetitions. Obviously fortified by my inane echoing, Boris clutched my knee. "I am the leader of the forty-five members of the Bulgarian Monarchist Front," he said.

"Forty-*five?*" I said. It seemed best.

"After our celebration I shall take you to a solemn service," he said, gripping my left ankle between his shoes. At the same time he looked at his watch. We left in haste. He took me to a church where the other forty-four members of the Bulgarian Monarchist Front were mustered outside the front doors. All entrances were locked.

"I myself shall get the keys," Boris said to me stylishly. "Because I am the leader. The keys are in New Jersey."

We took a cab to New Jersey and back. I paid. We went through the service at two in the morning. Some of it was very fine. The priests were out of voice through tiredness. At three, Boris took me home. He tiptoed from the elevator to the apartment door with erotic wheezes.

"I cannot lovemake to you," he said at the door, "in the house of our ancient Danish friends where you are the nanny."

"Never mind," I said.

But he came in all the same, not apparently wounded. He wanted a drink. The Airds had long since gone to bed. I felt no right to sit in their drawing room but no call to take Boris to my bedroom. So we went to the dining room. He dived gaily at my legs, like a football player. I thanked him in my head for so thoroughly putting pain to the past, at least for the moment. One of the Great Danes was simultaneously clambering into my lap, trying to get all four legs fitted into the available footage, under the delusion that she was some other size. It is a delusion that many of us have, including Boris and possibly myself.

"How I am jealous of the young puppy in your lap," Boris said.

Liar, I thought, and so feeling a trifle low but at the same time in his debt. By half past five he had drifted off to sleep underneath three paws of the other dog, which had taken to him. He had been muttering vows of romantic love, rather sullen. He slipped into Bulgarian and became not absurd. Other people, alive and kicking. Other people to blot out a face.

I went to sleep near him, on the floor.

Tessa came in at half past eight and looked overjoyed. She drew me into the kitchen and stretched out her arms, leaning backward a bit, and said, "How I love people who say 'Yes' to life." Then she asked why I was laughing again, and I said that that wasn't what had happened, and she looked angry, and I had a shower. I don't like showers, but the bathroom was the only place in the apartment where I could lock a door on myself. I wondered why the best-off nation in the world should have chosen showers instead of baths. Dreams of child-hood garden sprinklers, perhaps. I sat on the step of the shower and went to sleep and then wept. The voice of the dead rang in my ear. "Say 'No.'" The only time I cry now is in my sleep.

Days later, when I had decided to find myself a less cushy job, someone telephoned me and said, "You are ruining my life."

"Who is it?" I asked, unforgivably.

"So soon you forget a passion," said Boris.

Apologize. Explain. Say "How are you?"

Boris moaned. Silence.

"Thank you for the other night," I said.

"I am a wreck," he said. "You are making me a wreck."

"Why? Oh dear." Again, silence. I said, "Boris, I didn't mean why; I meant how? How am I making you a wreck?"

"You force me to sleep with a Great Dane puppy. I am a proud man." I started to laugh, but I don't believe he heard. "A Great Dane puppy. I am a Bulgarian," he said.

"I'm sorry. You'd dozed off," I said.

"My life is ruined. I have laid my life at your legs and yet you say nothing. What can I do to get you off the phone?"

"Should I ring off?"

"I'll kill myself if you ring off."

I looked at my watch. "Could you get yourself some lunch?" I said. "Treat yourself to a *nice* lunch, and go to bed? Could you?"

"I'd choke," he said, putting the receiver down. He rang back again at once and mistakenly carried on with the Airds' answering service, not realizing that the woman there had picked up by the time I got to the phone.

"You English girls are so cruel," he was saying.

The answering service said, "One moment, please."

"I'm here," I said. "It's me. I was getting your number from Tessa."

"You are ruining my life, I tell you."

"Could I take you out to lunch?"

"You ruin my life all by one little word."

"Which little word?"

"The most terrible word in your cruel language," he said, putting the phone down.

He rang back several times to say that the word was "no." Twice he had his mouth full. Once he said it to the answering service.

Tessa grew testy about the line's being used all the time, and said that the Bulgarians were the worst lovers in the Balkans, as though that were a world-known fact, like the trying nature to others of our gentle Scottish weather. I was laughing, which was the debt I owed him. But what if he wasn't faking? What if he wasn't funny?

F.R.A.N.K.

Matthew Paget, a cyberneticist at work on a Family Robot Adapted to the Needs of Kinship (F.R.A.N.K.), looked down from the eighteen-eighties Russian novel he was reading to speak to the four-year-old daughter sitting under his desk on his right foot. She was called Aston.

"Your mother sends you her love," he said.

"Where is it?" said Aston.

Matthew stomped out of the room, anxious not to weaken. He cultivated grievance in the pantry for a few minutes. My wife gallivanting in Rome. (She was working, in fact.) Leaving me to the devices of an enemy housekeeper. (Mrs. Trumbull, his ally.) He went back into his study, glaring on the way at a prototype F.R.A.N.K. in the corner, which was plugged in and idling like an electric typewriter with nothing to write. He dismembered its initiative for the time being and sat down at his desk again.

"Your mother may well be away for *months*," he said dramatically, although he knew she would be back next week. "She has obviously deserted us. You and I will have to stick it out as best we can." He sighed and joggled Aston with his right foot, where she had resettled. "We can only hope she's having a good holiday."

"She's working," said Aston.

"Humph," Matthew said, lonely.

"Ho," said the child, hearing that. There was a pause.

"Of course, I may become ill," Matthew went on. "Or you may. Who can tell?"

"I'll look after you," Aston said. "Can I show you my somersault? You're not watching."

"I have to go riding now," Matthew said, as if that were grim.

"Can I come?"

"I'm going with the rabbi. No."

The child did a handstand for relief, and Matthew went riding. A young Englishman teaching in a New Hampshire university, he had struck up a friendship with the local rabbi partly because they shared a style of high dudgeon. Matthew's was the fiercer, by a particle. He clung to it. He was eminent for it. Indeed, in this time of the politics of happiness, when people were privately much sobered, his friends and fellows looked to him for it, since the thundering held an energy that was at odds with the doom he alluded to. It was entirely cheering. The man overruled the matter. He did not know this of himself.

Cherishing rancor and pretending to champion the drab, he was actually a dashing man with a buried admiration for exuberance and mayhem. He had hopes, well hidden, that F.R.A.N.K. might suddenly develop boisterous tendencies. At the moment the robot struck him as rather craven. The prototype in his house could reply to typed messages, harmonize tunes, wave in answer to "Hello," and hold a conversation of a sort, drumming up self-assured remarks about the topics it had been rehearsed in. It could also trundle its way from room to room in answer to a properly put shout, negotiating a road through the imported English furniture by bumping cautiously into things and then backing away to try a forty-five-degree variant. The blind pains that it took were a triumph of programming. All the same, Matthew would have liked it better if it had shown some wildness; he was much interested by the machine's intellect but not by its temperament, which reminded him of his mother's. The elder Mrs. Paget also had a trudging nature, insuperably sunny and anxious to fit in. Whenever she stayed with them—with himself, his wife Molly, Aston, and the sceptical Mrs. Trumbull—there would be a closing of the ranks, and scorn for the alien pussyfoot in their midst would run through the house like flu.

Matthew had gone hacking today in fine black hunting boots

and a beautiful purple stock. The rabbi got the quieter horse. They took this one by turns. The other was extremely nervous. Matthew looked at the rabbi, who was cantering contentedly, and shouted in envy, "That animal's moping!" His own petrified horse naturally bolted at once. Holding on by the reins, he yelled to the receding rabbi that this was the horse's natural gait. Much farther on, half a mile away and out of earshot, he said aloud that he was scared and called for his wife. ("She sends her love." "Where is it?") He crashed through branches, sawing at the horse's mouth, and then found a hill to aim the animal at in order to slow it down. He rode horses on the hypothesis that they answered the rules governing bicycles. The assumption generally worked, more or less. The horse was successfully braked today. It finished in a state of lathery obedience, with Matthew not fussed. All the same, when he came home, he told the rabbi and Mrs. Trumbull that he had been killed "as near as makes no matter," and there was somehow an implication that the peril to him continued even now. The rabbi ate some English biscuits calmly.

"The die is cast," Matthew said in Latin, stalking about the study.

The rabbi translated for Mrs. Trumbull.

"Not *again*," said Mrs. Trumbull. "And another thing. Mrs. Paget telephoned from Rome. While you were out. She said there wasn't any point in your trying to ring her back because she'd be out by the time you got through."

Overcome by what he had missed, Matthew sent the rabbi away and watched television with Aston. "This is the politics of happiness," he said, looking at the President's wave and teeth.

"Is he any good?" said Aston.

"What do you think?" said Matthew.

"Lousy?" said Aston, after looking.

"You might be right," said Matthew.

Then there was a newsreel film of a boy burning himself to death in protest against the war in Vietnam. Matthew turned off the switch just in time, and directed Aston's attention to the robot in the corner, and thought of the students in his classes who had gone to jail for defying the draft. Aston watched F.R.A.N.K.

"Come to point D_2 from point F by the shortest way, please,"

Matthew shouted to it in a level tone that was quite unlike the shout he used to the rabbi.

"He knows this room very well by now," Aston said, watching F.R.A.N.K. feeling a way to the fireplace. "He hasn't bust anything for ages."

The robot came to a stop by the mantelpiece and sang "Climb Every Mountain" from *The Sound of Music.*

"Oh lord," said Matthew. "Where did he get that from?"

"Professor Gregson taught it to him while you were riding."

"Shut up!" Matthew shouted to F.R.A.N.K., and the song stopped.

There was a pause, and then the robot typed out a message: "I have completed a sassy peregrination." Matthew held his head.

"What's the matter?" said Aston.

"The death of slang," said Matthew.

"It's not F.R.A.N.K.'s fault," Aston said.

F.R.A.N.K. went on typing. "As of that time when I commenced the excursion, it was six thirty-five. At the present time, it is six thirty-eight and thirty-three seconds. Hopefully, I shall improve on this track record."

"Come to point B_3," Matthew shouted.

F.R.A.N.K. buzzed and stayed still.

"Please," Matthew added, and F.R.A.N.K. trundled to him. Matthew typed a message on a control keyboard: "Strike out 'Hopefully, I shall improve on this track record.' Learn instead 'With any luck, I shall get better.' " He fed the message to the robot grimly.

"He was only trying to chat," Aston said.

F.R.A.N.K. whirred and waved a tin arm and typed out: "Now we have another topic on the griddle. Let's kick it around."

Pause.

"Why are you grumpy with him?" Aston said.

"My house is being turned into a gymnasium for gobbledygook," said Matthew, as if the robot had nothing to do with him. At the same time he tinkered with it tenderly. "Things are quite impossible enough as it is, with your mother gadding about like this and telephoning while I'm riding. Well, we shall have to push on, in the teeth of everyone, I suppose. Give

F.R.A.N.K. a word. Anything in this room."

"Sofa," said Aston in a loud clear voice.

F.R.A.N.K. digested and typed. "Our sofa is soft," it wrote. "Is your sofa foreign?"

"That's a bit better," Matthew said fondly.

"Do you enjoy sofas of foreign origin? I have observed sofas from Chippendale and New Jersey," F.R.A.N.K. wrote.

"Isn't that an interesting mistake?" Matthew said. "Aston, do you know what the mistake was in that sentence?"

"Yes," Aston said. "New Jersey isn't foreign, it's here."

"Well, that's true, but it's foreign to F.R.A.N.K. As far as F.R.A.N.K.'s information goes, England is still home. It's one of the things I never reprogrammed. The mistake was classifying Chippendale as a place, like New Jersey. The Chippendales were a family who made furniture."

"Oh yes, I forgot. You told me that before," Aston said.

Matthew admired her memory, and then made a mouse for her out of his pocket handkerchief, folding it formally and getting it to jump up his coat sleeve by flicking it from behind with his middle finger. The trick came off stylishly.

"Do it again," Aston said.

"No!" he said, slumping. "I'm *exhausted*. None of you seem to realize. You wear me out, all of you."

Aston took no notice, as he wanted her not to. "What does the robot learn next?" she said.

"How'm I expected to work when there's this shambles to be put to rights?" he roared, glaring at the room, which was tidy.

"I'll do it," Aston said, looking round for anything to clear up and finding an ashtray with some of his pipe tobacco in it.

"The robots at the lab are better than this one," he said, watching her. "In a year or two they'll be tutors and secretaries and research assistants. You'll see. This one's more for company."

"He's not really much company," she said, though not wishing to wound.

"He will be soon," Matthew said. "Would you like to do an experiment?" He sat Aston under a black hood with a hole in it, and showed her a drawing, part by part, through the hole.

"What's this you can see now?" he said.

"A leg," Aston said, muffled under the hood. "A drawing of an animal's leg."

"What animal is it going to be?"

"Well, it might be a cow, it might be a zebra, it might be an elephant. Who drew it?"

"Me. I was disguising the style. O.K., that counts as one move. Now suppose you're only allowed one more move to tell what the animal is. What do you want to look at?"

"The head. It might be a man with peculiar legs, but I could tell that from the head, anyway."

Matthew took the hood off her excitably.

She said, "Oh good, it was an elephant."

He said, "It's brilliant." He strode quickly up and down the room with his hands in his pockets, skipping round the robot, whom he had set to tacking back and forth on the carpet.

"What's brilliant?" said Aston.

"The way you did that. F.R.A.N.K. still spends three moves counting legs to decide whether the drawing's a man or an animal before he asks himself what sort of animal. You went straight to the head in one, and you're not five years old yet."

Mrs. Trumbull came into the room and tried to sweep the child to bed.

"Don't take her away," Matthew said. "Please," he added, seeing mulishness and remembering the robot. "We were having a nice time. It needn't be bed quite yet, need it?"

Mrs. Trumbull suddenly burst into tears and stood with her head bent down onto the top of the marble mantelpiece. Matthew looked at her, feeling pity and panic, and gestured Aston out of the room. She went as far as the hall and looked back at him. He nodded, and she waited by the doorjamb. Mrs. Trumbull's shoulders shook. She dried her eyes with a Kleenex and threw it into the fire, where it hissed.

"What's the matter?" Matthew said, trembling. "Aren't you happy?" He looked at her strong back. "You're *always* all right!" he shouted at her. "You've never done this before. Are you homesick?"

She went on saying nothing and leaning her head against the mantelpiece.

"There was once a slave leader," Matthew said, "who led a rising in the West Indies, and he was shipped off to prison in

France, a very cold prison, damp, where he taught himself to read, alone, and then taught himself French so that he could write to Napoleon to ask for his freedom. He died standing up. He was propped against the wall. He seemed to have decided just to stand there. They found him with his forehead against the stone. I'd forgotten it. His *forehead*. . . . He must have died while he was *thinking*. . . . Against *stone*."

Pause. Mrs. Trumbull moved. "Thank you," she said.

Matthew took in again that Aston was standing by the door. "Could she have heard that?" he said in a low voice.

"Of course," said Mrs. Trumbull, still facing the fire. "But it wouldn't be the first mention of it. There was that kitten dying. She never did believe our tales. She sorted it out in her mind later."

" 'Strewth!" said Matthew, starting to back into anger. "There's never a day without some upset."

"You're not really a hard man, whatever they say," Mrs. Trumbull said.

Alarmed by her rare open fall into the giving of compliments, his mind fled. He remembered playing billiards in Paris one night. He got up, and put on his coat, and rasped that he was going to take her and Aston and the rabbi to shoot pool in the village.

"It's too late for Aston," Mrs. Trumbull said.

"Don't be stuffy," he said. "We can dress up. Aston can pretend to be a hippie. We'll take her on the horse. The *easy* horse," he added bitterly, the bitterness being for form's sake. "Not the one that nearly cost me my life."

He corralled the rabbi, and they went into the village. Mrs. Trumbull looked stoic again. Aston wore ropes of her mother's beads, a hippie scarf round her forehead, her father's riding gloves, and her own gum boots. She sat astride the horse while Matthew led it. The rabbi followed slowly in his Peugeot with Mrs. Trumbull. The car once came too near, and Aston swayed. Matthew caught her before turning round to bawl. "You were deliberately trying to run me down," he said. "Is there no *end* to it?"

"I can't listen to you for the moment. I'm in the middle of changing gears," the rabbi said. "I suppose you think it's easy, driving a non-automatic at this crawl." He put the car dolorously into first. No mean playing partner for Matthew, he could make even a need to change gears seem the blow of a fate hellbent on singling him out.

Mrs. Trumbull said, "I see you double-clutch. It's the mark of a generation." She smoothed her gloves.

Then Aston nearly fell off again, and whimpered, and Matthew vaulted up behind her. He moved her onto the horse's withers, where she felt magnificent. "Now *Aston's* getting in a state," he moaned to the trailing car, holding on to her, and she to him. "There's no consideration. She *knows* I can't stand her getting in a state." He carefully gave her the snaffle reins, which would do the horse's mouth no harm, and told her they might as well both hang on to the saddle.

Mrs. Trumbull looked at him for a while. "I wouldn't mind putting my slippers under his bed," she said to the rabbi.

"No good will come of this jaunt," said the rabbi.

Near the village they passed some Sorbonne students on an exchange year at Matthew's university. They were chatting and shouting to each other in bunches strung across the street.

"Is that Spanish?" Aston said.

"No, it's French. French is another language, just as Greek and Latin and Russian are other languages."

"What language does F.R.A.N.K. speak?"

"Nearly English, but partly maths. Robots don't quite speak English. There are other robots that speak things called COBOL and FORTRAN but they're fake languages. There are some kinds of words they haven't got. They can tell you you've drawn an elephant but they can't tell you whether they think it's a funny drawing or a rotten drawing. If we could ever get a robot to do that, we'd have done something new. It would be the first time."

Then it occurred to him that a four-year-old was constantly doing things for the first time, that Aston was riding a horse for the first time, and so there wouldn't be any reason for her to share that excitement, but she caught the note.

A troupe of twenty-year-olds sailed by on roller skates, blowing soap bubbles and weaving in and out of the people parking cars at the cinema.

Matthew and Aston shot pool. The rabbi and Mrs. Trumbull changed places with them later. Some of Matthew's grad-

uate students were there. One was playing a guitar and singing his own love poetry in a corner. A physics major. Another
was reading Allen Ginsberg aloud. It slowly seemed not the
worst of times but a wild and hopeful year. Matthew sat for a
while and listened. He pushed up his eyebrows with his fingers, one after the other, which was a habit he had, and thought
of young men in St. Petersburg reading *The Possessed,* and talked
to a scientist he liked. It was an evening that made him want
to speak every language. "Books for Sale or Rent," a notice
said in the main street of this village in the continent that was
held not to be reading any longer. In my sere and unruled
state, thought Matthew, without my wife, banging against the
sides of strangers like a ship hitting a quay in the dark, the
thing to do would be to write her a letter. It had best be a
good letter. Though it will never get to her, the posts in Italy
being what they are.

"When Mrs. Paget rang," he said to Mrs. Trumbull after
they had gone home, "was there the usual echo on the line or
was it all right?"

"You couldn't hear much," Mrs. Trumbull said. "She kept
going off. I thought she was opening the door to a waiter.
Several times I imagined her going to open the door to her
dinner, but then she said she'd been there at the desk all along.
Goodness knows what we lost."

"Idiots say that the problem is communication," Matthew
shouted. "The problem is *communications.*"

"I daresay."

Matthew wrote a letter to his wife. It went badly, to his mind.
Not my business, he muttered in his head, to have to produce
this soup. What one says is usually a poor substitute for thought.
And yet it's only when one says things that one feels a man,
alive and kicking. He looked at the letter with the disgust that
he reserved usually for minor ailments, and was in the act of
tearing it up when he gave it to the robot to rewrite in its own
way; thus:

GENTLEHEART,
   You are my hungry fellow-feeling. My awe curiously
cleaves to your footprints. My liking yearns for your spec-

tacle. Aston and I travelled on the silent horse and played
a game of skill with Mrs. Trumbull. The rabbi is a terrible
motorist. Please come back. You are my wistful sympathy.
I feel heavy-shouldered.

Yours,
M.

He kicked the robot, and then sat down and did some experiments. The effect of F.R.A.N.K.'s company as they played
draughts together unfortunately began to bring back the
sprightly grownups who had come to see him when he had
had measles as a child. They had played games with him by
touch in the darkened room, speaking in bright voices and
laboriously explaining the rules as if he had lost his wits. Tonight the robot started by winning, describing with the same
intolerable cheer the strategy of its success, and then it annoy-
ingly didn't change its tone when it began to lose. Matthew
routed it three times in a row, galvanized, and prowled around
the house to look at Aston, and eventually tore up both his
own note and the robot's. There was something awry in the
place, although he couldn't put his finger on it. It would have
to do with the lateness of the hour, he said to himself. I can
feel a wound somewhere in the house and I don't know if I
delivered it. There's a scar somewhere and I don't even know
if it's mine. We are supplanted as soon as we're born, that's
the feeling. Deposed heirs, that's the feeling. No armies. He
fleetingly saw his species in the grip of this innate sense, an
old intimacy with dispossession that human beings seemed never
quite to lose, although it had always been better known to literature than to politics or to his own science. He picked a few
scraps of the robot's letter out of his wastepaper basket and
decided to send the thing, pasting it together and meanwhile
going over and over his thought, like F.R.A.N.K. tacking to
and fro on the carpet. Well, we may be something after all.
Unlike my goddam, happy, likeable horse. It's time we got out
of Asia.
The telephone rang and he had a severe conversation with
a smug but scared colleague whom he suspected of plagiariz-
ing the research done for a paper published by one of Matthew's assistants. At the same time as the row, he was wonder-

ing what it was that had made Mrs. Trumbull cry.

"You don't like me," the colleague ended up by saying. "You never liked me. If you spread this . . . this calumny, you'll be disliked by everyone."

"None of us is liked by everyone," Matthew said. "And some of us by fewer than others. Especially me."

He went into the kitchen to find Mrs. Trumbull, needing her company. She was drowsing in a rocking chair by the oven with a letter in her lap, which she put quickly into her apron pocket. She was looking troubled again, and he suddenly guessed that she must have had news that her husband in England was ill. A goose walked over his grave as he feared for his wife.

"Letter from England," she said, shaking her head and banging her left ear with the heel of her palm as though she had been swimming.

"Have you had a bad dream? Did I wake you?"

She looked at the letter sticking out of her pocket. "It's all strikes and Prince Charles in England, isn't it? The stamps used to make you think of home, and now they make you think of the cost of living."

"Your husband's not poorly?"

"He got a cold the day after his birthday, but then people often come down after a birthday, don't they."

"Wouldn't you like to go back sooner than the summer this year? It's been a good three months since you saw him." He paused, hating the opinion he was going to put next but making himself carry on. "You should pack it in with us. You could afford to stop by now. You've been working since you were twelve. With you abroad like this, he must feel as if he's married to a merchant seaman."

She avoided the point and started to steam the English stamps off the envelope because Aston collected them. "Well, I'm due for my pension, but it's nicer to keep working, isn't it? Anyway, I can't get the pension while Mr. Trumbull's still at his office, and he'll never leave. He's been there forty years. They must like him. Of course, he knows the files."

Matthew sat on the kitchen table and let her go on. Middle-of-the-night monologues. The present tense, used of someone away. He understood that.

"The Queen came round to his office the other week. He's doing something hush-hush. I'm sorry for the Queen, poor thing. Four or five changes of clothes a day, and always smiling, and always all the people she sees being so *old*. Those ambassadors. No chance of a bit of platonic friendship or a bit of fun, is there? All those old codgers. No chance of slipping away for a fling or a flatter."

"Shall we have some toast and marmalade?" Matthew said.

She made some under the broiler, which was more like the grill she was used to than the toaster was, and Matthew looked at the envelope, which was sticking out of her pocket again.

"Mr. Trumbull's a genius with the files. He remembers every paper that comes in and out. Ministry of Defence. I don't know much about it."

"Would you like to go back straightaway?" Matthew said.

No reply.

"I sometimes ask him, how can you stand it? I couldn't. All that fiddling about. He has to check the papers in and out, and then there's a security man who comes for him to hand over the keys. He knows every sacred thing in those files. There's a lot of young chaps coming up but I don't think my husband likes them because he doesn't tell them much. They're in the dark. About two years ago with the spy scare the Ministry started checking up on us, in Wales even, with my family. Questions. What was my politics, all that. Who were our friends. Well, my husband's a terribly shy man and we don't have friends really, but they couldn't believe it. They even went to the dairy. The *dairy*. And asked things there. The woman that kept the shop took me aside one day and said a gentleman had been in, nosing about, and I said what was *he* doing, pray, and she said he asked if I had any debts. Going somewhere I'd been dealing for twelve years. Damned sauce. I felt like writing to them. I've never owed a penny in my life. Well, as I say, my husband's a miracle for memory. He can figure income tax just like that."

She gave Matthew the jar of marmalade, avoiding his look, and sat down again by the range with her eyes closed. "He used to do the butcher's tax and sometimes the grocer's in the country, near where we kept a pub. He used to spend five or six afternoons and earn ten guineas. You've got to be an expert these days, haven't you? There's all sorts of little bits of money you can save yourself if you know how. Things you can put against the tax. He always loved to absorb himself in things. He must know every piece of paper in the Ministry. Every high-up who hasn't sent some letter back at the end of the day. They have to sign for things they take out and they're not supposed to keep them overnight, you see. There are records written down, but he always knows who's doing it without even looking it up. Often he comes home and goes to bed at a quarter to seven after he's had his tea, and I sit downstairs and hear him swearing at those colonels as he drops off. 'Those bloody colonels,' he says."

"You miss him," Matthew said.

"Time enough," she said, opening her eyes and looking at him hard.

"Mrs. Paget would understand." He skipped a beat. "Hard to cope." (*Speaking for myself.*) "But you need a sight of him, woman."

"You've no call to be bossy," she said in the softest voice, watching.

"What's happened?"

Pause. Then, "I had a letter from Mrs. Paget," she said.

"You didn't tell me."

"She said she'd be away for a while."

"Not coming back next week?" The floor seemed to hurtle downward.

"I expect that was what she was phoning you about. I only got the letter after you went riding. It came special delivery. 'Express,' she wrote on it."

"Did she say why she had to stay away?" he said.

"She's tired."

"How bad?" he yelled. "Everyone keeps things from me."

"I couldn't say. She's thinking of being away until the summer."

"Where?"

"There was the address of a place somewhere."

"*Where?*"

She showed him his wife's letter, and the sight of her handwriting smote him. "I can't have an ill woman drooping about the house," he roared.

"She's just under the weather for a bit, I daresay," said Mrs. Trumbull.

"She *never* gets tired," Matthew said. "People belong together." He roamed the room and then said, "I'm sorry," for no obvious reason. None of us is liked by everyone, he repeated to himself.

He played with the robot most of the night. He telephoned Rome.

"What's this you wrote to Mrs. Trumbull?" he said to his wife. The connection was terrible.

"What, darling?" she said.

"What?" he said. He pushed on.

"I wrote to you a week ago," she said in the end, "to explain that I'd better have a holiday, but obviously you didn't get the letter."

He cursed blue murder, at one thing and another. "Suppose I get ill?" he said. "How ill are you?"

"What?" she said. "I didn't get anything after 'suppose.' "

"How ill are you?" he said, desperate.

"I've only got a temperature," she said.

"Help, it's not even Easter yet. How long do you need?"

"What? Perhaps if we try waiting a few seconds each time between speaking. I think the electronics get muddled if we talk over each other," she said, and he grinned at the very different intelligence of his wife, which had never conquered the concept even of a fuse but which still interested him more than anybody else's.

"I miss you," he said.

"I miss you," she said, but she was inaudible to him.

"What? I didn't get a word of that."

She started to laugh, and repeated herself loudly as the sound came back.

"Well, there's that," he said sombrely. "I thought you'd gone for good."

"What?" she said. "All I heard was 'there's that.' It's something you say, isn't it? Are you all right?"

"Given some things."

"What? The line went off again. I heard 'given,' " she said.

He snorted, pretending not to laugh, and said, "You won't be away long, will you?"

"What?" she said. "You'll have to yell."

"Take care of yourself," he said, refusing.

"What?"

"We should get out of Asia," he said.

"I'm not going to Asia. I'm going to Africa. Of course, you didn't get my letter."

"No," he said. "Take care of yourself."

"Could you hear about Africa?" she said, over him. "It's only because I need a break. I don't know why. I tried to write it. I love you very much."

"I'm hard on you. That's what you're really saying."

"What?"

"I love you," he yelled, and hung up, and felt an ass.

He spent the night working. He came into the kitchen only in the morning to make himself a thermos of coffee. Mrs. Trumbull was still there, making coffee for him herself. Her husband's letter was out of its envelope and lying beside the kettle. He did something that he had never done before in his life and read it, making a pretext to send her into the pantry for a muffin. Mr. Trumbull indeed badly needed his wife back. *But obviously she doesn't want to desert us. With my wife abroad. Help. My wife. I drive them all away.*

"I'm afraid you must leave, Mrs. Trumbull," he said. "We should have someone local." At the same time he again did something quite against the habit of his nature, and put his arms around her and kissed her neck fiercely. "I don't know how *Mrs.* Paget's going to manage, of course," he said.

"She's depending on me to look after Aston," she said. "I couldn't go."

"Ah, but I spoke to her in the night and told her to come back at once. I can't have her away." This is my affair, he thought. Mr. Trumbull needs his wife. My wife needs leeway. People do what I say.

He bought Mrs. Trumbull an air ticket the next day and packed her off in a hurry, afraid that she might hear again from his wife with instructions about how to look after him. Mrs. Trumbull said she would be back in a trice.

"When is that?" said Aston.

"I'll be glad to taste some decent bacon again," Mrs. Trumbull said in a hard voice as he and Aston drove her to the airport. "Though I'll give you that the bottled mayonnaise in America can't be bettered. I'm sure I don't know how you'll manage. In fact, we could put off my going, couldn't we? Just until Mrs. Paget's home." She looked out of the window and wept at the idea of leaving him.

"Best done now," said Matthew. "You'll be back in the summer." They drew up at the sign for departures. "I can't stand airport farewells," he said. "I'm a busy man." He again put his arms around her, after Aston had climbed from the back seat into the one beside him, and then Mrs. Trumbull shook his hand and said, "We won't say goodbye, we'll say au revoir," except that she got it the wrong way round. "We won't say au revoir, we'll say goodbye."

Back at home, he put Aston to bed and arranged for a student to look after her, and waited for his wife's reply to the robot's letter, which would certainly come very soon. He fed F.R.A.N.K. some recognition problems. The robot did well. Matthew improved its system slightly. The robot did better. Matthew moved some of the furniture around.

"Come to point E from point G, please," Matthew shouted levelly, "and sing 'Greensleeves,' beginning after collision two." F.R.A.N.K. blundered through the rearranged room. After the second careful bump, a Dresden vase toppled and broke. It was one that Matthew and his wife had always hated. The song began.

F.R.A.N.K. reported on the journey.

They went on working together.

F.R.A.N.K. deduced that not all dogs were spaniels, made a planetary calculation, rewrote a Yeats poem, and detected an undistributed middle in a syllogism.

Then, trying to engross himself in the news on television, Matthew spoke to the robot at a pitch it was not programmed to understand: "Have you anything to add?"

Staying in Bed

"We have always been a very tired family," Finch said loftily to Henry, both aged twenty-eight, Finch lying back in a large bed with his cello on his ex-girlfriend's pillow and Henry standing up by the gas fire. Finch was one of the most famous cellists in Europe, and Henry was known to a few as his accompanist. Finch pulled the bedclothes over his nose.

"You should get up more," said Henry. "I mean, you should get up at *all*. You've been there for over a month."

"I take furtive strolls to the fridge."

"You're too young to vegetate."

"I'm not young. I told you, tiredness runs in the family. Would you mind pulling down the blinds? The sun hurts my eyes." Finch turned on his side with an upheaval that he hoped to look final.

"What do you mean, tiredness runs in your family? When I've known you all since kindergarten and any one of you can wear me out?"

"My Aunt Belle was confined to her bed for many years," Finch said, blowing his nose in his health. He hummed something from a Beethoven cello sonata.

Henry hummed the piano part without thinking and then stopped himself because he had meant to argue. "Hell, old Belle was always beetling around," he said.

"You know I hate inner rhymes," Finch said faintly, eyes closed.

"Your Aunt Belle never stopped going until she fell off the mule. How old was she in Tibet? Eighty?"

"Only seventy-eight," Finch said. "Anyway, that isn't the point. She always felt secretly whacked. All her life. She really always wanted to stay in bed."

"She went to prison seven times to get the vote, and she went to Ethiopia and Nuristan and the back of beyond on a mule, and you tell me she was always whacked?"

"It wasn't obvious to the naked eye, but we could tell. The family." Finch covered his head with the bedclothes and fingered some double-stopping on the mattress. He heard Henry's voice through the blankets. It was like the sound of someone blowing through a piece of pipe. They had done that together as children in the North of England, experimenting with different lengths of pipe.

"You're practicing," Henry was saying.

"Who said?"

"I can tell because you're humming. You've no idea of the racket you make when we're recording. I don't understand how anyone so musical can hum so out of tune with himself. You don't seem to be listening to yourself."

"I'm probably listening to you," Finch said happily. He came out of the bedclothes and said, "While I'm laid up like this, why don't you do a few concerts on your own?"

"It's not right, lying in bed all the time at twenty-eight," said Henry. It's not like him, he thought, contemplating their long life together and their long history of loving each other's girls. He was married at the moment, Finch not. They had a great passion for women, a great passion for each other, a great passion for music and trains. They would go on long train journeys together. In America, where they often performed, the trains struck them as poignant chiefly because uncared for, but they had found a friend with a long New England face who was a fireman on the run to Boston, and his professionalism and high interest in the topic of transport were entirely cheering. The trains in India and in Morocco had impressed them on recital tours as some of the most distinctive they had ever seen. Finch especially had the English love for nineteenth-century public transport. Ships, trains, buses, trams. Those elegant and ingenious objects of use. He and Henry had been going all their grown-up lives to the British Transport Museum in Clapham, running their fingers over the polished wheels, regretting the end of brass fitments, and taking in the beauty of the fishnet luggage racks. Finch had grown up in Northumberland, twenty miles from Henry, near the Roman Wall. Work had brought them to London, which they regarded as Down South. Anywhere in England south of Durham was still Down South to them. What Southerners called the North—Yorkshire, Lancashire—they called the Midlands, meaning scorn.

"You're a Celt," Henry said, brusque to his friend. "You're a born gate-vaulter. You shouldn't lie about in bed. You're not ill."

"Of course I'm not ill. I'm just tired."

"You should go to an analyst."

"An *analyst*? You've been brainwashed."

"It's unruly of you."

"To stay in bed?"

"The agents are going crackers about it."

"In the eyes of anyone who has noticed history, unruliness is a great virtue in mankind. Would you like this pear?" Finch lobbed it at Henry and then lay back.

Good throw if he's that tired, Henry thought, suspecting something, but not finding it.

"I lugged that pear from the kitchen in the small hours," Finch said in a remote voice.

Henry wondered if his chum, the great young cellist, had taken untimely to bed because he was trying to keep out of Henry's marriage, or perhaps because he was nursing loneliness. He had no idea that Finch was trying to get him to stop being an accompanist and to work on his own.

"You don't exactly *lug* a pear," Henry said, eating it gratefully.

"You didn't say please," said Finch.

"It seemed a waste of time."

"No, it wasn't. Try it."

"Please," said Henry.

"Thank you," said Finch.

"Not at all," said Henry.

"Quite a bit," said Finch, suddenly perked up by throwing the rhythm out and hoping that Henry would follow him because he wanted to see how it worked in canon. "Please," he said.

"Thank you," said Henry, getting it.

"Not at all," said Finch.

"Quite a bit," said Henry perfectly.

"I think I may have a doze," Finch said, closing his eyes in thanks. "Ring the agent and do the Ohio concert on your own." He meant to look forbidding, but found it difficult when eyes that should be glaring were shut. "You owe it to me and to Betty. Your wife."

There was a long silence. "What are you actually thinking about?" Henry said.

"About my father," said Finch. "And that I have had to get through a lot of long silences with both of you."

"If memory serves—" said Henry.

"It doesn't. It rules," said Finch. "Go and practice."

Finch was a lanky man whose cello made him look even thinner. He had a peculiar droning voice that reminded people of summer days and of buzzing from high up. It was often imitated, even to his face, but he paid no heed whatever. He had a copious nature with a touch of riot in it. Henry liked his company because it was convivial; the staying in bed disconcerted him partly because they went on having a good time together however energetically Finch adopted inertia. Finch was a man with no zone of indifference and a lifelong distaste for milky kindnesses, which made his present wish to push Henry away and into a career of his own both powerful and covert. What he would do without Henry, lord knows. His mild-mannered and gifted friend had a contagious sense of what was interesting, amusing, noble, or important in life, though his bearing was lugubrious, like a plumber's. Finch had always found him altogether reviving. Before they had met, both aged six, Finch seemed to have lived alone for eons. He was an only child who had learned to read at three and quickly began giving characters to the numbers in arithmetic because he had no one to play with. He devised adventures for them. The number one was reckless, two was blithely intelligent, three was inclined to wickedness, four was heroic.

As time went on, Finch found himself more and more attached to bed. He read a lot.

His daily woman said in the butcher's that he wasn't poorly, he was taking a holiday.

"Some people!" snorted the butcher.

"Well, I daresay it's work really," said the daily. "He's doing a lot of thinking in his head. If looks are anything to go by, he's thinking in his head all the time."

Henry went to Ohio and gave the concert on his own. He telephoned Finch when he was back at his flat in London. Finch lived in Cheyne Row. Henry was about to move out of a place in Tite Street.

"You sound as if you're still in bed," Henry said.

"Why shouldn't I be?" said Finch.

"I've got the name of an analyst. A very nice man who's been struck off the register because he married a patient. And then she tried to kill herself but now she's all right. Fairly."

"You've got a nose for the washed-up, I'll say that for you. How do you know he's nice?"

"I've just had a drink with him."

"Well, I'm not going to him. There's nothing the matter with me."

"You should be up."

"I like it here."

"You'll run out of money."

"Not for a while."

"I've fixed for you to go and see him on Thursday. Or he'd even come to you."

"If he's offered to come to me, he can't be much good."

"I told you, he's been struck off the register. He's hard up."

"You do find them," said Finch.

"Then Thursday."

"No. I don't want another intimate. How many can a man have at a time? There's you and Betty. George, Peter, Anna. And there used to be Gloria, and I still have to think about her even if she isn't here. You don't not spend time on someone just because they aren't about any longer. That's six. I don't want some extra bogus friend."

"Gloria wasn't doing you any good."

"No, but I still miss her rather."

"So do I. I liked the way she muttered so you could hardly hear when she was being funny. Girls don't usually do that."

"Girls apart from Betty aren't usually funny."

"No," Henry said. He stalked about and thought. The receiver with Finch on the other end growled. He came back to it. "I've decided I'm not going to give another concert on my own until you start working again," he said.

Finch was so overcome by the brilliance of this counterstratagem that he yelled. Then he said, "In that case you can bloody well go and waste your own bloody time seeing your half-baked analyst for me. You can tell him anything he could possibly want to know about me."

"I'd have to make up your dreams."

"Feel free," said Finch. He sulked then for a moment. "Or you could ring me up, couldn't you? You could ask me what *I'd* dreamt."

"No decent analyst would agree to it."

"He sounds a rotten one, so there's no problem, is there?"

"He's not rotten."

"I quite like nursery rows sometimes." Finch leaned back on his pillows and tried one. "Yes, he is rotten."

"Isn't."

"Is."

"Isn't."

"Is."

"Who says?"

"Says me."

"Who are you?"

"Finch James Borthwick hyphen Grantley aged twenty-eight years two months three weeks. Anyway," Finch said in his ordinary voice and coming out of the interesting counterpoint, "if he's not rotten, he's certainly out of the usual run of analysts. Most unrotten doctors haven't been struck off the register. As a generality."

"You're barking."

"Yes, I know. It's exhausting me," Finch said, though sounding splendid. He went on, absorbed in the endeavor of thinking of a ploy, "I'm worn out with all this." He thought of the ploy. "Your harebrained idea of going to the chap instead of me—"

"It was your harebrained idea," Henry said with heat.

"You shouldn't be going to some analyst every day for

someone else," Finch pushed on. "You should be playing the piano."

But Henry was hellbent on getting Finch up, hellbent enough to go to the analyst on his behalf. Day after day.

"What dream did you tell him?" Finch asked from bed after the first morning, trying not to sound too alert.

"The one you told me to tell him, of course."

"What did he make of it?"

"He doesn't seem to say much. I believe they never do. They mostly make you talk."

"It sounds an awful effort."

"He wanted to know what *my* motive was, and I said I didn't have many, and he said that wouldn't wash usually, but perhaps in this case."

Another day: "What dream did you tell him? You didn't ring."

"I couldn't get through to you. I hadn't got the change to ring you from the tube, and I'd had to rush out of the house to get there because I woke up late."

"So what did you tell him?"

"One I'd had. I thought it would do. It was about our childhood, so you were in it. It was about the time you dropped the raw egg into your great-aunt's letter box."

"Wasn't that a good day," Finch said, closing his eyes in commemoration and then opening them to look fierce at the effrontery of somebody's making up his dream. "But I don't *think* about being a child."

"The analyst said it was a very bad sign. The raw egg."

"I daresay, but it was a very good day." Finch ambled back to his point. "I don't *think* about being a child, so it's not a plausible dream. I hated being a child, apart from knowing you. I wouldn't dream of dreaming about it."

"They say we dream a lot of things we hate thinking about in the daytime."

"Well, I hate *dreaming* about them too, so I don't. Asses."

The visits progressed. Betty often came to see Finch while Henry was with the analyst. He liked her. Henry's cat wandered into the bedroom one morning; Betty and her six-year-old son had brought it with them. Finch thought, bestirred, that the cat was an advance guard for Henry and that Henry must be on his way back to see them, and he wanted to call out to the animal, but in his excitement he couldn't remember its name, so he lay back and assumed fatigue again. The child, who had been watching him gravely, said, "Why aren't you playing the cello any longer with my father? Are you going to die?"

"No, I'm just tired."

"I expect you've got a sore throat," the boy said. "Would you like some condensed milk? It's better than whisky and honey and lemon."

"Your father and I used to eat a lot of condensed milk when we were children."

"He's told me."

"Do you want some?"

"It's a bit sweet for me. I suppose it's O.K. if you're old," said the boy.

"We were getting on for ten when we liked it," Finch said. He felt animated; and then he remembered his obligation to be bedridden; and then he wondered what Henry was saying to the analyst, and whether his friend's loyalty and humor were visible to the man, and what was to happen next to them all. He turned over onto his side.

"What is it?" Betty said.

"I was hating the analyst."

"When you haven't met him?"

"I was wondering what I landed Henry with."

"He wanted to do it."

"I was wondering if the analyst is taking it out of him."

The boy honorably brought him a tin of condensed milk and a tin opener from the kitchen. Finch opened the tin and looked at it. The child went out of the room again.

"I was thinking about the irrelevance to psychoanalysis of wit and accountability," said Finch.

The six-year-old came back, carting a telephone directory. "I remember a number that I think might interest you," he said encouragingly, starting at the beginning of the book and going down the columns to look for it.

After a while, wishing to support the undertaking, Finch sat up on the side of his bed and played something buoyant on his cello. "It's not much without your father doing the piano part," he said.

"What part?" said the boy.

Finch got up, for the first time in company for many moons, and went to the piano in his drawing room next door, shouting, "I can't do it properly." The pedals under his bare feet were interestingly strange to use and slightly painful. "Have you found the number?" he bawled to the child in the middle of a difficult run, thinking at the same time that the business of Henry's going to the analyst for him was actually doing the opposite of freeing his friend.

"Probably nearly," the child shouted.

Finch finished the movement and then came back to the other room, thinking of how much time he had spent with Henry and Betty over the years. "There's a special word in Russian for someone who moves in on a household indefinitely and has the right to complain about the arrangements," he said, "and I'm it." He climbed back into bed, laying the cello on the right-hand pillow, which was more practical since the telephone was on the left-hand side, and read some music while the child went on going through the numbers in the telephone directory.

"Almost any number you liked would be nice," Finch said.

"No," the boy said, not lifting his head. "It was the same backwards as forwards, and it had a six in it. It was a special one."

Henry came into Finch's flat one day and refused the usual catechism about what he had said to the analyst.

"You talk as if your dreams were, I don't know, pieces of new music," Henry said. "Sometimes you think you've done all right but often you say they don't hold water or they won't stand up. A man's *allowed* to have second-rate dreams if he feels like it. The dream you were lamming into yesterday was a perfectly good dream, the doctor said. He said you mustn't victimize yourself."

"Victimize!" said Finch.

"He said a lot of tyrannical people are really masochists."

Finch groaned and tried to go to sleep.

"Now what?" said Henry. "The man's doing his best. He's very nice about you. He bought your last record."

"*Our* last record."

"He's going through a lot because of your not wanting to see him."

There was a long pause while Finch committed murder in his heart, and then sat up in bed with his cello and played arpeggios.

"That sounds like a nutmeg grater," Henry said.

"Yes. I haven't been practicing. I've been in *bed* all this time. I'd been trying to go to sleep. I know: instead of going to sleep, let's go to Tunisia."

"Why Tunisia?"

"There's a letter asking you to play at an out-of-doors arts festival in the desert somewhere. I'd come for my health."

Finch walked about Tunisia in fur-lined bootees to emphasize his frailty. The bootees were unzipped to the anklebone because of the heat. The festival was a theatre-and-music fiesta devised for the villagers and attended by the experimental cognoscenti of the world, many of them Jews. Henry played the piano out of a van on forays into the hinterland to introduce the Trans-National Drama Research Gymnasium. Surprised villagers, grateful at first for free entry to anything, crept away from improvised stage sketches in a prepared nonlanguage. The directors and actors had spent months in zoos recording the noises made by apes in emotional situations. A man working on a theatrical seminar called "Computers—Whither?" was angry because the ape recordings had thieved some of his points about the place of computer speech in the new drama. At the same time, a filmmaker was directing an underground picture that owed a certain amount to *The Four Feathers* and *Lawrence of Arabia*. He was an agreeable man with a small private fortune and a look of poverty. Finch rather liked him. His name was Cecil Colling. Cecil had imported a tribe of Bedouins to the site to play the spectacular scenes. The men in the technical crew, unpaid, were earning their way by filming the fiesta for the BBC. The Bedouins, whom Cecil cared for and saw to be poor, were being paid in private out of Cecil's own pocket.

"The raid scenes are terrific," he would say after a day's

shooting, flushed with love of his work. "The Bedouins are really getting the hang of it. So are the camels. When I fire one gunshot, they go. Two shots, they stop in a flash. You'd never find English animals as good as this. It's the speaking parts I'm having trouble with. Film's a visual medium; you can't get away from it."

Sometimes, when Henry was trying to write a letter of apology to the analyst for having quit, and wondering whether the man was all right—and when Finch was pondering the need to do the same thing—they would wander off together and watch Cecil coaching the people he referred to as "the speaking parts." It was against his convictions to call them "actors." The Bedouins and the camels, both groups equally bored, would gather round a portable gramophone of Henry's and nod to records of *On the Town* and Schönberg's *Moses and Aaron,* listening carefully while the sand blew into their faces.

An English statesman arrived for a feast he had arranged between the Jews present as guests and the Arabs who were their hosts. The meal was a gesture to compromise, lying in an Anglo-Indian recipe for curry and a strawberry blancmange. The statesman knew he was going wrong somewhere: a kindly man, stocky, given to blunders, with misleadingly piercing blue eyes and a stoop. "Is that so?" he would say when he hadn't actually grasped a point; or sometimes "Quite." But people felt generally the better for his "Quite" at conferences, and so did the guests at his baffling feast. His presence was not a bad one to bestow, and his words carried across dead air with a kind of comfort. He would say "Is that so?" at the compromise meal, and immeasurable non-English-speakers would feel in touch with him. Or "Quite," and they would know what he meant. He had brought along with him an underling ex-ambassador, now in the U.N. Department of the Foreign Office, who was possessed by a sense of the fatuous that had often threatened to wreck his career. The statesman made a speech at the dinner. Finch was sitting next to the underling. The speech was in support of Arab-Israeli understanding. "Let the lion (whichever is the lion—I don't know)," said the statesman in a tactful bellow, "lie down with the lamb (whichever is the lamb—I don't know)." The underling sealed the end of his job by laughing. Finch had picked up some Arabic and heard the interpreter translating the image into a metaphysical nonsense about a camel (whichever is a camel) lying down with a camel (whichever is a camel).

Loafing about Tunisia in his unzipped bootees, Finch missed his cello, among other things. The courtly interpreter of the festival, a Tunisian, after giving him some hashish jam, said to him in a tent that he hoped he had peace of mind.

"Yes. I have a prior attachment," Finch said, to his surprise, but thinking not to be understood.

"Attachment to what, if I may ask?"

"To railway carriages. To bikes. To Sickert." At home in Northumberland long ago, there had been a painting by Sickert whose poignancy and brilliance had stopped him nightly on his way to bed. Finch lay back, lulled by hash, and thought of the Botticelli in the billiard room and the Angelica Kauffman on the half-landing and the Landseer in the downstairs lavatory. Not a man to fall prey to fabricated regrets, he remembered clearly that the Angelica Kauffman was a bad one, and pondered the question of people's nerve to achieve the first-rate. Henry would never lack it.

In Tunisia, doing nothing, Finch mooched and grumbled and read, and what he was thinking about had room to expand. He found himself responding to some of the ideas that the Tunisians gently explored in their tents. Their attitude to life was not unlike Henry's, he thought. Finch had a temperamental dislike of the physical idols of Greek literature and of English public schools. He found only Ulysses deeply human, with his craftiness and patience, and Oedipus, who wished to find out the unaccommodable truth about himself, and Perseus, who kept his heart from turning to stone.

One night he wept with rage in the desert cold. That's what comes of not practicing, he said to himself furiously.

"What is it?" said Betty, who was with him, and Henry.

"I don't like the times. Bad times," he said, without meaning to.

"Have you been having hash?"

"No."

"What's wrong with the times, apart from politics?"

"We've got no remorse. Only guilt, that's the trouble. It's

better here. It's also better in bed. And I like it with you two. What can one do in a time when no one is ashamed of having done something? When people are only guilty, as a weapon?"

"If you despised the times as much as you pretend, you wouldn't be angry with them," Henry said. "You've got yourself out of bed. Now take off your bedroom slippers."

"They're boots."

"All right, they're in the historic line of Aunt Belle's cardigans in Tibet, but zip them up."

"Henry's found a cello for you," Betty said.

"I've given up the cello for the moment," said Finch.

"I can't imagine going on performing without you," Henry said after a wait. "I don't want to."

"Your nurse once said to you, 'Some can, some can't, some do, some don't, and you're a can and do."

"I don't remember that."

"It struck me."

Unwilling to act in his proper person, Finch went back to London and started to live too high. Henry rose to fame on his own. Bank managers and accountants tried to depress Finch, but for all the limbo he was in, his spirits were kept up by the strongest curiosity to see what would happen next. I am a pirate and an exhibitionist, he thought, but not a cynic. He remained the best of all friends to people. After Henry had outstripped him in celebrity, he grew riotous. Refusing to teach or to perform, he started to compose, which much pleased his daily, though no one else knew of it. By night he kept himself from the usual evenings with Henry and Betty, thinking to leave them some space for a time, and he would often take a sleeping pill at eight, before dinner, because sleep had grown difficult. On account of all the months in bed, no doubt, he decided. On top of even a glass of wine the effect of the sleeping pills was dramatic.

One evening, lonely, he was taken to meet a great harpsichordist of nearly ninety. She was known for her acerbity, her cucumber sandwiches, and her insistence on decorum. It was uncertain whether she was offering him tea or dinner or nothing, since the time she gave was a quarter to six and she would never have had anyone to drinks. Out of nerves and hero wor-

ship, he had three double Scotches before setting out and two
more on the way, and then made himself self-destructively late
by going into a greengrocer's to buy some mint to chew so as
to disperse the Scotch. He arrived, having picked up his com-
panion guests, in a vast flat in West Kensington. There were
no carpets on the polished boards. Upright chairs were placed
around the walls of the drawing room a large distance from
one another. The great woman came in: standing four foot
eight, using a gold-topped cane. She sat firmly on one of the
upright chairs and spoke about the breeding predicament of
her mare. No one knew that she had a mare.

"I was thinking of putting her to a very nice stallion I've
seen in the district," she said. "She's getting on, and it would
be pleasant to have a foal. She's nineteen. It isn't unknown to
have a foal at nineteen."

"Really?" someone said.

"I'm afraid I lied about her age to the stud farm. Do you
think it matters? I said she was sixteen." The old woman took
a lace handkerchief out of the tapestry reticule hanging from
her left wrist and rolled the handkerchief into a ball between
her hands, which was a gesture everyone in the room knew
from her concerts. "I daresay I shouldn't have done."

Finch lost his head and said to this woman whose fastidi-
ousness he most revered, "You wouldn't lie about your own
age, that's the thing."

She gave him a basilisk gaze and he tried to dispose of his
long legs around the legs of the Sheraton chair.

Later on—days, he thought glumly—they moved into the
dining room, which was an equally august and unmerciful place.
The sherry in the clear soup put him out entirely. When he
woke up his hair was in the soup and his head on the rim of
the plate, and his hostess had left the table.

"We'd better go," someone said. "We'll take you home."

"I don't want to go home," he said, quite out. His rescuers,
a couple, decided to take him to Henry's new flat in Shepherd's Market, which Finch had prevented himself from in-
vading.

"Num quid vis?" he said to them in the taxi. " 'Is there anything else you want?' It's what the Romans said when they
assumed the answer was no. The answer is yes. A common

leave-taking, they used to say at school. *Num* expects the answer no. *Nonne quid vis.* The Romans never said that, I think. People don't. *Nonne* expects the answer yes."

"We're dropping you at Shepherd's Market," the woman said loudly, as if to someone disabled. There's nothing wrong with me, Finch thought.

Henry and Betty took him in. He accepted them without noticing them or where he was, because of the naturalness of it and the sherry on top of shock. He spoke to them and they to him of books and girls and other things. His bulk, thin but long, was hard for them to get up their spiral stairs, so they left him on the sofa below, on the floor that lay over an iron-monger's shop. At six o'clock the next morning he came stumbling up their stairs, threatening to crack the banisters, having the strength and the weight of a buffalo. They heard him in the bathroom, running the water, then breaking a tumbler between long pauses.

After a great while his footsteps lumbered in their direction. There was a knock on the door.

"Come in," Betty said.

"Who is it?" said Finch, without opening the door and still knocking. "Whoever it is, I've been looking in your books and you haven't got your *name* in your books. Every other time I've been in somebody's flat like this I've known where I am by the books."

"Come in," Betty said again.

He opened the door. "Good lord," he said, hitting his head against the top of the door frame. "Oh my friends, I am glad it's you. It might have been anyone."

The Position of the Planets

"Good lord, I'm a genius," the impresario wailed, as if crying for help. He held his hand to his forehead and loped across the bar toward the beautiful girl in the corner. "I'm a *genius*," he said again, and the hand again went to his forehead. He might have been taking his temperature. "I dreamt about you suddenly last night, and now here you are in New *York* of all places. You won't remember me."

"Nearly," the girl said, trying. Also still trying to write a letter.

"Well, it's a great piece of luck, to break a dream. I've been having wonderful luck ever since May 25th. I'm Scorpio. In the dream you were in London, of course. What are you doing here? We were both in London. We were in the National Theatre bar, the downstairs bar, the place where I last saw you. You won't remember. Can I sit down with you and have a drink?" He loomed over the table and spilled a pile of show-business newspapers from under his arm. "What are you doing in New York?" he said.

"Writing a book about the longshoremen's union," the girl said. "And washing up."

He was gazing at her left cheekbone, though, and absently swatting the air.

("Libra ascendant. You will encounter fiery 'reminders.' Sign of mutable air. Easy-moving gait in 'speculation.' ")

"I'm trying to find an actress I once saw who looks just like you. Can you think who it is? American. I'd have to get her past Equity."

"You could probably wangle it," she said, squinting at her letter.

"Do you know anything about unions, then?"

She gave up and said, "Are you buying plays?"

"So there, you do remember me. That's wonderful. Doesn't one roast in America." He pulled off his jacket in a hurry and left one sleeve turned inside out, like a small boy's jersey. A waiter came up and made him put it on again.

He leaned forward as if he meant to kiss her and then said in a low voice, "I'm going to give you the name of a first-rate lawyer."

"What I need is a vet for my cat," she said. "I don't think I need a lawyer."

"I can find you the best vet in New York. I know someone. But put this name down. He's the top lawyer in New York. For example, 'I can't pay you straightaway,' I had to say to him. 'That's all right,' he said. 'We can wait until doomsday, or August, whichever is the sooner.' 'No, you won't have to,' I told him, 'my luck's on the turn; it's going to be a tremendous year, though it's true that just now one's recovering from a few debacles.' Get out your book and write his name down. And while we're about it I'll give you the name of the best dentist in America. You'll say you shouldn't afford it here and neither should I, but in dentistry they've got the edge on us and you can't begrudge teeth. Liz says that. You've never met her. I always wanted to introduce you but there never seemed to be the chance of it. You haven't seen me since the bad time with the lawyers."

"This lawyer?"

"No, in England. My own company sued me, didn't you know? Making me carry the can. 'All right,' I said, 'sue me.' I moved out of my office the same afternoon. I found a place in West Kensington. No reason why a theatrical manager has to be in Shaftesbury Avenue and pay those rents. They tried to intimidate me by holding my furniture. There was a desk I was fond of, it's true. But by then I was into my new place and I felt well shot of the stuff. 'All right,' I told them, 'keep it; I don't want it now, I'm perfectly happy, thanks.' That was our bad year. I didn't know it was all coming, of course, which is just as well. Fortunate that things don't happen all at the same time. Insofar as time is constituted by duration—"

He had a think, and blew his nose, noticing after a moment that her mind was fixed on his words in a way that made him feel quite light. A five-pound note that had got muddled up with his handkerchief fluttered to the floor, and he looked at it accusingly, though without making a move.

"Next month we had the burglary," he said. "Liz lost a winning I'd given her on a horse. We'd kept it in cash. You can't insure cash, as you know, but who cares, and it seemed a good present. A Christmas stocking—no, a pair of red tights, actually—filled up to here with pound notes that we'd won on a strawberry roan named Cordelia. I'd just had an idea for a way of doing *Lear* and it had brought me luck. The idea. At the time. Though the money went later, as I said. In the same swoop they took my father's silver cigarette case. The first time I ever got bashed around the earhole was when I put my dirty fingers on that cigarette case. His letters went too, for some reason." The impresario made a face. "Rotten year." But a minute later he looked buoyed up.

(**"You have recently had a 'bad' year. Ignore this. Gamble on 'profits.' Journeys ahead. Your assets will be enfervoured. Lucky colour gold or gilt."**)

The girl rescued the five-pound note, because he was obviously going to let it lie there. "Oh, thanks very much," he said in a courtly way, stuffing it back into his handkerchief pocket. *"Lousy* year. Good riddance."

He paused, and she said to prompt him, "I heard you were poorly."

"Well, I had to have my tonsils out when we were in the middle of producing *Tamburlaine*, which meant that the stage management made a right old mess of pulling on the chariot. I daresay you heard about that joke-night among the London literati." He stared at her. If she doesn't answer me seriously, he thought, if she's listened to the chatter about me, she's had it.

"No," she said. "It came on fine the night I was there. I think it was on a truck. Have I got that right? From the prompt side."

Relieved, he talked volumes about the technical problems of chariots.

"And after the tonsils something else happened?" she said, looking for more, because he didn't seem a man to make a fuss over tonsils, but he evaded her and said only, *"Foul* year."

"What else happened?" she said, digging away.

"I couldn't seem to get back any vim, that's all. In the end I dropped in on Oliver Craddock, just out of curiosity, and he saw everything without my telling him a word."

"You mean an astrologer?"

"You're laughing at me and I laughed at myself, but he's the best astrologer in London. As I say, I wasn't feeling particularly well at that point. All right, I thought; yes, it's womanish to go to him, but they're poor times, and maybe an astrologer's a rug to put over you when you're wintering. I'm going to give you his address. I've never fancied the stars, having been a computer programmer in early life, but it may be a truth that mathematicians are often superstitious."

"I wouldn't have known you'd been in computers."

"We're not a breed."

"What made you stop?"

"It began to seem a craven sort of job. Also lonely, and without much dash, to my mind. I'd do most of it at night. I was learning at a place where we hired the computer's time and it was cheaper to get a night run. The engineer would go to sleep soon in a corner. Liz would have given me a thermos and a book. I generally didn't drop off till four or five. The computer would be burbling away and the lights would be fluttering around the console. One calls it a console and it looks much like an awful cocktail cabinet. But the nights there gave me an idea later for a psychedelic light show, so they weren't all wasted? If you dozed off and the computer happened to break down, the silence generally woke you. A comforting feature of that particular model was that you could store drinks in the back of its refrigeration compartment. I'm feeling splendid, aren't you?"

A waiter came up to him and handed him an airmail copy

of some newspaper. He folded it open at a page of stocks and shares, and as he was looking down the lists he gave the man two dollars.

"You tip too much, don't you?" the girl said.

"Hang on a moment, I've got to telephone," he said. She started to get up but he said, "Don't go, don't go," and hurried out of the bar, running with his body crouched and his right hand holding the newspaper low down, like a soldier carrying a slung rifle running in to the attack.

Someone came back with him to plug in a telephone. "Do you want to be on your own?" she said.

"Don't go," he said again, getting a London number and ringing his stockbroker late in the English night. She read while he talked. He has the sound of a desperado, she thought. Hanging on to the cliff face by his nails, gaining small purchase on it.

"I was just talking to my bookie," he said crisply, which was the way he treated money troubles, "While I was about it, I put a fiver for you on a nice little filly called General Motors." He had a drink, and then a double, looking at her. "You're a very pretty girl. Delicate. I don't mean unwell."

"Actually, I have seen your wife. At the Lyric one night."

"Liz has a small face, too."

No, the girl thought, it was a big, strong face, remembering it quite clearly, and then putting aside that puzzle. "What happened after the computers?"

"Liz made me stop. We wondered what to do next, because the only other thing I'd ever done was box. I was in and out of work. More out than in. I took a job at a place where they did greeting cards. We put out a lot of get-well cards and deepest sympathies, which was a bit of a con when the only thing I knew how to do apart from programming was punching people. I hadn't been any great shakes at boxing, but I'd thought as a young man that I might be. Everybody needs to shine at something, and I thought I could box. I used to have quite a complex about being beaten, but I met Liz after I'd been beaten hollow all year and she still married me."

"You looked happy, the two of you. She was wearing a red suit with red boots and a pleated shirt."

He blinked strangely.

"And you look fine now," she said, pushing on. "People revive very fast." Some people, she thought, he in her mind. The diligence of cheering up.

"Well, it's true that one isn't always sure that life can continue under its present auspices, but I am at the moment," he said, "and especially today. Oliver Craddock told me this would be a good time. 'It will be full of travel.' " He ate a peanut and went over his own words, having a perfect verbal memory, which was an aid in his profession. " 'Auspicious' is something Indians often say. I had an Indian friend in the bad year, a lawyer from Udaipur who kept up my spirits when the partners were after me. 'Today is an auspicious day,' he would say. He was quite superstitious, generally leaning to one's own advantage."

And then she read, in a copy of *The Stage* that happened to be turned in her direction, a paragraph about him which made it clear that the wife whom he was talking about in the present tense had died a year ago, and that he had had a row of flops in London.

"New York's a shot in the arm," he was saying. "I've bought the biggest shows in town. I'm going to make a fortune, and your little flurry on General Motors will keep you in mink for the rest of your life. No, not mink. I can see you wouldn't like mink. Fun furs. No, I daresay they've gone already. A beautiful pale-auburn fox down to your ankles, with a high collar to turn up. You'd look like a very small Katharine Hepburn. Witty. Have you seen that thing called *Thighbone?* Do you think it'd go? Barbra Streisand wants to do it with me."

"She'd make anything go," the girl said, a second after reading a paragraph on the front page of *Variety* about two big London managements—no mention of him—that were bidding against each other for the show. "What made you want to go into the theatre?"

"Well"—and he waited to be certain he was putting it right, for she gave him scruples—"well, as we were saying, one isn't sure of the ruling hand any longer, so there is an inclination these days to take over oneself."

"Is it that? Isn't it the risk?"

"No, the control. That's what I didn't like about computers; you have to truckle. Anyway, I'm not a man of the disciplines.

I thought to myself, Computers are in danger of making people furious, but the theatre as a job of work might be just the meat."

"Isn't it the gambling? The cheek?" The backbone, she thought, on her way to the newsstand.

When she got back, he was charging their drinks to himself and ordering more. "Room 605 or 505, whichever floor it is. You know it," he cried to the waiter. And "Oh, I am having a nice time!" he exclaimed to her. Another waiter came up to him then with a bundle of letters and cash that he had left behind in the foyer and forgotten. He gave him ten dollars and put the clump of valuables underneath his newspapers and a heap of message slips and theatre programs.

"Liz isn't a bit theatrical. She's Pisces, I'm Scorpio. Oliver Craddock saw it all. He said it would be hard for a time." He pulled at his tie. "When the lawsuit was beginning, before he could possibly have known about it, he wrote this down for me on a bit of paper." The impresario scribbled on a copy of *Arts-Spectacles* and turned it round to the girl.

" 'Legal, psyche-regenerative.' That's what he wrote," he said.

"What happened after the greeting cards?" she said. Some strong feeling roared along her bones.

"You could use words like 'fantastic' or 'spectacular.' I was in Cook's getting our letters because we hadn't an address at the time. We were living here and there, and I was looking for investors, so we gave a care-of-Cook's address. I was watching someone else picking up his post, a nice-looking man with a stoop, and he was reading his letters and he came to one where he cried bitterly. So I introduced myself. It was a letter describing the last hours of a friend of his. None other than the greatest mathematician in the world. You'll guess what I'm leading up to. Well, he said he was a writer, and I said I was looking for plays to invest in and why didn't he write one about his friend, and a couple of months later he'd written something pretty splendid, hadn't he? The luck began to run the other way and we made a bit of a fortune that six months. Who would think it of Cook's. Or of American Express, for that matter. A benediction from Cook's." He flapped his jacket. He had a nose like a snout, long and inquiring.

"It sounds more your doing," she said. "I don't believe much in luck."

"Ah, all I did was have an idea," he said. "Having an idea is nothing to go by."

She didn't intrude.

"Don't you be nice to me. I'm known as a bit of a bastard," he said proudly, heaving the pile of newspapers onto the floor and in the process dropping his wallet out of his jacket pocket. "Don't you be taken in, I'm not to be trusted," he said, noticing that his spectacles were steamed up. He rubbed them with a paper napkin and then put them away in his jacket because they seemed ugly in front of this pretty girl. As he was doing that, he saw the paragraph about himself in *The Stage* and planted his shoe over it. " 'Things will improve from May 25th,' " he repeated to himself silently, but moving his lips a little, which the girl noticed. He looked at her and said, adopting roguishness, "Would you like to come on a long journey with me? While I do a deal? Neptune is moving into Scorpio. I've got two first-class tickets. One always has two. On the firm."

But he's the firm, she thought.

"The most splendid hotel in America," he said. "The modern Chartres."

(*"Things will improve from May 25th. Forget bad 'symptoms.' "*)

"When?" she said.

"I'm going tonight," he said, scuffing the paragraph in *The Stage* hard with his foot as if he were rubbing cigarette ash into the carpet. "I won't promise to keep my hands off you, mind. And I'll be busy. It's a business trip. You won't see much of me." Then he said seriously, "It's a stingy offer."

People may blunder, she thought, and their actions can still have a fine echo; or they may act all right and the echo can be bad. "What plane?" she said. She paid for her own ticket, as it turned out. He forgot.

On the plane, which had armrests a foot wide, made in a plastic that looked like jellied gold lamé, he pretended suddenly to have remembered something and drew a rumpled piece of paper out of his wallet.

"Oliver Craddock wrote this down for me the first time I saw him and I'd forgotten all about it," he said. He smoothed the paper with his fingers and gave it to her. "I haven't looked at it since," he said, but it was much handled. She gave it back after reading it, and he went through it carefully as though he had never seen it. "Oliver Craddock said last year, 'There will be a removal of something or someone around May 25th.' Liz said, 'Christ, I hope it doesn't mean we're going to have to move.' 'No,' I said, 'We'll stay put in old West Ken,' but Oliver had seen it all, and I came to America the first time on May 25th. You may say an aeroplane isn't much, but it's a sign of activity."

(**"Do nothing 'more' in the present year. Neptune is moving into Sagittarius. Spark your income. You are very 'tired,' but this will change."**)

"Isn't it splendiferous?" he said in the hotel, gazing up. The lobby soared: twenty-eight floors high. At the top a glass cocktail bar slowly revolved, and drinkers exclaimed gaily at the changing spectacle of industrial buildings under construction. The racket of cement mixing was masked by the sound of Muzak. Lifts of glass and gilded plastic in the shape of water beetles darted up and down the outside of concrete columns four hundred feet high. Greenery dripped like candle wax into the lobby from the surrounding balconies; possibly *was* wax. Water lilies in a pool outside the coffee area were made of tin sprayed to look like copper. The impresario and the girl stood and watched, both shy. The hostess of the coffee place thought they were waiting for a table and corrected them for not standing in the queue. She was wearing a red velvet skirt cut like a skating skirt, with an alderman's neck chain slung round her hips and clanking between her legs. A diamanté brooch on her chest read "Miss Christmas." "No room," she said.

At *this* inn? thought the genius, whose gift was his trade's invaluable mixture of the sceptic and the buccaneer.

The impresario got two bedrooms. "In case Liz rings," he said to the girl, handing her a separate key and holding the back of her neck. She nodded, wondering why on earth, since Liz was dead and they were obviously going to be sharing a room. They had a drink and went to bed, and afterward he talked to her about deals and projects.

"You like America, don't you?" she said, raising her voice because of the uproar of building outside the hotel and the din of business conventions inside it.

"I went to Los Angeles on the last trip, and Las Vegas," he said. "Let's have another bottle of champagne. Las Vegas is a beautiful place. Perks one up. You perk me up. You've got to go there."

"I've been there," she said, but he rode over that, bent on ignoring his unreasonable jealousy that she had gone there with anyone else.

"I was feeling a bit tired," he said, "but it was wonderful there. I took Liz. Huge carpeted slopes in the hotel, like a golf course."

He turned away to the bedside table and found a souvenir sack of nickels from Las Vegas among the things he had unpacked from his pockets. "Here," he said, and threw it to her. "Save it for when I take *you* gambling in Las Vegas," juggling this chance in his head with the unthinkable odds that he would never see her again. "And then I went to Los Angeles, and I spent Thanksgiving on Malibu Beach, and there was a picture window"—he stared around him at the shoebox room and rejected it—"let's not exaggerate, but it would stretch from here to the lift. You should have seen the bed. It would have taken seven. It was as wide as a bus. What a beautiful day, right at the end of November. I went swimming, and I was so happy I cried into the sea for three-quarters of an hour. I don't know why. I never do that. Then I saw Rock Hudson and closed a deal. Well, and then I went on to Rome to look at a Goldoni production and I had to see the Pope, but I tell you—I hope you're not Catholic—the sight of the old pullet being cheered up the aisle of St. Peter's. They don't know how to deal with the times. Children living in the streets, peasants arriving from Sicily without an idea. Anyway, I signed all the talent in Rome."

The Muzak played "Raindrops Keep Fallin' on My Head" and they talked about Italy and then about nothing very much. Her dark brown eyes were like a Memling portrait's. "I signed a beautiful new actress," he said, leaning on his elbow and gazing at the girl. "Bilingual. Wonderful wrists. Eyes nearly black, which is unusual. And the bone structure!" He stroked the girl's collarbone devotedly. "I'm going to groom her, and then I'm going to show her to the National Theatre. She's the Latin Maggie Smith. I want to put her with Larry and John G. and Emlyn on Broadway and see the chemistry."

He gave her some more champagne and she asked if he had children.

"Three sons," he said. "Fourteen, sixteen, and twenty-one. Our greatest joy is that the twenty-one-year-old wants to go into the car industry."

Our.

"He's got the mathematical background that's needed for the future," the impresario said.

"You don't want him to go into the theatre with you? Or be your bookie in the City?"

"The flair for getting away with things doesn't descend unto the second generation."

Then he went to his own room. "I've got to lay a few more bets," he said.

A couple of hours later he rang to ask her to pick him up. The Muzak reached a gap as she was about to knock on the door and she could hear he was being told by the hotel that his credit wasn't good. "There must be some mistake," he was saying with an air. "The computers as usual, I suppose, but you'd better ring my solicitors and ask them to cable you the cash. I'll give you the number later. I've got an international call coming through."

She drew away to the balcony over the lobby, feeling incapable, looking down at the bawling men in dinner jackets far below and the women with stiff hair. After a while she went back again, and heard him talking to his broker about checks that were bouncing.

She asked him to come to her room so as not to overhear any more, and then they went downstairs in an express lift: a glass-and-gilt beetle that hurtled the twenty-eight floors in nine and a half seconds. He hung on to the semicircular rail around the outer edge, where they were standing because the businessmen who had got in after them had jostled them there, and she saw that his eyes were closed and that he had gone gray with fear about the drop. "I love you," she whispered under the Muzak. His eyelids fluttered for a second and stayed shut until they reached the ground floor.

They went out, he in a white suit, and he told her they were going to shoot pool. He clutched her shoulders on the way: a big shambles of a man, with shapely legs and a tendency to put on his overcoat with the collar turned inward. "Pool always perks me up," he said. "We'll have some more champagne in a moment. Champagne's the best drink. It doesn't give you a hangover if you remember to get down half a pint of water before you go to sleep. It's not easy to lay your hands on decent champagne here, but I know the manager."

"I can't believe my good luck sometimes," he said to her later in bed. "You're always in such demand."

Then he paused, and sounded tired, and said, "I've got something I must advise you about. If you are to prosper, as you should—" and she waited, but he had dropped into sleep like a stone.

He woke in a fury two hours afterward, and said that she had upset his rhythm and that he had to make some calls. From his room, not this, he seemed to mean. "I'll come with you," she said, risking intrusiveness. They dressed quickly and he again closed his eyes in terror while they were riding in the lift. His white suit by this time was crumpled and the Muzak seemed louder than ever. "I love you," she whispered under the din of other people's exclamations about the phenomenal machine.

They went into his room. "I'll give you a drink and then you'd better leave," he said angrily, clutching the back of her neck with great fondness, as before. "I want to ring Liz."

She went down to the lobby to settle the bill so far for both their rooms, and then changed her mind and paid only for her own and the booze. While she was waiting for the computer to do whatever it had to do, she rested her elbows on the counter with her back to it and the man next to her said in a heavy voice, "Are you an actress?"

"No, I'm just here with somebody."

"Come have a drink with me. You're a very lovely girl. You're not a feminist, are you?"

"I can't. Thanks."

"You *are* a feminist."

He went on needling her. "Are you an intellectual?"

"No, I do washing up."

"You're putting me on. Why would a lovely girl like you do dishwashing?"

"I need the loot."

"*Any* guy would keep you! You *are* an intellectual! What are you trying to *do* to me!"

She had to wait until her passport came back because she had cashed a traveller's check to pay the bill. She watched the lobby and suddenly saw that, in one of the lifts hurling down the middle of this Chartres, the impresario was standing with his hands clutching the railing. It didn't seem that he was looking for her, since he immediately went up again. Merely testing a hallucination, perhaps. Or himself.

She knocked loudly at the door of his room and carried in a tray of caviar. He was on the telephone.

"Marlon, it's a wonderful play for you, and Sophia wants to do it with us. Let me know tomorrow morning, eh?" he said.

Then he had some caviar and rang Italy and said, "Sophia, this play I sent that Marlon's going to do, he only wants to do it with you. Ring tomorrow, eh?"

Then he rang some film company in London and asked for one of the most junior men in the public-relations office, and the girl could hear the phone being put down on him.

"Is this your caviar or mine?" said the impresario. "I ordered you some. I wish Liz were here. What are you thinking?"

"Nothing."

"When people say it that fast, it always means they were thinking about something in particular."

"Nothing."

"I've got a lot to do. I've got to get some sleep," the impresario said, eating a spoonful of caviar and looking at a column about grosses in *Variety*. "Marlon and Sophia," he said. "Quite a double. '*Molto* boffo.' What do you think of ringing Albie Finney? I could get Albie. He's a friend of mine."

She went to sit beside him on the bed and read something tinny and long-winded about the recovery of Wall Street. "Have you got a lot riding on the market's getting better?" she said.

"A fair amount."

"Is it what you live off? More than the theatre?"

He stayed silent, quite obstinately, and she switched tone and said, "This is a trip about cheering up, isn't it? About keeping one's spirits up if one's a late capitalist?"

She was grinning as she said it, but he didn't take that in and yelled at her about Women's Lib claptrap. After a bit, he took off his debonair jacket and lay back on the bed in a beautiful fluted shirt, much creased, holding her newspaper over his head to look at the article she had been reading. She stabbed a finger at a line she remembered laughing about.

"What is it?" he said, declining to be humored.

" 'Investors used the summer doldrums as an excuse to stay away from the market in droves,' " she read out. "The shirkers."

"Ho hum," he said.

A couple of hours later, when he had been talking nonstop on the telephone, she was sitting in a chair half asleep.

"I'm going to make a fortune," he said. "Oliver Craddock was right. What *were* you thinking when you wouldn't tell me?"

"Nothing. Sorry, I've gummed up. It wasn't anything."

He threw a piece of ice at her and called her frigid.

She said in a rage that she had been thinking it was rough on him to belong to a society with a theology of gambling.

"You're in it too, mate," he said.

"Not half as much as Oliver Craddock."

"Marxist garbage."

She flounced into the bathroom, and then tried to think how to flounce out again in any way that would get her past his indispensable face and into the bloody lift. The telephone went, which was a possible cue, and she came out and heard somebody's secretary giving him a brushoff. He let only a moment go by before filling a teaspoon full of caviar and feeding it to her.

(*"Don't give way to 'anxieties.' Hearty awakening is in you."*)

"What time is it in London?" he said.

She looked at the fob watch round her neck. "Eight in the

morning. Don't you ever stop working?"

"Do you keep that watch on London time when you're away?"

"Yes."

"Who do you miss, then?"

"England."

He set the hotel alarm clock, touched. "There's an hour before anyone'll thank me for ringing them back," he said defiantly. And then he wondered who she was in love with in London, to have kept a watch on another time; and asked himself why in Christ she had come with him, in that case; and at the same moment reflected about some plays, for he truly liked the theatre.

"Need for subplots," he muttered when she thought he was asleep. "No, for sub-characters, to say there's something else. Fortinbras coming in at the end, when Hamlet's dead and everyone's dead. They're always cutting Fortinbras. I tell you, I wouldn't care to put on *Hamlet* without Fortinbras."

"Who were you with at the Lyric? Who was it in the red suit? What are we pretending about?"

"Red suit?"

"It wasn't Liz, was it?"

"No. Liz died a long while ago."

"Why didn't you tell me that before?"

He went silent, so she apologized.

"It was ages ago," he said roughly. "I'm not where they think I am. This is a *good* year."

She got up and stomped around.

The other room would be for telephone calls about being broke, of course.

"Come to *bed*," he said. "I've got a lot of deals in a minute."

She wished there were the faintest chance that he would drop being breezy. She lay down, and he drifted off, and five minutes later the central heating was hissing and clanging like a forge. He raised his head. "It's all right," she whispered under the noise, and he settled down again on his side with his back to her. Pause. Asleep, apparently.

"The truth is," he said, "I've been very eager to see you. They think I'm a dead duck, but it's not been a time you could write off. If I sleep through the alarm, will you wake me? Scorpio is coming into Aquarius. I've got to talk to my bookie."

After a pause he said, "Go if you want to."

It happened that she was propped on her elbow and could see that he had his fingers crossed.

"Thanks a million, but no thanks," she said, and he uncrossed them.

"Will you live with me?" she said, after thinking about it.

"Of course. Why the hell didn't you ask me before?" he said, and went to sleep at once. A few minutes later he was jerking around in the grip of an atrocious dream, and she woke him up.

"Go away. I'm asleep," he said.

"Weren't you having a bad dream?"

"No, just strenuous."

Foreigners

"Oh, god, I wish the shops were open," said the great atheist economist, near tears, to his terror. It was an ice-cold June Sunday. He had eaten roast mutton and apple charlotte. Three people in his Wiltshire drawing room slept, and so did his dogs. He looked at the fire hard enough to dry out his eyeballs, or perhaps to singe them.

"Sundays are impossible. I can't stand Sundays," his voice said, again frightening him. The voice was shouting. His hands were shaking. Sunday lunch, sleep; radio, muffins, sleep; gin-and-lime, the cold roast, radio, sleep. His English life, his English wife. On the opposite side of their English fireplace, Sara was answering letters on her engraved English note cards: "Mrs. Thomas Flitch, the Dower House." And so on and so on. His Indian mother was in a wheelchair by the bay window, reading. The sight of her brought back some Sunday in India. Himself a child on a bicycle. Dusk, nearly dark. Groups of young men sitting on the ground near a closed library, reading and talking by the light of flares in petrol cans.

His stepson, Simon, a tall stockbroker, guffawed for no obvious reason and kicked the chin of a sleeping dog off a pile of Thomas's books, although he didn't go on to pick up any of the spilled books.

"It'll be Monday all too soon," Sara said, with the brotherly grimness that Thomas had learned to read in her as a style of intimacy. Now she was doing household accounts and checking the milk bill. She looked fatigued and drawn. He loved her, and wished to save her the frightful inroads of Anglo-Saxon activity, and hated her hat. She was still wearing the ugly straw hat she had put on for morning church. She had cooked the lunch in it. Thomas liked her hair and loathed all her hats. In fifty-odd years of high regard for Englishwomen and awe of the fortitude and grace he saw in them, he had never accepted her defiling hats.

Simon's daughter, Pippa, a beauty of six who had one blue and one green eye, swarmed watchfully into the room on her stomach with Thomas's encouragement and bounced up with a war whoop behind the chairs of two sleeping visitors. So she was as oppressed by Sunday as he was. He admired her for dealing with it so capably. There was an interlude of chaos. A pot of coffee was spilled, and Sara had to get a damp cloth for the trousers of one of the visitors, who was involved in an unwise pretense that he hadn't actually been asleep. Thomas seemed to be seeing things through the wrong end of a telescope. People appeared to be very small, and their voices were too loud for their size. Pippa was much scolded.

"I've brought something for Great-Granny," she said several times, while the storm went on around her pigtailed head and finally spent itself. She heard her father and Sara out, and meanwhile held the present in her closed hand.

After five minutes, Simon attended to what she was saying and assumed a look of astuteness. "Have you got something in your hand?" he asked. Pause. "Something for Great-Granny?" he carried on shrewdly. "Let's have a look at it, in case it's one of the things Great-Granny doesn't eat." He tried to force open her fingers. "Let Daddy tell you. You're old enough to know by now that in the country where Great-Granny comes from they don't eat some of the things we eat. It's not that they're fussy, it's because they think it's wrong. You know that now, don't you, Pippa?"

"You told me before," said Pippa.

"Ah, yes, you see; it's a chocolate. So we're all right. I thought so. Why didn't you show it to me in the first place? Run and give it to Great-Granny," he said, sometime after Pippa was already there. "Granny, Pippa's brought you a special chocolate," he went on, some time after the old lady had thanked the child.

Thomas's mother was named Arathra Chib. Although his father had acknowledged the son in due time—when the boy grew up to be phenomenally educable—he had never married Miss Chib. She had stayed in a Delhi shack made of biscuit tins and a tarpaulin. Mr. Flitch, not a bad man, had worked most of his life in India in the tea business. When his bastard turned out to be studious, the boy was accepted into the English bachelor's house for a short time before he was shipped off to prep school and public school in his father's country. He spent the holidays in England with any parents who would have him. If nothing worked out, he lived in the empty school. Some master, equally lonely, would be set to giving him extra essays and physical training to keep him occupied. Thomas bore England no grudge for the youth it dealt him; on the contrary. After getting a double first at Oxford he married Sara, scarcely able to believe his luck. She was a pretty young widow with a small son, and Thomas went to law to give the little boy his own surname.

"Well done, Pippa. Chocolates are perfectly safe," Simon said laboriously in the direction of the wheelchair.

Thomas was already in the grip of a disorder not at all native to him, and now he suddenly confounded everything he believed he felt for Simon by remembering with hatred one of his adopted son's practical jokes. Some like Sunday long ago, the child Simon had crept up to his Indian step-grandmother when she was asleep in the same wheelchair and thrown a blanket over her, shouting that she was a canary in a cage. Thomas had kept the memory at arm's length until now, when it occurred to him that Simon's sensibility had not much changed. The insight cracked Thomas's heart slightly before he got rid of it again.

His mother's vegetarianism had been carefully respected at lunch, with the usual faint suggestion that it was aberrant and therefore embarrassing, although Sara did try to conceal her opinion. Before the apple charlotte, Miss Chib was given a bowl of pea soup with a spoonful of whipped cream on it. Thomas had noticed the cream, which represented effort. It also represented license, an unusual small expense on a treat beyond the necessities of Sara's food budget. Though Thomas was greatly revered he had never been well off, and now that he had retired from government advisory jobs he earned nothing much except by writing. Simon, who was well on his way to becoming a millionaire through his dealings on the stock exchange, had leaned over his pleasant young wife to peer at his step-grandmother's plate. "I say," he said jovially, "I see my mamma's been lashing out a bit."

Thomas's house, which he could barely keep up, was run mostly on the income from a small chain of modern toy shops that he had built up for his wife over the years. He had given her the capital for the first one on their twentieth wedding anniversary, when he had already bought a Georgian pendant that he dearly wished her to have, but before he chanced giving it to her he had asked her what she would like, and she told him. She had ideas about how a toy shop should be run in these times. Strong plastics, instructive building toys, things that would save women trouble. After a long while of keeping the pendant hidden and unlooked at in his sock drawer, Thomas had to bring himself to hunt for someone to buy it back, for he couldn't afford both presents. He got nothing like the price of it. But Sara's idea had obviously been the better one, he told himself, though without believing a word of it, for where would they all be now without "Mamma's business venture," as his stepson warmly pointed out to him on a walk round the garden this afternoon.

"Why don't you let me take over the accounts?" Simon said.

"What accounts?" Thomas asked, sheltering in slow-wittedness. He seemed to be fending something off. Nothing he was doing was like himself, and Simon looked at him oddly before poking a black pig in the belly.

"You should keep more pigs and run the place as a farm," Simon said. "And all this could be ploughed up, too." He gestured across the lawn that ran down to a stream and then up again to his own cottage, which Thomas had given him as a wedding present. "The expenses of this place are ridiculous. Mamma's a Trojan, but she's looking pretty whacked."

"She needs more help. I must see about more help."

"As I say, I could do the papers of the business. You wear yourself out with them."

"They seem to be taking longer at the moment. You wouldn't have time."

"Oh, I could do them on the train to the City some morning every week."

That fast? He probably could.

Simon looked around at the bigger house with an alert eye. "This place is potentially a gold mine. It's madness to run it as a private house. If you turned it into a business, you could keep six maids and gardeners if you wanted and write them off against the pigs. Or whatever else you went in for. Mamma's been talking of sugar beet."

Sugar beet? Sugar beet hadn't come up. Thomas steadied his eyes on the Tudor stable yard and his library window. "I won't have it," he said, shaking.

"Buck up, Father. Nobody thinks it's your fault. You're one of the world's thinkers. Been doing much writing?"

Thomas lied, against his temperament. "Quite a bit." Pause. "Preliminaries." Oh, come off it. But the ground seemed to be moving away. He felt as if Simon were lifting him by the collar and dangling him so that his feet were off the earth and his toes straining to reach something. Simon's big head and loose mouth loomed above him against the ridiculous English summer sky, which was the color of iron.

"Your last book was very impressive," Simon said. "Prunella and I both thought so. Reflected glow, you know." He blew his nose on a red spotted handkerchief that he wore in yeoman moods. "A bit above my level, I'm afraid, some of it."

"Oh, dear. Was it hard to follow?" Thomas asked, taking him to mean what he said. "Which passages?" But Simon had never got beyond page 27, and after that he had merely left the book out in case his mother and stepfather came unexpectedly for drinks. So now he was at a disadvantage, which angered him, and he lost sight of the gratitude he usually summoned up for the stepfather who had spent much of his life obliging his adopted son's ambition for parents with a big house and a dashing car. At many moments of weakness, or love, Thomas had spent far more money than he could afford or even wanted for the sake of Simon's joy in the holidays. The days when he could do it, or would, were now over. Their town house had been sold, lingeringly, with rearguard modernizing actions to keep up its price. The eventual loss kept Thomas awake at night. For the present, in the daytime, he was abruptly fed up with the lot: himself, his insufficiency, the toll that his financial state seemed to be taking of his wife, and the colossally polite head of his stepson, hanging over him now as if it had a miniature keg of brandy around its neck.

"Men are not made better by calamity," he said. At the same time, he was engaged in disliking his own state of intellect at the moment, which appeared to own no responsibility for the production of that sentence and buzzed around small problems without much resource or repose.

"What's that from? Is it an Indian saying?"

"What? No. Where was she thinking of putting the sugar beet?"

"Hey, I say, chin up. No calamity in this house, eh? Mamma's full of beans."

"She's very tired."

"Take her to the sun. Take her to Greece. A friend of mine's got a yacht. You could charter it."

"It would be rather ludicrous." When we can't afford someone to clean the house, Thomas added silently.

"I could put it against the farm and it wouldn't cost anything. A conference yacht." Simon laughed loudly. "Mamma could be entertaining foreign buyers. I do think you should let me go into the pigs."

Thomas told Simon to leave. He said he had work to do. Simon walked down to the stream and across the bridge to his own cottage, waving with his usual cordiality, which was unfailing because it depended on no cordial impulse. Thomas came back past the drawing room. He could see his mother playing with Pippa, and his wife talking to a woman friend by the window. Thomas looked at them all, and then at Simon, who was now a small figure and in another sense no longer monstrous, because he was walking exactly as he had done when he was a very young child and most moving to Thomas, with his hands in his pockets and his back arched. The familiarity of everyone eased the strangeness in Thomas's head. I wish I had them all here, he thought. I wish we were together. I wish we were having a picnic, and that it was hot, and I do indeed wish that we were all together; though even if I were to hold the whole world against my chest, it would probably save us from very little. The longing was unaccustomed. He came to the drawing-room window, which was open. His mind had at last found its way back to its usual cast when he heard Sara's friend talking to her.

"—start bestirring himself, for heaven's sake. Leaving you to do everything. What's a brilliant mind—"

"He is brilliant, that's so," Sara said over her. "But he's never made the career he could have done. He won't use his elbows."

But I am not that man, Thomas thought, shivering in a heap on the flower bed where he had dropped onto all fours so as not to be seen. I am not that man, he thought again, straightening up now, for in the next instant it seemed entirely necessary that he should not hide, should visibly walk to the front door and into his library. I will not be that man. He sat behind his desk for a long time, skipping Sunday's cold-mutton supper, rousing himself to say goodbye to the visitors, trying to deal with the paperwork of Sara's business. Wholesale and retail prices, markups, running expenses, employment insurance. Nausea. Sara, beautiful Sara, appeared in the accounts as the manageress. Deductible, to be candid. *No. Once not.* She had left samples of toys and plastic playthings among his books and manuscripts. Garbage. Her piercing household face swam across his eyeline, even more changed from its former self than now, and hermetic in its enthusiasm for nursery objects properly researched by child psychiatrists to be fit for the middle-class children who would lose them without a pang. There was a pale-pink celluloid rattle on his desk. It was decorated with an overdressed pale-blue rabbit in nontoxic paint. Long ago, he had found Simon a Hindu rattle made of chased silver with an ivory handle shaped for a child to hold. *What shall we leave behind us,* he thought. He stared at a Rajput scene on the wall among his books. "Won't use his elbows." I know as little of love as I do of painting, he thought. The days of smoking a pipe suddenly came back to him, and he realized that he was biting down on his own teeth. His mind seemed to be acting like mercury. He saw it slipping around in a pool and then dividing into drops that ran apart. He leaned back often for a rest and once he got up to type an envelope on an old typewriter in the window. The typewriter had been made in Delhi many years ago, copied from an English Underwood and reproduced in every detail except for the vital spring to drive the keys back. In the machine's heyday, the deficiency had not been regarded as crippling. Labor was cheap, time ran slow, and a girl sat beside the man typist to return each key by hand as he pressed it. Thomas had grown up in the neighborhood of the machine and one day he had bought it, bringing it to England by boat and vaguely intending to explore the possibility of supplying a spring, though he also like it well as it still was.

He delayed going upstairs for as long as possible, partly in a hopeless pretense of getting the papers finished with, and partly to avoid Sara. But she was lying awake. He guessed her to be worrying about money. Temper defeated pity and he attacked her rabidly for, of all things, going to her Anglican church. It appeared to him suddenly that there was a link between her flouted ambition for him and the ethic of a religion more alien to his own thought than he had ever dreamed. He sounded to himself like some tendentious student with balloon words coming out of his mouth.

"Jesus was the first Catholic and therefore the first Mr. Success of the profit motive," he said, putting on his dressing gown and feeling foolish. "Christianity and capitalism are inseparable. Why do you go? Why do you spoil Sundays?"

Sara said, "You're not well. You're losing your grip." She watched him quite carefully. She got up.

"I daresay. We can't stay in this house. We simply can't keep it up."

She was quiet.

So he snarled. "Does it mean that much to you?"

"What do you think?" Now the rage poured out: All these years, our things, deserve, owe, our time of life, all we've been through.

Help, he thought. I can't go on. I can't manage any of it.

Earn, she threw at him.

Relearn, he thought, adding the first three letters to her word in his head as if they were playing a game. "Church!" he shouted.

"You never shout," she said, staring at him.

"You spoil Sundays!"

"Socrates was the first man who thought about thinking,"

she said, sitting on the window seat and surprising him in every way.

"Uh?" he said over her.

"Jesus may have been the first man who understood the power of some actions. The power of forgiving an enemy, for instance."

"You mean me, don't you?" He held his head.

On Monday, when Sara had left the house early to see to things in two of the toy shops on the other side of the county, he could find nothing at home that he felt up to doing. He drove to a café in the nearby market town and simply listened to pacify himself. It was a tea shop, with one half that sold honey and homemade scones and the other with tables where the walls were decorated with a mixture of horse brasses and psychedelic posters. One of the middle-aged women who kept the shop had ordered a set of posters about the Paris rising of May 1968, because she had gone to the Sorbonne to study when she was a girl. The tea shop was next door to one of Sara's branches. Remorse had drawn Thomas there and it kept him pinned, though he was also wild for flight. An arthritic woman came into the café, alone, with a paper bag carrying the name of Sara's shop.

"You feel safer at home than what you do further away," she said after a long silence, addressing no one. "Further away you might be a nuisance."

Unplaced impatience felt like burrs on Thomas's skin. He leaned over to her and said, "No, you should get out and about more," which affronted her. He had broken the fourth wall.

In the late afternoon, slow to go home, he dropped in on an elderly doctor friend and played tennis. His hands shook and his friend prescribed a sedative.

"Work a strain at the minute?" said the doctor, watching.

"That sort of thing."

"Take two a day," said the doctor. "Sleeping all right?" The whole circumstance startled him. He expected limitless serenity of a man half Indian, and indeed Thomas had sustained the expectation for twenty years or more.

"Mostly," Thomas said.

"Let me know. Keep in touch."

"I can't concentrate. I don't understand myself. Sara's being a brick."

"Your English is more English than mine," the doctor said, not really to make conversation but to find more time to see. Thomas's mind seemed to be elsewhere, and there was no perfunctory laugh in return.

The doctor was concerned enough about him to trail him on a journey that Thomas then made to London Airport. He merely sat at the coffee counter there, hour after hour, alone. The talk of strangers alleviated something. At one point, he inquired at the Air-India desk and made a booking. Then he went back to the coffee counter, where two girls were talking about pop singers.

"I wouldn't mind marrying Paul," said the blond girl of the pair. She had a beautifully high forehead and an upper lip that twitched softly, like a cow's in a fly-ridden summer.

"Paul?" said her freckled friend. "Ringo any day."

"I think Paul's sweet."

"Ringo's more of a husband. More masterful."

"Well, if you're talking about *masterful*," the blonde said vaguely.

"Don't you want to be mastered?"

"Not much."

"I don't think a marriage with Ringo would work if he wasn't the master."

"There's always divorce."

They paused, and then the freckled girl said, "What about the cooking? I can't see me cooking."

"I wouldn't mind doing Paul a steak," said the blonde. "Or spaghetti. As long as it wasn't fish with the eyes left in, or a chicken. Not a whole chicken. Nothing with innards."

"Would you look after him if he was ill? That's what I'd have to do for Ringo, you know. I wouldn't mind. I should think he'd be very demanding. Anyone in the public eye."

"Paul's kept his sincerity. He's not spoilt."

Thomas quietly bought them another cup of coffee each, and they giggled when they realized it and clinked the thick coffee mugs with him before carrying on with their conversation as if he weren't there.

"What sort of ill, anyway?" said the blonde.

"Sick, say," said freckles.

Thomas saw Sara in his mind's eye. She was never ill, but now she looked beaten and angered by something he must be doing to her. For richer, for poorer.

"What sort of sick? English sick or American sick?" said the blonde.

"What's the difference, then?"

"Don't you know that? American sick is just ill. When they mean English sick, they say throw-up sick or sick to your stomach."

"English sick."

"Come to think of it, I'd look after him anyway. So long as he didn't carry on about it. You wouldn't catch Paul carrying on."

They ran for their plane, thanking Thomas for the coffee. He missed them and paced around and made another booking at the Air-India counter, stalling grandly about actually buying the ticket without even noticing that the people on duty were the ones who had humored him before. After a time, his doctor friend had seen enough of his extremity and took him for a drink in the airport bar.

"Funny, meeting you," Thomas said, refusing any ordinary guess that it could be no accident.

"Off somewhere?" said the doctor.

Thomas suddenly started to shake so badly that the ice in his glass chattered. He fished the cubes out and put them into an ashtray and found it all he could do not to weep at the mess they made with the ash.

"You need help," his friend said.

"What for?" Thomas said. "The pills will do the trick. It's mostly that I can't sleep."

"There are things that pills don't do so well as a rest and treatment. You need a rest."

A county hospital treated Thomas that week for acute depression. He was greatly humiliated. He was also in fear. To the family, who were breezy, referring to "Daddy's trouble," he revealed nothing. Sara drove him scornfully to the hospital three times a week, for he wasn't supposed to drive. This on top of everything else, she seemed to be thinking, although she did what she might to eliminate exhaustion and scorn from her voice. On the car journey, which took an hour and a half each way, he would talk to her with all the will he could muster about the toy shops. It was barely manageable. He found it impossible to believe that he had ever been able to write a book or give a lecture, or advise a government. Other scholars heard that he was unwell and sent him notes made remote by their instinct that his straits must mortify him. Sara felt many things, including affection, balked control, trouble over his loss of weight, and enmity toward one of the weak. Sometimes she tried talking to him about India, with a genuine impulse to do what she could. She did not feel shame, or any sense of partaking in the very view of life that was nearly extinguishing him.

At the end of the hospital treatment they went away to the Caribbean on holiday, by a plane that belonged to a director of Simon's firm. An old friend of Thomas's lived on the island, but he was a Negro politician with a mind in the world that Thomas had lost for the moment. Sara had letters to people who owned polo ponies and valuable land for development. So Thomas played bridge with them, and swam, and learned to use an aqualung. He began to feel like a king, more or less. Or fit, at the least. One day he slipped off alone, out of interest, to look up a local doctor, who took him on a tour of hospitals. Maternity wards with two women to a bed. Children with rickets. He didn't tell Sara much of it.

When they got back to England Simon had a surprise waiting. He had exchanged houses with them. Sara and Thomas were to be in the cottage, and Simon's household of three in Thomas's place. The point was the running expenses. Most of the move had been accomplished already. Sara knew of it. "We didn't tell you, because you were too ill," she said. "We decided to wait, so that there was a secret for you when you came back. When you were your old self."

"It's a fine idea," Thomas said to her, expounding it to himself and meantime walking around Simon's cottage with resentment for every stone of the place. "They're an expanding family. There's less work for you to do here. It's very good of him. Where will I work?"

"I thought you'd be relieved. The financial burden. Young

shoulders. Besides, he can write a lot of it off against tax, you know. So it's better in every way."

(Where will I work?)

"It's very good of him," he said, going across to the window to look at their house and then turning away in pain. He went on to bump his head on a beam. His state of mind was so much lighter than before that he laughed. "If *I* hit my head, at five foot nine, no wonder Simon wanted to switch," he said.

"It has nothing to do with his height," Sara said stiffly.

The only things left to be moved were Thomas's books. The Sunday after they came back from the West Indies, he and Sara and his mother—who was living with them now in a room not much larger than a cupboard, although the view, as Simon constantly said, was staggering—went formally to lunch in their old house. Sara started off in her hat, left on from church.

"For heaven's sake, take your hat off," Thomas said.

"Do you need one of your pills, dear?"

"No, I just hate your hat. We're going to our own house, aren't we? We're not going out."

"We are going out. You've got to adjust. The doctor said that about the income." This was the way she spoke of it: "The income." She meant his earnings, not the yield of the toy-shop business, but she had never been in the habit of referring to them so distinctly, let alone to the fact that money was thin on the ground at the moment. "We *are* going out. We're lunching with Simon and Prunella in their new home."

He threw a bottleful of his pills into the kitchen sink and tried to get them to go down the drain with the handle of a dishmop. "I hate the word 'home,' " he said. "It's like 'doggy.' The place is a house."

"It is my language," Sara said. She saw then that saying this had been unpardonable, but the odd thing was that he did pardon her, and laughed, and quietly fished some of the soggy pills out of the sink in case he fancied one later after all.

Simon was sitting in Thomas's armchair, which was too big to be moved to the cottage. Prunella had nicely been trying to prize him out of it before they came, but she was timid of him. "Better not to make an issue of it by my shifting," Simon said. "No need to treat him like an invalid."

At lunch, where there were maids to serve, Sara kept watching Thomas's plate. "Eat up," she said when he left something.

"No, thanks."

"The stomach shrinks. He's doing very well. He's put on six pounds," she told the table. She looked splendid herself, said the table. She did. But it seemed to Thomas that she was too doughty for him, somehow, and the hat finished it. For years and years, her frailer beauty had made him feel physically famished for her, but he had generally subdued the longing because she seemed worn out with housework. And now she was as strong as a cart horse, and he didn't give a damn. He suddenly felt farcically drawn to Simon's Prunella, which seemed a sign of health if nothing else.

"What's the joke?" Prunella said gently.

"There's a Russian story about a peasant who dreams night after night of having a bowl of cherry jam and no spoon to eat it with. And then at last he goes to bed with a spoon, and he doesn't dream."

Simon poured some port into the Stilton and talked of a hot tip about buying shares in a firm called North-East Gas Enterprises Limited. Thomas got up at last from his new place in the middle of the table, which he had quite liked because it had leg access to a rung where he could wriggle his feet when he was bored. He went to his old library, and Pippa followed him, equally enlivened to leave.

"Would you like to see my filthy sculptures?" she said.

"Very much," he said.

"They're in your library." They were made in Plasticine, and obviously based on photographs of Hindu sculpture in the art books on his bottom shelves. The six-year-old instinct had made them curiously abstract, and Thomas was much moved. The two were poring over them when Simon came into the room. He absorbed the little gray figures in a few seconds and his face bulged. He left the library and came back with a riding crop. Thomas found it hard to believe. He tried to block things but they went fast. The little girl was held by the back of her bent neck, and the lash of the crop swished down onto her cotton dress. When Thomas tried to grab the child away, the lash caught him in the eye.

"Stop!" he shouted, reaching again for the child and closing his red-hot eye.

"You speak of stopping," said Simon. "You led her on. Five, six, seven." It went on to nine before Thomas put an end to it. Simon by then had heavily said, "This hurts me more than it hurts you" to Pippa, and when the chaos was over Thomas began to laugh, for he had seen that the lash of the crop literally had curled round onto Simon's back between each stroke, probably quite stingingly, though the man had been too excited to notice it. Picking up the child, who was breathing in gulps like an oarsman at the end of a race, Thomas bent down to save her sculptures and carried her through to her mother. "I want these kept always," he said, thrusting the figures at her face.

"What are they?"

"They're sculptures of Pippa's. They're to be kept in my library. My books are to stay, too. I have a lot of work to do and there isn't enough room in the other place."

Sara said, "What was all that noise?" She looked more closely at the figures and turned away from him.

"What is it?" he said, watching her and flooded by a feeling that he had not expected. "You're not weeping?"

"You don't seem to be any better than before." She bent a little to lean her fists on the window seat, with her back to him. "You're not trying. You give in to these willful tempers. You're not yourself. I've got more than enough to do. You were never like this."

"Well, I am now. Simon beat Pippa for these."

"No wonder."

"He'd better have beaten me." Sara swung round, and Thomas was half touched by the horror in her. "She must have liked a book of mine," he said.

"They're in that wretched old-fashioned Plasticine," she went on, switching ground and speaking as if that compounded things. "Who could have given it to her? Prunella and I are so careful. She has plenty of the proper sort."

"This kind smells nice," he said.

"One of the *points* about the new kind is that it's odorless."

" 'Smell!' " he shouted. "Not 'odor.' You even take away smells. Actually, I think I probably gave her the clay."

"But we don't stock it."

"No, I got it from an art shop." In Sara's canon this was

perfidy. She looked betrayed, and tight around the chin. "You'll have to put up with it, darling," he said gaily, refusing to fall in with her mood.

There was a pause while Sara collected herself, and then she said they must go back and do the accounts.

"I've got some work to do," he said.

"Yes, we have."

"No, my own work."

"In that case there are all the books to move."

"I'll go on with it here. There's more space."

"Have you asked Simon?"

"Why the hell should I ask Simon?"

A dam burst again: All he's done for you. (Prunella left the room.) Picking up the pieces of your life for you. A foreigner accepted as if you were his own father. No real son could have done more. Difficult times for everyone. Your trouble. Everyone under great strain. You didn't mean. The subject of Pippa better not discussed (and then discussed at length). It occurred to Thomas as he listened to her that Sara had not changed a whit in the whole time they had been married. No hint or taint of him had touched her. She had remained her strong English self, and in truth she did put up with a good deal, for in her terms a scholar's life must always have stood for a life of privation, which would explain the furious resolve that clenched the lines in her face. All the same, he had work to do.

"Before you leave, you'd better apologize to Simon," she said.

He left the room, picking up the little erotic figures and locking them into his desk drawer.

Sara followed him. "What are you doing?" she said.

"Nothing," he said.

"What are you thinking about?" She pursued him.

"Nothing," he said again, smiling at her, for she was Sara. ("Remember the nine tenets of resistance in a country occupied by foreign forces," he said to himself. " 'We know nothing, we recognize nothing, we give nothing, we are capable of nothing, we understand nothing, we sell nothing, we help nothing, we reveal nothing, we forget nothing.' ")

"Doesn't it hurt your pride? It must," she said, not unkindly but in a rare and urgent search for a response of any sort at all.

After contemplation, he replied quite seriously, "A little. Very little. At first. Not now. I think it's harder on you."

"You've never been properly recognized."

"You mean well paid." He waited. "To choose to do the work one wants, I suppose one will quite often have to renounce the idea of making a fortune. Yes? I'm sorry, my dear." A few minutes before, he had tried to add "We apologize for nothing" to the rules in his head, but he knew that Sara would always move him to compunction.

Alone then in his library, feeling fine, his spirits began to mount. He thought about some work, and also about the world, as he had not since he was in India. The sense of being part of a general flux had been lost for years. There grew in him a wish to touch with his fingers a future that he knew was that of many others. The disorder that had seemed to him for decades to determine the course of events regrouped itself like a pile of iron filings suddenly organized by a magnet, and he had a flash of optimism when it appeared quite possible that men in the days to come might wish to find out more than concerned them at the moment. Probably this curiosity will be quite superficial, he thought to himself, as it is in me until I have more time to spend on it. But it will be better. He considered for several hours, making notes and getting up now and then for books. He felt he had his hand on a way to proceed, and one that might be of some consequence, with luck. Simon's heavy tread moved about upstairs and his voice shouted something at a maid. He was calling for a sherry. "And a tonic water with ice for Mr. Flitch in the library. No gin. He doesn't drink. Remember that. Pru, he is still here, isn't he? He hasn't drifted back to his own place yet, eh? Do you think we have to offer him a meal?"

Thomas looked out of the window. I'll leap into my life, he thought, if it splits my face to bits.

Nobody's Business

A big man with a municipal face was swimming toward Edward and Emily Prendergast across the glassy Mediterranean.

"Morning!" he shouted to Sir Edward, who is a judge. A tall, skinny man, with a soft voice that sometimes strikes the court as coming from behind his left ear. He has been married to Emily for nearly forty years. Emily is a woman of obscure stylishness who gardens, carpenters, reads science fiction, bottles fruit and pickles according to Elizabethan family recipes, and writes the most popular low comedies of the century. They are done weekly on the radio in the lunch hour, and people listen to them in factories by the million.

The big man splashed up to Edward and held his hand out of the water cordially, bobbing up and down.

"How do you do?" Edward said, turning his august profile with a politeness that Emily didn't believe necessarily to be lasting.

"Long time no see," said the big man.

"Have we met?" said Edward.

There he goes, Emily thought gaily.

"In the BBC canteen," the big man said. "You came to pick up your lady wife one day after a rehearsal. You won't remember. Long ago. I was the producer."

Two striking bodies were swimming after the big man, lifting themselves rhythmically out of the water with the butterfly stroke. Magnificent tanned shoulders consecutively emerged. One pair male, one female, probably, Emily thought.

"I don't believe you know Maximilian Keller," the big man said, making introduction gestures awkwardly a few inches above the surface of the sea, "and Jo-Ann Sills. Maximilian is from the University of Basel and Jo-Ann is from the University of California at Los Angeles."

"I'm the archivist who bothered you last April, and I wondered if you'd had any second thoughts," Jo-Ann said to Edward. Her long hair spread out in the water around her.

"Second thoughts about what?" said Edward.

"About letting us have your papers for the Sir Edward Prendergast Collection and the Lady Prendergast Collection— the *Emily Firle* Collection."

"The only papers we seem to keep are bills, and they're for the accountant," Emily said.

"But you must have kept your manuscripts," the beautiful girl said, and turned her head to Edward in the sea. "Your office surely must have kept your briefs over the years."

Emily stayed quiet, treading water and wondering where the others' breath for talking came from.

"And what about your memorabilia?" said Jo-Ann.

"*Is* there an Edward Prendergast Collection?" said Edward. "*What* Lady Prendergast Collection? What the hell are memorabilia?"

" 'Emily Firle,' I said," Jo-Ann answered in a voice of quartz.

"Don't ignore Women's Liberation," Emily said privately to Edward.

He made one of his expostulatory noises, seldom employed but powerful, and looked at her carefully from ten feet away in the water, lifting his spectacles to the bridge of his nose and then having to peer under them because they were crusted with salt, raising his head rather merrily, like a sea lion balancing a ball on its snout. "Are you all right?" he said, moving round so that he had his back to the others.

"Bored," she said softly.

"What's the big man's name?" he said in his lowest voice.

"I don't know." It was someone she had been to bed with. Long ago. Nothing. But indecent to forget. She made an effort: "David Willoughby, I think."

"Maximilian and Jo-Ann wrote a joint thesis about you both," Willoughby said loudly.

Emily had turned onto her back to save her strength and was staring at the sun.

"About us?" she said, turning upright again to go on treading water.

The talk in the sea lasted for another half an hour. Maximilian said grimly that his special interest was humor, and Jo-Ann said that her topic in the thesis had been the theme of male chauvinism in Edward's published legal opinions.

"What do you think of Women's Lib?" she said to Emily.

"I should think it's quite right, probably. Is anyone else tired?"

" 'Probably'? I hear doubt here," Maximilian said, raising a finger astutely out of the water.

"Shall we go in?" Emily said.

"Doubt, when you're generally so decided? Crisp? In your dialogue?" Maximilian said with disappointment.

"Doubt is the courtesy of the intellect," Edward said, sounding irritable and throwing his voice like a cat.

"And that seems to me a very uncharacteristic thing for *you* to say," Willoughby said firmly. He lifted his hand out of the water to smooth his hair. Emily tried to remember if she had ever known in the days of seeing him that he was such a strong swimmer, but nothing much came back.

At the same time she said, exhausted, "Not really uncharacteristic. If it weren't that a judge has to decide a case, quite a few of Edward's legal opinions would probably end in a question mark."

Maximilian drew out a plastic notebook from underwater with his left hand and started to make a note in it with his right, using a gadget pencil with his name on it in gold.

Emily only then took in that the others were not swimming at all but standing on the bottom, and that the reason she was worn out from treading water was that she was a good eight or twelve inches shorter than the rest. It made her laugh, and she sank. She had not had a violent case of laughing for years. She came up once and tried to get out a cry for help to the others standing there, but the laughing gripped her lungs and they thought she was fooling. She choked and spat out some seawater and then swallowed a lungful as she went into a spasm again. She sank slowly to the bottom and opened her eyes and saw the legs of the four underwater. One pair Californian legs, one pair Swiss legs, one pair forgotten legs, one pair Edward's legs. My finishing-school clothes list: One pair plimsolls, one pair best silk stockings, one Liberty bodice, amen, we give Thee most humble and hearty thanks, we Thine unworthy servants. Damn. I can remember everything. Life up to its old clichés again. I suppose it means I'm drowning. The three of them are presiding over us like a tribunal. She lost track.

Her husband, seventy-four, was the one who fished her out. Willoughby helped. The hale and hearty young archivists stood by, worried that she might die—worried partly because of the venerable old man's fever that she shouldn't, and partly because of professional affront at the possibility of all that memorabilia going west.

"You have an immense output," Willoughby said severely to Emily a few weeks later, leaning over her desk as if he were a judge himself. "Would you say that you were first-rate or second-rate?"

She and Edward were sitting together in their Dorset drawing room, in their chairs on each side of the fireplace, where they always sat. Jo-Ann and Maximilian and Willoughby were across the room, where visitors always sat. A stenographer was taking things down. The archivists had won.

"You don't need to answer the question," Edward said to her.

"A bit ropy," she said to Willoughby.

"The arranging of work in a hierarchy is a fat-headed process," Edward said to Willoughby.

"Would you deny that Lady Prendergast's work has literary worth, then? Just because it's humorous?" Willoughby said to Edward.

"Just because she's produced over a thousand scripts and books?" Maximilian said. "Personally, I rank the *œuvre* very high."

Œuvre, Emily thought. Blimey.

"So do I," Edward said. "But then, for me, *she* ranks high, don't you see."

"But how would you place your work, though?" Maximilian said to Emily. "In the event of your death, will it stand up?"

"I shouldn't think so, should you?" she said.

"Gas about posterity," Edward said, making a sort of barking noise and then lighting his pipe.

"Huh?" said Willoughby.

"What matters is the needs which art answers," Edward said. "I think that may be right. Could we have crumpets for tea?"

" 'I think that may be right,' " Emily said. "I like the way you say that."

Willoughby was shaking his head at the stenographer. "You can leave all that out. Everything after 'which art answers.' It wouldn't signify. Don't bother about taking anything down when you see me shaking my head."

"Conversations about lousiness," Emily said to Edward.

"Yes," Edward said. They ran over a few in their minds, having acquired the same references.

"Huh?" said Maximilian.

"She means there can be a certain quality to the rotten," Edward said.

"Can we go into that?" said Maximilian, and Willoughby signalled to the stenographer to start again.

"No," Edward said.

After a pause, Emily said, "There was once a very popular act called the Apple Blossom Sisters. They were popular because they were so lousy. They were singers and they couldn't sing a note in tune. The management would put up a screen in front of them and provide the audience with bad eggs and moldy tomatoes to pelt them with."

"You're not suggesting you're one of the Apple Blossom Sisters?" Maximilian said.

"Probably," Edward said. "She has a low opinion of herself."

"Then how does she go on? Producing this pretty remarkable work?"

"She doesn't always. There are halts. Quite long, for her. In that case, she will carpenter or go on a dig. An archeological dig. You know that she read archeology by correspondence when she was at finishing school. And then she will take a few days off from seeing anybody except me and do a bit of work. I've never been made much aware of it. She does it at that desk and I'll think she's writing letters."

"She works easily, then," Maximilian said. "In your very different and distinguished field, do you?"

Edward barked again through his nose.

Emily said, "Of course he does. But he stomps off to have a think now and then. There's always the possibility of making a terminal ass of yourself, isn't there?"

"Is that a mule?" said Maximilian, in his perfect English, making a note. "The terminal ass? Is that a demotic idiom?"

"Could we talk now about humor?" said Maximilian.

"Couldn't we have the crumpets?" said Edward.

"What about having a kipper as well? What about having a kipper to our tea?" said Emily.

"What an interesting preposition," Maximilian said, writing it down.

"Our friends have an idea for a joint lecture on educational television about the mechanics of humor," Willoughby said. "To study it as though it were a problem of engineering. Which it is, of course, as you of all people know."

"With your ear. With your technical sense," Maximilian said.

"Can you and Jo-Ann deal with a kipper?" Emily said. "They're rather full of bones in England. We don't debone them here, I'm afraid."

"The idea is," said Maximilian, motioning Jo-Ann to stand up, "to show a television audience the effect of trousers falling down." He started to unstrap his belt and then let his trousers fall to the floor. "One would show them falling at the usual speed and hear the laughs." He pulled them up and fastened the belt again with a scholarly expression. "Then one would show what happened if the speed were different." He waved to Jo-Ann to stand behind his back. "One would see them lowered very slowly." The pretty girl behind him let down his trousers inch by inch. "Don't rush it," he said. The trousers reached his ankles. He looked up and said majestically, "You see, it isn't funny."

"Actually, I thought it was almost funnier that time," Edward said, freezing his face, as he was used to having to do in court.

Maximilian saw nothing and said, "It would be interesting to observe whether one got the same effect by slowing up the, say, motion of a shoe on a banana skin."

*   *   *

"Born?" said Jo-Ann to Emily.

"Edward was born in London and I was born in Russia. Why does one go so much by where people are born, I wonder. Where were you born?"

"Rumania," Jo-Ann said.

"There, you see, and yet you seem completely Californian to me. Do you feel Californian?"

"Do you mind not answering our questions with so many questions, Lady Prendergast?" Maximilian said.

"I'm sorry," Emily said.

"And how did you leave Russia?"

"I lived with my uncle. I was an orphan. My grandparents got married in an old people's home. It was rather a jolly occasion."

"That doesn't answer the question. How did you leave?"

"It's not very interesting. I had English relations. What I remember, as I say, is my grandparents' getting married in Russia. They'd been living together for many years. When they grew poor they had to be shut away in an old people's home, because poverty didn't officially exist in the new state. It doesn't officially exist in America either, would you say? So they had to disappear. They had a fine wedding. They were aged eighty-nine and ninety. Everyone was in black because their best clothes were for funerals, and everyone danced. There was only one record, and that was the Slovene national anthem. Somebody had brought it with him. It wasn't quite the thing, but it was very beautiful."

"And then?"

"She came to England," Edward said. "Her father was a playwright. He died soon after she was born."

"Yes, we know that," said Maximilian. "It's in *Who's Who.*"

"What I was going to tell you is that he had written her a part in one of his plays. A non-speaking part. It was her inheritance, so to say. May I have a glass of water until you've decided about the kippers? He thought she could always be an actress in a pinch, you see. He wrote the part so that she could always support herself in exile if she didn't speak the language."

"Edward and I met in England in 1920," Emily said. "I'd been kicked by a horse and lost two front teeth and he took

me out to lunch and gave me asparagus. Asparagus is extremely difficult to eat without front teeth, because it means
pulling the things through the side molars and it makes a mess
of the lipstick. Those were the days when girls wore lipstick."

"You still do," Edward said. "I like it better."

"It was a very fine lunch, to my mind."

"And do you care for the times?" said Willoughby to Edward.

"Inadequate," said Edward.

"Without belief? Without intellectual system?"

"No, thin news coverage. We both prefer the *Washington Post*.
We get it by airmail."

"Mr. Willoughby means the age, I think," Emily said. "Well,
as we're in the presence of two students—postgraduate students—I daresay you'll take me to be sucking up, but the times
are rather interesting, don't you find? The music and the clothes
and the courage and so on. The nerve. Something here, don't
you think? One doesn't want to go."

"Go? What did you say that for?" Edward said.

Maximilian laughed as if someone had made a joke.

"No question of it," she said to Edward. "I'm not a quitter."

"No," he said. "You hung on for twelve years."

"Isn't it odd, sitting here without quite having the face to
touch each other? It's like the time when you were in hospital.
When we could talk on the telephone every day and I couldn't
come to see you."

"Why not?" said Jo-Ann.

"Because he was married to someone else then."

"Male chauvinist. Why did you put up with it?" Jo-Ann said
to Emily. "Letting the man have it both ways at once. They
always do."

"Well, it was a poor time, but it improved rapidly."

"Where were you born?" said Jo-Ann.

"We've asked that already. Russia. Don't you remember?"
Willoughby said.

"I used to have a memory, like, but my mind has blown,"
Jo-Ann said.

"My dear girl," Emily said, worried.

"I got into this tragical area of experience, but I feel as if I'm coming out of it now," said Jo-Ann.

"What friend's voice were you speaking in just then? Are you going to a therapist?"

"Yes."

"Well, never mind," Emily said.

"Of course, my wife *holds* with the world," Edward said to Willoughby.

"You don't?" said Willoughby.

"Not necessarily."

"Is he a demonstrative man?" Willoughby said to Emily, pointing at Edward with his pen.

"No," said Edward.

"Yes," said Emily.

"What was that about hospital?" Maximilian asked.

"Edward could tell you."

"They put me in the bin because I suddenly had a talking jag," Edward said. "I couldn't stop chatting. I talked nonstop one day for twenty-three hours. Even with Emily I didn't shut up, and we have always had the capacity for shutting up. The doctors told me I shouldn't talk so much. I said, 'I know that as well as you; the fact I can't do anything about it is my complaint, don't you see. Cure me of that and I'll be well.'"

Emily said to Willoughby, "You must tell the stenographer to stop, and we'll have tea."

"Not till we're finished," Willoughby said with an edge in his voice, looking at Emily. "And then what, pray? Was it when we knew each other?"

"Did you know each other well?" said Edward.

"Very well," said Willoughby.

"I'm sorry. Is that troubling?" Emily said to Edward.

"No," he said, looking as if it were.

"The hospitalization was when you and Mr. Willoughby knew each other?" said Maximilian, motioning the stenographer to attend.

"Yes," Emily said. "He was having a small breakdown. Edward was."

"You betrayed him when he was having a breakdown?" Willoughby said. "And you didn't tell me?"

"There was no reason that I could think of to tell you, and some reason not to."

"You betrayed him when he was having a breakdown?" Willoughby said again censoriously, his face looming over the desk.

"It seemed at the time that he might not have much need of intimacy. By temperament, not have much need of intimacy."

"And?"

"I had. Is it very hot?"

"Yes," Edward said. He loosened his tie.

"That's the tie I like," she said, opening one of their two copies of the *Washington Post* and burying herself behind it.

He looked at her sandals. "She's not very forthcoming always about what's going on at the back of her mind," he said after a time in a soft voice to Jo-Ann, "but I can generally tell something about it from the way she moves her toes. She wears sandals a good deal, and bare feet. We were on holiday in the Aegean when I was getting better from this talking thing and she was reading *Crime and Punishment*, and I used to watch her toes and wonder which part she had got to. I could make a fair guess."

He leaned over Emily's shoulder to see what she was reading and turned back to his own copy of the paper. "Where's that part in mine?" he said jealously, rattling the pages.

"Middle column of page nine," she said.

He found it and grew absorbed.

"How worried were you, in those days, about him? When I knew you?" said Willoughby.

"Oh dear. You think I did it to take my mind off," Emily said. "Well, perhaps I did. He was very distant then."

"Harsh," Willoughby said.

"No, distant," Edward said. "Though the effect for her was probably harsh." He put out his hand in her direction and then used the movement to tap the ash from his pipe.

"You see, he's very interested in making distinctions," Emily said. "It's the legal mind."

"I also used to have a temper," Edward said, "but it seems to be drawn off now in work."

Emily came in with a tray of tea.

"Edward made this tray when he was doing handcrafts in

the bin," she said. "You can see that he didn't give himself the time to finish it. He made a quick getaway. He was having quite a bad nervous breakdown, as it turned out—"

"You said a small breakdown," Maximilian said.

"—but when he heard what the fees would be if he stayed he decided that he was hanged if he was going to spend all that money on being upset. So he drove himself away again. He had committed himself, you see, so he was technically free to go, but they apparently lock the gates on patients all the same." She poured tea. "It meant breaking the gates down. He did it with the back bumper of the car. Do you want some sponge fingers? The Daimler was barely dented."

"Why did you stay together?" Jo-Ann said.

"You don't have to answer the question," Edward said again.

"*Stare decisis,*" Emily said after a pause.

"What?" said Jo-Ann.

"It's the principle behind precedent," Edward said, looking at her. "The principle in the law. It means 'to stand by decided matters.' "

Jo-Ann said scornfully, "Instead of hanging loose."

Maximilian said, "Instead of deciding a case fresh. On its merits. The law is in love with the past."

"The law is an ass," said Willoughby.

"It's foolish not to draw on the past," Emily said. "People shouldn't have to start from the beginning every time."

"Why not? I was unhappily married once," Jo-Ann said, "and I decided the hell with it, I can't go *on* with this. My ex-husband and I just weren't meshing. It took me forever to find the maturity to say to myself how bad it was."

"But how old are you, then?" said Emily.

"Twenty-two. He had impotency fears and I was having trouble in analysis. He had a wonderful brain, but I guess we didn't know how to make it in bed. We tried to work it out. I went to a sensitivity-training centre and I learned body language, but it didn't help my marriage, because I was a tool of male imperialism and that was what I was really resenting all the time. So then I freed myself and had my first lesbian relationship and now I live on my own." She looked lonely.

"What's body language?" said Edward.

"Well, like, the way you're sitting now, it tells me you're interested in me. It's a giving position."

"What about my wife?"

"She's interested in me, too. That's a giving position, too." Jo-Ann looked around the room. "David's in a hostile position. I guess he's feeling excluded. I guess you two have a lot going for you. You're both hot right now and you've been hot all your lives."

"What?" said Edward.

"Not 'what,' 'hot,' " Maximilian said.

"I know that. I said 'What?' " said Edward, lowering his voice dangerously again.

" 'Hot' means in demand," Willoughby said.

"Good lord," Emily said, turning to Maximilian. "Like the hot side of a record. Well, how very kind of you. But even if it were true it wouldn't be the sort of fact to interest one in a person, would it?"

"Then how would you explain the relationship, leaving sexuality aside?" Maximilian said. "That's one of the things we've got to explore."

"Why leave sexuality aside, pray?" Edward said. Then he took a pause and Emily looked at him, and he looked at her. After a while he turned back to Jo-Ann. "For some people," he said, "sexuality is the water they swim in. Though I can see that for others it's toy ducks in the bath."

This man has always been a great study, Emily thought.

Maximilian, wanting to make sure he had got things right, repeated in German to Willoughby what Edward had just said, and Willoughby, who spoke German, nodded wanly. It was not a particularly comforting conversation for him to hear. Emily noticed that and gave him and herself a sherry.

"It's sometimes extremely difficult to be translated," she said talkatively to the three catechizers. "Do you know, Freud's 'Beyond the Pleasure Principle' becomes in Japanese 'Happiness Lying on the Other Side of the Water.' " She paused. "Though perhaps that's what he meant, of course, and maybe the English is wrong, too. What is it in German?"

"I'll look it up," Maximilian said, making a note. "Do you write first drafts in Russian?"

"No," Emily said, "and I don't do drafts much. I just bash it out. In English."

"So Sir Edward forced his language on you," Jo-Ann said.

"No, I had an English governess. And I like English, you see. My stuff seems to get into an awful pickle when it's translated."

"That's because you've always been in the mainstream of the English popular tradition," said Maximilian.

"It didn't feel very popular to me. The first things I did came a cropper. Has anyone pinched my spectacle case? Well, they weren't up to much, I don't suppose. A great man in those days who was trying to be encouraging told me I had a terrific eye for English weather. A great critic. It took me months to get over it."

"You regret the Edwardian summers?" said Maximilian.

"Lowering of you to expect me to remember. Though I suppose one looks quite old."

"We *are* old," said Edward.

"Some of the summers in the twenties and the thirties were glorious. And there were those evil beauties during the Battle of Britain. But then again, they've been very fine lately, haven't they?"

"Anything you'd like to have been able to keep about the past?" Maximilian asked.

"Not except from a technical point of view. And there was a time when one functioned better, of course."

"Technical?"

"It's a pity about godmothers and spinster aunts. They always had an interesting part to play in my sort of stuff. It's the same with mothers-in-law. One rather misses their ferocity in the work of the moment. You find you can't get the same effect with, say, shop assistants." She paused. "There may be hope in secretaries."

"There's a mouse behind the wainscot," Edward said.

Maximilian told the stenographer not to bother until he raised his hand.

"I'm afraid it might even be a rat," Emily said.

Edward listened and said, "Too scrabbly for a rat."

" 'Life's mouse-like flitting,' " said Willoughby.

"Who wrote that?" Emily said, turning toward him and leaning over the arm of the chair. "I meant to ask you a long time ago and I forgot to. I remember your saying it a long time ago."

"Pushkin," said Willoughby.

"You'd better get the exterminator in, Emily," Edward said, again in his lowered voice, which was a habit famous in court at points when an inexperienced barrister hadn't known where to stop.

"He came today," Emily said. "Pempie and he got on."

"Who's Pempie?" said Maximilian, still signally uninterested in all this as material.

"Our secretary," Emily said. "He wanted to take her out. I believe she's rather at a loose end, but she said she couldn't seem to fancy an exterminator."

"But on the other hand," Emily went on after a wait, "the girl also said to me suddenly one day, when I thought she was trying to read back dictation, 'I can't get through the spring without a man.' We were in the middle of working out a plot. It struck me about her, you know."

"Your plots are cast iron," Maximilian said.

"Well, they haven't the structure of a lawyer's work," she said. "I'm all right as long as I know where things are going, but it's not on a par with planning a legal argument."

"You betrayed him when he was having a breakdown?" Willoughby said again. "Suppose *I'd* been having the breakdown. Would you have betrayed me?"

Emily said over him, "—as long as one knows where things are going, don't you find?" And then, with as much of an answer to his question as she felt like mustering, "I've tried to explain. Couldn't we talk about home perms or cucumber sandwiches?"

"You haven't answered his question," Maximilian said. "Do you mind if I tell you what I really think?"

"Not especially," Emily said with a pause. "After all, it's what life does all the time, isn't it? Though I rather wish *people* wouldn't do it. One doesn't resent it so much when life does. This really is a bit like the Inquisition. The three of you sitting there. There's something I keep trying to remember about you. Well, anyway, don't let's get occult. I don't like occultism, do you? That reminds me. Pempie is terrifically keen on auspicious signs, and she cheered up no end the day after the exterminator, because she drew a winning ticket in the village raffle. Everyone around had donated whatever prize he could. The butcher gave a turkey, and the hairdresser gave a shampoo and set, and a rather humorless psychiatrist who commutes to Portsmouth gave an hour's consultation. Pempie wanted to go to the psychiatrist because she's very keen on astrology and sends away for readings. I believe she associates psychiatry with palmistry. But in the end something prevailed and she had the shampoo and set. I'll get some ice, shall I?"

"I don't know how you dare," Edward said to Willoughby while she was out of the room. "Bring up the breakdown I had all those years ago. That time. When you know perfectly well that it—"

"—painful?" said Maximilian.

"—that she's got amnesia about the time when she nearly drowned," Edward said. His temper rose, and his voice fell. "I don't know how you dare. She troubles a good deal about the three hours that she's lost. She wants them back. People want their lives back."

"Were you against capital punishment in this country?" Maximilian said.

"I gave you the press cuttings about that," said Willoughby, without much grace. "He's on record, along with all the other straight-liberal-plank reformers."

"Some ass of a doctor told her that her laughing was a sign that she was trying to kill herself," Edward said.

"Perhaps she was," said Willoughby.

Edward said, "You don't know her very well. It was a sign that she thought something was funny."

"Who can tell?" said Willoughby. "Perhaps it was a sign that she'd only just realized she'd done something wrong with her life."

"Doesn't everyone?" Maximilian said, and Edward looked at him with interest and regard for the first time.

"While she's out of the room," Jo-Ann said, "tell us why the marriage has lasted. When you intimidate her so much."

"*What?*" said Edward.

"Exploit her," Jo-Ann said, and Edward's look blocked her. "All right, then," she said, "tell us anything you admire about her."

"I love her."

"Anything you *admire* about her. Apart from the Elizabethan still-room stuff and the keeping quiet," said Jo-Ann.

"Apart from the skivvying and the fitting in and the shutting up," Willoughby said.

Edward held still and gave his mind to his wife. "You know, she's inventive, you see, and she has a much better brain than I have," he said at last. "She's a very subtle woman, not at all vulgar, and her intellectual instincts are probably as sound as anyone's I've known. I'd rather talk to her than to any other friend I've ever had. Of course, she's much more talented than I am. She has a beautiful sense of timing. Did you notice when you were badgering her how she got interested in remembering Pempie and then could leave the room? She's always known how to get the action into her own corner at the end of the round. It's like a great athlete. I once read about a boxer who did that. She doesn't even think about it. I always have to think about things. The boxer: the end of the round, the bell went, his seconds had put down his stool, he was there to sit, and his opponent had to walk the whole way back to his own corner. I read about it in a book and it reminded me of her. It was said that he learned it by practicing shadowboxing to popular tunes that ran exactly three minutes on the gramophone. He got the rhythm into the back of his mind somewhere. She'll be here in a moment. Do you mind not pressing her about the drowning? I nearly lost her, you know. She didn't breathe for a long time. May we talk about something else?"

Emily came into the room with an ice bucket.

Maximilian said, "The law has influenced you very much, hasn't it? And your plays and radio programmes have influenced Sir Edward."

"I've picked up a bit," Emily said, "but the law takes a kind of mind. Sense of history. When to move. I haven't got that. It's like an athlete."

"Why did you bring up *stare decisis* in front of me?" Willoughby said sharply.

"Don't be jealous, my love," said Emily to him.

" 'My love'!" Edward said, and she looked at him, and then back to Willoughby.

"I brought it up because this is where I am. Decided matters." She pointed unconsciously at her feet and the room, meaning her life, and then moved the subject. "I don't mean I've learned much about the law. I'd make a very poor showing in a court. Do have a whisky, all of you. You remind me of a tribunal. It's like the time when I nearly drowned in the Mediterranean with you."

"You *remember* nearly drowning?" said Jo-Ann. "Sir Edward says you've got amnesia about it."

"Well, this does rather manage to bring it back," Emily said. "Archivists. It gives one quite a strong idea of what it's going to be like to be a corpse."

"A tribunal?" said Edward. "I'm sorry. Is that what it was like underwater? Was that because of living with me?"

"No, I should think it was because of nearly drowning. And anyway, it happens all the time. One's always in the dock and being questioned, isn't one? In one's mind. It's quite easy to accede to the charge that one's badly guilty."

"Guilty?" said Willoughby with hope.

"Of one's life."

"How do you account for being acquitted, then? For being here?" said Willoughby.

"Him, I expect," she said, looking at Edward. "That's the way I remember it. I believe that's what happened."

"Everyone said you couldn't make it," Jo-Ann said. "Everyone wanted to take Sir Edward away, because it looked as if you couldn't make it."

"He seemed finished himself," Maximilian said.

"You caught a breath or two and looked at him in the end," said Jo-Ann.

"They said he was going to die of exposure, at his age," said Maximilian.

"Willoughby tried, but he couldn't do anything much," Jo-Ann said.

"Nobody can do what he can't," Emily said. She gave everyone a drink. "Unless he has a terrific wish to," she said, coming last to Edward. "Then I expect he could."

Splendid Lives

The Bishop of Hurlingham, aged ninety-two, radical, widowed, is a cousin three times removed of Queen Victoria and would not have troubled to endear himself to the royal mind, his own being well occupied with books, pigeons, politics, and worry at the moment over the self-imposed starvation diet of his beautiful Derby winner. And also—when he slept, fitfully, in his library—with thoughts of the Almighty, of his dead wife, of the blessings brought by the young, and of the noble father that begat him, whom he suspected of being more stoutly thoughtless than history recorded.

He sat this evening at the head of his illustrious family's oak table, this more than illustrious dissenter, and tried with native interest to create something cohesive of the three other people dining there. His younger sister, Biddy, aged eighty-six, sat facing him. Before the First World War, the Bishop had chained himself to the railings of the Houses of Parliament with her and his wife, and been sent with the suffragettes to prison, where he had joined their hunger strikes.

A local ear, nose, and throat specialist on his left, Dr. Spencer, had been trying for years to get him to his office for treatment for deafness. "Come on Tuesday and we'll play a rubber of bridge afterward," Dr. Spencer said to him loudly. "Apart from that, there is the question of your hearing. The treatment I'd like you to have admittedly went out quite widely between the two world wars, but it's still the best."

"Oh," said the Bishop, staring at the foot of the table and

missing his wife. "Is that so? What does it involve?"

"Copper wires."

"I don't hear you."

"Copper wires."

"That's what I thought you said."

"Through the nose and out of the ears. Thin as a moth's antennae."

"What's that you say about moths? I got the rest."

"No alarm," said Dr. Spencer.

Ridgeway, the American girl on the Bishop's right, shivered.

"You don't say," said the Bishop. He bent his head courteously towards Dr. Spencer and at the same time gave a push to a modern chrome trolley bearing plates of consommé in the direction of Ridgeway, a pretty, long-haired revolutionary girl whom he had sat down with in Trafalgar Square in a demonstration about Rhodesia.

"It was good of you to protest about Southern Rhodesia," the Bishop said to her. "Our government's behaviour hasn't been your fault."

"Certainly not yours," said Ridgeway.

"But I'm afraid one still tends to think in terms of countries," said the Bishop. "I hesitated about protesting against Vietnam in public, for example. I thought our own house had better be put in order first. Which requires a certain amount of nippiness in revolt by the English."

Biddy said, "I remember your wife once saying that any society that depresses free meddling is on the decline, however flamboyant its immediate spoils. The idea stuck in my mind. She said it when we were chained to Downing Street."

"Really a good treatment for him?" Ridgeway asked Dr. Spencer.

"I fancy copper wires would bring back to you the days of forcible feeding, dear Biddy," said the Bishop, who had also undergone it in prison in 1912 and who had been one of the only men to risk ridicule from other men in clubs and Parliament for his position. "Barbarous. And the doctors who did it wouldn't even make their courtesies in the presence of a lady when they were in her cell. That annoyed some suffragettes as much as the error of the procedure, though I privately think anyone who objected then about etiquette was being a bit of an ass. In fact, I thought complaining over politesse as well as over politics was wanting to have it both ways, though everyone is entitled to invent his or her own peccadillos. One of the things I like about America is that when it makes a moral mess of things it really makes an *unholy* mess. I must admit there have been times when I have felt on the verge of despair about us all."

The Bishop addressed himself to Ridgeway and congratulated her on keeping her swinging hair out of the soup. Conversation then ran into the sand. The Bishop restored things, as he generally did. "Well, let's plough on. Give the trolley a shove to my sister, would you be so good?" he said to Ridgeway, as it came to her for a second helping. "You'll have to take care it doesn't slop, being consommé."

"My brother's wife had an amiable cook who asked once if she wanted the consommé thick or clear," Biddy shouted.

"No need to yell for my sake, dear," said the Bishop, whose own voice was soft. "You don't mind our using the trolley, do you?" he said to Ridgeway. "It saves walking about for the butler and valet. For Wren, I mean. He got a nasty hit in a leg in the war and they didn't get all the shrapnel out. He's politically to the left, like the rest of us. He told me yesterday he got on with you. You were the first American he'd met, he said, apart from the Catholic Cardinal of New York, whom we were obliged to entertain when my wife was alive. The Cardinal and I found no difficulties between us apart from this question of Christianity's link with capitalism. I am afraid it is a question that has somewhat driven me away from Church dogma, though not from speculation, I hope. It is only in this matter that thought has caused me disappointment."

"Not your age?" Dr. Spencer asked.

"By George, age doesn't blight the fun. To go back, it has begun to seem to me all too possible that the great sin of capitalism—apart from usury, greed, exploitation, and so forth—may well be kin to the great sin of the Christian Church when the schisms set in. Capitalism in practice inclines to splits. So in Western capitalism, as in Western Christianity, we have created a magnificent theoretical ethic of the majority, but it is a majority that no one feels part of."

"We did in Trafalgar Square," Ridgeway said.

"No, I'm afraid we were no more than a handful of the whole. It was good of you to turn up. One looks to foreigners for help. I noticed at the time what pretty ankles you had."

"And her political opinions?" said Biddy kindly.

"First-rate, I should say. Yes! Yes! The scent of new ideas is very fascinating. Keep shoving the trolley round, Biddy. You'll find you can avoid the grated carrots if you're thinking of another plateful." He turned to Ridgeway. "The war, the Second World War, turned us rather against carrots. A noble lord, who was the Minister of Food at the time was very keen on root vegetables because the English could grow them in their gardens and allotments and so on. One might say he pushed carrots. They were said to be good for the eyesight of pilots, so we ate them in every form—carrot soufflé, carrot devil's-food cake—though none of the immediate family was a pilot. They also improved the possibility of seeing in the blackout, which of course we all had to do. My personal suspicion is that his carrot propaganda was a bluff, wouldn't you say? A way of filling us up," he said, turning to Dr. Spencer.

"I was rather young at the time," Dr. Spencer said.

"Stupid of me. All the same, it's history, therefore still with us." The Bishop took the crust off a piece of bread and ate the middle. "As to our noble nutritionist, who wasn't such a humourless soul as he seemed by any means; you might say he had quite a visionary approach to root vegetables in general. We all got rather bored with advertisements in the papers for a character called Potato Pete, who was drawn with the face of an unpeeled potato and who would appear over potato recipes. I look much like Potato Pete myself. It struck me while shaving the other day."

His sister studied him. "Potato Pete didn't have bristly eyebrows and he didn't laugh as much as you, though I'm blessed if I can often see what you find to laugh about."

"Well, Biddy, there's the rest of the world, which accumulates surprise and buffoonery as one grows older, and there are certain cheering steps forward here and there, and books that have an exact comic sense of folly: quite a lot of them new. And there's Bucephalus," he went on to Ridgeway, "our quixotic genius of a horse, whose mind is more and more interesting to get to the bottom of. And then there's this pleasant place, where one could hardly feel got down. Ah, pie."

Another trolley had been brought to Ridgeway's left by Wren. "Is it quail pie?" asked the Bishop, looking at the dish on the Georgian tray.

"Yes, My Lord," said Wren.

"What do you like to be called?" Ridgeway asked.

"Well, you try 'My Lord,' but I don't really care for it much in conversation, do you? It's a bit of a boulder. That leaves 'Dr. Hurlingham' or 'Bishop.' Is 'Bishop' rather burdensome? My Christian name is Paul. I wish I could say that I had had a visitation anything up to his, but you could hardly reduce me to Saul when it was not the name my parents hoped for, could you? In modern times, that name anyway belongs to the young man who does those brilliant screen credits, wouldn't you say?"

"You mean Saul Bass? How do you know about him?" Ridgeway asked.

"Oh, he's very well known, isn't he? Full of life. Lovely work. Poor girl," he said, looking at her dealing with the thing on the silver monarchical tray. "Quail pie is always a problem. You've just stuck a fork into a second bird, haven't you? It's a question of judging the width of any particular quail you're after, but I'm bothered if I can see how you can do that when you don't know where the edge of it is. The crust should have been cut in the kitchen."

Ridgeway had used up three forks by now and each time hit a quail, and to lift out the forks would have ruined the entire pastry crust. The pie looked like a bull near the end of a bullfight: on its knees.

"The thing is to use a knife and get under the pastry crust to have a look," said the Bishop. Ridgeway did.

Now well dismembered, the pie on its trolley with three vegetables and bread sauce continued round via the two women to Dr. Spencer. The Bishop said, "You won't mind if I skip the pie and concentrate on the other things? At my age, it's more trouble than it's worth, and there's plenty of pleasure in mashed potatoes and bread sauce."

"And in gravy," Ridgeway said.

"I'm sure we could get those teeth on their legs again," said Dr. Spencer.

"On their *legs*?" said the Bishop, laughing till his eyes poured tears and dabbing them with a beautiful lawn handkerchief. "Oh dear, the tricks that language can play. The poor Pope was praying for peace at the United Nations and was reported in translation as saying that he hoped the nations of the world would let their arms fall from their hands. It made me wish I could draw." He took out a felt pen and did a cartoon on the back of his cheese plate.

"You can do almost anything, dear," said Biddy.

"Well, it's a question of setting your mind to it. Though I've certainly set my mind to getting Bucephalus to eat for the next season and he won't touch a thing. My late wife could always get him to eat before a big race." The Bishop went on thinking of the shapely Derby winner off his feed in the stables.

"You'll excuse me if I don't stay for the pudding," Hurlingham said, getting up. "I foresee junket. The cook makes it for me every evening on account of the tooth problem but I can never touch it. Bucephalus and I may have something in common. I thought for a time that Wren, who has remarkable powers of observation, had hit on it. He noticed that the horse would only eat when a pigeon was in the loose box. The pigeon would generally sit on the horse's back. Then the pigeon died. Disaster for Bucephalus. Nutritionally speaking. Skin and bones. A pitiful sight. So Wren got another pigeon and the horse seemed to take to him well enough, but the oats were still untouched. You'll excuse me? You've scarcely begun your sherry," he said to Dr. Spencer. "It's left in the drawing room."

"I'm afraid I was late," said Dr. Spencer.

"Calls, I daresay."

"No, traffic."

"It's the cars that slow things up now. The anger. This is no time for hostility. It tends to have a leadening effect, don't you find?" he said to Ridgeway. He got up by himself to wander along the immense corridor, down the curling back stairway to the stables, and gazed at the beautiful horse. It gazed back, food untouched.

"He hasn't had his cream cheese, either," said Biddy, still in the dining room and looking at her brother's place. "If you could only get him in shape to enjoy summer pudding again, Dr. Spencer."

"What's summer pudding?" Ridgeway asked.

"It was always his favourite, even in the nursery. Mostly a matter of white bread and fresh raspberries. But the pips give him trouble now."

"I shouldn't say it's entirely his bite," said Dr. Spencer. "It may be that he has something on his mind. He misses his wife, doesn't he?"

"Even after six years. Yes, I remark on it to myself all the time and wonder what to do. A pretty girl with a well-read mind perks him up," Biddy said to Ridgeway. "I was noticing him with you."

"I'm too slow for him, though. Do you mind if I go to bed?" said Ridgeway. "I'm too tired even to read."

"The sloth of youth, the energy of age," said Biddy after she had gone, rolling up her dinner napkin into a cylinder for her napkin ring and then doing the same for Ridgeway's. "That girl is very good for him. I don't think she's encountered a linen napkin before."

"I don't believe she knew how to get it into the napkin ring," Dr. Spencer said. "Or perhaps she abandoned things because she was expecting a clean napkin for breakfast. Americans have clean napkins at every meal."

"My goodness, the laundering that must go on! The starching! The ironing! Why a fresh one every time? It's not as if she wore lipstick. In the twenties, when we all did, of course, one's napkin was often a wreck after dinner. It was a problem to eat asparagus and artichokes successfully without getting jammy around the mouth. And one would never have repaired makeup at the table as girls do now."

"He's a remarkable man for his years," said Dr. Spencer. "You shouldn't worry about him. His age doesn't seem to be doing any harm to his sense of curiosity, or indeed his rebelliousness."

"No, it's not," said Biddy. "A life needs weight in its tail, you see." She paused for a while. "The only great drawback for him is missing his wife, but he doesn't let it affect him. In fact, I've often noticed that someone's sense of option and possibility even grows when most has apparently been whittled away."

*   *   *

Ridgeway found her way to the stable yard and saw the Bishop leaning over the bottom of the loose box. The horse's beautiful head tossed up at the sight of a stranger and then settled back to watch the Bishop. The pigeon pecked at the oats and didn't look at the horse.

"I was thinking of writing a biography of that horse," said the Bishop. Three English sheepdogs stood beside him on the cobbles, balancing on their hind legs and reaching just high enough to rest their muzzles on the bottom half of the door. "When I woke up this morning, I found I had the article all planned. It would be poor of me not to do it. The things I have missed doing are vexing thoughts."

"A biography of a *horse?*" Ridgeway said.

"Yes. It would seem to me not in the least mad, though there is something essential I still haven't hit on about Bucephalus's turn of thought. Anyway, why not a horse? A most interesting, noble and innovative life, this one's. You have wonderfully pretty legs."

Ridgeway looked down at them.

"Would you like a holiday job as the sheepdogs' walker?" the Bishop asked. "They don't get enough amusement."

Ridgeway went on considering her legs. "Good legs or not, they don't necessarily make me a good walker," she said.

"No, but I have the feeling. Brood about it."

In the meantime, he thought about her legs, the pigeon, and his hungry, enthralling horse. "Naturally, it would be a test to do the article well enough."

"If it were vivacious, you mean you'd be on your way to it?"

"That would be essential. It always is. Ridgeway, what could be more puzzling than a Derby winner who so misses a pigeon that he's starving himself to death? Company, is that the secret? What's unsatisfactory about *this* pigeon?" He laughed, and his steel-wool eyebrows shot up. Then he said soberly to Ridgeway, "What are you laughing about?"

"Your gaiters, the pigeon, the horse, the mud."

"Oh, yes, it is muddy, isn't it?" He had a torch in his hand that he lowered to the level of his own legs, little though they interested him. "You see, I should like to do this biography adequately." He flashed his torch at her left hand. "Aren't you married? You live with someone in America, I expect."

"I'm getting divorced, I'm afraid."

"I daresay you're right. Why?"

"He was a banker, and I wasn't old enough until the last moment to know that I didn't like what he did." She paused.

"What did you discover?" said the old man, shaking his head.

"What difference does it make? Wouldn't it be boring to hear about?"

"No."

"He hadn't much idea of what was happening. Of consequences, let alone causes. He couldn't see himself."

"To leave an imprint somewhere by making the right snap decision, is that what was missing?"

"One spring we were on holiday in the West Indies and we bought a very good landscape by a young local painter. I was thrilled. And then my husband asked the painter if a bank could be put into the composition, and the painter gave him a look and painted in a bank in five minutes. He needed the money."

"I may be wrong, but I think your generation and country express themselves most fully in immediate behaviour," the Bishop said. "Other times, other places do it through sculpture or writing. It is a question. Ah, suddenly I have it about the pigeon; it's the wrong *sex*, of course. It is a question whether we have ever seen the really vivid expression of a nation's temperament except on a plane of"—she thought he was going to say "religion"—"art. In actions, we have hardly ever seen it. And religion has grown too confused with persuasion and prosperity. You know, of course, about the nineteenth-century offshoots that actually considered prosperity an attribute of God and made their followers feel shame for not reflecting it. It is also a pity that there is very little private prayer."

A stable clock chimed. The Bishop said to himself, "A *female* pigeon, a *female* pigeon, like the one that died."

"You miss your wife."

"Yes."

"I'm afraid I don't miss my husband."

"What was wrong with him, to your mind?"

"His boredom."

The Bishop hesitated. "I don't often talk about this, but I had a brother who died by playing hazard, and I think he did it in war against boredom."

"How old was he?"

"Seventeen."

"Young to be bored."

"Oh, no, on the contrary, things become more interesting as you get older. For instance, the case of this horse and this pigeon. If my brother had waited, I believe he would have grown interested in things. The nature of his thinking was too flat and stale for him to bear at the time of the accident's happening, you see. But later it would have altered."

"Do you look on suicide as a sin?"

"Oh, never mind about that now. Are you cold? I say, I am glad we hit on the idea of the female pigeon."

"You do distribute ideas. You thought of it."

"Did I? I must dust the mud off my gaiters if you are going to be perceptive."

"And he risked himself to get back the taste of things?"

"I was rather young, but I fancy he thought he could recover the savour of life by chancing the loss of it. He played Russian roulette by jaywalking just in front of a racing carriage. People nowadays find the tale picturesque. He deliberately stepped off the pavement in front of a carriage that was being driven very fast. You didn't do that, did you? When you and your husband agreed to get divorced?"

"When I decided to get married, perhaps?"

"Of course, people are at a disadvantage when they are dealing with anyone like your husband, to whom the idea of retreat is not a humiliation but a piece of strategy. I'm not speaking of your own nature but your position. I wonder if I could do a noble article about a horse. It should be possible. George Stubbs, now, his anatomical drawings of owls and so on had nobility."

"It's not what people expect of you."

"But therefore not a bad rebellion, in its small way. Neither of us can protest in Trafalgar Square all the time."

They moved towards the house after the Bishop had patted the horse's head and felt his ribs.

"No lustre," he said about the horse, his own eyes shining excitedly with ideas in the light thrown by the stable tower. "I wish you would be a dog walker, but I can see you wouldn't meet many people." Then he recognized the absurdity of what he had said, and picked her up and carried her over the mud.

"You must be careful of your frock," he said.

"I like that word," she said. "It's the first time I haven't worn jeans for ages."

"I like jeans, too."

"Pagan gaiters," said Ridgeway.

"I like them in Trafalgar Square, at least. Or for picnicking, or painting, or mucking out stables."

"You were saying something about justified rebellion. Is there any such thing as justified war?"

"What do you think?" he said, still carrying her, his feet stumbling over the cobbles and his mind visibly teeming to hear her reply.

"I believe the war against the Nazis was. I don't think the Crusades were."

"That's what I think. Now, the independence of India, the independence of Ulster, these are difficult questions. The thing would have been never to have behaved greedily in the first place."

In the following week the male pigeon was replaced by a friendly female. The horse ate and had a spectacular season. The popular papers disapproved of a Bishop who owned a racehorse, especially a winning one. The serious gossip columns ran short paragraphs saying that he sent his winnings to Black Africa. The Bishop wrote finely about his horse. Ridgeway went to prison briefly for making another and more violent protest about Rhodesia, after sitting next to a middle-aged white woman liberal from Rhodesia who had told her about a four-foot cell for black dissidents who were found dead after days without water. Their footprints were on the ceiling, perhaps because of the need to keep walking somewhere. With a finger dipped in dirt, one of them had written in shaky capitals on the wall: "HELLO OUT THERE." The signal had been inscribed by a man whom the woman liberal had taught to write English after she had herself learned Shona.

Ridgeway's memory of the Bishop, the stable yard, the horse, the pigeon, the dark, her sense of her own weight when the old man was lifting her, recurred and recurred.

"Are you against violence?" she had said as he was carrying her. "I'm a pacifist."

He had stood still to think about it carefully. "I am in general, too. I can see the possibility of violence being the only way to be gentle in the end. The difficulty is to be certain who is planning the violence and whether a gentle society is going to emerge from it. Most guerrillas are too disorganised." She was draped across his arms as if he were carrying a bridal dress stiffened with age. "Is that your shoulder blade or my watch strap?" he had said. "Either way, it must be painful for you. We're only a minute from the steps. I'm afraid I'm a bit of a slow stroller now when I'm carrying a girl."

"Am I heavy?" she had asked.

"No. I was just enjoying our conversation. I hadn't really noticed your lightness, which is rude of me, isn't it? You'll find the old do that. One gathers the mind to a point and the other things pass one by. It's a great blessing, age. There's more time."

Phone-In

Programme

"Hi-de-hi. Rise and shine. And may God give you many, many happy years ahead," said Mr. Rossiter in the radio studio at 7:30 in the morning. "Mr. Big Director, put through our first caller. Who's the lucky one?"

"Linda, Granny's going to be on with Mr. Rossiter. Eat up your eggs. Isn't this something?" said Mrs. Slotkin with her ear to the phone.

"You're on the *air,* Granny. I'm sorry I don't know your name yet," said Mr. Rossiter.

"Turn up my radio, Linda. I want to be able to hear myself," said Mrs. Slotkin, speaking over him for excitement.

"I said you're on the air," said Mr. Rossiter.

"Oh! You scared my mouth off."

"Are you hearing me? There's a lot of background noise."

"There's a steel band outside."

"Could you shut the window?"

"I'm sorry, I'm sorry."

"Hon, I can't hear you. Are you all right?"

"Yes, I'm very good. I feel extra good this morning, talking with you. It's like I'm taking a course for a degree. I respect the way you treat people."

"Is your radio tuned to this station? I can hear an echo."

"I respect the way you tell people when they're wrong."

"Never mind. What's your name, honey? What's your problem?"

"I'm Mrs. Slotkin senior. My son and daughter-in-law passed

away and I live with my granddaughter Linda Slotkin in a lovely mobile home and my problem is I'm lonely."

"You'll have to turn the radio down, honey. I'm getting the echo of my own voice. I can't hear you because I'm speaking over you."

"Linda, you heard what Mr. Rossiter said. What are you wearing that dress for on a weekday?"

"It seemed a special day," said Linda. "Your phone-in day."

"And what's your problem, again?" said Mr. Rossiter.

"Isn't that a pity? I can't hear us on the radio now. All I can hear is our voices on the telephone. Mr. Rossiter, I want to tell you what an appreciation I have of your deep sympathy for human beings. Can you hear me?"

"That's very nice of you. I like to do what I can. Is there a problem concerning your mobile home? Repairs? Leases?"

"No, I'm just lonely."

"With your lovely granddaughter with you? Mr. Big Director is waving at me to tell me we have just two minutes more for this call."

"I'm not lovely," said Linda, audibly to the audience. "I've reached the gangly age and I talk through my nose. Granny, ask Mr. Rossiter if I should have my adenoids out."

"Linda, sweetie, you mustn't interrupt your grandmother," said Mr. Rossiter, "but you just send me a photograph and your address and I'll also send you the name of a doctor near you. Mrs. Slotkin, tell me about your activities. Does your mobile home park offer you enough activities?"

"I never liked Canasta and I can't take to Bingo and I don't drink. I don't believe in vegetating so I proofread the telephone directory. When I've finished my work I go for a drive in my late husband's car to deliver the proofs."

"That's a full and adventuresome day, Mrs. Slotkin. Your trouble is that you're too hard on yourself. I expect you sometimes take your neighbours in the mobile homes for joyrides, don't you? You're a sociable person?"

"They turn me down. I'm a loner, you might say."

"Are you an experienced driver? I'll bet the scenery around you is something."

"I've been driving for twenty years but people get testy with me because I never did learn to make a left, its being across the traffic."

"How do you manage?"

"You can do it if you figure it out. I always had a head for planning. Right and right and right again, and keep going parallel with the left turn you had in mind as far as you want and then one block further, and then right and right again, and you're at your left turn. I also keep a sharp eye out for clover leaves, which are a great blessing to people who find left turns a trial."

"Mr. Big Dircctor is making his final signal. I'll have to ask you to hang up in ten seconds."

"I can't ever thank you for this."

"You've a good life, Mrs. Slotkin."

"Oh, help," said Linda. "Oh, hell. A cockroach has just gone into the toaster. Mr. Rossiter," yelling, "suppose it gets electrocuted?"

"Honey, if you have a bug problem in your mobile home you're entitled to help from the manager. God bless you both. And now come in, new caller, and a good morning to you."

"My name's Mrs. Wishhart, Mr. Rossiter, and I just can't believe this. My husband and I live at Peaceful World which is a beautiful place with a golf course and recreation halls and we sold our house to buy this to retire to. Only there's one trouble I want to talk to you about."

"And what's that?"

"You tell them, Mr. Wishhart."

"Mrs. Wishhart has always been an exemplary cook, Mr. Rossiter, and they won't allow her to cook in the cottage."

"Why's that?"

"We have to clock in for meals at the community centre," said Mr. Wishhart. "It's the only way they can tell if we're ambulatory. We're always ambulatory, one or the other of us, and one's enough to get the other along. If you don't appear in the meal hall for three days they put you in the hospital and that's the end. If one of us gets arthritis we just have to hope that it won't last for more than three days. We're very spry, you know."

"I can tell from your voices that there's something else on your minds, can't you, listeners? Do you regret selling your house? May I ask your age?"

"Our combined ages are a hundred and sixty-three," said Mr. Wishhart. "You've put your finger on it, Mr. Rossiter. Mrs.

Wishhart often gets up in the morning in our cottage and goes to the place where the bedroom door of our old house used to be. That's how much she misses it. We lived there with our unmarried daughter, you see, and we decided we were likely to become a nuisance when she got engaged, so we sold the house and had to pay everything we had for this cottage and the services. And then our daughter's fiancé was killed, and the management here won't let anyone under sixty come and live with us."

"And she's forty-one, do you see?" said Mrs. Wishhart.

"I'd like to look at that agreement you signed, Mrs. Wishhart. You give Mr. Big Director the address when you're off the air and I'll study it and see if we can't get you out of this. It'll mean fighting, mind. You've got to face that you've taken the wrong step. For the best reasons, but that doesn't help you in law. But we'll think of something. And send me copies of your wills. You know, sometimes we're up against a wall and we have to decide whether strong measures aren't the most decent. Suing isn't pleasant but we might be able to get you more freedom than you have at the moment on the ground of humanitarianism. Humanitarianism to your daughter, I'm thinking of."

Mr. Big Director slipped Mr. Rossiter a note reading "Pity about mentioning wills, but good about daughter," and the red light of another call came in.

Mr. Rossiter said, "This is a call from another mobile home. The Fleischer home. Now, I want you all to understand that buying a mobile home isn't just something for the retired to do. Three-quarters of the inhabitants are young married couples, or even unmarried. You'll find a sprinkling of young vegetarians. Remember your mobile van is never called a trailer if you're houseproud. You can get Hi-Rise two-storey mobile homes. Remember you're outside pollution, you're outside riot areas, you're outside high taxes. Mr. and Mrs. Fleischer, you said you wanted to tell listeners about your experience of mobile homes."

"You first, dear," said Mr. Fleischer shyly.

"I've got to make the tea. I wish I could offer a cup to Mr. Rossiter."

"Well, we're in a world of pretend, aren't we?" said Mr. Rossiter, laughing the strong laugh that got him through his shows. "Pretending we know each other."

"There's a wide variety of choices. You can get either a sunken bath tub or a flush bath tub, and the sunken costs no more. You can get a fireplace."

"Fake," said Mrs. Fleischer.

"Not all of them," said Mr. Fleischer. "I've seen a genuine WBF."

"Wood-burning fireplace," said Mr. Rossiter. *"Really?"*

"What brought us to mobile homes is that we like moving around, hunting and fishing, et cetera. I kept thinking we couldn't afford to move around all the time, travel being the price it is, but I found we could. It's also a way of not bothering your kids too much. It gives us our independence. You've got to think ahead. You've got to remember that when you become old, young people don't look for your company. Not that we're getting near the dangerous age yet."

"When I saw the mobile home I swear I was never so tickled in my life," said Mrs. Fleischer. "We'd once been to a demonstration about them and it stuck in our minds. An exceptionally nicely dressed conjurer with two white rabbits in a show made gold coins appear like magic when he was talking about the savings of living in a mobile home, and the rabbits would disappear when he was talking about the use of space. Oh, it *is* nice, sitting down like this, the three of us together. It must be awful to be old and lose transportation, mustn't it? That's one of the blessings about a mobile home. At first I was worried about their reputation. You hear a lot, of course."

"Roughnecks?"

"People drunk as polluted fish, the rumour goes. Not an ounce of truth in it. We had a humdinger of a party when Mr. Fleischer retired last year, and the office gave him $156 as a going-away present, but there wasn't a sign of debauchery and everyone respected our new home. I was thinking, the funny thing is that you go away twice in life. Once when you marry, and once when you retire. And each time it's a ceremony to remember."

"Splendiferous," said Mr. Rossiter. "I can see Mr. Big Director raising his eyebrows at me. The word just came to me. And what do you do when you're not hunting and fishing?"

"As and when we come to a stop, which won't be soon," said Mr. Fleischer, "I've got the cement to build a nice entrance. I've got cement and rocks. I've had enough of lawn. Cement's more aesthetic."

"That's not to say he's not a practical man," said Mrs. Fleischer anxiously. "For instance, he especially chose a conventional door instead of a sliding one, thinking of me with packages in twenty years' time. He was also against the extravagances that money can buy in a mobile home. Chartres ceilings, Roman tubs, wet bars."

"A couple buying is entitled to talk back to the manager about things like that," said Mr. Rossiter. "Listeners should look out for, say, swing-door alterations that have been promised but not made. This couple we have the pleasure of talking to are getting the very best out of the mobility of their mobile home. I don't have to tell them that there's a dreadful decline in resale value because there's no land attached, but I'm sure they've taken that into consideration and they're not going to want to move as they get older. Excuse me"—strong laugh—"not going to want to change residence."

"About hobbies, apart from moving about?" asked Mr. Fleischer.

"We're going to be older, in time, you see," said Mrs. Fleischer.

"As long as they aren't against doctor's orders," said Mr. Rossiter, "I suggest Air-ballooning, Axe-sharpening, Bicycling, Camping, Geology Trips, Glove-making, Harp-playing, Horseback riding, Horseshoes, Jousting, Juggling, Mountaineering, Picnics, and Yachting."

Mr. Big Director gave him a note reading "Most of those are moving about."

"What's Horseshoes?" said Mr. Fleischer.

"Looking for horseshoes. Horseshoes are lucky, and the search can take you to all sorts of places. And then you deduce the description and life-story of the horse. The life-story *so far,* that is. It's not necessarily over. If contemporary, a horse's shoes are being changed all the time, of course. Then suppose you have a talent that your circle keeps exclaiming about—cooking, uncommon shawls, hand-made baby clothes—you may have the makings of a good small business. There's fudge. Truffles.

Chocolate chip cookies. Mille-feuilles. Lampshades. Remember that failure to keep ledgers, slipshod delivery dates, over-generous credit, tend to lead to doom. You could start a sewing shop, or a repair shop for the sports goods you like. Have professional cards made up. You could go in for cooking dietary meals or feeding goldfish: $1 a day is the standard rate for feeding goldfish. You could run a mobile library, though this requires capital, and a stable emotional state is an important factor due to the sustained detail work and the perpetual interruptions. You could consider raising night crawlers. Large earthworms that come out in the night. I know a couple who made $80,000 raising and selling night crawlers for fish bait. You can get started for as little as $10 to $12 for 2,000 fine breeding night-crawler stock, and in about four hours of darkness you can pack and ship about $9 worth of worms. Am I losing you? Worms are a fruitful small-business hobby that I've just been investigating."

"You were talking about Geology Trips," said Mr. Fleischer. "My impression is that mineral people love to mingle too much. What's your main advice about planning for the future, Mr. Rossiter?"

"Keep the brain occupied and the physique seated."

"I'd go mad."

"There are ways and ways. I can see Mr. Big Director waving at me to tell you about my hobby. It's marionette theatres. I build them from scratch."

"A friend of ours, more sedentary than us, is doing that with a lot of his circle," said Mrs. Fleischer. "Mr. Fleischer does carpentry when the weather's bad."

"I'd like to tackle some of the bigger things but I can never quite get caught up with what I'm doing," said Mr. Fleischer.

"They're putting on 'Little Red Riding Hood' in hopes of the grandchildren," said Mrs. Fleischer. "We've only got children as yet but I daresay the group we're talking about is quite right in principle. You can't expect young people to turn up if there's no entertainment. The rehearsals have bogged down because no one wants to be the wolf who pretends to be the grandmother."

"Can I ask you something, Mr. Rossiter?" said Mr. Fleischer.

"Anything I can do. Of course."

"Why aren't you on television? My wife and I have been listening to you for the last five years and we have ideas about what you look like but it would be an ease to know. We choose to keep our circle small and you've become one of the set, you see."

Mr. Rossiter laughed his strong laugh and said, "Mr. Big Director will send you a signed photograph of myself with my best regards if you'll leave your address. Stay young. Stay healthy. We'll be back with you after this message."

Commercial break

Mr. Rossiter, aged eighty-one, which was the reason he didn't go on television, looked up at Mr. Big Director, his wife, aged eighty-two. She brought him a cup of coffee, moving the microphone away to kiss him on the mouth.

"I wish I didn't have to send out these photographs," he said, looking at a pile of signed and doctored ones of himself aged fifty. "Here I am, talking to people about fraudulent practices."

"It's legitimate."

"It got on·my nerves today, calling you Mr. Big Director. You went too high up on that gallery. I couldn't see you. You know I can't talk to people when I can't see you. Will you get me"—pause—"I'll remember in a minute."

Mrs. Rossiter waited two minutes.

"It'll come back to me in a second."

She waited another while: ninety seconds.

Mr. Rossiter said, "Did you get it for me?"

"You never said what it was, darling."

"I get like this when the programme's off the air."

"You mustn't fret about the Mr. Big Director business. It started as a joke and it should stay one."

"It's anti–Women's Lib."

"Darling, I'm eighty-two. Women's Lib wouldn't thank you for me. I was a lot more than a flapper when we were campaigning for the flapper vote in 1928."

"All that about hobbies!"

"Yes."

"Not to mention creativity! Bertrand Russell, Casals, Rich-

ard Strauss, Picasso; I say their names for good cheer until I
could walk out of the room at the idea of the giants being in
the house! But at least they didn't go in for hobbies. Who wants
work that's made up to keep you busy? You're like a prisoner
sewing mailbags."

"I remember feeling like that when I was a child at school,
soaking wicker to make trays nobody wanted."

"Well, we won't make any wicker trays now, my dove, not
for anyone. You're an eternal object lesson to me in this matter, I have to say. You've never had the time for invented work.
It's a great question, keeping the brain interested. Sometimes
one finds oneself thinking but knows one's not getting anywhere, however hard one works, that one's just shaving the
points of needles."

"I've been thinking about this business of violence," said his
wife. "This violence on the news all the time. It's nothing to
have in the house. I'm much gratified by this programme of
yours, you know. The news is full of adversity. My experience
is that violence is worst when you see it on television, next
worst when you see it in a newspaper, and not really bad at all
when it's happening to you."

Programme

Mr. Rossiter's first caller after the commercial break, Mr. Anthony, said vehemently, "Right now there are two hundred
thousand young Communists in psychiatry. That's where the
violence is coming from. They don't believe in the Almighty
but they want to change people's beliefs. A person's mind isn't
something to tamper with."

Mrs. Anthony said, "Dear, Mr. Rossiter may not agree. I
don't believe I agree with you about change. Think of the first
moon-shot, dear. Mr. Rossiter, we were all different after those
first boys came down from the moon. I'll never forget seeing
Neil's leg coming out of whatever it was: the module, was it?
Like he was feeling for the bottom of the ocean and didn't
know if he was in his depth or not."

"And kids! Apart from psychiatry, and Communism, there's
kids and drugs," said Mr. Anthony.

"We don't meet many kids, living here in a mobile home,

Mr. Rossiter. We don't meet the people in the other homes, either. You wonder what's in their minds. Of course, if they weren't here they could maybe see more of their kids, but that would depend on the kids, wouldn't it?"

"What's your question, Mr. Anthony?"

"Well, I'll say it for him," said Mrs. Anthony. "His father left all his savings to my husband's sister, thinking she hadn't got the earning power of the two of us. She tied it all up in a little house that's bequeathed to the Police Athletic League for use as a gym, and when she died my husband was forced to pay for her funeral because she hadn't left any money."

Her husband broke in, crying, his voice high in pitch. "And when I die, who's going to pay for *my* funeral? Let alone Mrs. Anthony's, a woman's always being more expensive because of the flowers? What I want to know is, Mr. Rossiter, can I sue the Police Athletic League?"

"You'd better send me a copy of the trusts and I'll put you on to a good lawyer, if you'll give your address to Mr. Big Director."

"And what'll *that* cost me, I'd like to know? In the United States of America?"

"Well, if you don't like it here, it's a free country," said Mr. Rossiter, distressed.

"Well, if it was a free country, he'd probably take a taxi free somewhere else," said Mrs. Anthony.

"Have you got some coffee there for him?" said Mr. Rossiter. "Are you sitting next to him?"

Commercial break

Mr. Rossiter shook. Mrs. Rossiter was standing beside him and had coffee with him.

"To talk about his wife's funeral being more expensive! To grumble about paying for his sister being buried! The stinginess we turn up in this programme!"

"Have you thought, dear, about getting a driver's licence? I think it's time. You can't depend on my always being here to drive us. Suppose I'm the first to go."

He glared at her and roared, "You *can't* be! There are some suggestions that go too far!"

They sat in silence while the commercial finished.

"What are we doing?" said Mr. Rossiter. "Doing this pro-gramme week after week? We're not exactly serving people who make events."

"It's difficult to serve someone who makes events. One can best serve someone who is subject to them."

Programme

Mr. Tyler telephoned. "Good morning, Mr. Rossiter. There were several things I wanted to talk to you about."

"Any help I can give."

"You're an ear, you see, like my wife. For instance, our for-eign policy. I never approved of the recent military graft."

"Draft," said Mrs. Tyler.

"Oh, it is draft? Well, graft's no misnomer. We're a little bit old."

"He's eighty-seven and I'm eighty-five," said Mrs. Tyler. "Our average age is exactly half-way between us every November because we were each born in a November. We still work three hours a day each, but it's not enough for us."

"People are lucky who work all the time," said Mr. Tyler. "Teachers, writers. Carpenters and electricians get paid by the hour but the trick in that is that they don't work the whole hour. If you were to ask me what I miss most, I'd definitely say working all the time, and the only work that lasts all the time is brain-work, which unfortunately my wife and I aren't up to any longer, apart from reading. The little luxuries you don't miss when you're on a pension, but the lack of interest you do."

"Go on," said Mr. Rossiter, alert.

"My wife's a real old dictionary. She does the crossword every day. She says it's not as hard as it used to be."

"I developed the knack when I was ill," said Mrs. Tyler.

"She doesn't take proper care of herself, Mr. Rossiter."

"You can't worry every time you sneeze," said Mrs. Tyler.

"How do you manage on your pensions?" said Mr. Rossiter. "Send me details of them, and your insurance plans, and your outgoings. Give your address to Mr. Big Director. We might be able to think of some extras that could come your way."

"One can cut back, you see," said Mr. Tyler. "I used to smoke the cigarettes in advertisements but now that the taxes have gone up I roll my own."

"We've had some wonderful pot-lucks," said Mrs. Tyler, laughing. "For instance, we won a raffle, long ago, and two other couples drove with us across the country in the fancy cars we had then. Oh, that was fun! Every evening, if we'd driven our ration, we'd get out beside the cars and throw something in the air. In the men's case it was silver dollars. In the wives' case, not having any, it was our shoes. Some of the roads were so rickety, and made worse by cars getting stuck with the wheels racing, that we used to drive across the sun-baked meadows and prairies out of kindness to our country's lovely automobiles, and because we had never before had the pleasure of seeing the continent at full stretch. Well, we had a lot of gaiety going, and we were all fools, and we're all alive."

"You've lost your health again since yesterday," said Mr. Tyler, his voice fading as he presumably put down the receiver and went into another room to look at his wife.

"I'll tell you a story about where we live, Mr. Rossiter, as you've been kind enough to ask for our address. Well, outside our front door there's one of these old-fashioned mail chutes. It has a notice on it. I copied it down; I'll read it to you:

'NOTICE.
Discontinuance of Mail Chute Service.
The management of these premises having notified the
undersigned of its intention
to discontinue the rental of this mail
chute, notice is hereby given that the
service of this chute will be discontinued
on or about
February 1, 1951,
and thereafter the chute will be removed
from the premises.
Signed, for Euphrates Mail Chute, Inc.'

"Well, you see," said Mrs. Tyler, "now it's nearly twenty-five years later, and the chute's still here, and I'm still here."

Catering

"With the divorce-rate you'd think it'd die out, but no," said Angelica, the daughter of Mrs. Pope the wedding caterer. She spoke to her father, sounding taxed. The smell of roasting turkey rose through the Popes' small Putney house like the smell of bonfires seeping through things. Angelica's boyfriend liked it. He would nibble her hair and taste gravy. Angelica thought the place stank. The weddings Mrs. Pope catered were always on Saturdays. One turkey was cooked on Thursday night, the other on Friday at dawn, because the oven wouldn't hold two at a time. It was a ritual. This was a Thursday.

"Your mother and I can carve two turkeys and feed a hundred and twenty people with white meat only," said Al Pope.

"Breast," said Angelica.

Mr. Pope was a thin man with a collarbone like a wire coat-hanger. He was one of those people who are tolerated or even held in affection for being a good chap and always staying to pay for the last round of drinks at the end of an evening. He was an engineer. He had gone to night school in the Depression. To get his learning he had trained himself to sleep only four hours in the twenty-four, with half an hour allowed for recreation. Now there were three hours an evening with the television. These were the palmy days, to his mind.

On Thursday evenings he could hear one bird loudly roasting in the oven. The other would be laid out, trussed and full of onion, on the table in the living-room beside his elbow ("taking my attention away from the set"). Any other day of the week he chose to watch television from a part of the room that could be closed off with frosted-glass doors, but he made Thursday viewing from the dinner table a point of principle. On Thursday the table was extended with two extra leaves, and it practically filled the room to the glass doors. The table also supported a hundred and twenty rolls of raw bacon, a vast bowl of fresh white breadcrumbs for the stuffing, tins of fruit and packets of jelly, bulk orders of cheese biscuits and ice-cream wafers and chocolate digestive biscuits.

"Aren't you enjoying your supper?" Mrs. Pope said from the kitchen. "You haven't come back for your seconds."

"The provisions upset my concentration," said Mr. Pope.

"A steak-and-kidney pudding doesn't call for concentration, dear," Mrs. Pope said. "It's for enjoyment."

"I mean my concentration on the telly," said Mr. Pope. "You didn't take my meaning. It's nice steak-and-kidney."

He heard his wife starting on the giblet stock. He recognized the symptoms of the activity without turning his head. "I don't know how you find the time on a Thursday," he said. "To make us a hot meal."

"I should think she could do a steak-and-kidney pud in her sleep by now," Angelica said.

"She doesn't do it in her sleep at all," Mr. Pope said. "It's not always steak-and-kidney and you know it. It may be always the same turkey for her weddings, but it's always something different for the family. A steak-and-kidney's a lot of work."

"Yes, when she's been on the go since nine in the morning seven days a week and up all night on Thursdays and getting a lousy ten quid for the whole caboodle," Angelica said. "What the catering comes down to is that she's being had."

"It's ten pounds net, though," said Mr. Pope.

"Net is gossamer," said his daughter.

"Net means no tax, the way she works it. Net is ten pounds clear. Ten pounds clear doesn't grow on trees."

Angelica snorted, in a pretty way.

"Anyway," her father said, "she enjoys it, and don't go asking me why. You can ask her. It's her business."

"She'll get clobbered one day by the tax people for evasion of the law," Angelica said.

"You want to watch your tongue, my girl," said Mr. Pope.

"You're right there. You're not wrong," Mrs. Pope said to him from the kitchen. "Do you need a glass of something, dear?" There was a pause. "What do you want to drink?"

"Well, I haven't got very much choice, have I? Considering there's only the one thing I like," Mr. Pope said.

She brought him a pint of mild-and-bitter. Thursday was the only evening she ever found him trying. Her name was Ada and they were fond. She had a harmonious face with a merry aspect. A large woman. Their one child was Angelica, a name her mother had thought beautiful even before she found it was a kind of cake decoration. As Angelica grew older, Mrs. Pope started to foster-mother small children for the local town council. Angelica, who called herself Andy after going to secretarial college, had grown up among a horde of farmed-out toddlers whose predicament had made them rampageous, demanding, or expectant of small fortune according to their natures, before being stamped with Mrs. Pope's ample view of things and returned to other lives in due time. The departures took a toll of her. And of Mr. Pope, fiercely attached to the kids in the middle of calling them a bloody nuisance or too quiet to be right. To his wife's mind, he must have had enough of children and deserved a bit of peace. Anyway, she became a private-wedding caterer when Angelica left school.

"How does she manage it? Does she borrow a kitchen?" the headmaster of the secretarial college had said once to Angelica, who worshipped him and was in the habit of secreting what her mother did because she was determined to have another sort of life herself if it killed her. The headmaster had found out because his sister-in-law had used Mrs. Pope for a function in his family and the name had made enough of a connection.

"She does it all at home, every cupcake and rock bun," Angelica said bitterly.

"Must take a bit of organizing, all on her own."

"She's got her girls. She's been using the same ones for years. She calls them girls but they're ancient. Three pounds each a time. One of them can't move about much so she stands there in the wedding hall and does the washing up. The others do the laying and the clearing."

* * *

A wedding took the whole week to do it properly. Mrs. Pope always rented the same small community hall. Sunday could be a day off, but if she had had a wedding the day before she had to count the cutlery and the crockery to make sure nothing had been pinched, scrub out the tea urn, and carry everything out to the garden shed where she stored it in the week. In the early days she had hired the stuff but by now she had saved up enough to get her own and hire it out herself. Sunday was also the day when the napkins and the tablecloths were washed. Ada had a spin dryer but it didn't get the linen better than damp. If it was a good drying day, she pegged the load up on the lines in the back garden. If it was raining, the pile stayed stacked in the kitchen.

Monday was the day for ironing, and for icing the wedding cake she had made the week before, and for what Mr. Pope called the final conflab. The final conflab was with the couple and their parents, and he saw it as the day when future trouble raised its head in the form of arguing about which set of parents was to pay for any drinks at the table. The bride's parents paid for the food, the bridegroom's parents paid for drinks at the bar in the hall (trestle tables, administered by Mr. Pope, transformed into a flashing barman), but drinks at the table were often a stumbling block. Mrs. Pope was also used to sniffing trouble. If there had been a bit of frostiness at the final conflab, she foresaw an edgy affair on the Saturday. She would call it a gannet wedding. ("I bet this is going to be a gannet wedding," she had said this Monday.)

"We'll have wine at the table," the bride's mother had said.

"Is wine at the table drink or food?" the bridegroom's mother had asked.

"What's the hassle?" the bridegroom had said, who knew some American to cover events like this.

"What your mother means," the bridegroom's father said, "is that *our* wine or *their* wine? It's not food, you see, but it's not the bar, either. So who pays?"

"I will," said the bridegroom, holding his girl's hand because she was appalled.

"That's always a good solution," Mrs. Pope said quickly. "And would you like to have my cake stand or is there one of your own? Mine's only plated but it's quite nice, I think you'll find."

"You can't afford it, not on your wages. Wine at the table," the bridegroom's mother said.

"Belt up," said the bridegroom.

"Your mother's only saying what needs to be said," said the bridegroom's father.

"Well, if we don't have wine at the table, what are we going to toast them with?" said the bride's father, intervening with authority. "That's a cost *I'll* assume. *If necessary.*"

Al Pope spoke up from the little part of the room that could be shut off with the folding doors to divide himself and the television from his wife when she was having her conflabs. "Let the groom do it," he said. "It usually turns out to be the best." He came into the other part of the room: their talk had brought to mind something he had been wanting. He helped himself to a mild-and-bitter after passing around a bottle of ruby port in order to soothe things.

"Happy wedding day, if and when it comes," he said, toasting them lugubriously and then winking at his wife.

"I'll pay," said the bridegroom's father. "May as well go the whole hog."

In the weekly order of things, a Tuesday and a Wednesday were the light days. Ada would check through the shopping lists and go to the cash-and-carry shop where they let her buy things wholesale. (She had a wholesaler's card, because her first do had been for a confectioner and he had let her borrow his card. It was for confectionery only, but he naturally broke the rules himself when he fancied a bottle of sherry, and the transgression passed into legality with the issue of Mrs. Pope's card.) She handed on only the cost price of things to the client, and Angelica called her a nit for it. The dry goods would be stored in the hall, beside the foster children's old dolls' prams and tricycles, and Mr. Pope's bike, and huge tins of biscuits and nuts and sweets, flour and dried fruit and stout and icing sugar for wedding cakes, and the parcel from a local printer holding a bulk order of matches engraved with gold and silver hearts and the couple's Christian names. The printer was an old mate of Mrs. Pope's and did the job for her cheaply. The turkeys, the two looming birds, would sit around in the living room to thaw out.

* * *

A Thursday was the longest day, controlled by the turkeys. While one was in the oven, Mrs. Pope would mix the wedding cake for the next week, and then the rock buns, and then the flaky pastry for the fancies, and then the short-crust pastry for the sausage rolls. That was the night when Mr. Pope had to have his supper on a tray.

"It's the one night he *has* to have it on a tray," Mrs. Pope had said once to Angelica. "Why he always wants it at the table on a Thursday when he chooses a tray every other night of the week, Lord knows."

"Inevitable," Angelica had said, doing the shorthand outline for the word in her head.

If Angelica came back early enough on a Thursday, she would be pressed by her father into helping her mother with rolling and filling and egging the pastry for the sausage rolls. They worked at the living-room table, using pastry brushes so old that they slanted like a rocking-horse mane, dipped into cupfuls of whisked eggs to glaze the pastry after it had been pleated at the edge with the back of a knife. Mrs. Pope could crimp a foot and a half of succulent, buttery pastry in twenty seconds. Mr. Pope would sometimes come into the room to watch and to lick a spoonful of raw cake mixture.

"There was a chef at Lyons in Leicester Square who used to break two eggs at a time onto the griddle," he said this Thursday. "One in each hand on the edge of a cup and never an egg messed up. I used to watch him. He was behind a lovely clean piece of plate glass."

Some other Thursday he had said to Angelica, "You're not as fast as your mother yet, my girl."

Patience came sullenly to Angelica; or perhaps only patience with her parents. She was a beautiful girl with raised eyebrows and poignant circles of pure white skin around her eyes. She thought her parents had a bad life. "I don't want to live like this," she had said back to Mr. Pope that time.

So Mr. Pope had put his finger into the raw rock-bun mixture to taste it, and said, "What's the matter with it, then?"

"It's so cramped and you're both so old-fashioned. I can't even bring a boyfriend back on Thursday because of Mother sitting up all night down here." Angelica slept upstairs in a tiny room and she was ashamed to have anyone there because of the creaks in the sagging single bed, not to speak of her unease about her parents' twenty-first-birthday present to her, which was a reproduction Jacobean dressing table with mirror lights that Ada and Mr. Pope had bought for her on hire purchase. If they'd only get out of Putney, she thought, there's plenty of nice modern stuff for half the price. (Her boyfriend Ron was in design.) It was enough to break your heart, but there was no telling them. Angelica took them to be conventional.

On Friday the finished fancies, iced and delicate, were stacked in crates in the hall, and the second turkey went on being basted, having been put into the oven by Mrs. Pope in the middle of the night. She would also peel four hundred potatoes and finish preparing the stuffing and the green vegetables: one stuffing and two veg for an ordinary wedding, two stuffings and three veg if the family wanted it grand. Delicate little brussels sprouts floating in great pans, plates piled with chopped chestnuts and sage-and-onion mixtures, wooden boards of chopped parsley, crockery jars full of turkey dripping. Sometime after midday Mrs. Pope would have her bath and then go to get her hair set for the Saturday; if she'd had the bath after the hairdo it would have spoiled the set. On Friday evenings she got the linen ready in the hall, and telephoned her friend the van driver to make sure everything was ready for taking her to the hall the next morning, and made a list of what she wanted from the garden shed. The turkeys were laid out for Mr. Pope on the living-room table and he carved them. In the old days Mrs. Pope had done it, but the time came when Al decided to take it over. He had a collection of beautiful old carving knives that he arranged in a neat row and sharpened in turn with a steel. Mrs. Pope would relax so that she was ready for the do.

A Saturday was the pinnacle, obstreperous and exhausting. The van arrived at a quarter to seven. There was the loading of all the crates to be done, and the hanging around for the bread to be delivered, and the picking up of the girls, and the chilly hall to be warmed by lighting the gas rings in the little kitchen off to the side, to the left of the dais where the band would play. Then they set up the tables, and roasted the potatoes in the turkey dripping, and cooled the champagne if champagne was called for. Champagne meant a lot of extra work because of serving it at the last minute, but it made things festive.

"Something on your mind, love?" Mrs. Pope said to Angelica this Thursday evening, slipping the rolled pastry over the long strips of sausage meat.

"No, why?"

"I thought there was something on your mind."

Angelica went on basting a turkey with her back turned.

"Answer your mother," Mr. Pope said.

"All right. I'm fed up with not being able to bring Ron back. The place is so full of bloody poultry and fancy cakes you couldn't have a cat in. Ron'd go off his nut. Not to speak of nowhere to sleep."

"It's a lovely smell, really," said Mrs. Pope.

"Not week in, week out."

"Only two nights a week," Mrs. Pope said. "And you get your changes. It's not turkey all day. Some of the time it's the fancies."

"I've got to get a place of my own."

"Who's Ron? Your current?"

"You've *met* him, Dad."

"You can't get a place of your own, because you're not earning yet," said Al, "and that's that. We're not keeping you. Not keeping you from doing anything you want to do, I mean. Any other night of the week he can sleep on the couch in here, but not Thursday. Not when your mother's up and down all night with the oven and might get a chance of a stretch-out."

"Why can't I have your room? Why can't you sleep in here with her?"

"I can't sleep sitting up. Where'd I go? You can't have a working man sleeping under his own dining-room table. What's wrong with your own room? Many a time I've slept two to a single bed, and don't think I didn't creep up the stairs when I was a young 'un. What the eye doesn't see . . ."

"Mum wouldn't like it."

"I don't mind, dear," Mrs. Pope said.

"Well, and there's the dressing table," said Angelica.

"What about it?" Mr. Pope said.

"Ron designs contemporary furniture, and it would upset him. Phony Jacobean."

"Your mother saved up for that," said Mr. Pope.

"Tastes change," said Mrs. Pope.

"Yours don't," said Angelica. "You're stuck in the mud. You want me to have the same life as you lot and I'm not going to, see? White weddings all the time. It's not modern." Pause, looking for a fight, but none offered. "I'm getting out."

"We couldn't stop you, love," said Mrs. Pope.

However, something about the scene with Angelica bothered her so much that on Friday morning, when she had gone upstairs to put on a cardigan, she found herself sitting around with one arm into it and one out, and she had been there so long that she couldn't even recall whether she was in the act of dressing or going to bed.

At lunchtime, as she did every weekday, Mrs. Pope cooked an extra main meal and covered it with tinfoil and took it down the road two stops on the bus to her old friend Willy, a widower in love with her. She had been doing the same thing for seventeen years. Willy would give her a glass of sherry, and she would sit with it to watch him eat for twenty minutes, and then come back again on the bus with the clean plate. He fancied different things to the Pope family and liked her cooking. He took to her experiments with pizza and spaghetti and French cassoulet, things her own family wouldn't have touched. Fifteen years ago she had had a child by him. Mr. Pope hadn't wanted another. He knew about the daily visits but not about the enduring devotion. They hurt his pride, though not so much: not so long as his wife stayed. The two of them had talked about the child all those years ago, and he had taken her away to Morecambe to have it. Angelica had been left with a maiden aunt. Mrs. Pope brought up the baby for a while as if it were one of the foster children, but after three years she felt the strain on Mr. Pope and had it adopted by people far away. Willy had acknowledged the child and saw her quite often. Another daughter.

*   *   *

This Saturday, Ron had been spending the night with the Popes. Al had carved the turkeys and put away the knives and then lain down for the night on the table, which Ada had covered with two eiderdowns. He had said he preferred it, to get a jump on the Saturday; he held to his changed position with dignity, but it was so that Angelica and Ron could have the bigger bedroom. Mrs. Pope slept on the sofa with her neck propped up on a rolled cushion and her head unsupported to keep the set in. Al twice noticed her lying awake in the night, and the second time he got off the table and went into the kitchen.

"You're not disturbing the fancies, dear?"

He came back with a mug of cocoa and said, "Not when they're all wrapped up for tomorrow. My watch has stopped. What time is it? I've had this watch for thirty years and it hasn't done badly, but perhaps I need a new one."

"The new ones don't last unless you go to Bond Street," Mrs. Pope said, meaning to go to Bond Street on Monday to get one with his name engraved on the back of it.

Dawn seemed to come slowly. Both of them slept in fits and starts. Ron appeared at six-thirty: a nice, dapper boy with a mouth as pink as a baby's, wearing jeans and a mod sweater, so that he could help with the day. Ada wore her best, under a white overall.

Angelica came down and made them all tea and toast, to give her mother a respite from food. The beautiful cakes and pastries lay on bakers' trays in the kitchen and the hall. The van came. For the first time in her career, Ada failed to take in that the bread hadn't been delivered before they left.

Ron had come in his own car. "I'll go back," he said when they realized in the freezing hall.

"Don't leave," Angelica said, to her mother's surprise.

"Somebody's got to," said Ron.

"That's best," said Ada, looking at Angelica. "Then we can get on."

"It's always the men who suffer," Al said ritually. Nobody took much notice, not being meant to.

The women stood in the little kitchen unloading the trays of cakes and the crates of cutlery and the cardboard boxes of turkey wrapped in tinfoil. The gas rings were heating up the place; the people looked like coachmen on Christmas cards. Ada turned on the fluorescent lights in the hall and they started to set up the caterers' long tables. They wore white flat rubber-soled shoes, like nurses, and moved fast. Florence, the girl of sixty-five whose legs were bad, stood in the kitchen mashing hard-boiled eggs and cress for the children's sandwiches that were to be served at the buffet after the wedding breakfast.

"It's less children than usual," she said to Ada. "Is it going to be a nice wedding?"

"There was a bit of trouble over the drink."

"I once met a girl who knew someone who'd got engaged at a place called the 400 Club. I always wanted to meet someone at a restaurant that was just a number. They're always the gayest."

Al Pope was getting the bar ready. Ron helped.

"They've decided to have spirits, even," Al said. "We'll make them some wallbangers."

"What are wallbangers?"

"You know, like people who bang on the wall when you're having a good time. If you're dealing with vodka you need something to kill the taste. A wallbanger is a vodka or a gin or whatever you please with orange juice. It's much the same as what they call an orange blossom, but the name of a wallbanger goes down better with the men when they're at a function. The vodka gives you a lift, you know. A lift, like people need."

There was a lot to do. Spirits rose through the morning. Angelica undertook the cutlery. The band arrived at half past three. The place had warmed up by then and smelt delicately of turkey and roasting potatoes. Florence was basting the potatoes and washing lettuce and dicing cucumber and buttering bread for the buffet. The wedding breakfast was to be at four-ish. The band had their instruments wrapped in transparent plastic, like frozen food. One of them was hungry, and Mrs. Pope made him a bacon sandwich.

"The turkey is the bride's mother's, and though I daresay she wouldn't miss a slice—well, I'd rather the bacon," she said, worrying about Angelica.

"There's something up," Al said in a low voice in the kitchen.

"I expect she's sickening for something," Ada said. "Perhaps she shouldn't be working?"

"She's got an easy life compared to what you had," said Al. "You'll find out what it is, I daresay."

Al talked to Ron about the beer question. "When you're being a barman in this situation," he said, "you have to watch the froth. Your barrels of beer are hot because of being moved, and you're apt to get half a glass of froth if you don't watch it. People at a wedding don't like that. They can turn naughty if you don't do it right."

The guests came very promptly at four. There was anxiety and social effort. The band played. People slowly settled down at the tables with glasses of sherry. A lot of them had push-chairs beside them with babies sucking rusks or kicking under fluffy blankets appliquéd with rabbits. Full-scale prams had to be left at the door but pushchairs were allowed, though they made serving a nightmare. Ada and the girls rushed through the hall with the soup plates and then with the turkey, pota-toes, and veg: four times round a hundred and twenty people, plus the obstacles of the pushchairs. Angelica by now was with her father and Ron at the bar, doing the table wines and rub-bing the champagne glasses.

"Champagne's a pest," she said. "You have to serve the soup and clear, and then serve the main course, and then wait around while they eat their pudding and their cheese and biscuits, and then you have to belt around like hell to give them all a glass of champagne for the toast; and you *say*, 'Don't drink this, it's for the toast,' but they all drink it too early and you have to go round again. It's the pushchairs that are the biggest bind. Mum's got about forty pushchairs tonight."

"What's the trouble?" Al said to her while Ron was away with an empty barrel of beer.

"What do you mean?" Angelica said.

"Are you pregnant?" Al said. "You could say."

"No," she said, rubbing up a trayful of champagne glasses fast with a glass-cloth. "Ron and me's not serious. I want my freedom."

Her father went into the kitchen to talk to Ada.

"I haven't got time now," Ada said, flying about clearing the plated dishes of turkey and stuffing and bacon rolls.

"I think she's pregnant and Ron won't marry her."

Ada brooded about it while she was working. She said, "You'd better get back to the bar. Tell her I want some help in here."

Angelica was tearing around the hall serving champagne. Her father saw that she was crying. The band was playing very loud rock. The guests, the older ones, were complaining to Angelica that they couldn't hear each other. The ones in love had left their food and were holding hands and wanting to dance. One of Angelica's false eyelashes had come loose, and at the same time as dealing with tears she was also dealing with eyelashes and champagne and pushchairs. Al sent one of Ada's girls over with a message that Ada needed her.

"Your father says he's worried about you," Ada said in a soft voice, getting the plates ready for the buffet. "You do the rest of the sardine sandwiches," she said more loudly. Florence was washing up at speed, resting one poorly leg against the other.

"I work all week," said Angelica, reasonably quiet. "I'm fed up with having to do one of your bleeding weddings on a Saturday every time I can't manage to stay somewhere else over the weekend."

"Weddings are what I do," Ada said. Pause. "I didn't know you stayed away on purpose." A nail seemed to have been tapped in somewhere. Angelica looked irate and claustrophobic.

"Are you having a baby?" Ada said.

"Ron and me aren't serious, Mum."

"That's what your father said you said."

Angelica started to cry again.

"Get on with the sardines, you'll feel better."

"I'm fine, Mum."

"You think we'd be shocked but we wouldn't. You have it and I'll foster it. You've got your schooling to do and you couldn't look after it, I see that."

"Don't be daft, Mum. I'm not pregnant now. I went to a doctor. I had an operation for it."

"Oh dear," Ada said. "Oh dear."

"It was an abortion," Angelica said.

Ada stood there, feeling dreadful. "You must be feeling dreadful," she said.

"I'm all *right,* Mum. If you dare tell anyone I'll never speak to you again."

"Your father probably knows."

"I mean Ron."

"You haven't *told* him?" Ada turned away to the gas ring and dealt with the tea urn, feeling as angry as she ever remembered. "Well, I expect he knew really and didn't like to bring it up," she said.

"He wouldn't have guessed. He's not a noticer."

"You can never tell for sure about what people cotton on to."

"The thing is we're not interested in all that. He's got his designing and I've got a life to lead, haven't I? I told you, we're not serious."

"How *could* you not tell him," Ada said, laying out the plates. "When we'd have looked after it."

"You'd never. You're too conventional."

"I looked after one of my own like that," Ada said with difficulty. "I had a baby like that, you know. But I thought I'd better give it away in the end."

Angelica wasn't hearing properly. She was doing dishes of jellies and iced biscuits for the buffet. "Well," she said, "that's what happens with fostering, Mum. That's why Dad wanted you to give it up, because he saw you getting upset when the kids left."

She went out of the kitchen, grumbling about the heat to get herself away, and started again on the champagne.

"What was it?" Al said to Ada in the kitchen a few minutes later. Florence was there, trying not to listen, washing up faster than ever.

"She was having a baby and she went to a doctor. You know what I mean. It wasn't her fault. She says Ron and her aren't serious." Ada was piling mashed bananas onto bread and butter for the children.

Florence nearly dropped a plate but caught it efficiently and said, "That was a close one. It's a different washing-up powder. Slippery."

"You'd better go out there again, hadn't you?" Ada said to Al. A woman guest came in and asked for some hot water to warm a baby's bottle, so Ada had to help Florence move the tea urn, which took up all three gas rings.

"It's getting near the speeches. You'd better get out there," Ada said again.

Al wiped his forehead with a spotted handkerchief.

"I can hear they're into the cheese," Ada said. "Who's looking after the bar?"

"Ron."

"He's a nice boy."

"He doesn't like our dressing table."

"Well, he's got a degree from an art college, hasn't he. It stands to reason."

Al started to carry out a tray of cups. He looked back. "That about the doctor would have upset you," he said.

"I wish she hadn't done it."

Al put down the tray, and she stopped thinking about the lost baby and watched his face. He was good to her.

"You could always have looked after it," he said. The volume of the rock outside was terrific. "She shouldn't have got rid of it."

Two of the girls raced in with piles of dirty plates up their arms.

"Well, it's the modern thing, isn't it?" Ada said.

"It needn't have been difficult," he said, thinking of Willy's child, whom they never spoke about.

"You wouldn't have been glad of another brat in the house," Ada said.

"I wouldn't have minded."

"No, you never did. That's something you say, isn't it? 'I wouldn't have minded.'"

Al went out to stand on a chair and start the toasts.

"Boys and girls," he said to the guests, "I am calling on you to get into the spirit of giving this young couple a happy day." He was good at this, but today it came harder. The casualness. "A happy day. Here on my left is your host, Mr. Pickering. Look at his happy face. He is not gaining a son-in-law, he is losing a daughter."

The best man had gone into the street ten minutes ago, feeling unwell, so Al did his job by reading the telegrams. There were rather few, so he read out all the cards too, and added an old chestnut of his own that always worked. "I have here," he said, "a cable from a friend who seems to be in the fruit business. The message reads, 'An apple a day keeps the doctor away, but what can a pear do at night?' " He looked at the wedding couple and thought that they seemed fairly all right, given the circumstances, and then at Angelica and Ron, still both racing about with champagne, and thought that they were more than a bit all right, given a little good fortune. Ada was standing at the door of the kitchen so as to watch him, before she set up the narrow side tables for the buffet.

The girls and Ada and Al and Angelica cleared away the trestle tables. The guests sat around the edge of the room while they were doing it. One or two of the men made straight for the buffet tables unasked, but Ada stopped them. She always held it was right for the bride's mother to see first the spread that was laid out; after all, the bride's family was paying.

Florence was washing up as fast as before. Three buckets for the cutlery: one for the knives, one for the forks, one for the spoons. There was a beautiful box for the untouched remainders. They belonged to the bride's mother. Angelica and Ron were in there helping. Al was carrying a message from the bride's father to the band, asking for a conga. After a long wait, the band struck up: piano, drums, two guitars (electric). The combination was small, but it achieved a resplendent racket. Some people grumbled, but other couples danced. There was the feeling that ahead were thousands of lives that might be lived.

Autumn of a Dormouse

"Energy and pride are the roots of the best things we do: I think that's right," said Mrs. Abbott loudly to herself one night, winding up her alarm clock and setting it for five in order to think, five A.M. being for her a long-tested good time for thinking. "Without them, men and women are barren and without mercy." She poured herself another cup of tea from the brown English teapot she had brought from London long ago, and nodded off in a bed covered with travel brochures.

Mrs. Abbott was seventy-four. Her widowed son, Grafton, shared with her the legal custody of her grandson, Alexander, but the child had actually been brought up by her since his mother's death when he was two and merely visited by his father. The old lady and the boy had an affinity. They made imaginary trips through tropical forests and to strange islands far away from any mainland. Footprints in the sand, finger-marks on the mind.

Then Grafton, a rich stockbroker, married an heiress called Edna. He decided in a loving but rather theoretical mood to commandeer the boy. He and Edna had come to Mrs. Abbott at the beginning of a school term and taken Alexander away. The boy didn't want to leave his grandmother and the world of atlases, and he was miserably homesick at his new boarding school. It was the first time he had been away from what he thought of as home. He stuck it out for a term and even for a vacation spent at school. Grafton had thought it the least disturbing way to cope with the boy's time off, because he was going to be in Germany on business. Edna took Alexander out to tea twice. His grandmother refrained from telephoning because she thought it might be disturbing. Privately she cried for the boy.

Eventually, when the interminable next term had begun, he had telephoned his grandmother at her Detroit home secretly from a telephone booth, calling collect, three hours before she had taken herself to bed to think.

"I hate this place. Can I come and live with you like before?" he had said. "Why don't you call? Are you off me?"

"No, darling."

"Then why?"

"Because I thought you were someone else's business."

"Whose? Edna's been here. She's O.K. I think boarding school stinks."

"What are you eating?"

"A Baby Ruth."

"Oh, good."

"But why can't things be like they were?"

"Things never are."

"Damn, I've finished the Baby Ruth," the boy had said, kicking the telephone booth. "I suppose you'll be like grown-ups and say this is costing you a lot."

"The thing is, your father wants you with him, now that he's married again."

"But I'm *not* with him. I'm in this place. Anyway, Daddy's always abroad. The only person I see here who I know even a bit is Edna. She took me out to tea, and the food was great, but I upset her by not liking the clockwork toy she gave me. I tried to explain that clockwork toys are for children and she got cross and said she had a *rag doll* for when father was away and I wasn't making the proper adjustment. She wants me to go to a psychiatrist."

"I don't know about therapy for children," said Mrs. Abbott. "We never had it in England when I was a girl."

"That's what Edna said father expected you to say. He forbade me to write to you in vacation. He forbade me to telephone you any time at all."

"Then where are you?"

"I escaped from a botany trip. I'm in a phone booth."

"Why aren't you allowed to phone if *you* want to? I didn't want to break into things myself, as I said."

"But I've got your letter. Edna said that father said he thought a telephone call would be disturbing. What's disturbing?"

"He meant getting in your way. He meant it might throw you off balance."

"What's therapy?"

"A sort of doctoring. Therapy is for people with a lot of past, and by the time people have a lot of past my own hope would be that, given more experience, they would know enough to sort things out for themselves. Though some clever people don't agree."

"I don't want to go back to that place. Could you ring father? Edna said that she thought he'd be back by now for two days."

"I'll have a think about it."

The old lady nodded over her tea tray all night. At five o'clock the alarm went off. The sun was coming up, in its usual way. Mrs. Abbott got up with it, in her usual way. She dressed in sporting red, made the bed, and went downstairs to the atlas. At eight o'clock, when she had carried thought to a conclusion, she rang Edna.

"I'm still asleep. Who's that?" said Edna anxiously.

"Alexander's grandmother. I don't think he wants to go back to his school. He says he hasn't seen anyone he knows apart from you. It's been good of you to go."

Edna whispered, "Could I call you back? Grafton's still asleep and he might want to be on the extension when we're talking." (More loudly.) "Even the *birds* are hardly up."

Birds. Flight. To keep things in the air: that was the thing. Small Edna, intimidated, spending her time with a rag doll.

Edna rang back at nine o'clock and said loudly, for the obvious benefit of a listening Grafton, "We think Alexander belongs with his father and stepmother, even if Grafton's away on . . . Alexander would get fond of me."

"I could fetch him from the new school. He said to me in a

letter that it's like a swanky prison. I could look after him again willingly," said Mrs. Abbott.

"His brain would turn to mould if he went back to live with you. Forgive me. With an old lady, though," said Edna.

"But he was so happy, and now he seems so troubled."

"When?" said Edna.

"He rang me last night."

"Your imaginary trips up the Amazon. Though he *is* crazy about them."

"I have a plan for him. I promise you and his father that it will work. I've got it all thought out. Something more interesting and educational than joshing in changing-rooms."

Grafton finally spoke. "Hello, mother. You're not the right company for a young boy."

"It's as well that you declared yourself to be on the extension at last," said Mrs. Abbott to this man of affairs who was, she still couldn't forget, her loved child. "It would be different about Alexander if the boy ever saw you."

"Let it be, mother," said Grafton. "He needs other boys, and men schoolteachers. The constant companionship of a lady of seventy-three isn't appropriate for him now that he's growing up."

"Seventy-four."

"Mother, let it *be,* I said. Leave it to us. You're bigoted about therapy. You're being fuddy-duddy." Grafton cut off the call.

"Or concerned," said Edna. "After all, she has looked after the boy a long time."

Edna kissed her husband goodbye. He was going to Japan. He always made it clear that it would be "A waste of your time to come with me. You'd be lonely." She started to look at an atlas in melancholy, and tried laughing at herself, though anyone else would have considered her one of the most fortunate and beautiful brides in America.

The child rang his grandmother again the next night for fortitude. He was running away and coming tomorrow, he said. He had his knapsack packed.

After her think, the old lady had withdrawn $69,000-odd of savings in cash from her bank. It was money her son didn't know of. She had been keeping it for hospital bills, old-age home bills, or to leave to Alexander. At a Detroit travel office she had bought eighteen open return tickets to Rome from Kennedy. "First Class," she said. "Mrs. Abbott, initial E for Emma, and Mr. Abbott, initial A for Alexander."

"One passport as you're a married couple, or are you on separate ones?" said the girl in the travel office.

"Mr. Abbott is ten."

"'That's a half fare, then." (No humour, poor child, thought Mrs. Abbott.)

"And one and a half one-way first-class connections for Mr. Abbott and myself from Detroit to Kennedy."

Alexander arrived, sobbing, with a knapsack. Mrs. Abbott told him what they were going to do. "Fly to New York, then take an evening flight to Rome, which arrives at breakfast time in Rome, though it's the middle of the night for us."

"You're not serious," said Alexander. "Daddy would be furious if you took me abroad."

"It's only abroad in a manner of speaking. Just to keep us both amused while they think about things for you. I don't think they've had a jolt yet. Grafton often needed a jolt when he was a little boy."

"Granny, this would be more than a jolt."

"I've sorted out the timetable. We'd catch our breath and take the lunchtime flight from Rome back to New York."

"It would cost a lot of dough."

"The lunchtime flight arrives at early suppertime in New York, except that if you hang on for a couple of hours you can have a terrific dinner on the plane when we do the turn-around to Rome again that evening. And so on, every day. Think of it! Rome!"

"We'd hardly have time to see it," said the boy excitedly.

"We never do anyway, on our most successful trips. We can read on the journey. We're going first class. Nothing but the best."

The boy looked at a pile of travel books held by a book strap at the front door, beside other smaller things neatly stacked.

"Suppose father tried to stop us," said the boy. "He went on and on about wanting to have me now that he's married again."

"Your father's away as usual. Japan. Then the Common Market countries. I thought of Japan, but the flight times don't fit. This works perfectly." She planted her slim hands down firmly, as if they were paperweights to save a rare manuscript from flying away in the wind.

"Suppose Edna tried to stop us, then?"

"She's got no technical right. But do you want to ask her about coming with me?"

"Not much."

"Don't be short with her, Alexander."

"She's all right, but she doesn't give herself time to think."

"Don't worry about Edna taking us away from each other, if that's what you've decided upon. She's got no legal rights. I'm your next of kin after your father. And as far as poor over-travelled Grafton's concerned, what we'll do is leave him a nice letter on the door here to save a stamp and the give-away of the postmark date. We'll just say something reassuring and permanent. 'Dearest Grafton, Alexander is quite safe. He and I have gone to Rome. Returning to Kennedy tomorrow.' "

"You're not doing wrong," said Alexander. "School is boring. I learn more with you. Edna's kind. In fact, I feel sorry for her, never seeing father. Though he's not very nice to her when he does see her: he sleeps, mostly, and talks on the telephone to Hong Kong."

"Perhaps it's jet-lag."

"Isn't that what we'll have? Jet-lag all the time?"

"We'll stay on New York time there and back. That's the great merit of daily flying. That, and the first-class service, and the fact that no one could say anything about non-consultation when we'll be in touch with your father or Edna in your own country every single day. We wouldn't actually have to go through immigration in Rome, even. Not every time, if we were tired."

Alexander looked at her alarm clock, which was on the tea tray she had brought down to do the washing up, and noticed the time it had been set at.

"Could you have a nap?" he said. "I'll guard the door."

"We've got our plane to catch to New York. For between, I have a plan for us, involving a boat. I won't say more. A short travelling surprise between flights; I can tell you that much. And I'm bringing some provisions. Chocolate for strength, biscuits, fruit, glucose tablets."

"They eat glucose and chocolate when they're going up Everest."

"We shall be flying very high ourselves. Did I tell you we weren't going economy? First class! Think of it! It's the only way. Not that I ever have before, you understand. This is an adventure. I wish it could be the Nile or Tibet but I thought your father might be angry or worried with our not being able to get back in a day."

"Why not Greece? I should have thought you'd want to go to Greece, being a classical place. My new school gave up classics long ago. We can take Spanish, or the Spanish guitar if we're dumb." He paused, and said with bitter pride, "I take Spanish."

"I thought of Greece," said his grandmother. "In fact, I longed to show it to you as much as Rome, but we wouldn't like the present politics and the flights are very long. Rome is perfect. Did you know I spent my honeymoon there?"

"What happens when the money runs out, Granny?" said Alexander, looking at her carefully.

"We'll have to see. The right things flow from the right decisions, and this is a right decision, wouldn't you say?" He still looked concerned, so she played a game of chess with him until they could leave by the taxi she aristocratically ordered. The driver took a long time to come, scenting in her a thrifty nature, but she tipped him handsomely.

"Isn't it fine," she said, putting her arms round Alexander's shoulders, "travelling so light? You in your jeans, with a change of underthings and shirts. Me in my travelling suit, which adapts to any climate."

"And your books," said Alexander. "And the provisions, and your spare clothes. Do you always carry an open basket?" Someone long ago had called her a frank packer.

They took the plane to New York, and then a taxi to a park with a lake that offered electrically driven bumper boats. The chaos of children steering so as to bump into someone else's rubber fenders as hard as possible was controlled by a woman in naval uniform with a megaphone.

Mrs. Abbott climbed into a boat. Alexander steered. Their boat was number fifteen.

"Number four, keep away from number six. He's younger than you are," shouted the lady with the megaphone. "Number thirty-six, this is your fifteenth trip! Come in this instant!" (Pause.) "Do as I *say*, number thirty-six." (Pause.) "Number twenty-four, you'll pay for behaviour like that! I'm going to turn your electricity off." Number twenty-four suddenly floated silently in the middle of the water, becalmed. The little boy in it dived desperately into the lake in his jeans and T-shirt, swam for the shore, and ran.

"An adventurous spirit," said Mrs. Abbott admiringly. "Have you ever heard of Judy Holliday?"

"No," said Alexander. "I like the name."

"You'd have liked her. She was very funny. She was an actress. She would have acted that lady perfectly. Isn't the naval uniform dashing? Though I don't think she was quite fair to number twenty-four."

"He was a good diver. Can you still dive?"

"If I'm on my mettle."

Alexander didn't know what mettle was, but guessed it in context. He bought his grandmother another trip with his own pocket money and let her steer. She did it with panache. The woman with the megaphone looked nonplussed and made no comment on her skillfully taken risks.

The old lady and her grandson drove to Kennedy by taxi to check in. "Only hand baggage," said Mrs. Abbott.

"Duty-free goods can be collected on the flight," said the check-in girl.

"We shan't be needing anything as we're travelling first class. We don't smoke."

"Mementos? Perfume? Accessories?"

"We'll be back shortly. As to accessories, I don't suppose they have anything by Molyneux here, do they? Molyneux seems to be a forgotten name," said Mrs. Abbott.

"He's something to do with show business, isn't he?"

"No. He made my wedding dress, but it was long ago. Never mind. Other people recall him. Memories for old details are probably limited to people with time, and you must be very busy. Do we need to book our return flights from Rome for tomorrow?"

The girl raised her eyebrows but punched a computer. "A return trip straightaway would be very tiring."

"My grandson needs to be back. But you say it's not difficult to get on any flights we want."

The airline official looked at her, having seen the wadge of tickets in her bag. "Are you planning to take many flights? You realize you'll be subject to search of the person as well as of hand baggage?"

"Very wise. Is there somewhere we could rest until the flight is called? I saw you looking at my other tickets. You have to realize that I come from England and the English have always been great travellers. Lady Mary Wortley Montagu, Lady Hester Stanhope, Byron, Lawrence of Arabia, to speak of only four. Of course, they had to do it largely by camel and mule. But a 747 can be made to seem quite spirited if one tries. Unfortunately our schedule doesn't allow for camels."

"You asked for somewhere you could rest. You could go to our first-class lounge. Would you like a vehicle? A wheelchair?"

"We've just been on a bumper boat and we're used to getting about ourselves. But thank you."

In the first-class lounge she had a lime-juice and Alexander had a Coca-Cola. Then she had a cup of black coffee. "I don't want to miss the fun. Though we must get our sleep. We arrive in Rome at two in the morning by our watches. I think we should stay permanently on American time for your father's sake. It makes a link. I wonder if he does the same for Edna's sake in Japan? Rome will be buzzing and we don't want to be drowsy for that."

On the aeroplane they had champagne and then caviare, smoked salmon and *foie gras*. Alexander liked the *foie gras*, especially the bread and butter.

"Don't fill yourself up. There'll be more to come," said Mrs. Abbott.

There was a choice of chicken à la Kiev or roast beef. Mrs. Abbott told Alexander about the cathedrals of Kiev. Later on they watched a film so bad they took their headphones off. Alexander produced a bottle of aspirin.

"I smuggled these through the search area," he said. "I swiped them at school for you because I know you don't sleep very well. I've got your chocolate. I prefer chocolate as a way of going to sleep. Counting sheep never works, but rationing the squares of chocolate does."

Mrs. Abbott put on a pair of dark glasses to rest. Her grandson was quietly impressed by her debonair ease as a traveller.

"Are you asleep?" she whispered, after a time.

"No."

"Do you want a comic? I bought a supply."

Alexander read himself nearly to sleep and then said, "Tell me about learning Latin."

"I'm wondering what would interest you. Not the ablative absolute, not *ut* with the subjunctive. There are some jokes in Latin, but they're not exactly funny jokes. For instance, '*lucus a non lucendo.*' That means, 'the sacred grove ("is so named" is understood: that's ellipsis) from its not shining.' "

"I expect it's a pun. That would be why it doesn't make us laugh," said Alexander sympathetically.

"Yes. *Lucus* means sacred grove. There's a lot about *lucus* in Virgil and Cicero. It also means light, which is the pun about it and the paradox. There isn't much to the remark nowadays on account of the sacred grove being out of date," said Mrs. Abbott.

"And Latin," said Alexander.

Mrs. Abbott lifted her dark glasses up onto her white hair.

"You look like a woman pilot in the old days. The aspirin haven't worked, have they? You must get some sleep," Alexander said.

"I was thinking about people saying 'no.' It might interest you to know that there's no formal word in Latin for 'No.' Or 'Yes', for that matter. You just construct the question with *num* or *nonne* in the right place, expecting the answer 'Yes' or 'No.' The difficulty is the answer, but there are ways to do it. In fact, I think 'Yes' and 'No' come too easily in English." She pulled her glasses over her eyes again. "For instance, if I'd been able to construct my questions about our trips to your father expecting the answer 'Yes'—if I'd been able to speak to him in any civilized circumstances instead of on an extension, that is—then I think we'd have been able to spend weeks in Rome together seeing all sorts of things. As it is, we'll imagine them."

"Will you be sued for libel?"

"Libel is about something written."

"But you're still taking a risk."

"No. We're taking a trip. We're taking a step. Nothing legally wrong or morally unkind. Do you know what I mean? You listen very well. You must be a joy to teach."

"But there's danger somewhere, I can tell. To you. At my age, I should be looking after you when Daddy's away."

"Your grandfather, who knew you quite well though you can't remember him, is a great source of strength. We're having a spree. One should be allowed sprees. People will tell us we're eccentric, but everyone's eccentric when you get to know them, thank goodness."

"Another aspirin wouldn't hurt you." Alexander read the label on the bottle. "It says two or three for an adult dose, and you're much more than an adult." They slept.

In Rome they decided to stay in the transit area without going through immigration. "Immigration's a waste of time," said Mrs. Abbott. "This way we can have a nap before catching the plane back, and read my books about Rome." She bought a few more travel books with pictures at a bookshop and said, "I don't understand Italian apart from musical terms and lines from arias, but one can generally puzzle it out with the aid of French and Latin."

"Don't they speak Latin even in small parts of Rome any longer? What a disappointment for you."

"I managed at the newsagent. The young lady was very nice."

"Tell me about your honeymoon here."

"I brought some photographs with me. This is the Colosseum. Your grandfather took the pictures. I had to stand absolutely still because the exposure was very slow."

"You were pretty then, too," Alexander said. He studied her now, lost in the way she laid her hands flat and hushed her voice when she was finding something exciting. "I hadn't realized you were pretty even when grandfather knew you."

"You're the first man who's said to that to me for a long time." She paused, shy. "About Rome: let's see. It's built on seven hills."

"What are they?"

"Palatine, Quirinal, Capitoline, Viminal, and I forget the others."

"I expect you forgot because it's boring."

"Romulus traced the outline of Rome in 753 B.C. Romulus and Remus were twins and they were thrown into a river called the Tiber and abandoned to a she-wolf."

Alexander decided against saying, "Like me."

His grandmother said, "It might cheer you up that St. Peter's is built on what used to be Nero's Circus."

"Oh good, but don't Roman Catholics mind?"

"None I know."

"You're not at all like a she-wolf."

"The twin who founded Rome turned into a god." She hugged the child, who so abandoned dignity that he curled up on the plastic airport sofa and went to sleep in her arms. She looked out of the window and thought of her husband, of her son, of Rome. When the child woke up she said, "You've only had three hours' sleep but we can rest as we're flying back."

In the plane, Alexander said, "Did you sleep at all?"

"Now and again. I will in a minute."

"Try now."

"The trouble is, I'm hungry."

More champagne, caviare, *foie gras* and smoked salmon. "Could we both have bacon and eggs?" said Mrs. Abbott. "It's breakfast time for us."

The airline purser, after some hubbub in the galley, offered two hamburgers. "We carry these in case of smaller children," he said cautiously, not wishing to offend Alexander. "We can't manage bacon and eggs. Beverage? Bloody Mary, perhaps? A virgin Mary for the young gentleman?"

"What's a virgin Mary?" said Alexander.

"In this case," said Mrs. Abbott, "it's tomato juice and Worcestershire sauce. You haven't any tea?"

"We could make you some, I suppose. There'll be espresso coffee later," said the purser.

"It would keep my grandmother awake," said Alexander, craning across Mrs. Abbott to look at things. "Look, there's an island bang in the middle of that river. What a place to live!"

"The Tiber."

*   *   *

In New York they did a quick turn around, pausing only long enough for Mrs. Abbott to send a telegram to her son saying "Alexander very well love mother," and caught the flight back to Rome. They were again offered magnificent wine, Beluga caviare and *foie gras*.

"We're hungry for it this time," said Alexander.

The stewardess looked at Mrs. Abbott and asked if they had been flying recently.

"Yes. This morning we came from Rome and they kindly offered us these things at breakfast time when we wanted bacon and eggs. I think we'll splurge again on headphones."

The stewardess called the purser, who knelt beside Mrs. Abbott and said, "Don't forget you can order anything you like in first class provided you order it in advance. If we'd known you wanted bacon and eggs . . . Our film is *Mame*."

"Oh, we've seen it. What a pity. About the food; champagne and Coca-Cola and caviare now is splendid. It was earlier in the day we wanted eggs and bacon."

They both slept well through the film, and woke with enough appetite to tackle the breakfast croissants.

"I haven't told you about how your grandfather and I came to Italy," said Mrs. Abbott. "We travelled by what was called 'hard.' Fourth class. Wooden seats. On the Simplon-Orient Express. We couldn't get over the excitement of it. At every frontier the wagon-restaurant that the well-off used would be unhitched, and luggage would be inspected, which took time. And then, at five one morning, we were over the Italian border, and people on the platform were shouting 'Cappuccino,' and we drank strong sweet milky coffee."

"What's Rome like?"

"The sky's a beautiful strong blue. There's a lot of golden stone that looks as if the last of the sun has soaked the place, like a street left by strolling people at dusk. And a great deal of marble, and old walls, and high columns. Three of the columns belong to a temple to Castor and Pollux that was built two thousand five hundred years ago. Now we'll do some school work. I bought a book about mathematics so you can teach me about sets. When I was at university we did maths by a different system."

Alexander groaned, and went to sleep. When he woke up

they were over Rome and his grandmother was looking down at the Circus Maximus. "It held twenty-five thousand people. Think of Domitian standing on the highest towers of his palace and looking at all the people he commanded. He wasn't a good ruler. And look at the aqueducts, see? Where it's green. That's the Roman Campagna. And do you see the triumphal arch? The Brecht theatre company in East Berlin has a beautiful plaster model of a Roman triumphal arch for *Coriolanus*. It swivels round on a revolve, and there's a stockade on the other side for the battle between Coriolanus and Aufidius. I saw the revolve. The company travels with it. *Coriolanus* is by Shakespeare."

"Was that a real journey to Berlin?" said Alexander.

"Yes. Your grandfather liked the company very much. Do you know something? There's a temple down there that has the most ancient inscription in Rome. It was found in 1899. It's what they call a boustrophedon. One reads it first from left to right and then the next line from right to left. You used to make up notes that way when you could first write, as a trick for me to puzzle out. I was very impressed, though for some reason your father thought it was a sign you were unhinged when I showed him one. Remember 'boustrophedon.' Though it doesn't really matter what things are called. It's having the new ideas that counts."

That day they washed some drip-dry things in the Rome cloakroom and went through immigration to hang them up in two lockers to be worn next day. They took thirty-seven round trips altogether. When the money was getting low and Mrs. Abbott was wondering where life could run to next, Edna and Grafton and an attorney were standing inside immigration in New York. Airline officials who had started by happily accepting the huge scale of ticket-buying had to begin to investigate to look responsible, and leaked the story so that there would be publicity for the airline. Newsmen and photographers jostled behind Grafton and Edna as Alexander and Mrs. Abbott hugged the family.

"We tracked you down through the telegrams," said Grafton.

"You didn't even use false names, which was foolish of you," said the attorney.

"How long have you been back? You speak as if I didn't want you to find us," said Mrs. Abbott to Grafton.

"A week."

"Poor Edna," said Mrs. Abbott. "With you away, if she was worried."

"I started a law suit against you in Luxembourg but I'll drop it now that you've brought Alexander back."

"I never took him away. We were in New York every day."

"What were you doing?" said an aged newsman.

"My grandmother likes travelling and so do I," said Alexander.

"What made you come back every day? Very tiring for an old heart," said a ruder cub reporter.

(Alexander had been asked that once, too, on their first rapid return. His wits about him, as usual, he had said: "We forgot to lock a screen door back home and had to take care of it.")

Edna tried to hug Alexander and take him away. Alexander kicked and screamed. "I want to stay with Granny. I want to be an airline pilot."

"We'll meet next weekend?" said Mrs. Abbott to Grafton, Edna and Alexander.

"I'll be in Brussels," said Grafton.

"You'll be hearing from us," said the attorney quietly to Mrs. Abbott as the group led the hysterical boy away. Suddenly he skipped loose to run back to his grandmother. He gave her the locker key for Rome, where her clothes were drying, and the remains of his pocket money. And half a bar of chocolate; "Instead of *foie gras*," he said.

"I'll write to you from Rome at once," said his grandmother. "And then I'll take a breathing space, and then I'll be back."

She had enough money left for an economy flight back to Rome, and a quiet hotel life there for a short time. Her son grew in admiration of her. Her address was the Hotel Inghilterra. Grafton remembered it was where she had spent her honeymoon. "What I don't understand is the money you spent," he said in a letter to her just as the cash was starting to run out, and her life with it, as old lives do. "You usually economized so much."

"Ah," thought Mrs. Abbott, "but it was worth the try. He'll see the point later."

Those of the hotel staff who had been there for fifty years remembered her as always having been a courtly woman. They were pleased at her deftness at learning Italian at her age. However, as she had said to Alexander, it wasn't knowing the names of things that counted, it was having the ideas. In her last days, while she was standing in the Forum and wishing Alexander were there, whom she wrote to regularly, she was planning to get a visa for China.

Stephanie, Stephen,
Steph, Steve

She had been christened in 1929. Stephanie Angelica Bysshe Talbot, with the surname of Duncan, at the Cumberland family seat. One of the family seats. There were three. Her mother was also named Stephanie, it having been laid down by her overbearing great-great-grandfather Stephen, on her father's side, in his will, that any and all descendants and descendants' spouses or beneficiaries were to be christened, or to adopt the name by deed poll, Stephen or Stephanie, in honor of the aforesaid Stephen's repute and his fortune.

And as to these three family seats, the baby Stephanie's mother, Stephanie, had been saying to her husband for a long time that she wished a fraction of this withering fortune could be spent on chairs designed for sitting without bruises, adapted to reading, or writing, or thinking.

"A total of two hundred and seventy-one Cromwellian studded-leather chairs in three counties cries out for a few reading chairs, doesn't it? Upholstered, possibly? Some cushions?"

"The places were not originally architected to be originally furnished that way."

"But originally was a long time ago, seen from now. It isn't as though we had roast swan for dinner every night."

"I don't see how such things as you suggest would fit in."

"We could make at least one room *possible* to live in. Without offense to the rest of the house. Couldn't we?"

"I don't see how."

Seats and chairs. Stephanie drove into the market town and bought six deck chairs. Visibly glad that Stephanie had made the move, Stephen even liked the chairs' canvas.

"I haven't ever seen canvas before, except as sails. Interesting. I must say you look much more comfortable now. Stephanie, you *are* much more comfortable?"

"Yes, much. I don't suppose one's ever exactly comfortable when one's eight months pregnant."

"You've made the room very pretty." He looked round again at the room: the yellow cushions, his wife in muslin reading, the white voile curtains blowing. He touched one of the curtains, thinking not to be seen, and she laughed and said, "That was like the business with hugging the bookcase in Chekhov. The curtains are made of nearly the same stuff as my dress." She held out her hands. "You *could* even touch the dress." He was not then alert to irony, but she remembered that he had once said—later apologizing—"When you hug me you hurt me."

"There are some chocs over there," she said: she making time, and he glad of it. He brought them and said quickly, "I've got to go away to the shipyard. Before that, I'm going to sail round the country. I shan't be here when the baby's born. And don't plead."

She stayed quiet.

"And don't hold your tongue."

"You've left out 'either.' You need it. Because of the contradiction," she said. Pause. "Don't worry. There'd be nothing you could do anyway, and births happen every minute, and I know it would be wretched for you not to be able to help. Let's play Truisms. The truisms that aren't true."

"The trouble is that we must have played them all by now."

"Stephen, let your mind wander. What about the dinner party we had the night before last? That was fairly flush with them. 'The best things in life are free.' "

"That was said by the woman who'd inherited sixty-five million in tinned soups."

" 'You can always tell a lady by her accessories.' "

He said quickly, pleased, " 'You deserve the best.' It's the hallmark of stinginess."

" 'New York isn't America.' "

" 'It's not the heat, it's the humidity.' "

"Have you been seeing a lot of tropical people lately?"

"No, but one stores things up."

"This is one turned round the way it should be," said Stephen. " 'When you've lain on your bed, you must make it.' "

"Yes," said Stephanie. "Well done. 'When people are angry they say a lot of things that they mean.' When are you leaving? I could tell it would be soon."

"Tomorrow."

When the baby Stephanie was born, she had a sprouting of red hair. It was the chemical color that hair can turn on the skulls of the long-buried. "One of us here to straddle time," thought her mother, as if quoting. There are many clichés about the hope carried into a house by the newborn, but this one's character was different, and everyone who spent time with her saw it. She clearly already knew the dark side of life, though she was rapturous company from the start. Her mother foresaw in flashes the course of Stephanie's youth, prowess, age. In one dream she dreamed "Bankrupt of life, yet prodigal of ease." She woke, still thinking of Dryden, and looked at the baby in her cradle. She wrote a letter to Stephen saying that the baby was a girl and that, as she was going to have to be called Stephanie, her mamma was ready to answer to Steph if absolutely necessary, or to anything else except Stuffy, which her governess had called her before her adenoids were taken out. She had nowhere to send the letter except to the shipyard, where her husband was not due for two months. She died that night.

A few letters, necessarily without return addresses, arrived from her husband during that time. Unemployment was growing all over the North, but it took him a while to gather the situation. Starting as he did from Land's End, he noticed first the swing of the sardine harvest away from the coast of Cornwall. He did what he could about the fishermen who were out of luck. At poor times of night, when he was incapable of saying to himself how much he missed Stephanie, he would stomp into the cabin of one or another of his crew and bring out maps to get on with things, though once he bawled, "I should be up there! Driven out of my own house!" Then, of course, a difficult apology. First babies, thought the crew, sleepy and resentful.

A letter, 1929

My darling,

Today—no, tonight, I can't sleep for my concern about you—a St. Ives meeting about the sardines.

Tomorrow we set off. Our itinerary will come to you as soon as possible.

S.

A letter, 1929

My darling,

Sleep still impossible. A lot of fishermen still out of work, though some moved to tin mining. Now: St. Clears, Carmarthen, Llandovery, Trecastle, Brecon, Hay, Hereford (a few miles further inland—nearer to you, my heart), the Outer Hebrides, many other places you wouldn't know of, no addresses of inns or pubs or digs to give you, so we *are* in the dark, aren't we. I am sure you are looking as beautiful as ever. Then I go to the shipyard. How I long to see you. Would you be your usual sweet self and ask Mrs. Watson to get in plenty of salted butter and a supply of potted shrimps nearer arrival, because there will be quite a few of us and I know that would go down well? Have snatched some time from the tiller to write some of the poetry of mine that you like, though I remember being v. hurt by several literary experiments that you said were "pensive-couch department." You see how seriously I take your criticism. I trust you will be as rapt by these endeavors as I am; and how the baby will enjoy them. Any letters you have written, though we know writing isn't your forte, will best find me at the shipyard.

Again and again,
my dear love,
Your husband

A letter, 1929

MY DARLING,

High winds. Shall have this posted as soon as possible.
I forgot to mention that the crew greatly likes beer, so
Mrs. Watson should get in a goodly supply.

> In haste,
> YOUR HUSBAND

When Stephen eventually reached his family shipyard on
the Northeast Coast, he found two-thirds of the men laid off.
He had had no idea of what the crisis could come to. He also
found many letters from Stephanie, carefully dated, giving him
newspaper cuttings and, at length, her own understanding of
the national situation. She had the intent focus that he was
later to find in his daughter. It was in her last letter that she
had given him the news of the baby's birth. And then telegrams from Mrs. Watson and from the Cumberland doctor,
telling him of Stephanie's death. His secretary, Mary, at the
shipyard, still working but without income, had opened the
telegrams and thought it best to put them on top of Stephanie's letters to him. He seemed to Mary to wish her to stay in
his office for a while.

"We must do something about these office chairs, mustn't
we," he said.

She made a note.

"I don't know what to do next. I mean what to do first."

She waited a long while indeed.

"Can we get hold of Mrs. Watson? I'm sorry, can *you,* and
when you do I'll come in straightaway? I've got to go out for
a breath of air." He lifted his spectacles and consulted her face
in request, for the first time in their knowledge of each other.
"You must have been working for months for no money," he
said.

"There isn't any."

She got Mrs. Watson and then the doctor. As she heard
Stephen speaking, he sounded so ice-cold that Mary found him
a blanket and some hot water. In the deserted shipyard there
was no chance of tea.

"Where are the other directors, Mary?"

"Down South. There's a certain hostility from the men, sir."

"There are some documents I need." Agreements, contracts, his own bank statements, his assets. He wrote a list. He telephoned the other directors to tell them what he was going to do. They disagreed violently with him. So he acted on his own. He telephoned the unions concerned. He spoke to them with liberty, and they agreed to call a mass meeting of the laid-off men the next day. In the night, in his office, it could be said that he had a crackup. From three to five was the worst time to get through. The men gathered without sense of purpose at seven-thirty or thereabouts. No point in being on time when there was no work. He thought that he wasn't an open speaker, but his character seemed to Mary much changed.

"Not much doing, is there? Well, there should be, and I've talked to the other directors, they're all down South, and I've talked to the unions, and we ask you to build a ship."

A voice from the crowd yelled, "What's she called?"

"*Talbot,*" shouted Stephen. "H.M.S. *Talbot.* Who's willing? To get back to work at your proper wages?"

Another voice from the cloth-capped crowd: "Who's paying?"

Stephen: "Our company."

A ship engineer: "Bliddy company. Like enough *they'd* fork out. I'd eat my hat. You're the only bigwig who's shown his face at last. Known how much the dole is?"

Stephen gave the wretched amount. Though he didn't like separating himself from the directors who were making their way on the stock market down South, he came out with it: "I'm paying for this ship. The unions have your contracts, underwritten by me. You've got my word. You've turned up and I've turned up and I want you all to sign and you can stand me a pint when I'm broke. Who'll come in?"

The hands went up. Over three-quarters of the men.

Stephen went on: "Your contracts are in the office, with Mary and me. We want this ship by the end of the year."

A voice from the crowd: "You weren't here for two month, mate."

"See here," shouted Stephen. "We all turned up, didn't we?"

Having financed the ship from his own shares in the company and with much of his own fortune, Stephen was hardly a rich man any longer. He managed to keep his place in the company, though none of the other directors agreed with his compliance with the unions. He sold all three of the family seats, thinking often of Stephanie's wish for comfortable chairs and of her amicably combative presence. Living now in the West Lodge of the Cumberland house, lying in the double bed that he and Stephanie had so long shared, he had the docile hallucination that she was lying beside him. He got up quietly and shaved and made their breakfast. In the kitchen he thought of the bed, still the same, the yellow curtains she had wanted, the deck chairs. Even if they were in a minute cottage, nothing of consequence had changed, he thought. A man should shave before breakfast, and Stephanie should have breakfast in bed, he thought. He carried the breakfast up the small stairs. He talked to Mrs. Watson through her bedroom door and went into the nursery to whistle to the baby. Covering the tray with a pram blanket, he whistled bits of a Handel sarabande and "Voi che sapete" and the mandolin song from *Don Giovanni*. But when he went into the big bedroom, no movement from the double bed. Still stirred by the force of his wish to meet obligations about which he knew himself to have been faulty, he looked at the grandfather clock that had been moved from the big house, found it telling 5:10; corrected his own watch that told 8:45, thinking that it had stopped the night before; and sat with the baby. At 6:15 by his newly set watch, Mrs. Watson came in to the small Stephanie. He picked up the breakfast tray for two and said to her, "I'm just going down to redo our boiled eggs and heat up our coffee."

"Coffee boiled is coffee spoiled, sir," she said, nodding, wondering what to do with this man out of his wits.

"Mrs. Duncan still asleep, Mrs. Watson."

"Yes, sir."

"Sleeping quite heavily. On the usual side of the bed, of course. Not that anything else is usual for the moment. But the ship's coming along. That's one thing." He took the breakfast tray back to the kitchen, timed two new boiled eggs, made new coffee, carried the renewed tray upstairs, and sat at the bottom of the hump in the bedclothes for a while, until he realized that the hump was on his side of the bed and marked where he had briefly slept that night. Stephanie's side of the bed was now quite flat. But she had been there all night with him, he felt sure. He thought for a long while, rang the local telephone operator for the time, reset the clock and his watch to the time the watch had been keeping in the first place. But he had been perfectly awake. The making of the breakfast had been no dream. A man gone bonkers wouldn't be able to time boiled eggs, would he? He ate one of the cooling eggs, then the second one, so as not to be faithless to such a powerfully rational tray. Even as he drove to the shipyard, still not late, he found it hard to believe that a reasonable man could make such a dark error. In a half-awake nightmare, possibly. But fully awake, and in daylight. At the shipyard, he telephoned Mrs. Watson and tried to be level, to ask her to clear away the breakfast tray, to say lightly that he had made a mistake, to ask about young Stephanie. He missed his wife more than ever. He used the word "hallucination" to himself with severe irony. "*I* should have washed the breakfast tray," he muttered to himself. "It can't be so. She must be there. I'm *not* bonkers." He thought, with his chin on his hands, and then signed a pile of checks that Mary had left for him in the folder marked "For signature today." Today being, presumably, today.

"Is today today?" he asked Mary, pulling down the points of his waistcoat.

"Yes, sir."

"And I haven't gone mad?"

"No, sir," she said, looking at the date on the checks he had signed.

"In that case, the folder you yesterday must have marked 'today' isn't very clear, is it? A dive into delirium, I should call it. Put the *date* on the folder in future, in pencil, then rub it out, and when you're writing 'today' on what will always be yesterday, put the *date* of the next today. Is that clear? Oh, and this folder about things to be done, which you call 'Bring back.' Apart from its sounding like a command to a dog about a bone, and you know I don't like dogs, I think you mean 'Bring *forward*.' The folder holds the things getting nearer to us. So it's obviously 'Bring forward.' Nearer to us." Angry with her for not being Stephanie and for being alive, he added, "It's a matter of asking for action *sooner*, don't you see? For movement *forward*. Not *later*, movement *away* from you. Unless the you is someone standing at the end of the time continuum? Look up 'continuum' in the *O.E.D.* if you don't know it."

"I only have a *Secretary's Friend*." He looked at her minute dictionary, with its dolefully wrong information about subtleties and roots, and thought it no friend. In the shipyard's lunch hour he went out and bought her the two-volume *O.E.D.*

"It's called 'The Shorter,' " she said. "Shorter than what? It's huge. Oh dear, it would have been costly." She went to the office kitchen, saying "Thank you," and made him a cup of the deep-black coffee that he liked, from the freshly ground beans called Continental.

"The proper one, the plain *Oxford English Dictionary*, volumes and volumes of it, would be a weight to look things up in, I thought." He took the coffee and thanked her. "But I can picture you being very happy with the complete, so we can go a bust on it later as an office expense when there's anything coming in to put expenses against."

"You do cleave to the next thing, sir."

"I'm afraid I don't. This morning early I slithered downstairs and got a breakfast tray for Mrs. Duncan and me, because she was asleep in the bed beside me and I waited, and she wasn't. Wasn't there."

Mary read the dictionary. "Interesting word here, sir. 'Wanhope.' Why should it mean despair? It says 'archaic' anyway."

"What would it mean to you?"

"Hope despite everything." She had some of her own tea— very sweet, a blend that was free if you collected enough coupons—and said in the manner of a dictionary, "2. Fragile hope."

"As there's no reliable country address for me now, let's address everything from the shipyard. Even personal letters, you see. If I have to go down South, you'll open everything. Otherwise I'll be here every day as usual. But starting at twelve noon, because I want to see Stephanie in the mornings. The baby Stephanie."

Stephen employed a tutor for Stephanie when she was ten. The tutor, called Steve, which further complicated things, was just down from Oxford. Steve and Mrs. Watson got on, except that Mrs. Watson had trouble with his habit of asking her in to sherry at six-thirty each evening in his bedroom, heavy with the smell of his pipe.

"This room has a Scots mist of your tobacco, Steve. You don't seem able to read a book without smoking. There's a shaggy Highland-cattle stink about the place. Cumberland isn't Scotland, Steve."

"Your usual sherry? Let's choose another topic."

"Pardon?"

"At an Oxford tutorial one always agrees on a topic. Then one—oneself and one's tutor—talks about it."

Mrs. Watson smoothed her apron and felt young. She got up, using the bottom of Steve's bedstead as a ballet barre, and danced. High kicks, done facing away from him, because she wasn't dressed for it.

"You've got an extraordinary turnout," he said, responding. "I'd no idea."

"It's not my own. It's modeled on Jessie Matthews' in *Evergreen*. I think I could have been something of a star if I'd had enough of a mirror. You can't practice without a nice big mirror. Mrs. Duncan gave me one when she saw my interest. It must have cost the earth. But a bird got into my room and smashed it, and I wouldn't have asked for another. That being in the big house, of course. There wouldn't be room here anyway. So I do it in the bathroom and while I'm washing up. I got a biggish old mirror, and I prop it up under the sink so that I can put in an hour or two of work after dinner. Propped on the floor, you understand. An acrobat once said to me that he liked to work full figure."

"What are you drinking?" Steve asked when she had sat down.

"It's a port-and-lemon. I can't quite get on with your sherry. It makes me feel fuzzy. Not that I'm not accustomed to wines. When I'm simmering a salmon, there's always two tablespoons of white cooking wine in the stock. I expect you'll have noticed."

"I thought it might be vinegar."

"It may have gone off. I'm not a taster. You see how a conversation can move? It doesn't need a push from your Oxford things. We've talked about smoking, Oxford, Jessie Matthews, mirrors, wine, and very pleasant it's been."

"What happened to Mr. Watson, if I may ask?"

"We were in service together. Nineteen twenty-one it would have been. I was a book learner then, like you and Stephanie." She drank some of her port-and-lemon. "One day, after the dinner, he came into the kitchen and found me reading a book. Very angry he was. Reading in front of the cook, me being a betweenmaid, you see. As butler is to bootboy, so is cook to betweenmaid."

"And what was the book?" Forgetfully, Steve filled another pipe.

"I was interested in women's rights, you know, and much taken by the sea. The book was rather narky about the idea of women seamen, being written in the last century, but you could put up with it. Always interesting to hear the other side. It was called *Let Them Be Sea Captains If They Will.*"

"Unkind," said Steve.

"Well, I learned quite a bit. Knots, rigging. It wasn't the time when I could really have been a sea captain, so he'd got me in a way, but I can't complain. I can sail a three-masted schooner quite well, given a good crew."

"Really?"

"It's in the mind, you see. When I was Stephanie's age or a bit older, I used to rub the palms of my hands up and down tree trunks to make them rough. As if I'd been hauling on ropes. Of course, the dishwashing does it now."

"And Mr. Watson?"

"He left me that night. But that's not to say that his getting into a tantrum about my reading a book has put me against books. They don't necessarily lead to the end of a marriage. Where would you say young Stephanie was bound for?"

"I'm worried that she's lonely. A man's no company hour after hour for a girl of ten."

"Children are hard to come by in this part of the world. It's mostly sheep. And the big houses here and there, of course, but the owners all send their children to public schools down South. Well, we'll put our minds to it. There's a very nice little girl just her age in the fishmonger's. Would you say she liked boys yet?"

"She says all the boys she's ever met are rough. I shouldn't be surprised."

"There's a nice lad who's the son of our organist. At least, it's a harmonium, but I've heard him at the organ in the Abbey, so we've decided to collect for an organ for our church."

"Perhaps the organist could teach her. She seems interested in music, and who knows where it might lead."

During the Second World War, Mrs. Watson had to leave to work in munitions. Steve, being ill, was exempt. Stephanie regretted that she was too young to go into the Wrens. Perhaps the war would go on for years and years and the minimum age would get earlier. The shipyard was working at full speed. Stephen was so tired that he sometimes slept in the office. Ringing Stephanie whenever he was likely to be away overnight, he caught himself saying, "There's a hitch this end, so I may not quite be there. No, I may not totally be there." Stephanie laughed, not seeing the difference, and Stephen said, "Your mamma would have explained."

"That's the air-raid siren your end."

"It always goes about this time."

"I think I'd like to be with you."

Stephen considered that for a moment and then asked Steve to bring her to him by train, saving the rationed petrol. She arrived and typed two short letters for him, with many mistakes, but dexterously. Though the carbon paper often went in backward, she would always begin again.

"You do that pretty fast," said Stephen, working at another desk.

"It's like scales."

"Do you like the organist?"

"Not much."

"Why?"

"He's so hairy. Also he makes jokes that aren't funny. How close was that last lot of bombs?"

"1 should say about three miles. They missed what they wanted. The ships."

He took her home when the all-clear had gone, and set up a camp bed for her in the office. Again, disapproval from the other directors.

A battleship was lost off Norway. That was a bad day.

At home, Stephanie insisted on doing the shopping after

lessons. Stephen and Steve and she ate a lot of stewed rhubarb out of the garden, sweetened by her with golden syrup on rationing points, because the sugar made from sugar beet had practically no taste. She did what she could with whale meat, but it would have taken Escoffier to drown the fishy taste. She studied Lord Woolton's advertised recipes featuring Potato Pete, potatoes being about the only thing available off ration apart from parsnips, swedes, and turnips, which the three of them united in hating, and carrots. The carrots she censored because their only merit was that they were said to improve R.A.F. eyesight. She wanted to go to sea. The household's favorite dinner was her invention of raw potatoes patiently grated, mixed with dried-egg powder and water, and fried as fritters in whale oil with a slice of the prized but rationed Spam. There was plenty of rabbit. Stephen, a very tall, thin man, would help himself to a piece of bread and margarine after he thought she had gone to bed. She never failed to hear the rattle of the bread bin. He found himself growing in love with her, and remarried when she was fourteen. Stephanie withdrew. Her stepmother was crass. Stephanie was not so much sad as amazed. Being in the habit of making lists in her five-year diary, she entered, "Difference between distress and dismay."

After the war, big houses were so impossible to run that they were going for a song. Stephen bought back the old house for his growingly enormous new family from the living he earned at the shipyard, where the other directors, who had held on to their shares in the company, had reduced him to the level of an employee. Stephanie went South. She earned a living at a paper-pattern shop, took her Ph.D.—Steve had been a fine teacher—and used the Westminster library every evening. Jobs progressed. She was a blithe conversationalist and funny.

At a garden dinner party in Notting Hill Gate, she was seated next to a famous philosopher with a face that made her eager to understand. The lower part of the face was cold, and it chattered with talk, but the eyes were warm, and the forehead was wrinkled through being lifted by incessant interest. But how the bottom half did harangue. He seemed to find Stephanie engrossing. Eating nothing and allowing her to eat nothing, he set her a mathematical problem about the weighing of twelve balls in a balanced scale to find out the single one that was heavier. Or lighter. The heaviness or lightness not being the point, only the difference. The answer had to be achieved in two weighings, or was it three?

"I'm sure a monkey could do it," said Stephanie. "I don't seem to be able to. You do it."

The philosopher looked delighted. Later, he took her up to dine in Hall at his old Oxford college.

"This is delicious Burgundy," she said, when she thought it all right for a woman to speak.

"Claret."

"What kind?"

"Can't you tell? We take the labels off here, of course, because everyone can tell and anyway it's decanted."

There were many long gaps in talk. A celebrated historian said something about poodles making very good gun dogs. A French woman professor with a plait round her head and a face like a muffin was pointed out as being the expert who bought the wines for the college. "What a breakthrough for the suffragettes," said Stephanie, in the gay voice that she knew would cause no one to pay attention. The women were allowed to stay for the port. She had been warned in advance that the penance for that privilege was silence. Quiet as a Trappist, she was surprised to hear that these men over their port—confident, upholstered men—exchanged not political opinions or blue jokes but information about home carpentry by mail order. There was a place in Weybridge, apparently, where you could get nuts and bolts and screws by the pound for a third of the usual price. It seemed that each of the dons was engaged in making a bedstead or a library stool as a present for his wife, and one, a chattering historian, even a very tall desk for himself to write at standing up. "Like Hemingway, you know. Spain littered with these desks. Carpenters very good there. Desks probably better than the general run of the prose."

No longer surprised that women had never battled particularly for the right to stay for the port, Stephanie thought of many things. Of her father, of sailing, of photographs of her mother, of how much she wished she had had a brother or sister. Going back to the philosopher's rooms, she slipped because a strap on her sandal had broken. With the knowledge that he had of woodwork, he could have been the best to help.

"Well, go on, help," she said.

"How?"

"A hammer and some nails? Glue?"

"They're in our country place." (Our. She hadn't known that he was married. Never a mention.)

"Or carry me."

He looked round the courtyard in case of onlookers. "Take both the sandals off and throw them both away later. They're beyond redemption."

"They're Yves Saint Laurent, and you don't throw Yves Saint Laurent away. I saved up for them. Thank you for dinner." She took the sandals off, carrying them as obviously as possible, and went to the station in bare feet. This was not her world, not her world at all.

After six months more in London, teaching Greek at the Polytechnic, she went back North to live in the same old West Lodge. Her piano was still there. In the big house, Stephen had taken to reading more and more and working less and less. He seemed poorly but denied it. The house was beginning to sag with books. His second wife, Sandra, must certainly have had her saving graces, but Stephanie found them hard to detect. Sandra read expensive Harrods books on roses and new ways with basements. Her children, now five of them, were brought to her regularly at five o'clock for tea by Mrs. Watson, who was revived beyond words by the sight of Stephanie. And Steve was still there, tutoring the new batch.

Living uncertainly in the lodge, playing the piano and thinking about jobs, Stephanie one night found a note slipped under her door. "HURRAH! BRAVO! WELCOME!" It read like a telegram from far away, but when she quickly opened the door Steve was outside in the rain holding some papers and a collapsible music stand under his mackintosh. They tried to shake hands, for some reason.

"I suppose we could go in," she said.

"You're already in." She thought briefly of carrying him over the threshold, remembering the philosopher's signal failure about her sandals. She was wearing them now, mended with glue, by herself.

"Is there something wrong with your leg?" said Steve.

"I have to be careful about the glue in my sandal. The directions said 'Set under a heavy weight for twenty-four hours.' You can't exactly pile *The Decline and Fall* onto a sandal, so I thought it would work if I stood on it."

"Don't tell me you stood up for twenty-four hours for the sake of a sandal."

"No, I did it in shifts. Eight hours, three days. What are you carrying?"

"Some music."

"Whose?"

"Mine."

"By who?"

"By me, I meant. I've been composing a bit."

His pile of music paper was twelve inches high at least, and the music stand, which had a lip no higher than an inch, was at an angle of forty-five degrees. He played for her, leaping up now and then to alter something in his manuscript, and each time he did it the papers naturally scattered. When it was five in the morning and the papers had been collected by the two of them for the fortieth time, she said, "Would you mind if I meddled with the screws on the music stand?" He said nothing, troubled about getting the papers straight, and she did what she had been wanting to do for hours, which was the obvious matter of turning the screws with a penny so that at least the stand was level.

"Oh, dear, I know I had a useful diminished seventh somewhere," Steve said from the floor, defeated by the muddle of his manuscript pages. His notation was small and beautiful.

"What key?"

"Submediant in the bass, in C minor, I think."

She played it.

"Yes. Or try it in the relative." Which she did. "That's better. Let's write that down somewhere where we won't lose it."

"The best place would be the place where you want it, wouldn't it?"

Another twenty minutes and the notes were in the manuscript. Steve lay down on the sofa. She played the passage for him to make sure it was what he wanted, not noticing that he had gone to sleep. The music was rapid and exuberant and quite new to her ear.

"I'm sorry, I dropped off. I know the music too well, you see," he said when she stopped. "Are you tired?"

"Play Scott Joplin," she said. She danced a bit. Then he made a cassette of himself playing Scott Joplin, and they danced together.

They had breakfast. No time to go to bed. He had to leave his bacon and tomatoes half eaten because he was due up at the big house to teach the children.

"What subject?"

"Latin for the older two. The little ones are doing what I think they think I think is finger painting. It looks a lovely mess to me, much like your being allowed to lick the bowl of raw cake mixture when I was teaching you. But you can make a packet now with finger painting, at the right gallery. One boy of three should have done marvelously out of it. By rights."

"What happened?"

"They swiped what he'd earned, his parents, and put it in trust for his children."

"Trusts, overbearing wills. It never works. Look at Daddy. Is he O.K., do you think?"

"He misses your mother." To avoid betrayal of Stephen's new wife, he got quickly onto his bicycle to whip himself along the drive. Stephanie was pleased to see that he didn't any longer use bicycle clips. When he had first come into the family, the bicycle clips had seemed immutable. He had often worn them when he was teaching her. It struck her how untrue the psychiatrists' truism is that people don't change. Her father, she had heard, had been a hypocrite and self-absorbed in the days before she was born, but look at his history since. And look at the disappearance of Steve's bicycle clips. To her, bicycle clips had perfectly exemplified caution. But now there was humor and boldness, which led to their spending the next night together. In the interval of that day she had got a job as a classics teacher in a faraway village, Cumberland not being all sheep.

In the big house, Stephen said to Stephanie, "Having an affair with Steve?" She didn't answer, thinking the answer obvious, and Stephen said, "This is your father, Stephen, speaking, Stephanie. Steve?" Outside, the nanny was shouting, adding to confusion, "Steph and Stephie, come here at once if not sooner." The child—which child, all of them similarly encumbered by the now emptied but still onerous ancestral will?—came running and said in strong protest, "I couldn't be here sooner than sooner." The overheard incident reminded Stephen of his first wife, and he smiled at Stephanie, who was laughing.

"Look on it as euphony," he said.

"Darling Daddy, the names in this house are so impossible now that it would be better even to be called Euphony than Stephanie."

He tried the word for sound, didn't care for it, and said, "Clearly, you are Stephanie, because your mother was, and you are very like her."

"And you are Stephen. I don't forget that you called the ship H.M.S. *Talbot.* The ship you built in the Depression. Have you got any photographs of her before she was sunk? I don't know about her history. The records aren't very good. I looked things up in the newspaper library and the Admiralty."

Stephen pulled some dog-eared photographs out of his old navy-blue wallet, which was full of holes. Stephanie noticed its age and kind, and determined to find a new one exactly the same. He sorted the photographs carefully. She could see that there were many of a woman, and many others of a baby, but he kept these on his lap. His hands were arthritic but strong, and he had the sort of eyes often seen in the stock of the North of England, so brown that they are nearly black. He had never had need of spectacles. He handed over the photographs of the *Talbot,* christened after her, of course, as she well knew. There were pictures of every stage of the ship's building; even a photograph of the victuallers, North-country faces, thin, with bony features and big eyes. Engineers, fitters, a woman she didn't recognize. "That was Mary," he said. "The secretary who stayed on. All stayers, that lot. I can see you've got to the launching. Down she went, down the slipway, everything perfect. There wasn't any champagne, of course. We used cider. We couldn't do anything for her when she was torpedoed. Thirty-two of the men were saved. You won't remember, but you came out in one of the search boats with me." He paused, said, "It seemed the right thing to do, considering the bombing and all the rest of it. You were likely to be killed anyway. That's all past but not over, don't you know. I don't think my heart would go out to anyone who didn't love ships."

She played a Handel sarabande for him on the harpsichord he had refused to sell. He listened without moving and approved, saying nothing. "And there's Steve, and he tells me you've learned Greek, and I want to take you to the shipyard, and there's grouse for dinner. You'll come, both of you. That would be my hope."

Teeth

"Why don't you get married, darling?" said Mrs. Chancellor to her daughter, Amanda. "Are you living with that dentist?"

Mrs. Chancellor was on a bay horse, forging through branches along a green tunnel of path in Windsor Great Park. She was in front. Amanda was on a black mare. She is a sculptor. Pretty. Taut young figure. There was the sound of twigs crackling and leaves being swept aside. The riders ducked.

"I said why don't you get married? I asked if you were living with that dentist. Sorry. Did that branch hit you?"

Amanda said, "Didn't hurt. Living with, er, that dentist. Yes, I am. Well, no." She ducked another branch. "I'm not actually *living* with him. We're in different houses. He says we're living together, but I keep saying living together means *living* together. Having both of us and his razor all in the same place at the same time."

"But he's a dentist, Amanda."

"Yes. So?"

"If only he were a doctor, or even a vet."

"He's a very good dentist."

They came to a copse and made a halt in the ride. Horses tethered, Mrs. Chancellor passed Amanda a thermos flask of steaming coffee. "I suppose it means he understands your oxy-acetylene welding, though."

"What?"

"His being a dentist."

"Filling a hole in a wisdom tooth hasn't got much to do with sculpture," said Amanda.

"But something."

"More than you and Daddy have in common, you mean?"

Mrs. Chancellor accepted that tacitly. Pause. "We're fine," said Mrs. Chancellor. Pause. "It doesn't matter." Pause. "Politics draws us together. We got engaged at a very political time. He never minded my being a Tory. I wish your vet were a Tory."

"Not vet. *Dentist*. Could you call him 'him' or 'Andrew'? You did when you met him."

Mrs. Chancellor struggled with plastic glasses full of coffee and tried to make a level place for them in the grass to prevent them from burning her fingers. "Your father always managed to be a Socialist even when I did well on the Stock Exchange. He never took a penny."

"What's the matter with the glasses?" said Amanda. "Are they burning you?"

"Plastic carries the heat."

Amanda drew two silver cups in leather holders from a saddlebag and gave them to her mother.

"When do you and Andrew use these? I pictured you with enamel mugs. Something more earthy," said Mrs. Chancellor.

"They're for you. They're a present."

Mrs. Chancellor inspected them, taking the cups out of the leather holders and looking at the hallmark. "George III."

"I was waiting for the right moment."

"Did you make them?"

"No, I'm afraid not. I'm working in steel at the minute, and I knew you wouldn't like steel cups. You'd have called them mugs."

"You think I don't like your work?"

"Yes."

"The women in this family have always done things, darling."

"Your playing the Stock Exchange?"

"Despite Daddy. But we gave the winnings to Uncle Willie. I do it instead of bridge. I used to like bridge, but you never took to it and I can't abide having to collect a four."

Amanda said frantically, "Why doesn't Daddy like your betting on the Stock Exchange? Don't you want him to keep you company?"

"Perhaps it's that in the case of *doing* things one does them best alone. Like welding, I daresay. But I wish you'd marry Andrew."

"Even if he isn't a Conservative?"

"That could be changed, darling. One doesn't *live* best alone."

Andrew's surgery is visible from the Fulham Road. There are reflections of chimneys in his windows. He was drilling a middle-aged male patient's tooth. The sound of the drill was mixed with John Cage music. The record came to an end. Andrew stopped the drill but left a hooked steel thing bubbling in the patient's mouth as he turned the record over on the gramophone beside his instruments. His stereo equipment is beautiful. Andrew is a tall, thin young man with horn-rimmed spectacles. He was wearing blue jeans under his dentist's white coat. Thick curly hair; thin nose; a decisive, modest temperament. He once agreed strongly in a dream with an imagined man who looked all too like himself; the man confessed to fear that he lived on the opinions of others. But in Andrew's waking life he has much resolve.

Above the record, Andrew said, trying to help his patient give his mind to the music instead of to dentistry, "Isn't that interesting?" Silence. "Or would you rather have the Beethoven late quartets?"

The patient said, through the instrument in his mouth, "No. I haven't heard John Cage before. One doesn't often get the chance."

"This is a new issue. These are also new speakers. Though I'm afraid you're not hearing the music at its best, with my working on you. I had the speakers specially positioned for the patient's chair." He waited again to go on working, drill poised. "All right? What a musician! I know it seems a pity to hear him through the bubbling. If you should be in acute pain later, feel free to take an aspirin."

The patient said, "Just a minute, could you? My mouth aches when I laugh." There was the sound of a door key being used, and footsteps. "Or are you in a hurry? Is that your wife?"

"No. It's Amanda. You've met her." Andrew carried on drilling, gently. "All right? Only two minutes more. It could be *two* aspirin. Shall I stop?"

The patient said, "Sorry. Aspirin as a pain cure always strikes me as funny." Andrew put on another John Cage record; the patient took the bubbling instrument and the wadding out of his mouth. "Excuse me, old friend, I'm not talking as a patient, but why don't you get married to Miss Chancellor? I was very struck by her when you introduced us."

Andrew thought, the drill in his hand. "It might wreck her career, you see. A sculptor is not cut out for marriage." And then, to defy his dream, "I don't live on the opinions of others."

The patient voluntarily put the instrument and the wadding back into his mouth and guided Andrew's hand to the tooth in question, nodding. He said, mumbling through the John Cage record and the bubbling, "I can see you're one of those chaps who worry about other people's problems. It's just a tooth to me, and it shouldn't be a grief to you."

In Andrew's black-and-white kitchen, there is a small water heater over the sink. Black-and-white tablecloth with black-and-white napkins. In the big space—for sleeping, eating, talking—that extends from the kitchen, a spread of cushions around a white V-shaped sofa. A slate floor, a low round white marble table with objects on it, lit by a black hanging lamp with points of white light coming through punctured holes. White muslin curtains blowing in the breeze.

Amanda was wearing white jeans and a white silk shirt, with her hair pinned back in a ponytail. She had turned up her sleeves to cook, but she had stopped for the moment to go through a first-aid box, with Andrew's pair of spectacles lying broken beside her. Andrew had changed from his dentist's white coat into a navy polo-necked cashmere sweater and brown velvet trousers. Over this, though, he was putting on yet another white dentist's coat.

Amanda said, "You don't need a dentist's coat for dinner. It's going to get bouillabaisse all over it. It's already got a bit of my makeup on it."

"You may be right." He took the coat off. "I can't see much without my spectacles."

Amanda tried a gauze bandage on the broken bridge of the glasses. "They're too *loose*. They shouldn't have fallen off when you were just bending over a record. Supposing they'd fallen onto a patient."

Andrew said, "They're not loose generally. Only when I've had my hair cut. I had it done today."

"Would you mind an Elastoplast for the spectacles?" Amanda said. "There's nothing to be done about your hair. Have a look at the soup." She mended the spectacles, winding the Elastoplast round and round the nosepiece, watched by Andrew, who peered at the task and then at the bouillabaisse.

"When can I try the specs?"

"Have a go now."

Stopping the bouillabaisse-stare, Andrew put on the spectacles. Amanda started to wash mussels at great speed. Andrew looked cautiously into the pot, holding his spectacles with his forefinger. "What is it?"

"Don't you know? I said. Bouillabaisse. Mussels and things."

"Are all sculptors such good cooks as you?" He looked into the saucepan with apprehension. "Oh, I see. Mussels? I was afraid they were turnips."

"The mussels are the ones in the shells. Those are potatoes."

"When did you do all this?"

"This morning, early, before I had to pick something up at the foundry. I thought it would be all right to have garlic as it's Friday, but then I realized you might have a patient on Saturday and wouldn't want it, so I may make do with onions and dill."

"Yes, I could try that. Dentists can't be garlicky." He touched her neck. "Thoughtful of you. I have got a patient."

Amanda laid the table.

"What is it?" said Andrew.

"You see, that's where it would help if we were living together. Then I would know if you had a patient."

"That pot's too heavy for you. I'm stronger." He grinned, holding on to the Elastoplast. "My vision's now eighty percent better."

"Only eighty percent. Oh dear."

Andrew shut each eye in turn. "Or rather, I should have said a hundred percent in each eye separately but only eighty percent together. I think the glasses are not quite aligned, maybe. I don't like wasting your time. I'll get them done on Monday."

"I could do a more decent job on them in the workshop."

She had been holding a heavy black iron pot as she talked, absorbed by his spectacles problem. She put the pot on the table and looked at his hands. "Dentists always have nice hands. Mine seem to be full of clay dust and the nails are broken, however much care I take." Andrew took hold of one of her hands and kissed it.

After the bouillabaisse and starting to wash up, Amanda piled the plates in the sink. Andrew laughed and moved her over, using soap powder and a washing-up bowl.

"*Why* will you not let me wash up?" said Amanda.

"Darling, you're a terrific cook, but you're lousy at washing up. You go too fast."

"I've done those," said Amanda, watching him rewash some plates.

Andrew looked at her.

"With eighty percent vision they must look done, at least," she said.

"If I leave them on the sink rack, I'll think they're clean and put them away. Or the daily will."

"What's the name for a daily who comes in twice a week?" Pause. "Andrew, do you want me to go?"

"Of course not. Hang on a minute. The iron saucepan can soak. Is it yours or mine?"

"Ours."

"I mean, shall I take it out to your van?" Andrew said.

"The van is full of bags of cement and things from the iron-monger. I found a beautiful piece of steel tubing that he gave me for nothing. And I had to get an oxygen cylinder filled up."

Andrew looked at her rubbing her foot. "What's the matter?"

"I've got a hole in my foot, I think."

"What?"

"I've dropped some molten steel onto it, and the steel seems to have made a hole in the bone." She studied the hole in her sock, then took the sock off. "It's a very small hole. Is it the sort of thing a dentist could fill?"

Andrew bent down to look at her foot and said, shaking his head about his ineptitude, "No, a doctor. Doctors are better."

"You sound like Mummy. Mummy's never going to get over your having spent your birthday-present money for me on a van."

"Sweetheart, you couldn't put bags of cement into the back of a Jaguar. I suppose that's what she wanted. But you're quite right that she doesn't think I'm up to standard. On account of the van. No more than she's ever going to get over my being a dentist."

"Or my working. Or our not living together."

Andrew pushed up his bandaged spectacles to finish the bouillabaisse pot with wire wool, using one eye only to get the fishy remnants in focus.

Amanda in her back yard. Black jeans this time. She was draping a clay molding of a head in a wet cloth. There were armatures of horses and leaping men and women standing in the yard. Many sparks from her welding equipment. She finished what she was doing and went in the van to buy maps from the little local shop that sold everything. "One to Dover and then French ones from Calais onward," she said.'

She looked through the maps carefully. "And a knapsack." She also looked most seriously at different brands of chocolate. "Which of these is the most sustaining?"

"Are you going mountaineering?" said the shopkeeper.

"No. I just like to keep my van stocked up, in case."

"A van's a useful resource."

"I once heard my grandfather say that about his rabbit hutch. He said he didn't like his family a lot and that he was terrified of his governess but that the rabbit hutch was a great consolation."

"How do you come to have a van, if I may ask?"

"Someone who understands me gave it to me."

A few days later, Amanda was again in her back yard, with goggles on, using the welder. Her mother was at the gate, shouting at her over the noise. Eventually Amanda noticed and pushed her goggles up. "I'm sorry," she said. "I didn't hear you."

"You should be out somewhere, darling. Oh dear, this van instead of the nice young two-seater you should have. *And* living alone." Pause.

"Is that why you came?" said Amanda.

"I thought I'd find you in now. I knew that you generally worked through lunch. Whereas it's the essence of marriage to have lunch together, I used to think. Or now of living together. Even that." Pause. "But then, to tell you the truth, Daddy used to be on the telephone all the time at lunch anyway, so the maids started to give him something on a tray in his study." Pause. "I wish you had more fun."

"Darling, I do. My bloke just doesn't want to seem to spend the day with me."

"That's what I meant. If he's in love with you, though? There's room for you both in either place, from what you say." She looked up at Amanda's little house. "This would be a splendid place for a dentist."

"I think it's room in his head that he's talking about. Space to move."

"Would you like a present of a course to brush up your Greek? You'd meet people. We won't need to tell your father. He would think you were unhappy."

Amanda said, sitting on a trestle table, "I'd rather sell a few more sculptures." She got up again, summoning resolution. "Do you mind if I work while we talk?"

"You'd enjoy it, you mean? Yes, I do see that."

The voices of small girls—maybe not so small, maybe eleven—floated over the fence. One said, "What perfume are you going to use tonight?" Another said, "I can't decide. What are you going to use?" The first girl said, "I thought the one called Perhaps."

Mrs. Chancellor said, "Darling, on second thoughts perhaps this would *not* be a suitable area for a dentist. And you *certainly* shouldn't be living here alone with children going about talking like that. Daddy would have a fit." Pause. "I'm having a fit."

"Mummy, they were just schoolgirls who'd probably been wandering around the chemist's."

"They sounded like what your grandmother would've called 'girls of the town' to me. I've seen a lot of it, as a magistrate.

Oh dear, I've broken part of one of your wire casts."

Amanda looked at it. "How did you do it? It's very strong."

"Worry."

Amanda inspected the armature and threw it experimentally across the yard to test its stamina. Everything but the damaged wire remained intact.

"You can see, darling, it's much stronger than you thought," said Mrs. Chancellor.

"How on earth did you bust it, then?"

"I said, I was worried about you."

"So you broke a piece off my horse." Then Amanda melted. "You must have iron fingers. You should have been a sculptor."

The telephone rang inside the house. Amanda picked up the nearest receiver, in the kitchen. Her mother waved and left, having mended the iron base of the armature with a strip of Elastoplast ripped off her own finger. Inside the house Amanda said to Andrew, "No, nothing in particular's happened. I'm sorry. Mummy's just bust something. Darling, yes, I'm off. France, I think. I'll ring you up when I'm across the Channel: no, I'll do it from a hundred kilometres inland, wherever that gets me to. I'm not sure. I've got the van piled up. I probably won't get farther than Dover, as usual. You couldn't come with me, I suppose? No, yes, I know you need to be on your own, and there are the patients." Explanation to herself, it seemed. "You need a rest from me. Hello? Hello? Oh, damn."

She went into the yard again, looked for her mother, found the hapless piece of Elastoplast on her armature. Laughed, as much as was possible in the circumstances. Another day of Elastoplast.

After a while, having mended the damage, she went back into the kitchen to ring Andrew. He was out. She had to leave a message on his answering machine. Difficult to speak privately to a machine, but she tried. "Darling, I waited for the bleep, I was hoping you were in, I was wondering if your Elastoplast's holding but I expect you've got another pair of glasses by now. I'd better set off." A sound signaled the end of the recording. She said to herself, "Oh, blast," and redialed the number. While the machine talked in Andrew's recorded voice and she couldn't yet be heard, she muttered to the air, "Perhaps I should say I'm a patient with an abscess and an impacted wisdom tooth. Then I *know* you'd ring back." Bleep sound. She talked. "Andrew, I couldn't get the last bit in before the answering thing cut off, but I was saying I thought I'd better be off now and obviously I wanted you to know. Write to the *poste restante* at Nice. . . ." The machine shut off. Amanda spoke softly to herself. "I wonder where you are, whether you're just not answering, whether you know that I love you and that this is the trouble about not living together. Best not said, I suppose."

Amanda was in the Nice *poste restante* reading a telegram from Andrew. "Come quickly." She fled to the telephone and asked in French for Andrew's English number, but the connecting operators responded negligently to the idea of the call's being urgent. She drove very fast along the roads of France, reading maps beside her as she went.

In England, she put two pence into the nearest coin box, got the operator, was told to put in sixteen pence. She reached Andrew. "Darling, I've only got enough change for one go. You might have to ring me back. I'm at Dover seven-three-five-one-o-six. I don't know the code. I called you from—" Click. The usual telephone hiatus. Andrew rang back. She said, "I was saying I rang you from Nice, but you couldn't hear. They cut us off. What? Yes, I've got the van. You said you needed me. I'll drive as fast as I can." He suggested, in a voice so calm that it worried her, that they meet at the Bear Hotel. She went along with him. "Yes, that would be about halfway between us, I suppose. You'll have booked a room, or do you want me to?" They were cut off again.

She drove very fast through the South of England. The Bear Hotel. Perhaps all would be well. She tried once to make an emergency call to the hotel, emergency services being free, but she had to agree that this was not a question of "Fire, police, or ambulance" and had simply to drive on. She got to the hotel, still hoping that all would be well and that this was an assignation. Andrew's car was there. She got out and sat beside him. He had a week's growth of beard on him and could barely manage to get out of his car to hold her.

"I raced," said Amanda. "Did it seem ages? Why haven't you shaved?"

"I can't manage without you." He talked too fast. "Could we go for a walk?"

"Will they keep a room this late?"

"What room?"

It seemed best not to say that he wasn't attending.

They walked round and round the country green. "You won't leave me, will you?" said Andrew. "I told you I had a map in front of me and that this is exactly halfway, but you were late."

"I still don't understand why you haven't shaved."

"I haven't been seeing any patients, if that's what you mean."

"I thought you'd booked a room," said Amanda.

"We've got plenty of rooms of our own. Two *houses* full of them."

Amanda stroked his hair. "That's what I mean." He jerked away from her. She said, "Do you want to sit down? You either talk so fast that I can't understand you or you wait ten minutes before you open your mouth. Why didn't your secretary notice you're stalemated?"

"I wanted to marry you, but I realized it wouldn't work. I'd spoil your career. I'd spoil your life if we got married."

"Why?"

He jerked away again. "A drill's too like a welding machine." Pause.

"Could you rest?" she said.

"I'm selling you short." He kept on saying it.

"No, my dove."

A church bell in the village struck two in the morning. They walked about for a long time, going back to the hotel car park and driving to the green in his beautiful old Alvis, which was done up with straps like an Edwardian picnic basket. They lay down together on the green on the tarpaulin they had brought from the back of her van. She tried to get him to rest. When that didn't work, she tried to get him to talk to her, but then he would sit up and almost fight her off, like a swimmer in trouble grappling with a rescuer. In the way that banality has of interrupting crisis, a policeman with a torch suddenly loomed up and shone the torch at her.

"Having trouble, Miss?" the policeman said.

Amanda said, "Thank you. No. It's *my* tarpaulin." "Tarpaulin" was the first word that came into her head in the effort to make eloquent Andrew's straits to a stranger, and the absurdity was some mild relief.

The policeman persisted. "Your car, Miss? Your husband, is he?"

Andrew roused himself. "No, it's my car, and I'm not her husband, officer."

The policeman said, "So it's your car, is it, you say? Number of vehicle?"

Andrew looked for help to Amanda. "What's the number of the car, darling?"

"I don't think I've ever known," she said.

The policeman looked at the back of the car and wrote in his notebook, speaking out loud as he did it. "Can't remember number of own car, so-called. Lying on the grass with girl not his wife. Driving license? No driving license on him, witness asserts."

Andrew said, "It'd ruin her career if I married her."

Amanda looked at him gently.

The people at the police station were unexpectedly benevolent. They kept Amanda waiting outside a night cell but gave her news of him.

Next morning, while walking back to their parked cars, Amanda asked Andrew why he had kept saying all night, according to the police, that it was a bad time.

Andrew said, "Because I'm ruining your life. You just come and wash up."

"No I don't. You won't let me. You leave me the interesting part."

"What interesting part?"

Amanda: "Cooking."

"Cooking's a burden to a sculptor. I'm a burden to a sculptor."

"No." She remembered that a police inspector in the night had said, "He keeps putting those broken spectacles on in the cell. He says someone he's fond of gave them to him and they're not a very good mend and they give him double vision, and then he's able to go to sleep."

*   *   *

Family conclave. Mr. Chancellor, Mrs. Chancellor, sitting in their drawing room. Amanda crouched on a footstool. Mr. Chancellor sitting at his desk, looking at a Reg Butler sculpture on it of a naked woman with her arms upstretched, shrouded as if in gauze by the dress she is taking off. Next to it, an Elisabeth Frink head of a warrior. A chintz-and-Chippendale room with a big log fire and many books. A Labrador on Mr. Chancellor's feet. He played often with the dog and, more often, pretended not to be hearing. Amanda's arcane ways alarmed him. A sculptor living with a dentist.

"Thank God you decided against him," said Mrs. Chancellor.

"I didn't," said Amanda.

Mrs. Chancellor said, "I didn't want to influence you, but a *dentist*. Henry, you know what you feel."

Mr. Chancellor said, "What? Of course I know what I feel. Oh, I see, you want me to say what *you* feel." He turned to Amanda. "Your mother feels that a dentist is not up to scratch for you."

Mrs. Chancellor said, "Your father's often said that if only Andrew had been a surgeon we wouldn't have minded."

Mr. Chancellor said, "Never said any such thing." He played with the Labrador with his foot.

"We don't even actually *live* together, technically. He could not see me anytime. Daddy, I think he's troubled. Whenever I go over to him now, he keeps picking fluff off his pajamas."

"He's in *bed*?" said Mrs. Chancellor.

"I put him there, but he won't stay there. He wants to get on with things. He hates holidays."

"So do you," said Mrs. Chancellor.

Mr. Chancellor said, "My experience is that people don't stand suffering well when they're in bed."

"He's stopped even being able to speak to me. It's as if he's got dentist's wadding in his mouth," said Amanda.

Mr. Chancellor said, "I think he means that he feels he shouldn't speak to you, perhaps. In case it causes you distress."

His wife said, "In any event, it's just as well."

Mr. Chancellor said to his wife, "Dear, it would be different if Amanda hadn't got such a lot of skeletons in the cupboard."

Amanda stood up and went to the desk to look at her father. Mrs. Chancellor said, "Skeletons?"

"Me, for instance," said Mr. Chancellor.

He plugged in an electric kettle and warmed a teapot from a tray, heating it over the fire. He wished to save the maid trouble.

"You?" said Amanda.

"That's the sort of thing he means," said Mrs. Chancellor. "A Socialist for a father. It's ridiculous for a busy man to be making tea just because the daily's lying down."

"She's not feeling well," said Mr. Chancellor.

"Good heavens," said his wife. "No one's well around here. The whole conversation seems to be about invalidism of one sort or another. People need to pull themselves together."

Amanda said, considering talking on behalf of her father but rejecting it, "Mummy, Andrew's going to be all right."

Her mother said, "The trouble with your father is he won't use his elbows. And Andrew's out altogether."

Amanda said, "It's my fault he's gone silent." Pause. Pondering her words: "He thinks he would get in my hair, you see."

Mr. Chancellor said, "Anyway, it was never anything much but pain for you. Was it?"

Amanda went over and helped him with the tea tray. "Darling, it was always one of the best things that ever happened to me," she said.

Mrs. Chancellor said, "Masochism." Mr. Chancellor looked at the Labrador and then at his daughter.

She said, "Of course, I may have bungled it hopelessly. Beyond recall, I mean."

Mrs. Chancellor said, "It's over anyway, quite rightly. I'd seen it coming." And then, to her husband, forcing him: "Hadn't we?"

Amanda said, "I haven't. I'm not giving up." She looked at her father, and he nodded.

"I wish I could help. Your mother seems to have it all organized," he said.

Mrs. Chancellor spoke over him to Amanda. "There's a nice clever young man coming to drinks and I expect he'll want to take you out to dinner. You've got to promise to be good to him, because he was having an affair which has just broken up.'"

Amanda said, "Oh, darling, if you said that to me about him, what did you say to him about me? The same?" She looked at her father. "Daddy, the same?'"

"Roughly," said Mr. Chancellor. Pause. "I'm afraid I've made things difficult for you most of your life. Weak of me, probably. I think you *might* like this man. Your mother does. His name's Jasper. I think he's probably a twit. But he's written several Fabian pamphlets."

"What about?" said his daughter.

"The last one was rather difficult to follow, for me, but it sold out. He seems to have a populist touch."

His daughter said, "What was it called?"

Mr. Chancellor said, "It was about Freud. I have always thought Freud a great prophet and possibly a left-winger. Your Conservative dentist isn't by any good luck a turncoat, is he?"

Amanda answered, "No, he isn't." Pause. "What's the pamphlet called?"

Mr. Chancellor said, trying not to cause further trouble by looking at her, " 'The Libido Off the Leash,' I seem to remember."

Amanda and Jasper walked, without finding much to say, in the garden of her parents' house. Mr. Chancellor could be seen in the window of his library, writing.

"Daddy's working," said Amanda.

Jasper said, in a rather high voice, "Your mother's the more interesting one, don't you agree? Though I noticed you talked mostly to your father. When we were having sherry, I mean," and anything he had meant melted into a high laugh.

Amanda said, "I'm sorry. Is it that you're sad about your girl?"

"All for the best. You sound well out of your chap."

"Ah. I'm glad you think so. Shall we go in? It's starting to rain."

Jasper put up the umbrella. "I always carry a brolly. I suppose I should take you out to dinner."

"It's only six o'clock still. No, six-fifteen. We can't possibly walk in the rain for two hours. Though I suppose we can't give up in front of Mummy and Daddy."

"No, that would be dropping a bit of a brick, wouldn't it?" Pause. Witless. "I tell you what, I've got a brilliant idea, I'll take you home. Are you a walker? I hope so. I'm rather a keen walker. I get jumpy legs at plays and reading books and things. Where do you live?"

"Miles. We could get a bus."

"Where to?"

"My dentist's, I think."

A look of distress on Jasper's face. But here at last something for him to do. "Poor girl, which tooth? Show me. Open your mouth."

"I feel like a horse having its age told."

"I've got a splendid, frightfully expensive dentist in Harley Street who would see you tomorrow morning if I rang him up. What's your name again, actually?"

Amanda and Jasper, he with his black City umbrella, walked for two hours. Little to say. Outside Andrew's house, they saw Andrew at work through the lighted window of his surgery. Jasper said, gallant, searching for a topic, "Aha! I spy a patient in the throes! Are you sure he's any good, practicing all the way out here? We could've run to a taxi. Does his receptionist work late?"

Amanda was already halfway up Andrew's steps, getting wet as Jasper tried to hold the umbrella over her. "He doesn't need a receptionist as late as this. I've got a key."

"A key to your dentist! I say, how grand. While you're waiting for your appointment, shall I come in and read you one of my pamphlets? Some of it's rather abstract."

"No, really not. The thing is, he doesn't seem able to talk at the moment."

"How peculiar." Jasper peered at Andrew through the window. "It isn't as if he's got any instruments in *his* mouth."

She kept silent. Nonspeaking, beloved Andrew.

"I'll give you a buzz," said Jasper. "What about getting sort of engaged? It could be unofficial, if you liked." He pursued her up the steps and put the umbrella over her in a way that touched her, in spite of the impossibility of their hours together. He gave her a copy of his pamphlet with his telephone number written on it. He kissed her. She saw Andrew catching sight of them but could hardly do anything except return the kiss and take the pamphlet. Then she shook Jasper's hand and watched his back disappearing in case he should turn round. He didn't. Disconsolate? It seemed not so, not at all. She sped into Andrew's house to tell him her shame about what she had said by mistake to Jasper on the doorstep. It released his tongue and soothed his concern for her. They talked far into the night, as they always had, as they always would. In her excitement about seeing Andrew, she had bade Jasper good-bye with the words "It was nice meeting me."

As Is

"For you to be such a close friend of Professor Chalcott is a craziness," says Professor Anna Krzyżowska, a Polish émigrée physicist in a laboratory at an Eastern American university, to an English-born student named Fiona Cairns. It is 1969. "He's forty-five years older than you are. He'll die before you. Then where are you? Fiona, I ask you, where are you?"

"In the cupboard. Closet. Looking for a pipette."

"Did you hear what I said?"

"Yes. I'm in the closet. I think we may have lost that pipette. To be frank, I think you may have busted it."

"You're not answering my question."

"I told you, I'm in the pipette closet. The closet for pipettes."

"I think you would not recognize a pipette from a pipe," says Professor Krzyżowska, blowing into a complex of linked tubes and producing a sediment that gives her satisfaction. "What I said—and the correct response is not in my closet—was that it is a craziness for you to be such a friend of Professor Chalcott when he's forty-five years older than you are. And then I said he'll die before you. And then I said where will you be?"

"Without him."

Fiona is nineteen years old. She is studying comparative literature, but to earn money for textbooks she helps in the physics laboratory. Cross about the pipette, Professor Krzyżowska says, "You're certainly not born to be a physicist."

"No. I know."

"And what is more, you are a foreigner," says Professor Krzyżowska unreasonably. "You even stumble over cupboards and closets. That is, over usage of cupboards and closets."

"I know."

"You failed to respond to my statement. I am so very tired of being treated as the Polish Corridor."

"I'm trying to forget which statement you mean."

"That for you to be such a close friend of Professor Chalcott must stop. You must protect yourself."

"Aren't those *injuctions?*" says Fiona, head in closet, crying.

Professor Krzyżowska, who pretends to a godmotherly role toward the pretty Fiona, feels herself to be ugly. It is beyond her confidence to see herself with the good wishes of others: to see the full mouth, the middle-aged nobility plucked out of danger. She has been forced to learn distrust, wishes to forget the learning, but finds it impossible to erase. The chalk marks of Poland's history are not to be washed off the blackboard of her mind. Sometimes when she tries to dream the phrase in English, "blackboard" becomes "backboard," and the next day her shoulders are braced and her neck is stiff as she lectures. Her courage is invisible to most and taken for severity. In the large and jealous frame that shelters her, she strenuously chides herself. She hides cost. Later that day, alone, she breaks an essential piece of her research construction. She, too, weeps. Then she works, speaking to herself in Polish. The true small self that aspires and chugs along in travail.

Professor Chalcott is of another stuff. He teaches musicology. His house is large and so full of books that he has never thought of having the interstices repainted. He was born there, married there, saw his wife die there, continues alone to entertain friends there with undiminished heed. "I'm eager to know what you have been reading," he will say. Innovation of any sort, in any field, excites him. "You've taught me something I didn't know," he will say, leaning his chin on his silver-headed cane, his dog at his feet. The dog is brown, and the

Professor, typically, having spent some time pondering the question of a name for him, called him Brown. Fiona and he love and comprehend each other. He preserves that careful literalness, that adherence to presented facts, which is so often the staple of conversation in people brought up in houses such as his.

The day after Professor Krzyżowska's effort to detach Fiona from him, he comes into the university library. Fiona has just finished three hours of work as a junior librarian to earn another two dollars an hour. All the returned books are back on the shelves. As a last act of tidiness, she has been trying to clear a fellow-student in a yoga trance off a reading table.

"What are you doing?" Professor Chalcott asks her.

"I can't wake this girl."

Professor Chalcott peers at the cross-legged yoga practioner, says nothing, and goes into the librarian's office. He drops down like a sack of flour into a green plastic armchair.

"Are you bored?" he yells. "I've been bored for the last ten minutes."

She lugs herself to the door and considers. "Yes, I am. But what would the option be?"

"Would you like to come to a magic shop? I'm bored with deciphering Beethoven's shorthand. I like you better than his quartet, now that it's ten past four."

They set off. Professor Chalcott wraps himself in a muffler and takes a bookbag and a briefcase. He says, "Can you decide on any way of avoiding the man at the reception desk? It's unpleasant of me but I don't care for him. A weakling and a dullard, I think. He has the sort of face that seems to want to swallow its chin."

So they climb a stairway, Fiona pausing in the pretense of doing up a sandal, to give Professor Chalcott a chance to catch his breath, and they leave by a door from another floor.

At the magic shop, Professor Chalcott is known not as a learned musicologist but as an expert in magic. He is warmly greeted. Shown things.

Professor Chalcott: "No, no, no, you know perfectly well I've seen the disappearing egg over and over again. Perhaps something with cards." He practices a trick needing both legerdemain and fast patter, and then says, "Arthritis puts the kibosh on that idea. Some silk scarves to vanish up the sleeve, in pretty colors? Colors that would suit my friend? Yellow, deep pink?" Again he practices with what the admiring manager produces. "Yes, that's within the range of possibilities. My physical possibilities, apart from possibilities of enchantment."

Fiona says to him outside the magic shop, "Professor Krzyżowska says we shouldn't spend so much time with each other."

"Because I'm going to die first, I suppose."

"I don't give a damn."

"Don't you believe her, anyway. I'm here. Beckett once said, 'The young pop off. The old hang on.' "

A sparrow that appears to be blind in one eye then crashes into Professor Chalcott's briefcase. He picks the creature up and strokes it and then puts it into the briefcase, making a nest of his handkerchief for the bird and leaving the case open. "'Do you know," he says to Fiona, "there are one thousand three hundred and fifty-nine feathers on a sparrow's neck? I fear this one may have lost a few."

"What a lot you know. Beethoven's shorthand, magic, sparrows."

"And you your languages, and being able to do a backbend. Combined"—gaily—"we could take everyone on. I forget if it was Archimedes who said, 'Give me a lever long enough and I could lift the earth.' We'll look it up."

"I like it when you say that," says Fiona.

"What are you reading today?"

"*Antony and Cleopatra.*"

"It describes a world so immense that time yawns in it. We could discuss that, too."

They walk back to the campus. Professor Chalcott suddenly stops, and Fiona worries. "I find it difficult to talk when I'm on my pins," he says, seeing her concern. "A joke. Your Arab oil-producing new populace of London. An Arab rings up—an Arab with a good many women in his rented Georgian house—and says, 'This is your husband. To whom am I speaking?' "

Fiona says, "Jokes lighten the weight, don't they? The millstone on the chest in the middle of the night."

"You feel that weight?"

"Sometimes. Last night I was dreaming in dialogue, as usual, and woke myself up by speaking aloud but couldn't make myself hear myself because my throat was so dry."

"What did you get? A glass of water, or a pen?"

"A pen."

"That would have been my choice. Did the dialogue make sense in the morning?"

"Yes."

"What a folly, to ask such a question of you."

Nearly at the college, Professor Chalcott takes her arm and says, "Shall we go and see *Long Day's Journey Into Night* this evening? It's a German company."

"Yes, please. Though you know I don't speak German."

He does not pull rank about the tickets. Their seats are very high up. Fiona keeps pausing on some pretext or other to give him a rest on the stairs. His hearing is bad. She has to attend carefully, though German is arcane to her, because he wants to know the details of the staging. She begins to feel like a guide dog for the blind: he can barely see. When the mother in the play comes downstairs to her suspicious family—she pacified by her secret fix of some drug—Chalcott knows by heart that the character must be carrying her wedding dress over her arms. "What does it look like?" he says.

"Cream tulle," says Fiona.

"No, I mean the way she's carrying it."

"Like a pile of freshly ironed fine laundry."

"A reviving idea, when the dress is old."

Again, the next afternoon, he sits himself down heavily into the green plastic armchair in the library. He says, "Shall we go to see Dietrich tonight?"

"Live?"

"A swift scoot to New York?"

Fiona has already seen Dietrich in London, aeons ago, but a repetition would be worth it with him. "My right trusty and well-beloved friend" comes into her mind: the adjectives of English citations. And again she feels like a guide dog. She

can repeat the English and the French to him; the German is
once more a problem. The verbal information he wants in all
languages has to be exact. Miss Dietrich is wearing her beautiful sequined body stocking. Professor Chalcott, that most distinguished and noticeable man, suddenly says, straining his eyes,
finding that useless, and employing a loud voice, "Can you see
her nipples?"

There lies between Professor Chalcott and Fiona a gentle,
unexacting variation of humor and event. He appears brusque, but few people have ever sought to punish him. After the
Dietrich evening, he takes Fiona back to her dormitory and
they find Professor Krzyżowska on the doorstep waiting for
them. Fiona, knowing that violence makes Chalcott sick at heart,
grasps his arm and steers him to his house. A tugboat guiding
a great liner perhaps soon to be broken up, except that liners
can be replaced by christening some new hulk *The Professor
Chalcott II,* and there is no analogy for such a man as this.
Fiona comes back to the dormitory. Professor Krzyżowska is
still lurking. She says, "I must repeat myself. He's going to die
first. You must protect yourself."

"We're on a doorstep," says Fiona. "Do you want to come
up?"

"It's for your own good."

Fiona has a room to herself. She sits on the bed, Professor
Krzyżowska in the only chair, a desk chair that reminds her of
the backboard/blackboard confusion.

"You must see younger men," the Professor says.

"What are you trying to do? Are you in love with him?"

"I'm thinking of you. You should be going out with other
students. A safeguard. I saw you taking him home. It's I who
should have taken him home."

"You *are* jealous."

"You'll suffer."

"Self-protection hasn't much to do with friendship."

"I'm on my own," says the Professor, without meaning to.

"I know. I'm sorry."

"I'm going to *stop* this nonsense," the Professor shouts.

It can then go either way. Peril is in the room, the likeli-
hood of real damage; or the Professor can be touched on the
arm. Fiona chooses to brush her teeth.

"Why are you brushing your teeth?" The danger starts to disappear.

A pause. Fiona says, "Sorry, my mouth was full."

"I know some apt young men on this very campus."

"Why apt?"

"As I said. They're your age."

Fiona sits on the bed and then stands, feeling it wrong to slouch when the Professor's frame of mind beseeches respect.

"You see," says Fiona, trying yet once more, "I don't want to be with people of my own age all the time. Not just for the sake of it. I mean, I was trying to get someone my own age out of a trance in the library a while ago. I've never had to wake Professor Chalcott up. We have fun. I've never enjoyed myself so much with anyone. Are you saying that I'm in your way? Troubling you?"

"I wish you spoke Polish. All your Russian is no good to me. I abhor."

"Your English is perfect."

"No."

"You mean not fluent enough to say what's at the back of your mind?"

The Professor gets up and walks about the room to command it. Fiona says, "I don't understand the age-ghetto principle we have in America. I don't want to go around with some husky athlete just because he's nineteen."

"You'll see I'm right later."

"If one only knows one's contemporaries, how is the past to be handed on?"

"I'm talking about the inevitable loss. Guard against the future."

"But we're happy *now*."

"You can't afford this. It's against nature." The Professor goes over to the bed and yells, "Someone's been sleeping here!"

"Me."

Impasse. Fiona takes the Professor's chair, but sits on the arm of it. "You see, he is my *great* friend. How many great friends does anyone have in a lifetime, including husband and brothers and sisters and children and parents? Twelve? Fifteen? With luck. I'm not talking about acquaintances or well-wishers."

"I'm just telling you that you are laying yourself open." The

Professor picks up a pencil and vents helpless anger by breaking the point off. "I suppose I should apologize for this," she says. "I'll get you another."

"The contagion of the world's slow stain," says Fiona.

"Who said that?"

"You did, once. You said it was Shelley," says Fiona. "A friend to you, and not even Polish. Certainly not your age. I wonder if I could get you something? The Coke machine's just down the corridor."

"A glass of ice water."

"It would have to be a paper cup."

The Professor throws the slept-on pillow out of the window.

The next afternoon, Chalcott meets Fiona on campus and says, "Lot of swansdown outside your bedroom window."

"Professor Krzyżowska threw a pillow out of it."

Professor Chalcott drops his cane, bends down to get it, can't reach. "Would you mind picking up my cane?" Project achieved. "One of the things I like about you is that you wear dresses with waists," he says. "Also you remind me of Cleopatra. Interesting that you should have been reading that play. Shakespeare's, of course, not Shaw's. Shaw isn't very good at women. You're *very* good at it. At being one."

Fiona stays quiet. He goes on, taking her arm as they walk. "You always suggest something around yourself. The past. Beethoven carries Mozart around with him. Anyway, what was that woman doing, killing a swan outside your window?"

"I wasn't speaking loud enough. She wasn't killing a swan, she was thrashing around with my pillow. I think she thought you'd been lying on it. You can't blame her."

"I can and do."

They walk to his house. Chalcott says, "I'm eager to play you something I believe I may have deciphered from Beethoven's shorthand. I want to talk to you about whether you think I've got it right. Then I want to play you Cole Porter."

"Important about the shorthand."

"I nearly called you up in the middle of the night, but I didn't think you'd welcome being woken. So after playing the piano, and having some sardines, I simply wrote out the idea on staff paper and imagined your being there."

"I was awake anyway. I nearly rang you to tell you something from an encyclopedia I was proofreading."

"Why proofreading?"

"It's one of the jobs on the bulletin board. I can think about better things in the back of my mind, so it's bearable. I get the encyclopedia free, too, but it's not up to much. I was going to read you an entry about the character they had as Friar Tuck in *Romeo and Juliet*. Friar Laurence turned into a Toby jug."

"I should say a researcher just chose the most familiar Friar."

They go later into a store where Professor Chalcott has tracked down a Virginia ham. Professor Krzyżowska is there and looks at them askance. She takes Fiona aside. "Virginia ham is too salt for him," she says. "You'll kill him, you and the Virginia ham."

"He wants me to taste it. He says it's the taste of his country as he remembers it at my age," says Fiona. "He was brought up in Virginia."

"A mistake, the salt, for his digestion."

"I don't think so," says Fiona.

Professor Chalcott appears from behind a smoked turkey and says, "Mistake?"

Professor Krzyżowska says, "The salt. At your age. Fiona shouldn't allow it."

"Bunk," says Professor Chalcott. "Fiona doesn't make mistakes." He leaves again to settle the bill. He thinks as he goes that some things one does seem correct but out of pitch, and that other things one does can seem errors but in pitch. Alone with the Polish Professor, Fiona says, "The point is, Virginia ham gives him pleasure."

When Are You Going Back?

"How is your sister these days?" said the owner of a chefs' outfitting shop in Soho. "You must miss her. She went back the best part of a year ago, as I recall. Are you the older or the younger?"

Juliet said, "I don't have a sister."

The owner said appreciatively, measuring her waist, "She's full of fun, isn't she? You're the spitting image of her. You must get a lot of people saying that. Though she's taller, isn't she. And so where do you both come from? I remember serving her a pair of trousers like the ones you're after now and I think she said Idaho. Or was it Ohio?"

"Cincinnati."

"Geography was never my fiercest point. I imagine she'd be the younger, wouldn't she?" He took her inside leg measurement and shook his head for some reason.

"No, you see, those were always my trousers and I want another pair exactly the same because I've dribbled paint on them from painting a tub."

"You're saying you're the same person. Well, I can verify that by the trousers now you've explained it. It would be the same blue and white checked trousers with the bagginess taken out."

"Do you always identify people by what they buy?"

Taking this to be a compliment, the owner of the chefs' outfitting shop bowed over Juliet's hand and said, "It's my profession, isn't it?"

"When will you have the trousers ready?"

"It's a big alteration but we'll be ready for you at the end of next week. Give my regards to your sister when you write to Cincinnati. I'll remember that now. It's in my head." He tapped his forehead. "Safest place to keep things."

A man waiting at the counter said, "But she hasn't got a sister, she said."

"Good morning, Mr. Neal," the owner responded, and then shouted down his back stairway and said, "Help up and in a hurry, we've got the butcher-boy trousers standing here inside-leg thirty-six."

Mr. Neal, a good-looking man of fifty-odd, said to Juliet as she was leaving the shop at speed, "Don't distress yourself. How long have you been here?"

"A year, in a dump, after a quick exit from Cincinnati to 'New York, New York, it's a beautiful town,' " which she sang.

"What do you do?"

"I'm at the London School of Economics on a grant. The new pants, trousers, are because of doing up the dump."

"I heard. And you like it here in spite of all, and you're about twenty-two?"

"Twenty-three and I'm called Juliet and thank you for catching on." She went quickly into Old Compton Street.

Friday morning. By tube to a lecture at the London School of Economics. Juliet was wearing a spotted muslin dress under a thick coat that her parents had sent her from Cincinnati, thinking that anywhere so far across the Atlantic was likely to be freezing. The coat was far too hot for London, but the fragility of the muslin dress made up the difference. While they were waiting for the L.S.E. lecture to begin, Juliet told an English girl named Harriet about a dream she had had the night before.

"You threw an india-rubber at me," said Juliet. "An eraser."

"I'd never do a thing like that."

"Harriet, I know you wouldn't, but in the dream you did. You also flicked some ink at my dress and it spotted it."

"It's spotted muslin already. Where's the spot?"

"English people are so literal. It was a dream."

"But you wouldn't have a dream without a reason." Harriet

searched Juliet's dress and said, "There's a faded spot here. You've no right to have a dream like that."

"It was followed by a crummy business in a caterers' clothing place."

"What happened?"

"A man kept on sending messages to my sister when it was me he was measuring and I haven't got a sister anyway."

"Was that another dream?"

"It happened, and it's always happening here. People are always saying 'Oh, are you here?' or 'When are you going back?' They don't mean to be rude but do I have to wear a label around my neck? I'm beginning to feel like an ectomorph."

"Good heavens," said Harriet. "You've been here long enough, haven't you? You're not that much of a solipsist."

Talk bogged.

"Say something," said Juliet.

Harriet shook her head. "I've got nothing worth saying at the moment."

Juliet said, "You're turning me into someone garrulous and I'm sure I'm not."

"I'm not up in Freudianism." Harriet went on reading *Language, Truth and Logic*.

Juliet said, "The Lord protect us from high-bred English silences." Wait. "I mean, you let a conversation go off the rails and then there are casualties and people are getting killed because the carriages are on their sides by then and you don't have the slightest idea how to hoist them up again and the hell with it."

Before the afternoon lecture Juliet found on the reading-flap of her chair a bottle of black ink and a note from Harriet saying "This is to fill in the faded spot or dot. Use a pen, not a brush, or the ink will run. I'm sorry about the dream." In a million years Juliet would not have thought her likely to have so acted on an insight. The note was signed "Anyway. H."

Anyway. Friday evening. Back to the dump, which was in Soho. Juliet shared it with two English girls: a gym instructress called Victoria, and a personnel manager called Joanna. The evening took the usual course of any other Friday evening.

"Have some sherry," said Victoria to Juliet. "I'm flaked, aren't you?" She looked at her watch and said, "No, Jim's coming in a moment to pick me up and they hate people being late for dinner."

"Who's they?"

"The people we're staying with. Upcountry."

"Derbyshire as ever?"

"The telephone number's on the kitchen pad but there won't be any calls for me. They know I'm always away for a Friday-to-Monday."

"It sounds forbidding. You always say a Friday-to-Monday but it's only a weekend, isn't it? You work yourself to a standstill on Friday and Monday so it isn't as if you had four days off."

"It's just what we call it," said Victoria. "It's not meant to seem foreign to you." She put her hand on Juliet's arm with a gentleness that Juliet associated with vets, Cincinnati, animals, a hen-house being built by her brother-in-law. "You must come up to us one day," said Victoria. "Let us know when you're free. It's not at all intimidating. It's a frightfully big house so you'd have all the room in the world and there aren't any rules apart from listening for the meal-gongs. It's not that sort of place. You're left alone as much as you want."

"I bet," Juliet said that, and then "Erase. Sorry."

"You really must come up one day. You'd enjoy it. I don't like the thought of your being here alone every Friday-to-Monday. Think about it and I'll put it to our hosts."

There was a honking car outside, and Victoria ran downstairs with her usual leather grip, after leaning out of the window to shout to Jim, "We have got saddle soap up there, haven't we?" Jim shouted up, "Do you want to polish the old grip?"

And there was Joanna still to go.

Juliet said, at the door of Joanna's room, "Is there anything you want? I'm going to do some shopping."

Joanna came out, looking vivid, with a bundle under her arm that she regularly pretended to be a load of food though both Victoria and Juliet knew that it was her clothes and books for the weekend at her boyfriend's studio. The silence about his name and her whereabouts had been shyly insisted upon for so long that even her flat-sharers observed the code.

Kicking the code, Juliet said, "To be practical, so what's his name?"

"Henry," said Joanna. "I'm just taking him some salami."

"Soho being rampant with salami, alive and kicking with Chinese bean sprouts, and would you both like to come and have dinner here with me tomorrow night?"

"I'd have to ring you. He may have fixed something."

"You don't have to fix salami. There's nothing to be done about salami. You just have it."

"One can put it in a cassoulet. When *I* said fixed something I meant he may have arranged something. He often does. For Saturday night. He's a bit difficult about weekends. Could you and I have pizza together on Monday night? I know Victoria's got people coming and we'd be in the way."

"You're sure you're free?"

"I've never heard you use sarcasm."

"It was an attempt to be funny."

"Yes." Joanna took her bundle from under the smock she was wearing and smelt it.

"Garlic. Henry doesn't like garlic much because of his ulcer."

"Salami *is* garlic. *Denotes* garlic. Anyway, that's all clothes and books and notebooks."

Joanna looked bruised and said, "Honestly, there is some salami in here, though not all. I admit that, and I've found a place that does it with much less garlic than anywhere else so all one can do is hope. We'll see each other on Monday at seven and go out at once because it's not right this business of lurking when one of us is using the kitchen."

"I don't understand why we don't get asked."

"I know, but Victoria wouldn't see it that way. This way you've got the place to yourself all weekend."

"And I've got the paint-stripper for the tub so I've that to do."

On Saturday Juliet spent four hours in the empty bath patiently stripping yellowed paint off the original porcelain. The smell of the paint-stripper was noxious.

Harriet rang and asked her to a cocktail party that evening.

"I'm in an old pair of chef's pants because I'm stripping the bath and can't make it but thank you a lot," she said.

"How are you doing it? The bath."

"By sitting in it."

"Why aren't your flat-sharers doing it with you?"

"They're away for the weekend."

"Do you want me to come over?"

"Two of us in a tub already guaranteed to burn your skin off?"

"You shouldn't be left alone in a bath."

Anyway. Tomorrow was a Sunday. Of course, Juliet woke unusually early on this day to be rid of. She made coffee. Her Soho street was full of shops selling coffee beans out of huge sacks: beans that you were encouraged to run your hands through and to smell before you bought. She did some necessary work, found it engrossing for five hours, and then got out her address book and rang everyone she knew, including Harriet. No one was in. "One's forefinger gets fatigued with dialling. Also one's mind," she said to herself. It was a day and evening nearly impossible to get through, though reading Jane Austen helped. That grace of moral order.

Early on Monday morning, she telephoned Harriet to ask her if she would choose some people to come to dinner far ahead in the Soho flat, and if she would do it now, before they were likely to have gone to work. Harriet did some quick telephoning and rang back. Dinner the Thursday after next. Married couples, all of them. "People do seem to get booked up. These particular people are more interesting than nice, if you know what I mean. I could have a look for an extra man for you at the L.S.E.," said Harriet; but Juliet said, "I'd be getting up and down with cooking and plates, and anyway who cares about *placement* now?" The phrase "extra man" rang in her head.

She cooked cassoulet, new to the peculiar ingredients ("pig's knuckle, or trotter if unavailable, a quarter of a goose . . ."). The butcher knew what she wanted. The one she liked best had a particularly beautiful shop window, with crowns of delicate lamb cutlets dressed in chef's frilled caps of miniature size. The cuts of meat were arranged on bright green artificial grass. She had never seen grass like this except in Hollywood.

She thought of Beverly Hills, and the huge rolls of such stuff that were used for celebrities' dinner parties to protect the real grass.

She also made taramasalata. Her cohabitants in the flat helped with setting the table. They had asked their own boyfriends. Henry in person at last. Victoria's had brought his guitar. Juliet said to him, "Would you mind a lot if you played the piano instead? There's one in the bedroom. Or maybe you don't play the piano."

"It would mean cutting my nails. I need my nails for my guitar." The nails were as long as a mandarin's.

"Yes, you'd regret it," said Juliet.

"Juliet's against regret," said Victoria, a ready translator of the clear.

"There's bound to be somebody else who can play a piano," said Juliet. "I suppose I even could, in spite of the cassoulet. It's only that we've had such a heap of guitar music at home since protest songs, and people sitting on floors in jeans, and there isn't much room for sitting on the floor here with three sofas in the room. Also, no one listening to guitar songs knows when they're going to stop. Whereas with a piano you do."

Some of the people who came, at helpful Harriet's suggestion, were politicians; some literary editors; some photographers; one a titled writer of an expensive and inept cookery book illustrated with witty drawings of disaster in the kitchen with *noblesse oblige* going on in the drawing room. A man who had been identified only as "Could-we-bring-somebody" was introduced namelessly as "This-is-who-we-meant." He was the Mr. Neal of the chefs' trousers encounter. Both he and Juliet remembered very well indeed. He came with her into the kitchen, which was as small as a broom cupboard.

"Something in the oven smells splendid. What is it?"

"Cassoulet. What are you called before Neal?"

"Nick. It's nice of you to have me. What can I do?"

"Remember for me where people are sitting. I've written it out on my hand." She showed him the palm of her hand with a table plan and initials on it in ink.

He studied the palm as if he were telling her fortune. Realizing what he must look as if he were doing, he said, nodding to the drawing-room-cum-dining-room, "Most of the people here aren't exactly lifelines." He soaped off the ink after he had convinced her that the two of them had safely committed the drawing to memory. She had put him on her right, but he said that the shadow minister present had to be on her right. So Nick, that source of help, was to be far away.

"I always wonder how long one has to soak real haricots," said an antique dealer named Clara in a tenth-hand Victorian evening dress that, as she explained loudly to no one in particular, had cost her a year's salary. Leaving no space for an answer, she said, "If it hadn't been for Christopher, who's getting thinner and thinner on his yogurt . . . Sorry. Lost my way. Oh yes, if it hadn't been for Christopher living near his flea market I'd never have found it. Christopher has pull in lace."

"Twenty-four hours," said Juliet to Clara.

"What?" said Clara.

"The beans."

"Must have been awake all night," said a highly mooted Tory M.P. called Bertie.

"They don't need watching," said Juliet. But Bertie had the habit of making statements rather than asking questions, and he had already gone on to ask the table at large if anyone knew whether Piggy was still footing it in Nuristan.

"No," said a literary editor called, it seemed, Chips, "but Bimbie's still out there."

The wives, called Emma (two), Pit-Pony, Becca, and Caroline (two), listened carefully to their husbands and spoke across everyone willy-nilly about a distinguished couple from South Africa who had been under house arrest for five years. At last, mention of people whom Juliet knew about. She tried to get a word in about their pamphlets and the wife's novels.

"One *must* read something she's done," said Clara. "One hears about her books all the time."

"They do loom," said Bertie.

The witty artist drew a witty drawing on the back of his bread-and-butter plate. The ink would come off the plate, but not the butter now on the tablecloth, Juliet thought. Then the mooted young politician spilt his glass of red wine.

"Salt," said Clara.

"No," said the politician. "That turns it black immediately. One trick. Foolproof. Pour some very *good* claret on it at once, and then wait three seconds and put at least half a bottle of Sauterne on it. Chemical reaction. It's got to be frightfully good Sauterne. I've seen it work even on Aubusson carpets. I daresay it's because of the age of the claret and then the counter-reaction of the sugar in the Sauterne."

Equipped only with Chianti, it seemed to Juliet that it was going to be cheaper to buy a new tablecloth. The incident any-way passed in an instant, and only Nick looked at the cloth and then firmly got up and put soap and water on the mess.

"One still misses old Fruity," Bertie said out of the blue.

For a moment even Harriet forgot his invariable freedom from context and looked for fruit for him in the kitchen. This in spite of the Brie and salad on the table. And then she re-membered that a man called Fruity had been Bertie's best friend who had died two years ago of an undiagnosed illness in the midst of writing what had promised to be an innovative book.

Bertie, Fruity, Bimbie, Piggy, Pit-Pony. "It's all names," Ju-liet shouted suddenly and very fast, crying; "I mean, I know they're your friends, but I don't even seem to get time to ask you about them." She ran down the stairs and out into the street for a few moments. No one noticed except Nick. When she came back she had mustered herself and said, so low that people at last attended: "Look. I know I'm American, and I don't expect you to have heard of Eudora Welty or Peter Fonda even, but there must be something English we could all talk about. Or some*one*, if that's easier. Inigo Jones? Sickert?" No luck. "Britten?"

"Oh, you mean the E.E.C.," said the mooted politician. "One doesn't think of it as Britain any longer."

"She means Benjamin Britten, I think," said Nick.

Pit-Pony leaned over for some Brie. Juliet asked her about her name. "It's because the family comes from rather near the mines, the coal mines, and I used to go to the cottages of the miners' wives who worked in the house because they let me do things more than the family, and often I'd stay with them overnight." She paused, and couldn't go on with the cheese. "It's very bad up there now. We don't know much down South.

I wish people in London wouldn't call me Pit-Pony. Eliza's a perfectly good name up there. Do you feel a bit lost here, Juliet?"

Taking a cue of manners, as he saw it, the literary editor leaned forward to Juliet and said, "When are you going back?"

"She's here," said Nick. "Why do English people always ask that?"

"Why why?"

"Why what?"

"Why do you ask why?" said the literary editor.

"Bound to make anyone feel they've got no place here, isn't it?" said Nick. "Wouldn't it be more interesting to find out why she came?"

"Because of the L.S.E.," said Juliet, "and Shakespeare and Jane Austen and Harriet Martineau and the way English people love Nelson, and things." She looked quickly at Nick. "And other things."

"You haven't told us about the L.S.E. An exchange, was it?" said the shadow minister.

"No. I did it on my own." Ferocity, unusual in her. "And, apart from Shakespeare, I suppose Pope, Dryden, Swift, Chaucer, A.J. Ayer, Bertrand Russell, Purcell, the Beatles, as Harriet knows."

Nick stayed with her and helped with the washing up. Then he took her to his flat in Devonshire Street. For days they played truant and saw only each other, eating sardines or fried bread and tomatoes, walking in Regent's Park, looking at old bookshops, reading in bed.

"What exactly do you do?" she asked, after a couple of days spent mostly in the bedroom.

"Not much."

"But what exactly?"

"I was a waiter in Marylebone Lane, but I'll have got the sack by now for being absent without telephoning. I used to be a doctor but now I'm doing research. Being a waiter gives you time for thinking."

"That's what you mostly do?" she said, herself thinking, and then, "Could I be on the other side of the bed for a while?"

She climbed over him. He said, "Or I suppose it might be called thinking about thinking. I mostly keep a notebook and put things down that might lead somewhere one day. Also I'm learning electroencephalography. I'm teaching myself. I've got a place in a lab at hospital. Just being a G.P. didn't seem very adventurous at my age, so I chucked it at fifty."

"You talked about Hamlet in your sleep last night. I couldn't quite make it out."

"I put it down, whatever it was." His notebook was now on her side of the bed. "Look for it if you like. It's one but the last. It's only a note." She read, "Young man ransacking his mother for mislaid birthright of innocence. Magnanimous play." After that there was a note about electronics that she couldn't decipher.

Juliet dreamt of New York: of the noises of sirens, and car horns, and transistor radios held to the ears of pedestrians; and of Central Park concerts where she had often stood in line since early in the morning with her bike and a picnic to hear some great singer in the evening from a place on the grass near enough to escape the hubbub of the streets alongside. She woke abruptly, waking Nick, and said, "I said 'waiting in line' in my sleep."

"I didn't hear it. Why does it matter?"

"It should be 'queueing.' "

"Only here. You were in New York in your head. Either's all right. It depends who you are."

"Not where you are?"

"Both people understand both sorts of English, unless they're duffers."

Nick went to work at the restaurant at eleven next morning, hoping that his job would re-offer itself. Juliet read all day, which was her way of going to ground, and forgot about lunch. The telephone rang. She had the common odd instinct, just before picking up the receiver, about who the call was from and that it was for her. So she said "Nicholas Jefferson residence here."

"And this is Nick's Diner speaking and would you like to come and have a rather nice dirt-cheap load of abroad dinner at six o'clock? The restaurant is Pakistani and we'll have to eat in the kitchen. The waiters wait on each other." He gave her the address. He gave her a map. He made her draw it for herself over the telephone. As though in readiness for a long foray, she put on espadrilles. Following the map, which she had again drawn on her hand just as she had the seating of people to dinner, she set off. Many doctors' plates in brightly polished brass. A soldiers' hospital named after Edward VII. In three minutes she had reached the restaurant. Nick being the man he was, he had not wanted her to wait and was waiting there himself at the door.

They had tandoori chicken. The chicken was hot, the kitchen very hot, the prices very cheap. Many of the people there, mostly men, were reading as they ate. Languages got mixed in her ears. The voices she had been reading: Flannery O'Connor, Burke, Beckett; and the voices she was hearing: Nick's, her own, Pakistanis', waiters' answering dinner orders in languages she couldn't understand or sometimes even place. Her own accent she found imprecise and slurred but Nick understood it well enough. Again, he saw where her attention lay, and he explained that a lot of young foreign doctors worked here when they weren't on call.

"Doctors in America earn a fortune."

"Not here. Not if they're working on their own time to be specialists. Or if they're juniors on the N.H.S."

"I thought the N.H.S. was going downhill."

"Most people think that about everything about England, including a lot of English people and including some ex-left-wing waiters who've made a pile and taken to hunting. But some of them get it right. One who's got it dead right has been working so hard that he's just had a nervous breakdown."

"Is he in a clinic?"

"No, he's working. He's got a job to do."

"Doesn't he need help?"

"What does that mean?"

"Psychotherapy?"

"Help doesn't mean that in England."

"Then what?"

He went through a few of his notions of help. Friends. Company. Books. Work, obviously. Humor. Sense of ancestry. He thought even of saying "Mercy," but put that aside and instead paid the bill, which turned out to be a matter of subtracting the amount from his wages. Juliet listened to the Tower of Babel sounds in the kitchen. He said, "This is what the big English cities are like now. Swinging London had always been a magazine invention. Gave rise to a great many very bad pizza places and a great many W.1. houses turned into gambling joints. W.1. is what abroad calls Mayfair. And estate agents, of course. There's a Czech playwright eating over there. He speaks English but he won't write in it. He says he can't. Terrible thing, for a writer to be plundered of his language. He signed the Civil Rights manifesto. That's why he limps. The police shot him as he was escaping but they only got his ankle. It's a very bad fracture."

Nick went into the dining room to work. She had the spare key to his flat. She did some unnoticeable housework for him, thinking to be useful. She had asked him again about whether she might read his notebook and, being an unfretful man, he had said, "Of course. They're not journals."

All the same, she waited until he came back, and then she read in another room after he had fallen asleep. One passage struck her because she had had no hint of the part of his mind that would have prompted it. A note about a man in the time of the Gospels, and his function in that society being accessory to his character, and society something he could control. "Now a man is an annex of his social function and there's nothing he can do when the bias of his character and the edicts of his job happen to conflict." And immediately after that, a note about her in the caterers' shop. About the clothes she wore, and then an exact report of the words, and then "Edicts of her undertaking v. instinct to quit?"

She thought about Nick: the way he had listened to things in Soho, the way he worked at the restaurant. She went to sleep in the room where she had been reading and dreamed all over again, word by word, the ungentle dinner party in Soho. Jumping awake from thirst after that was over, she had a drink of water and went immediately to sleep again until she was wakened by the noise of Nick shouting. She went fast into the bedroom and shook him awake. "You were having a nightmare."

"Was I talking in my sleep?"

"Screaming."

"No way to lead a platoon," he said, still in the nightmare. "Was it in the Ardennes?"

"I don't know."

"A tank's blowing up there. It's in flames. Six men inside. I can't see. My eyelids are too hot. Everytime I run back to get one of the men out it gets worse."

"Sit up. You're still in the dream." She got him some hot broth because he kept saying, "Hot sweet tea."

"It's a *dream.*" She thought of slapping his face, but it seemed quite the wrong thing to do. "It's not as though you're hyster-ical," she said, explaining out loud without noticing.

"One gave them hot sweet tea for shock," he said. "It was all they wanted. There was one of them I couldn't get out." At least he had moved into the past tense. He went suddenly to sleep and she thought it best to stay this time. She overslept, of course, to his scorn. He brought her breakfast in bed. "You were talking in your sleep," he told her.

Not the moment to bring up the Ardennes, she said to her-self. Out loud, "What about?"

"New York. You do miss the sticks and stones of New York, don't you?"

"Not in Devonshire Street. I thought eggs were short here. You've given me a boiled egg."

"They're not short now. That was in the war. Forty years ago. I'm very old for you."

"Old to be a *waiter,* perhaps, but not a waiter learning elec-troencephalography."

"Old to be an extra man."

"Some phrase."

"Worse things. What exactly were you dreaming about?"

"That awful party.'

"England isn't all like that. You won't skedaddle, will you? I thought I'd go into the lab today. I think I may have left the sterilizer on."

She bought food on the way back from the L.S.E., and a kaftan, and started barbecuing steak on the toasting grill of his gas cooker as soon as she heard his key in the door. The place immediately reeked. She opened the windows and went back to the stove. He yelled at her, turned off the stove, and shouted, "Turn back those ridiculous sleeves, you idiot. You can't do a cookout in a kimono. You might have been a cinder."

"It's not a cookout, it's a cookin. This isn't the first time I've cooked steak. And there's ratatouille."

"Garlic makes me sick."

The steak cooled. They went to bed without dinner. She kept the ratatouille in the fridge, hoping for improvements in appetite. That night she had violent dreams about petrol thrown on to flames: because of the row, the flaming steak, the flaming tank. Next morning it seemed that he had had much the same dream. Things healed. They had the cold steak for lunch. "The ratatouille's still delicate ground," she said.

"Yup."

"Do you want to chuck it out?"

"Not on your life."

He worked in a notebook and then among his long charts of electroencephalographs. She wrote letters to America. He said suddenly from the floor: "When I was on the tube yesterday a woman said her doctor had told her that her liver was on a knife-edge. That was how I felt about the ratatouille. But I shouldn't have shouted at you. I'm sorry."

"Well, you were in a war."

"I had a very easy war."

"I've heard a lot of Englishmen like you say that."

He thought and then gave a barking sort of laugh.

"What was that about?" said Juliet.

"My sister. She was the private secretary to somebody top-secret. She was the ideal private secretary because the most fascinating things went right over her head. She'd be reading women's magazines and serials and horoscopes, you see, between using her high speeds. So you can safely ask her about the most confidential decisions and she hasn't an idea what you're trying to find out. And so you could say that women's magazines won the war for us."

"At the dinner party, did you notice how people much too young to remember the war kept on saying how American food parcels kept Britain going?"

"There are pockets of English people who are condescending to America."

"But not your restaurant. There were a lot of very young American students there and they knew more about the Czechs than I do. They'd been there."

"I've been to America twice, actually. The Medical Research Council helped. Oh, by the way, I think I may have left the sterilizer on." She had begun to recognize this as a ploy. He said, "As it's a Saturday, we wouldn't be disturbing anyone if you came in with me. Would you like that?"

As if he were giving her a treat, he told her in the lab a little about electromyography. "It's a matter of sinking needles into the right place, basically." He laid himself down on the examination couch and told her to watch for what happened on something that looked much like a television screen. Green waves. She turned round, and shouted to him to stop, please.

"I thought you'd be interested. It doesn't hurt at all. I know what I'm doing." But he got off the examination couch. Juliet, feeling ashamed, took Nick to see a revival of a poor film called *Green Slime* because the title had always interested her. On the way out, he said, "We might go back to America for a while together, yes?" Having a careful mind, he added, "Before coming back, of course."

Dame of
the British Empire, BBC

"It's extraordinary that they didn't get B.H.," said Yseult, an actress with elocution famous all over England. If only Wilde were still alive to write for her, radio listeners said. If only Congreve.

"B.H.?" said Bell, the young pregnant wife of the assistant producer. She had not yet grown used to the reign of initials at the BBC. The D.G. was the Director-General. She had once been engaged to the D.O.P.S., the Director of Overseas Programme Services. Baffled by him, though already keenly missing their future, she talked to the vicar and cancelled the wedding time reserved at the church.

Yseult, D.B.E. (Dame of the British Empire), sipped her wine. "B.H., dear. Broadcasting House. From the air, the roof is the shape of a battleship. Obviously the easiest point for a crucial direct hit. They got a great deal of Harley Street. But B.H. carried on. I remember the miracle of it, even though I was only a small child."

The second great actress at this dinner party was called Nora, also a D.B.E. The dinner, an anxious one, was at a refectory table in a house of wood and glass beside an inlet of the Thames near Henley. Nora said, "Yes, I remember. I was in the Wrens. I hadn't thought of you as being a child in the Blitz, Yseult."

"You *remember?*" said Yseult. "I've only really heard about it. From my father, who was on fire duty. My little nose pressed against the windowpane in Portland Place. I couldn't sleep. I've never been an easy sleeper." ("No, you haven't," her husband had said long ago, after banishment to the dressing room. Now dead, she thought, and I still upright, Lord help us.)

The two actresses were famous through the world for a radio duologue between haughty mistress and fast-thinking maid that was broadcast not only in England every week but also on the BBC World Service. Their enunciation was so clear, their writer so direct, that their soothed listeners in Africa flooded them with particularly devoted fan letters.

Yseult pursued the point about being old enough to recall the Blitz. She had been placed, at the last minute, at the head of the table, where the famous elocutory boom that gave sound engineers weekly trouble could do no particular harm to the people seated next to her: the obeisant assistant producer and the gentle, gray-haired head of drama, who knew the value of the series and the pitfalls of his actresses' pairing. At the foot of the table was the writer of the series, their host: a good cook, hostile to blenders and serf to a sieve.

The duo of Yseult and Nora worked on the air as it never could have done onstage. Yseult, who at six had changed her name from her baptismal one, Ann, because she thought the Arthurian motif fit for her, now stood six foot three. Possible for a character part, hard for a heroine. For ten years she had worked in opera, but her height made things difficult. The tenors with her wore the highest possible lifts inside their boots, but they still stood well below her. Costume designers always gave her long skirts, and she would sing with her knees bent; there grew into being so many cruel imitations of her Groucho walk that she was stricken. The last scald of fate's revenge came when she was singing in *La Sonnambula* and the bridge in the sleepwalking scene failed to break as it should have. The stage manager wondered whether to bring down the curtain. The conductor dithered. She led the orchestra, sang more, walked back, and tried the stage trickery again. Again the bridge didn't break. Music critics in the audience started to laugh. The third time it worked, and she fell safely, to the relief of the insurance company, who were being telephoned by the money-minded director of the opera house. Her noble common sense in this notorious opera debacle, practiced by a prima donna thought to be unmitigatedly vain, went uncommended. Her pride had been scraped, but she took action of a mildness not attributed to her. Only one other person at the table knew what she had achieved: the writer and host had been there. To the others, including the kindly Nora, no Ibsen door-banger, she was as she had always seemed: invulnerably sure of herself and prone to the stupidity that often goes with competitiveness.

So. Yseult at the head of the table, hastily placed there instead of at her host's right, so that she could lead the table in general without doing harm in the particular; Nora on the host's right; the host, tall, witty, with long legs that tangled like poles in a ski fall; the assistant producer; his wife, Bell, already feeling her own hand in her lap as separate from herself, as if the baby.

"Have some more of this curious stew," said the host.

"Curious it is," said Yseult. "In the vein of farce, as the cuisine modes go."

"Yseult," said Nora. "He had to cook for one person on the Scarsdale Diet, one person allergic to dairy products, one vegetarian, one person who swells up on anything farinaceous. So we might have had a hot-pot of polyunsaturated margarine and fresh basil and turnip broth, wouldn't you say?"

"How are your cows?" said the pregnant girl with true interest.

"Well, darling," said Nora, "we haven't had the right weather this year, so we've only been getting twenty gallons from the ones who usually give us thirty. So we've got to be patient until they have calves again next year and lactate again. It's the one thing we can't blame on the recession."

"I was thinking about them," said Bell.

Nora turned to her. "Yes. I've moved from the house, you know. After Billy's death it was too big. So I switched to one of the dairyman's cottages. My daughter called it the Old Cow's House and I thought it was funny at first, but now it makes me feel old. I hope a sense of humor doesn't pass, like the capacity to do backbends."

"Can you do backbends?" said the assistant producer. "Or could you?"

"Now only if I use a wall or a doorjamb." Nora made a

"May I?" face at her host and did a backbend down the door-jamb of the door behind the open-plan kitchen, the house within being architect-designed and short of doors.

Bell clapped. Yseult said, "Wonderfully achieved." She could have made "Hello" sound like a full line of Racine, if such a word had been in his vocabulary. She and Nora had played together for so long, with a warmth and ease owed mostly to Nora's sunny well-being, that not many people around even this table knew that the quick sophistications plied between the two great actresses playing domestic-serial situations in Restoration style emanated as much from Yseult as from Nora, or that Yseult was fighting for something. Her life, you could say.

"I noticed you didn't have the ratatouille on the sundeck," said the host.

"I don't care for a first course away from table," said Yseult.

"I like the garlic in it, and the Pernod, was it? An invention? Garlic makes you sleep without dreams," said Nora.

"Garlic makes you unknowable," said the assistant producer. He was frightened by having spoken, but sped on. "The first smell of garlic comes through the soles of naked feet. Been known since Roman times. You can tell from the amount of foot-washing in the Gospels that Jesus' feet smelt." He had a drink of wine, and said, "Shortest verse in the Bible: 'Jesus stank.' "

There was a pause of horror. "Dear heart," said Yseult, putting her arthritic but beautiful hand on his, "that remark is at the level of graffiti. It's a level not up to your instep."

There was a glance between Yseult and Nora, and Nora said, "Do you remember the mess we made about the poetry reading?"

"All too well. You may tell it. Except that the mess, the *confusione,* was not made by us. It was in the passive, not the active. The mess was made."

"We were asked to give a poetry reading at a car factory," said Nora, "by a young man full of purpose about bringing poetry to the people." She paused, not laughing, which was her habit when she found herself absurd for being trapped in the jargon of liberalism. She had been chased out of a job in Hollywood because she caught the note of Fascism rising in the anti-Semitism there long before most people had picked up the wavelength. "Yseult and I were to do a lunchtime recital. At this car factory. We made a new translation of 'The Wife of Bath' to lift their spirits."

"Very little of valuable lewdness has been written for many a century. Of true value. Not pinchbeck. Don't you agree?" said Yseult to the table at large. "Now, this table itself, being of the monastic, reminding us of the ethos of Mt. Athos, tells us everything about what we now think of as puritanism and therefore, of course, of its obverse or antithesis, which is to say the lewd in its own pure, though scarcely puritanical, sense."

"I don't understand a word you're saying," said the assistant producer.

"No," said the host.

"I have read in Middle English many times in the desert throughout Africa, and the people of the sand have clustered to hear. Have understood me," said Yseult. "At the car factory I would have been understood, Nora. It was simply the absence of the people that was at fault."

"Darlings," said Nora, "this nice young man was perfectly a Socialist, but brought up in Bournemouth, and educated at a quite expensive preparatory school before Modern Greats at Oxford, and he picked us up for a lunchtime recital at twenty to one and when we arrived the canteen was quite empty. For this friend of the people didn't know that his people's lunch hour is from twelve to one. If one starts work at seven, you see. He needed comfort for his mistake, but he only eats yogurt. Other people's yogurt. He believes in being badly off."

"Easily achieved by not working," said the host.

Yseult suddenly found the chronicle of the gaffe not funny and said to her host, "You told us that last episode was going to be repeated. I've thought of what to do about the lines that don't get the laughs from the studio audience. So odd. A dowager of the highest rank saying to her butler after a line from her friend, myself, 'In a crisis of lethargy one does not speak at one's best from a hammock.' Now, in the night I hit on it. We shall get the laugh if we reverse the lines. The preceding line, intentionally dulled of course to lead up to the next, should be spoken by Nora. The response, I take it over, and we have our effect."

"The laugh," said Bell.

"A question of collaborative creation," said Yseult. "By displacement we perfect."

"So who does get the laugh who didn't get the laugh?" said Bell.

"Dumper dumper dumper dum," hummed the assistant producer in warning, nodding to the head of the table.

The head of drama said he felt sure something of the sort would work out well on the floor. Head of drama not for nothing, he diverted and said, "Children write to us. A lot of them. One was invited to a studio audience and I had a long letter from him in the Gothic script."

Yseult said, drawing the letter from her bag, "Yes, I should say it was Gothic."

Nora said, "He sent me a carbon copy," and also drew it from her bag. "You read it, Yseult. I think the boy had been reading a lot. The letter is from Brixton."

Yseult used a lorgnette on an ivory handle and read aloud, " 'My dear Dames Yseult and Nora: Notwithstanding the lateness of this apology for my absence at your programme, I hope it is still a valid one. The cause of the lateness in question was the bloody (pardon me) tube. I had left my home at approximately 2:25 P.M., knowing that a journey to the BBC would not consume the greatest interval of time. I waited a bit and boarded an exceptionally filthy compartment. When I had arrived at the Oxford Circus halt, I was stalled in the train for some time. Estimating that I would arrive at the performance while it had already commenced, I decided not to do so and left the stranded compartment. I then directed my steps out of the station and professed to myself that I would walk home since I delight in walking. On reaching home, I decided to give an explanation to you both that very evening but neglected doing thus. For the past week or so, I have neglected my obligation to you, I regretfully must pray.' " Yseult paused.

"I think it's 'say,' " said Nora.

" 'Pray' is a funnier mischance from a prodigiously gifted young mind." Yseult carried on, " 'In any event, that is all I have to expound to you on that matter. It will interest you to know that I have finished *Wuthering Heights,* which made quite a signet on my emotions for its passion and different faces of human nature.' "

"Facets," said Nora, forgetting that Yseult had trouble now

with her eyes. "He deserves attention, darling."

Yseult went on, " 'Though I am making tentative arrangements concerning a gathering, to which you are of course invited, I would like to find occasion for meeting with you prior to the aforementioned gathering. My timetable for daily activity is exceedingly flexible: much of my days are spent at home. I know that you and I will have much to chat about for an afternoon's tête-à-tête. My heartfelt wishes to you. Yours ever, Nathaniel Fare.' "

Bell clapped. The head of drama, used to whisking away attention from an act impossible to counteract, said, "May I tell the table a story about you, Yseult? It caused great trouble to O.B."

"Outside Broadcasts," said the assistant producer.

"Now, many of you will have wondered what happened to our great Yseult when she dropped opera."

"The bridge incident. So I got married," said Yseult, playing with a fork.

"To a farmer in Lincolnshire," said Nora.

"We were married for six years."

"So you *must* remember the Blitz," said the host, as lightly as he could.

"I've lied about my age so often I don't know how old I am any longer, in truth," said Yseult. "What a pleasure: linen table napkins. A picnic laid on napery upon the greensward."

"Who said that?" asked the host.

"Yseult did," said Nora, giving time.

The head of drama went on, "We were doing our 'Farmer's Weekly' programme. Our breakfast programme each week, live. A farm breakfast at six-thirty in the morning because of the milking. We arrived, and the sound effects of teaspoons and cereal were excellent. We spoke easily of pigs, arable-land value, value-added tax for farmers, clay and iron content, the enviable Lincolnshire soil. Yseult was pouring tea, and to my shame I didn't recognize her inherent greatness. But there was a fine white wall and I told our excellent cameraman to put a rustic chair against it with Yseult, given her permission, upon it. We— I speak for the unit—wanted her contribution as a farmer's obviously hardworking wife. Our interviewer said that she must find the life very interesting. Do you remember what you said, Yseult?"

"Of course."

"What was it?"

" *'I hate it.'* That's what I said."

"We couldn't bleep it."

"I had to go on after that. My husband had taken the car keys from me, I said, in case I ran away."

"And then?" said the host.

"I went to the railway station after the programme on my child's bicycle, and came to London to find a job. My child was better in the country and she loved her father."

"How much money did you have?" said Bell.

"The stationmaster took the bicycle as credit for a ticket. I should imagine him to have been a man of the caliber to send the bicycle back somehow. I slept in Regent's Park. One of our Edwardian summers." Yseult played with her napkin, and took out her compact to hide her tears, using the napkin to blow her nose: an action observed by everyone. "That wretched agriculture has left me in a permanent state of flu," she said. "I wish our sound-effects man were here for me to pay him tribute. When we hear our playbacks, I have never detected my having a blocked nose. It would be a vulgar comic device for my character. That young man has perfect pitch for the self-absorption that is the tonic note of comedy." But no one found it funny that she was absorbed by her elegant nose, the nose of a Plantagenet with adenoids.

Addio

The London Victorian Wigmore Hall, where the cheerful cherubs had been not even so much as chipped by the Blitz and where the acoustics were better than the ones bought by any number of dollars for Avery Fisher Hall, in New York City, was less packed than usual for the great Madame Johanna Alba's master class. Her famed role for fifty years had been Cherubino in Mozart's *The Marriage of Figaro.* At seventy—"too late," many people said—she surrendered her sprightly young-boy part and became famous as the same opera's serene Countess. Retaining dignity, she then resisted even in her prized master class any urge to sing her great role of old.

The two dozen semifinalists, chosen from over two hundred applicants, sat on school chairs onstage. A few musicologists were allowed into the auditorium, a few other singers. Madame Alba was laced into her celebrated costume for Cherubino, even though she was to sing the Countess at chosen moments. Close-fitting white waistcoat, pink breeches, pale-blue tights not supposed to bulge, though they reminded several blackhearts in the audience of the legs of a hippopotamus in pale-blue surgical stockings. The lacing of the waistcoat had been no mean feat. At last, Madame Alba, who had the musicianship to value her breath control more than her figure, commanded three holes of her waistcoat to be eased.

"We could retain the bosom," her dresser of forty years said loyally. She had travelled with Madame from opera house to

· *302* ·

opera house, like the trunk holding Madame's famous pale-blue cloak for *Tosca.* Though suited neither to the role nor to the ominous plot, the forget-me-not cloak remained. Everyone objected. Nevertheless, Madame was to be obeyed. A resident director at Covent Garden had once contrived to put Madame into black for *Tosca,* instead of her beloved pale blue. He still bore on his forehead the scar of the marble mantelpiece of his club's main fireplace, which she had upheaved and thrown at him for vilifying her cloak at the after-opera party. Her Goliath strength was in a spirit equalled only by grand opera itself.

"Were we to retain the trimness of the bosom," said Madame sternly to her dresser at the Cherubino fitting, "we should only emphasize the natural musical fullness of the waist."

So the enlarged Cherubino sat on the thronelike armchair, itself upholstered plumply in a matching pink-and-white design that seemed to add further limbs to the diva's own. Indications of plot by way of odd bits of furniture were carried in. A gold clock, a window frame empty of glass, a high-backed sofa meant not for sitting but only for the blithe fancies of rococo conspiracy. One of the few lay people in the audience of Alba fanatics, a Gregorian-chant expert named Daphne, quite unfamiliar with *The Marriage of Figaro,* asked questions of her friend Gavin, a man knowledgeable in these things. She looked respectfully at the bareness of the furnished stage, at the meagerness of the props. "It's not modern, is it? It's not minimal?"

"No. Nothing simplistic here. The impoverishment is dramatic, not optic. It is also, of course, historically lateral. The Shakespearean mockery by Mozart, for instance, in the way Cherubino is dressed as a boy."

"But Madame Alba's going to sing the Countess, it says in the programme. The students are the Cherubinos, singing bits of him one by one. And also, the Countess is dressed as a puppy-fat girl."

"This is in memory of her great days as Cherubino. A page boy."

"He must have been horribly teased at school," said Daphne, who knew more about present-day upper-class cruelty than about eighteenth-century aesthetic conventions, just as she felt more about Mozart's death in a pauper's grave than about the honor given to divas. "On the whole, I'm on the side of paupers, not of prima donnas," she said to her programme.

"Where does it say that?" said Gavin, leaning over her.

"I did."

The master class began. Tape recorders were started. Daphne whispered, "Those must be elastic tights. I wonder where she gets them." Her overriding interest was in operatic memorabilia, in the sense of clothes. Even more than in Gregorian manuscripts.

"I should think that mews shop off the Charing Cross Road would have an idea." Gavin otherwise ignored her heavily. His interest was in opera from Gluck up to, but not including, Bellini. "My passion is for *Figaro,* per se," he murmured to her severely, somehow turning the sentence into a music lover's glance backward at a hummer in the row behind. Daphne was crushed as the harpsichord began. She looked up at one of the cherubs and pondered elastic tights.

Madame Alba did not speak. This would have been a misuse of her voice. She whispered to the audience that she was going to sing the Countess an octave lower "to save my instrument." The audience rustled in passionate comprehension. The padded, page-boy Countess sang "Porgi amor" at a school desk decked out as the Countess's dressing table, looking at herself in an ornate hand mirror empty of glass. Confusion grew. The chosen students on their uncomfortable seats controlled their breathing, one or another dashing in and out of hiding and through the Countess's window at moments sprung on them by the prompter acting as stage director, and prayed that Madame would lead them somewhere in the speeded chronology fixed upon.

Again and again, the same process was gone through. Semifinalist by semifinalist.

"Where are we?" whispered Daphne.

"Round about the music master, I should say." Scant evidence of men onstage, but Gavin had confidence.

Alba's voice, distinctly hers even at an octave lower, again and again led beckoned singers to stand and to sing, in spite of the contracted plot, "Voi che sapete." Notes were taken by judges in the audience. Now and again, the director continued to order that the contestants scuttle behind the sofa or through the window (stagecraft). Madame went on singing an octave lower. Not out of prima-donna exhibitionism but out of a wish not to be drawn into contest.

The last entrant, an immensely fat girl of clear-eyed beauty, eventually got up at Madame's beckoning. Again Madame sang the Countess in her baritone whisper. Little was left of her greatness except in her phrasing.

"It would be more difficult at that pitch," whispered Gavin, making a note of no consequence on his programme.

"More difficult altogether," whispered Daphne, her mind suppressing elastic tights. "Control."

"All musicianship is control. Or, rather, liberation controlled."

"I wonder why we go to concerts together." She wished her words back, and thought them again, as though using invisible ink to rid her mind of them.

"Liberation controlled," repeated Gavin, ignoring her trouble and gripped only by his own last words, touching her spinster hand to take the chill out of his edict. He had no idea that she was blaming herself. He was not one to impute impulse.

The big girl began "Voi che sapete." Solemnity gripped the audience. This was the voice of the evening, a voice that would never have a chance, because of the girl's size. The exquisite melody took flight. The rising cadences seemed to be drawn up by something more than the flowing of notes. No passion that music cannot raise and quell, thought Daphne in counterpoint. Dryden. Gavin looked round at her; a fidgety man, but she was not to be interrupted in her concentration.

Madame Alba rose from her judge's seat and softly joined the melody, recognizing greatness. First she sang an octave lower, then in unison. A marvel was occurring. The uncastable girl finished and went back to her seat. Madame stayed standing, without realizing it. No one in the audience knew what to do. Shout bravo at the brilliant bulk? Throw roses? Where from? The harpsichordist had his head on the keyboard. He had been told to keep Madame's voice down an octave, and he had failed. Then he got up and bowed to the girl's success, raising his hands. Madame Alba was still standing, hands clasped together like a singer's at practice, tears streaming down her face. Someone in the audience shouted, clapping, "Your career is at the BBC. Go to the BBC," and the applause broke out. Madame Alba said, "Yes, the BBC," her own bulk looking fragile as she went up to the girl and shook both of her hands.

"Very good rendering," said Gavin.

On Each Other's Time

"Are you as low as I am?" said Alfred Rowlett, aged thirty-four, yelling cheerfully on the telephone from Bolivia at eight-thirty-five in the morning.

"I don't know how low that is," shouted his brother Federico (born in Positano but English as they come), aged thirty-two, from Madras, where it was five past six in the evening.

"About the riots," said Alfred.

"Where you are or where I am?" said Federico.

"In Liverpool," said Alfred.

"Probably lower, though I'm more resilient," said Federico. He was at the perennial disadvantage of being younger, a disadvantage that unduly weighed on him, because it was by nature unmendable. This insistence on being the more resilient was a perpetual defense. "I can hear your breakfast coming in."

"That isn't breakfast, that's my bed. They don't do breakfast here. They bring the bed instead. I suppose so that they don't have to make it, because it's gone again in the evening. I have to sleep on the floor. I have to wait for the bed to come back again in the morning and tip them, because otherwise they make a mess of my notes."

"You must be flaked."

"No, there's a rush on and not having a bed saves time. Is it tiring there?"

"I don't seem to be sleeping."

"Try lying down," said Alfred. "You never remember that

part. No one can sleep standing up except horses."

"The thing is, I have to walk about from now on so as to be up for being woken. They do it about ten at night here if you order a wake-up knock for four in the morning. I think it's because the English were so fierce to Indians about unpunctuality for nearly two hundred years that we've made them nervous."

"Have you got the figures yet?"

Federico read out to Alfred facts about divorce costs printed in an article published in London. They were about alimony, maintenance, the rising rates to any harried and/or married citizen in a string of countries that had nothing to do with where either of them was and nothing to do with England either. This was the way the brothers often helped each other. They were both social cartoonists, working at their drawing boards and listening in far-flung places to dilemmas and gripes expressed through many a beard net or yashmak, and their notions were kin. All four in this generation of the family alone were working wits of one sort or another. They had early come to an agreement about pooling information on their offices' foreign telephone expenses. The method saved money on long-winded explanations to researchers in London, who were anyway no good at pulling together suspiciously obscured facts even when they smelled as high as rank herring; it also saved the tedium of being put on hold with a caption for a cartoon and then cut off after someone at a news desk said, "Hang on while I get a pencil."

Alfred, the eldest of the four, was a specialist now on Latin America. He had been drawing cartoon chronicles ever since Oxford, with a wit in the tradition of pamphleteers and broadsheet writers, about the doings of the flagwagging "peacemakers" in high office whom he found in most countries of the world. He and Federico, the brother closest to him, had in common an unusual lack of careerism. Federico was the more solid man, as the saying goes, but no Rowlett was dulled. He had high degrees in divorce law. His knowledge about infidelity in the countries of the world had brought him to a unique point in financial cartooning.

When Federico was born, already named, it was pointed out to their lucid father that Alfred's and Federico's Christian names would render them both Freds. *"Render?"* said Mark Rowlett. "Render down, as with lard, or render to, as with bills? No child of ours is ever going to be nicknamed." Being a satirist, he had no need to raise his voice. "To be fair, two Oxford friends have made the same point. But if anyone really wants to collapse into lingo, the boys can be Alf and Fred. Though over my live body."

Mark Rowlett in his married life had always lived somewhere in Cumberland. He had moved and moved, with his shortwave radio and a very old Remington, on which he typed articles and broadcasts. His wife, Constance, was a theoretical mathematician, a wool-embroiderer, and a breeder of local sheep providing the best wool. Her third child was Deirdre, a beautiful young woman of twenty-eight engaged in a series of prodigiously long and wry articles—wry in a dodgy way, dodging you for fifty columns of sober type every time—about trees' ecology on this planet. She lived mostly in Scandinavia at the moment, for the interest of the trees. She, too, was on the economical family plan of research shared by telephone. Her childhood had been lonesome, though Alfred earnestly looked after her. A lot of her time had been spent in counting trees, much as other children make list upon list of friends, but the tree familiars had been so often lost to her by the family moves that she early despaired of anything's having longevity, including study and species. Long before she had got distinctions in every Oxford matriculation subject, she got below nought at school in Scripture, deportment, tolerance, and basketwork. No one in the family was inclined to take this seriously, but her father, an investigative reporter, investigated. He found that the basketwork mistress was also the Scripture mistress, and that for two terms running an embarrassed Deirdre had been made to play Eve, lamenting Adam's torn rib between the school desks. After that discovery Mark took her away from school and taught her himself. They worked swiftly together and she well on her own. Whichever house they were living in at the time, there was the same Carolean chair behind the desk where she was allowed to spread books for classics, which they saved for the evening. The chair's ribbed legs left marks on her own, because she twisted them around the carving.

The youngest, twenty-four, was Peter, a tall, thin boy who

became stroke of his university boat and a half-blue at squash. As a child, when at long last he had begun to speak, he was loquacious whenever lonely. His mother saw that he felt apart from the older three. He even loathed food, this skinny lad, while the rest of the table merely found food the least interesting thing at any dinner. If ever he had to be mildly punished for not doing homework, the only punishment meted was to shut him away at his desk in his own unlocked room. Quite unresentful, he cancelled out the punishment by going immediately to sleep under the desk, his thin complex of limbs like coils of plumbing under a basin. Constance found a clue when he said out of nowhere that he felt underexercised, "like a dozy lion, the dangerous kind." She immediately took him rowing every dawn on Lake Derwent Water. She was a good oar herself, for reasons no one knew. Like Peter, she was left-handed, but she gave the left oar to him to lend him a sporting chance. At eight, he didn't notice this, but at eight and a half he did. Thinking to repay her in effort, he taught himself shorthand secretly at his coed school, though the girls scoffed. As soon as he left school he became a cub reporter in the dock districts of Northumberland and Durham. The loquacity ended and he became inquiring, with the reporter's gift of seeming invisible. It came, perhaps, like all the children's distinct talents, from one or the other of their parents. Peter's conciseness came very much from his laconic father.

Mark's fame as a satirist had begun at Oxford in the days of the Spanish Civil War. He was to speak at the Union against an undergraduate named Hogg, whose political views he very much disliked. Mark let loose a greased hog in the hall. He had since been trying to explain to his Oxford contemporaries that a greased hog is not satire. Prewar Oxford was a curious interlude in his life. Brawn, beefy minds, a lot of sunrise baying for lukewarm Chablis left over from someone's party the night before. His County Durham childhood, in Consett, had been poor and frightening. His seaman father was drowned when Mark was nine, an only child; at the age of twelve he was seen off to sit for a scholarship to Winchester. He went alone through the ticket barrier carrying a cello left to him by his father. It was bigger than he was, and the weight added to the twitchings in his kneecaps. Despite fear he got a scholar-

ship. After that one bullish year at Oxford, also on a scholarship, he joined up, in the Merchant Navy. Unwarlike, decorated for bravery three times when his ships were torpedoed,
and still wondering whether he shouldn't have stood trial as a
conscientious objector and chosen the hated option of sugar-
beet farming, he went back to postwar Oxford. What an Oxford. British-railways buffet sort of meals instead of dinners
in Hall, men too old and grieved to be undergraduates trying
desperately to make up the war years they had lost. Mark threw
in his hand after two terms and started to earn a living as an
apprentice typesetter up North. Then he married Constance
and added to his wages by proofreading the telephone directory.

"To think there was a time when I proofed it," he said out
loud.

"What, darling?" said Constance, peering in at his study
window from the garden.

"And now I can't even see well enough to find it."

"What?"

"The telephone directory."

"I put it away the last time the phone was cut off." The
quarterly, laggardly, unpaid phone bills were the insistent reason—professional habit, family links—for the many moves. The
moves were distressing to Mark because of his stacks of references and distressing to Constance as a sheep breeder. Mark
never had more than a penny, though he worked all the time.

"We must be able to phone," he said, as usual, though as if
the point had just occurred. "I've got to keep in touch."

"You've got your shortwave radio."

"That's incoming. I've got to have a two-way system, don't
you see. Bring me my chequebook and we'll be honest citi-
zens."

"We're overdrawn."

"We can always sell something."

"What?"

Mark looked around him. "We could flog the complete
Galsworthy. And there are plenty of other books I could be
without by now. Haven't we got a load of things somewhere
about Iceland?"

"Iceland? Wouldn't they be Deirdre's?"

"No. A friend of mine in the Big Apple wrote to me a while ago and happened to mention that there's an enormous Iceland section in a perfectly normal bookshop on Fifth Avenue. Colossal. Far bigger than all the European sections put together, he said. Which proves that there must be a mounting scholarly demand for commentaries on the Edda. Possibly, though not necessarily, even for the Edda itself. Sensing my interest, this kind chap sent me five feet of books about Iceland in return for some valueless tips about gold ingots. A solemn man. Illiterate, sadly. From a business magazine called *Know Your Capitalism*. Keen-nosed and a worker at heart, he detected a bookish man when he saw one and sent me these five feet. They must be somewhere."

"You could inscribe them with your name and that would add to the value. I'm told that the place to do it is on the title page, never on the inside cover."

"How did you find that out?"

"I was asking an antiquarian bookseller I happened to meet in the fishmonger's."

"Great. And you could sell some of your tapestry chair backs. They're great stuff. I'd help you fix up a show."

"They're not up to snuff, Mark. Not yet."

"Then I'll sell my old atlas."

"Not that one. It's the one with the marine map glued into it." Mark, by one of the many accidents that cling to childbirth and to seafaring parents, had been born on a British boat accidentally storm-tossed into someone else's fishing rights. This, he insisted, made him either a British diplomat entitled to a *laissez-passer* or an anarchist. Mark warmed to the idea of V.I.P. travel all over the world with no official rude enough to look at any of his passports (which happened, for brave and honorable reasons, to be forged) or, better still, made him a free port in human form, with the privilege of duty-free Scotch.

After a moment of meditation on that, he waved his hand at Constance and said, "Well, sell your car then."

"It wouldn't fetch a penny." She was certainly the only person in the family or at the local garage who could drive it. "Besides, I use it to *save* money on the telephone calls I'd otherwise have to make to get shops to deliver."

Constance was an excellent driver of this car, changing gears tirelessly to coax it up to its maximum speed of twenty-four miles an hour, uniquely knowledgeable about opening the boot. Even her athletic sons couldn't kick or prize a way into it when they wanted to carry their luggage into the house after she had driven slowly to Newcastle to meet a plane from Guatemala or China. The back seat was piled high with wool-embroidered canvases on their way to the furniture-maker. Constance, a chain smoker, had often been noticed using her cigarette as the ignition key at the first attempt to start.

"Not that the telephone's my medium," said Mark, "but we never know when there mightn't be an editor ringing about a typo, or a film producer, or the children. I can always tell when it's going to be them. Only thing that makes me believe in God, or gods, is when old planchette starts buzzing and I know it's one of them. Talking of God, darling, we really did have them in an abhorrently monarchical order. First a boy heir, then another boy as backup, then a girl who's probably going to keep the monarchy going for good in this age of Women's Lib and Queens by being the first woman on the moon, then yet another boy in case there's ever need of a dauphin if the others kick the bucket before me. Do you remember a particularly territorialist *Henry V,* where the Dauphin was a very small old man playing with a yo-yo?"

"Mark, that's got no connection with Peter at all. He was only small, ever, when he was a baby, and he only played with a yo-yo when he was a baby. Babies *are* small and they *do* play with yo-yos."

"He didn't open his mouth until he was four. The others were reading by two and a half."

"He talked enough to the other children. The youngest in families often do that."

"He's certainly shot up since," Mark said. "And spoken up. I've cut out a great piece he did this morning. It's on your dressing table. I couldn't find anything by any of the others, could you?"

"There's a nice reference to Alfred in *The Economist.* Quoting him."

"Signs of dangerous radical infiltration in *The Economist* at last. Great. I've *never* made *The Economist.*"

* * *

By selling Galsworthy, the five Icelandic feet, and a sheep by Landseer, Constance had the phone reconnected. Mark was sitting by his shortwave radio as usual, straight to work in his dressing gown from shaving, monitoring events in Ulster, Poland, and Albania, when the engineers came.

"Constance," he said, in the quiet voice she always heard.

One of the engineers said that he'd seen Mrs. Rowlett going out in her car. Then he himself left. Mark knew both engineers well. They were named Frank and Vic. They had been many times to disconnect and reconnect this telephone.

"Engineers and handymen and carpenters and American policemen always travel in pairs, don't they?" said Mark. "Where's Vic gone?"

"He's parking the van."

"Hard to find a place to park these days in the country," said Mark, looking out of his window at the deserted landscape.

Frank fiddled for a time, did the wiring, and then dipped into his back trouser pocket for a piece of paper. "I wonder if you could give me a bit of advice about this," he said.

Mark read carefully. It was a pop lyric written out in pencil. "I'm glad you did this. It's the real stuff, I should say. Have you got a tune in mind?"

"I'm known for my whistling, but I'm not satisfied with the last two lines. I want to say 'stygian' at the end of the seventh line, but I can't hit on a rhyme for the eighth."

Mark gave the matter his complete attention. He stood up, with a little difficulty because of a twinge of arthritis, and for the first time in years managed to get a grasp on a thesaurus that underpinned the whole wobbling pile of the *Oxford English Dictionary*. Mark and Frank worked on the problem.

Frank rejected many possibilities and then seized on one. "That'll do it." He started to whistle. "Yes. I can hear that. Very nice of you."

"I didn't know you did this."

"You've got to have another skill, haven't you. With unemployment." Frank started to pick up his tools.

Mark thought, and then said, "Vic's not back yet?"

"If you're interested, I'll just show you what I've done." Frank unscrewed the telephone so that the conglomeration of wires was exposed. "I cleaned it up for you, because they don't dust

much in the instrument shop, not secondhand telephones."
The telephone bell then rang, surprising Mark from this phone
offal. Frank said, "Receiving. Dry cleaner's, pickup at Mrs.
Fawcett, she's all right, she won't mind the other pickups. Going
to lunch, no trouble. Deliveries before we pick her up again,
pack that little lot in easily before the corroded jack at Ridleys.
Roger."

"So Vic uses the van as a taxi while you're working," said
Mark. Frank nodded, and Mark said, "Very sensible. It's what
you were saying yourself about writing songs."

"Two strings to your bow now if you're going to have half
a chance. My dad used to say that, but he never had the op-
portunity. As a miner. That's your telephone this time. I'll be
off."

"Keep at it," said Mark. He let the telephone ring once more,
said firmly to himself that he wasn't getting the planchette signal, but wasn't in time to stop himself from saying into the
telephone gaily, "Not by any chance a family conclave?" He
responded with just as much alacrity to the reply, from an
editor who wanted a long piece in a hurry. Mark was not a
man to live by one hope alone.

"Your phone was out of order for days," said the editor.

"I hadn't paid the bill."

"Can you do the piece by Friday?"

"That's late for you. Thursday."

"Telephone it in. Reverse the charge. Many thanks. Make
the copytakers read it back if you want. You use a lot of difficult names. In good spirits, are you, apart from the news?"

"Not much apart from news now, a lot of people say, but
with the amount of activity that's just been going on privately
in this house, I should say there was a good deal else. Fighting
off unemployment on all fronts up here."

"Write about that next time, if you would?"

"Maybe. If I could." Mark started at once to make notes for
the immediate piece. As usual, the notes were made in his head.

A young girl who lived in the house rent-free in return for
helping Constance with the sheep came into his study in tears.
"I can't stand the life here. I can't get things happening. I
don't like letting Constance down, but I want to pack straightaway. I need a lot of your old newspapers for my packing
boxes. They're full of earth, because we had them for the rho-

dodendrons. I'm sorry, but I'm going to be nineteen in a month. I've maybe still got a future, haven't I? And it isn't here." Crying most bitterly, she started to pick up piles of his carefully sorted newspapers and magazines, which stood in high stacks all around the room and on his sofa.

"You can't have those. They're work." Mark got up without the usual difficulty and put his arm around her shoulders, walking slowly to the door in his dressing gown and carpet slippers. "It'll be all right. You have to go by your instinct. Now, lining the boxes. I think we could snitch a lot of drawer-lining paper for you from the kitchen cupboards. You look in the bedrooms and I'll ransack the kitchen."

"Mrs. Rowlett will mind. I can't call her Constance any longer."

"She's very fond of you, but people have to move on."

"I meant about having to buy new lining paper. Even you haven't got enough to manage on, and you're clever and you've been at it for years. I've probably left it too late already." She ran upstairs, not looking back, shouting, "It comes of being self-employed, does it? But I can't think of anything else. A delivery girl or a waitress, if I could get it, and then something of my own in the evenings."

Mark went on stripping the kitchen of lining paper for her.

Without his knowing it, all of his children were due to arrive in Newcastle from their points abroad. And without telling him, Constance had gone off by car to collect them. They arrived at home, Constance taking out her cigarette to beam at the success of her surprise. Talk; private talk between Mark and Constance about the girl upstairs; questions; sandwiches of dressed crab.

"A binge," said Mark, eating little.

"What's the noun for someone who binges?" said Federico.

"It couldn't be 'binger.' If you read it, that would make it rhyme with 'singer,' " said Deirdre.

"Why not with 'harbinger'?" said Constance.

"Anyway, it would never in a million years describe Mark," said Federico. "He's the family skeleton. The skeleton in all our cupboards."

"None of us, not one of us, could ever aspire to be as disreputable as he is," said Alfred in homage. "What's all this about the girl upstairs?"

"Not girl. Mary. She's worried about going to seed," said Constance.

"What does she do?" said Deirdre.

"Helps Constance with the sheep," said Mark. "She plants grass with more natural vitamins in it. More natural than usual in Cumberland."

"Then going to seed would be an endemic worry," said Alfred.

"No. It's endemic to being nineteen stuck in the country with unemployment getting worse. Her brother in Newcastle has just been laid off," said Mark.

"So she's quitting," said Constance. "And now she's concerned about leaving us in the lurch on top of everything else."

"One thing always comes of another, that's what I always say," said Peter, with for him an unusual note of the Rowlett high spirits that were sometimes taken by the envious or the inattentive for callousness.

There was a family pause, each wondering about the others' doings.

Alfred stripped off his shirt and heaved some new rocks from a nearby cliff to improve the run of the garden waterfall. Federico looked after the departing girl and carried her boxes to the bus stop two by two. Deirdre went to work, lying down on her bed. Peter and his mother went to the nearest shops to buy food and to drop Mark's oldest jacket at the dry cleaner's. Mark started to work. Old touch typist that he was, he didn't bother to turn on his desk lamp. He worked for five or six hours, finished, switched on the lamp, and went to edit his top copy. He couldn't see anything typed on it at all. Fifteen pages, and nothing there. Hands shaking, he tried every pair of spectacles he had. There was no doubt. The thing he most dreaded for himself had happened. He leaned back to think. I must sprint now, now of all times, faster, now of all times, but I'm falling through a skylight in the blackout, someone was leading me and they didn't tell me it wasn't floor, I must sprint into work if it cracks my bones, I must think of something else to do but there's nothing but read and write that I want to do. My face feels slashed to bits, I wonder if I did that when I was shaving and just didn't notice. Because I didn't notice that I couldn't see. One wouldn't, with something like shaving. He said, loudly, "Deirdre?"

Her room was opposite his study, and she came in quickly.

"I've gone blind. I've got to reconstruct a piece for a deadline. Do we know anybody who could take it down?"

Deirdre came over to look at his typewriter. She tried a few sentences standing up and told him that he could dictate to her, to go straight onto the typewriter. "Sit down. Take your time."

"I'm better if I walk about. I wouldn't know what to do with my hands and legs." He strode around with his fingers pressed against his eyeballs. His fingers had always had a way of turning back a little at the last joint, but now, when he was trying to push his eyes away, the angle was much sharper than usual. Deirdre rolled a sheet of typing paper into the machine to practise, used as she was to electric typewriters.

"Daddy," she said, "don't you realize? You had it fixed at blank. The ribbon control. It's on the place that doesn't print. It's the one for cutting stencils." Then she looked around the desk and saw, on the left, the uncollated pile of carbons that Mark, old professional that he was, had automatically made of each page.

Mark said nothing about his eyesight and only "What a piece of luck" about the carbons.

"Have you only got one bit of carbon paper? This is like lace.'

"But can you read the sense?"

"I'll retype it and ask as I go. How much time have we got?"

"An hour."

They worked together fast. She said she wanted to give him time to make changes and would retype it if he wanted. It was a piece with a wide span. "I'll do it again when you've read it," she said, handing it to him.

"No, you'd better read it to me, as I'm blind," he said, so concentrated about what he had been writing in his mind that he had already accepted calamity. The old pro, though, working in another part of his head, started to read. "Mistake. I can see after all."

"You didn't notice the carbons?"

"Bloody carbons. Very good of you. I'll read the thing by the window. I'm fed up with that desk lamp. It looks like a ship's hospital. Round the Horn, steerage."

She left him alone. He said "Great" as she left. It was one of his words. He worked, telephoned the long piece, listened to his shortwave radio, and then sat back to think awhile. The thinking led to a note. Typed.

DEAR MARY,

I am sending this to you at the YWCA because that's where you said you would be, though I sensed hankerings after the YMCA. I suggest that you get in touch with a cousin of mine (male), no more decrepit than I am, who would put you up on the instant, gratis. He lives in Gosforth, and the telephone number is 2341618. He will guess immediately that you are a friend of mine, because you are asking for something free. Anyone else who calls him up is dunning him for unpaid bills or trying to deliver subpoenas about axe murders. He stands firm in the face of all such lugubrious calls, but yours will be cheerful and responded to. His name is Bodkin Rowlett, poor chap. Take him a bottle of a vile drink called absinthe, which he likes because he associates it with literature and the French Revolution. Send the bill to me and I shall recompense you when you next come out here.

Which brings me smoothly to my next point: that you must be missing the sheep. Alfred seems to think that he is Mr. Atlas, for reasons unfounded in my eyes. He has been heaving up a large number of hideous Cumbrian stones of exorbitant size that were impeding the spread of Constance's whole-wheat-germ sheep grass. I should value your alliance in heaving them back again. When you come, and I suggest the weekend after next, dig up anything that you think would grow in Gosforth. I doubt whether anything much flourishes in the YWCA.

I forgot to tell you that I went blind today but it turned out to be a technical hitch.

It's a lousy job, job-hunting, and you don't even get paid for it. I did it myself for four years and the situation wasn't nearly as bad then. But set the alarm every day, get out there, call reverse charge whenever in need of sheepish news. And no fear.

Love,
Mark